Clash of the Vikings

Clash of the Vikings

Peter Wilks

Copyright © 2018 Peter Wilks

The moral right of the author has been asserted.

Apart from any fair dealing for the purposes of research or private study, or criticism or review, as permitted under the Copyright, Designs and Patents Act 1988, this publication may only be reproduced, stored or transmitted, in any form or by any means, with the prior permission in writing of the publishers, or in the case of reprographic reproduction in accordance with the terms of licences issued by the Copyright Licensing Agency. Enquiries concerning reproduction outside those terms should be sent to the publishers.

Matador
9 Priory Business Park,
Wistow Road, Kibworth Beauchamp,
Leicestershire. LE8 0RX
Tel: 0116 279 2299
Email: books@troubador.co.uk
Web: www.troubador.co.uk/matador
Twitter: @matadorbooks

ISBN 978 1788038 027

British Library Cataloguing in Publication Data.
A catalogue record for this book is available from the British Library.

Printed and bound in the UK by TJ International, Padstow, Cornwall
Typeset in 11pt Minion Pro by Troubador Publishing Ltd, Leicester, UK

Matador is an imprint of Troubador Publishing Ltd

To Edna Griffin

Part I
When Dark Roots Take Hold

Chapter One
From the Sea

The night mist was caressed by the morning sun, the swirling grey wall slowly parting as it burned off in the warmth. Raised voices that had been muted and remote, grew clearer as their owners called the beat of the oars over the accompanying sound of splashing in the water. Something dim and shadowy emerged from the dissipating depths of the mist and as it quickly took shape and substance, another unclear image appeared behind it like a spectre followed by more separately or in twos until there were a fleet of seven Viking longships spread out in a ragged line.

The air was becoming unpleasantly hot and humid for the early June day. Shimmering in the distant heat haze the Northumbria coastline reared up over the visible horizon. The distinctive prows of the dragon ships cut through the choppy water like a knife. Rowers hauled with all their strength, the rasping, scraping sound of the looms caused wear against the surrounds of their sockets as the banks of oars propelled each vessel toward the shore with smooth rhythmic strokes. Clouds scudded across the blue sky and a few of the circling white sea gulls keened mournfully before descending on flapping wings, their shadows enlarging upon the sand as they landed to forage for mollusks and crustaceans on the beach backed by a range of hills.

A curly-headed young boy short for his age with his homespun clothes hanging loosely from his undernourished-thin frame emerged from a grove of trees atop of the grassy ridgeline and stared wide-eyed in fright at the fleet of longships displaying rows of shields along the sides of the gunwales, before he dropped the firewood he had been gathering for his evening meal and turned into the shadows, hurrying off down the reverse slope to tell his father what he had seen.

As the fleet crested the lines of waves edging closer to the enlarging shoreline a powerful crosswind suddenly began blowing into the leading longship called Mjöllnir's Might, plucking the long flaxen-hair of the youthful lookout standing on the roped-shrouds and rattling the mast decorated with the tribute carving of Thor's hammer. A crimson banner bearing the runed slogan 'Red Plague' fluttered from the top of the masthead.

Sweat trickled into the lookout's eye and he blinked and did a double take as he peered ahead and saw the jagged tip of something piercing the whitecaps just a stone's throw away from the fleet. Moistening his dry lips, he unslung the large spiral seashell with his free hand before raising the opening to his lips and blowing, emitting a deep, long blaring signal. Below and towards the stern of the Mjöllnir's Might, A fifty year old man furrowed his brow.

"Tjernagl," Gunnar the Skilful said to a young Norseman with curly, reddish gold hair sitting back on his haunches beside him, his hand hitting a crude, small-headed drum. "Take the helm and keep the craft steady."

"Aye, master steersman," Tjernagl jumped to his feet, his great plait swinging as he gripped the proffered tiller with a sore, splintered palm before Gunnar straightened his poor posture and limped his way forward.

Feeling the Mjöllnir's Might move through the blue water underneath him and working with the swaying motion, the bare-chested, master steersman passed between the seated rowers and then paused to glance up at the lanky, long-limbed lookout. "What is it you see, Olaf?"

"Hidden rocks under the surface off the starboard bow," Olaf shouted down.

Gunnar ducked under the rolled up sail to take a look for himself at what was ahead of them and then he had to raise his meaty hand to shield his squinting gaze against the fierce glare of the midmorning sun as it slid from behind the clouds to shine down on the sea and reflect the light in brilliant glittering flashes. The rhythmical sound of the drum was heard again as someone else in the crew took it up.

"By Odin's beard, you have the eyes of a hawk," said Gunnar with a shake of his grizzled head. "I foresaw sandbars paralleling the beach, but Pytheas the Greek mentioned not reefs along this stretch of shoreline in his sea charts. The fleet would have foundered as it manoeuvred in the shallows for certain." He spared a backward glance at Tjernagl and barked the first of a series of urgent commands at the crew. "Helmsman, bear hard-to starboard. Port side rowers hold stroke position for six beats, starboard side ply your oars."

The left bank of oars was raised horizontally and the rowers briefly suspended their stroke there, while the right oar bank continued the movement of the oars through the water. The nose of the Mjöllnir's Might swung swiftly, the keel pivoting into the direction of the wind. Gunnar came to a snap decision as he gauged the strength of the gusts, shouting and gesturing at three Vikings to do his bidding. They scrambled up the rigging to unfurl the sail and Olaf blew two strident blasts on his conch shell to signal the rest of the fleet to turn and follow along in its wake.

"Rein in the oars and seal the oar holes with the covers, we do not want the water rushing in," Gunnar ordered, explaining himself as he went. "The wind is blowing in the direction we desire to go. Helmsman, steady as she goes."

"Aye, aye," Tjernagl replied, hearing the sail swish and the ropes shuffle in the angling wind. Covers were repositioned over the oar holes.

"Fridrik," Gunnar turned to address a short, youth with big front teeth and a pointed nose sitting by the mast. "Slake my thirst and then the crew."

Clinging to the rigging, an athletic twenty year old Norseman was untying a section of the sail and asked, "And my father, master steersman?" His long free-flowing hair flickered in the wind, his brown eyes boring into Gunnar's back. "Shouldn't he be told we finally broach English waters? 'Tis he's wits that dominate and determine the course of this attack."

"Aye, Lokar; I have not forgotten that I am the hand that carries it out either. I was about to do just that," Gunnar replied irritably, without looking back. "Fridrik, go first to the hold and rouse Jarl Magnússon from his slumber. Tell him there are things to be done that will not wait."

The second and third longships named Long Snake and Bifrost's Bow veered sharply and withdrew their lightweight, pine oars but they didn't align orderly behind the Mjöllnir's Might. Instead those Viking vessels were astern and off to the left taking a diagonal course in order to maximize the benefit from the bracing northerly gusts, which blew in to strum the rigging ropes and swell the forty foot square sails; the stout beitass-spar fixed in place against the rear of the rough woollen cloth held its effective shape even when it was sodden with spray. Blue and black banners sporting symbols in the form of helmets and crossed battleaxes flew aloft.

The four remaining longships tacked sharply and spread out alongside Bifrost's Bow in a staggered pattern, the drumbeats onboard silencing as the fleet sped across the waves. The wind rattled the decorative lines of shields, but they were held securely with wedges within the inboard shield rack.

Mjöllnir's Might and Long Snake were a hundred feet in length with room for sixty oars, a few ranging in reach, consistent with where they were made use of upon the vessel, and a crew of over a hundred and twenty. They didn't differ greatly apart from the carvings on the prow of the second ship depicting Asgard gods wrestling with the fanged mouths and coils of long snakes. Bifrost's Bow and the other longships were a little shorter in length with fewer oars and wider, deeper hulls for carrying cargo, but their mastheads and stern-posts were just as lavishly decorated.

Their slender hulls creaked as the overlapping, oaken planks flexed with the movement of the in-beam waves, thin cracks appeared and lengthened from the nailed timbers, but no water seeped into the gaps behind the wood for reason that they had been filled and sealed by sheep's wool dipped in tar. Beneath the gunwales, a single uneven row of oar ports were cut into both sides of the ships' hull, so that all the blades could catch the waves and stroke in harmony. A single stern steering oar was fastened on their starboard side.

Onboard each longship, the rowers caught their breath and rested, wiping sweat from their faces with rags, whilst sitting on their own personal sea chests two to an oar, which now stood on the deck at their feet, as a teenage boy passed among them, filling their gourd cups from a bulging water skin. The tidal wave energy crashing against the hull made steering more difficult for the Mjöllnir's Might, exerting pressure on the after end of the keel, trying to make it slant into shore, but Tjernagl leaned into the steering oar and adjusted for drift.

Off the starboard side the coastal profile gradually changed as the beach narrowed along the base of elevating cliffs where notches had cut into them from waves having battered the bedrock surface. About half a mile ahead of the fleet, a spectacular rocky headland undergoing erosion jutted out into the North Sea inhabited by seaweed communities. The ruins of an old Roman signal station was still visible atop of the sea stacks many metres high and forming isolated pinnacles. The keels of the longships swept through the whitecaps at an average speed of ten knots as the wave tops splashed over their bows.

Within minutes the fleet had arrived at the crumbling headland; the Mjöllnir's Might swung wide round the outer edge to avoid Gunnar's grisly premonition of the steering oar becoming tangled up in the brown seaweed or colliding with the top of more hidden reefs just below the surface of the water. The Long Snake and Bifrost's Bow came after, cutting across the swath of gusts followed by the remainder of the Dragon ships, closing the gap somewhat between them all, their sails slackening for a moment or two, as the wind now abeam, abruptly died down, before the master steersman felt his chest hair ruffle, as another fiercer gale blew in off the sea, filling the sailcloth again and swelling them outward.

The fleet was driven onward, the longships repositioning themselves, taking the shape of an arrowhead configuration, as their course lines spread out in layered tiers on both sides at the rear of the Mjöllnir's Might. A dark smudge of land appeared in the sea about two leagues distance off the port bow of the foremost vessel. Waves began slowing the progress of the dragon ships as they lifted each of them up and settled them down again. The rugged cliffs lowered on the southern shore and these alternated with wooded ridges and sheltered embayments.

* * *

The surf crashed upon the island's beach and young children dressed in loosely woven linen made from homespun yarn, giggled and ran across the sand as they treated the vital chore of gathering kelp for animal fodder and crop fertilizer as if it was a game to be played. Two older boys though competed against each other for the affection from their parents. The foam lapped over their dissolving footprints and nearly surged up to where four of the overturned boats had been drawn up by the fisher folk above the tidal line, their worn hulls were either being repaired with new timber or encrusted with barnacles.

Arranged higher than them stood a collection of squat, wattle and daubed fishing huts and shacks topped with thatched roofs together with table-like stalls displaying oysters and crabs, shellfish, shrimp and prawns on sale to pilgrims visiting the isle. More posts had been planted into the earth about five feet apart and between these were cut tree branches that were in the process of being woven together to made a couple of the walls for more dwellings. A column of smoke slowly rose above the settlement almost obscuring a distance belfry topping a wooden tower backlit against the blue sky.

Wild goats grazed on what little grass there was on the parched hillsides nearby and a hardy flock of Cheviot sheep roamed in the fields beyond.

Outside the small settlement, men sat on crude benches or cross-legged on the ground, mending nets and women stood behind huge cauldrons stirring butchered fish soaking in a 80 percent brine solution, while other woman and their teenage daughters placed earlier catches of fish on robust racks to partially dry before the rest of the smoking process was carried out in kilns build from sun-dried bricks just a few paces behind the huts. Tendrils of smoke curled upwards from the smoldering wood in the fireboxes and the background noise snatched away the words of the inhabitants from carrying too far. A holy man riding a white donkey bareback pulled on the simple bridle with his free hand to bring his mount to a slow halt before dismounting and tossing the reins to a wagoner kneeing beside his wain, who was in the act of replacing a broken wheel on a greasy axle.

"Greeting fellow islanders," the monk raised his hand at the gathered onlookers and the voluminous sleeve of his black robe fell back to reveal his scrawny, pasty arm. Heads turned towards him and some stepped back to allow the monk room, as a big, beefy, broad, flat-faced man detached from the group. "A fine morn is it not?"

"It's a blessing that you came so quickly, Brother Isaac," the headman said ignoring the pleasantries, rubbing his aching shoulders with ointment. "We ain't aversed to tolling under the hot sun, alas…"

"Don't despair Malcolm, together we shall find the aquifer, for am I not a historian?" The monk interrupted, a sweaty sheen covered the reddening tonsure shaven into his short dark hair, as he stepped off the dusty Roman road and his sandals trod upon the drought-starved ground, riven with cracks, as he headed towards the piles of soil hiding a trench with two diggers standing within. Hardly any plants grew in the hard ground. "The old scrolls in the priory library told me aright, the water is underfoot hereabouts. Till then you are all welcome to keep drinking and filling your animal pails from the cisterns within the monastery."

"Methinks you are a prattling dullard, monk and this task is beyond your ken," a stocky young man said, feeling a surge of anger as he strenuously scooped another shovelful of dirt out of the widening hole. The monk blinked in surprise and the second digger paused to pick up a large stone and toss it. "I care not a whit who knows it. I wager we will reach a layer of hard rock again ere long."

A low murmur of conversation broke out among the peasant onlookers as they exchanged scandalized glances. The village headman's face went cold and firm as he turned, bent and cuffed the side of the digger's head. The monk tightened his grip on his riding crop.

"Forgive my boy, Brother Isaac," Malcolm said, trying to find the right words to say as he directed his sternest look at his son, but who set his lips stubbornly. The headman straightened and ushered the monk away from the excavation. "Stephen is wont to be rather brash and quick of temper when tired, but he is the salt of the earth." He paused to let the monk comment, but the silence lengthened between them until he spoke on with measured emphasis "As you know there's been nay a drop of rain for weeks to relieve the land and 'tis three such shafts he and the other youngsters have dug and lined with stone to avert cave-ins of late since the ground trembled and the old well ran dry."

The slightly protuberant eyes of Brother Isaac lit up in understanding and he simply nodded, relaxing his grip on the riding crop as he followed the fifty-five year old headman down a gentle slope. Piles of fish heads and guts and other refuse was dumped close by, flies buzzing around the summits. At the bottom, Malcolm edged around the line of kilns to emerge at the rear of the settlement, sunshine seeped through interstices in the walls and roofs of the huts and shacks supplementing the light of the lit reed tapers within the gloomy interiors. Teenager boys and greybeards were using axes to chop up cords of firewood into smaller manageable sizes to feed into the kilns.

"I do, so put your mind at ease, Friend Malcolm. For in the passing of the seasons I too would have felt a grieved if my efforts in the pigpens on my family farm had been all for naught." The monk went on with a sober assessment of the situation. "At least you will not have to dig a village latrine anytime soon. I shall take especial care and attention to the various soils and local plants ere choosing the new site should this borehole prove equally fruitless. Whether good or ill betide you, trust in yourself."

Malcolm sniffed, keeping his opinions to himself and gestured at the line of smoking kilns, each one was five feet tall and maybe six feet wide around the base. "Lo, Brother Isaac, due to the weighted nets and the fishing holes my people dug in the mudflats at low tide, we are now catching and preserving three times the amount of fish than was in my father's day. The increase in the workload has meant we are carting in hands from the mainland villages to help us out with the tasks, women mostly and the odd men who are too old or young to take part in hunting."

"Your tithe tax will be paid when it is due then, not in installments?" The monk's appraising gaze took it all in and he fingered his angular chin thoughtfully. "For the abbot is not satisfied with merely the bones and offal you have been throwing our way in the past."

Malcolm felt heat rush to his cheeks as rage took the place of the cold within him. "Yes, Brother Isaac."

"And what of the oak the wains carried over the causeway from the mainland?"

"We fare better burning this harder wood for fuel than the softer wood, for the conifers contain pitch, which imparts a bitter taste to the fillets. Come! Brother Isaac I'll show you the storehouse and the tannery." Malcolm turned, angling around the axe men. "This way if you please," the headsman made his way with long strides towards one of the wide gaps between two of the huts. The stink of wood smoke hung heavy in the air.

Just ahead of him, there was a sudden, loud, deep rumbling noise that resembled thunder. Before Malcolm could glance up at the sky he glimpsed a hatchet-faced old woman stop stirring her cauldron and her stooped frame stiffen, as she peered out to sea. The knee of a fisherman cracked when he untangled his legs and stood up beside her to block out the view beyond. With a momentary quickening of his pulse the headman thought something was amiss and he dashed forward. The monk frowned but blindly adhered to his heels.

"Four, five," the white-haired woman counted before asking her younger brother. "William, you had dealings with the merchants who buy our fish, what comes after five?"

"Six and seven, Bronwyn," William said, lowering the rim of his straw hat as he watched the unfolding scene as if he was spellbound.

"Who be these sailors bound for our shore, William?" Bronwyn asked in confusion, drawing her shawl around her head and shoulders. Several pilgrims turned from the stalls and moved to stand beside the fisher folk. "If its supplies they are a wanting…"

"Never have I seen such a sight," William sputtered in a self-assured voice, feeling cold with the beginning of panic deep inside. "And yet I heard fearsome tales of hairy men, northlanders by birth, whispered around the camp fires at nightfall."

Malcolm skidded to a halt and his mouth dropped open when he forcibly shoved himself between the pair of fisher folk and saw a line of longships riding the waves in the near distance, dragon prows poised above the decks like cobras ready to strike, their banks of oars rhythmically rising and dipping into the water. The headman's face went ashen and his gummy mouth dried up with fear.

"We must flee or be forever undone," Malcolm shouted, the volume and intensity of his words caught the imagination and disturbed the composure of the people around him as he pointed at the fleet of ships. "Death's shadow is upon us."

"What do you mean, Friend Malcolm?" The monk pulled up beside him, aghast and he gazed speculatively at him.

"Whoever is touched by the shadow is struck from the earth," Malcolm replied. William, a head taller than the headman, let out an involuntary gasp and clenched his liver spotted fists, as an arrow thudded into the soft sand up to the fletching. A few men wrapped their arms protectively around their wives and offspring, uttering expletives of anger and alarm as more barbed-shafts splashed into the sea shallows only paces from the beach, as the archers onboard the nearing longships tested the range.

"Have these sailors a name?" asked the monk.

"Nothing that's polite, I call them a plague of the seas after their chieftain. We should tarry not on this beach, Brother Isaac," Malcolm stepped backwards and ran a hand through his thinning iron grey hair. The monk joined him followed by William and Bronwyn, who from Malcolm's expression and words cemented the numbness spreading through their limbs. Bronwyn hitched up her skirt and her leg muscles trembled from tension as she cast a nervous glance back at her daughter and grandchildren.

"Come hither, my child," Bronwyn urged them. "We' are taking the little ones away."

Parents beckoned their children to them before taking them in their arms and hurrying from the beach followed by the pilgrims and the mainlanders.

"People need to be warned of the threat and arm themselves," Malcolm spoke on. "The women and whelps should hide in some bolthole whilst they are able else they shall be enslaved."

A youngish woman with apple blossom in her tresses and cradling a pink-cheeked two year old boy child in her arms approached Malcolm as he turned on his heel. "Flee to where, headman?" Unshed tears glistened in her green eyes, envisaging the fate of her child and herself as she stared at his grim, rigid expression. "All the fishing boats are out to sea and we are on an isle surrounded by the high tide."

"Come with me to the monastery, Arwen," the monk butted-in as he made a snap decision, a twinge of fear sending his stomach into knots. "The walls are high and the doors are stout. We should all be safe from their arrows behind them."

William took the hands of his two competitive boys, the grass crunching under their dirty, bare feet as they merged with the fisher folk and others flowing from the settlement. The adversity was bringing the people closer together. Another volley of arrows from the longships rained down a lot closer and a man dropped, gagging with a shaft piercing his throat and a young woman screamed and convulsed, blood spreading to stain the back of her dress as she crashed earthward. Her crying baby bounced sharply from the impact before panicking feet coming from behind trod on her head, caving in her skull. "Keep going and don't look back."

"Farewell brother," Malcolm uttered and veered off from the exodus towards one of the interior huts.

* * *

The podgy wagoner flicked his reins and the team of horses veered onto the road, easing into a gap in the outer edge of the flow of people on foot leaving the settlement. A number of children were already sitting in the body's sturdy box and the monk's donkey trotted behind the wain tied by rope to the backboard.

"I say, Enoch wait up I say," Brother Isaac came alongside the wain and banged his knuckles on the sideboards. The wagoner jerked back on the reins and the horses pulled up as most of the villagers moved onwards. A grouping of adults and children slowed and crowded around the monk. "Glad am I to see that you replaced the wheel, my friend."

"Aye, an easy enough task for a wagoner such as I after seasons of hauling fish, refuse and timber to the kilns. Alas never did I see a time of dire need when I would be taking children hither to the monastery, Brother Isaac," Enoch glanced back, his eyes darting back and forth as he took everything in. The monk untied the rope and snatched up his donkey's reins. Half a dozen of the passersby had the mind to haphazardly carry off a weapon, a pair of axes from the wood pile, an adze and a hammer lying about here and there, and a pitchfork; its slightly curved prongs had been embedded in a hay bale. "There be space on the back of the cart for the young'uns and the womenfolk with you, but hurry the sands are running out of the hourglass and ere long there be loud, angry snarls assailing our ears from all sides."

The Wagoner's utterance brought the others forward. Bronwyn and Arwen began hoisting up children to the cart bed.

"I must get going to relate the grim tableau I witnessed on the sand to my brethren," Brother Isaac looked at William. "Could I trouble you for a leg up, good neighbour?"

William nodded, crouching down and interlocked the fingers of both hands to form a stirrup. The monk put his sandaled-foot on the stirrup and it added him to mount the donkey.

"I prefer a straight road, alas I be following as fast as my nags can pull us to said destination," Enoch's fingers raked through his flat blond hair. "I just got to settle them down a mite being as how they be skittish around so many people travelling from place to place, but a league should allow the team to get accustomed to their presence."

"Of that I have nay doubt, Enoch," the monk heels nudged into the donkey's sides to set off at a canter. Here and there he saw gaps starting to appear in the fleeing line of people as the young and fittest left behind the elderly and the lame. Brother Isaac shook his head and muttered to himself, "How easily they forget their religious education. Do unto others as you would have them do onto you."

Back at the cart, William helped Bronwyn and Arwen aboard the vehicle before he climbed up beside Enoch and sat on the driver's bench. The wagoner flicked the reins and encouraged the horses to move.

***

The headman's son and a handful of young men ran into the settlement, coming to a stop in front of Malcolm. They looked around uncertainly; their nostrils wrinkling from the coppery smell of freshly-spilled blood till their eyes saw the bodies lying on the discoloured sand and the approaching longships lightly skimming the water, nearing to shore.

"What has befallen us, father?" he asked, giving him a searching look. "We saw our friends and neighbours taking flight and came to explore the reason for it."

"Be blind to the facts nay longer, Stephen; invaders we have," Malcolm saw the anxiousness in his son's face before risking a seaward glance over his shoulder, desperation lending an edge to his voice. "I am away to fetch my spear," he looked back at them, "grab whatever weapons inside the huts that have already been to the smithy. Our retreat is cut off by the tide and I am not convinced by the solidness of the monastery walls that hark back to the Roman age. We have not a choice but to stand and face the enemy."

"I am not afraid of any man, headman," a thin faced youth Malcolm recognized by his short, fair beard as the second digger.

"Nor am I, Doon," Malcolm said, giving him a down-mouth chuckle. "But it is the hundreds with him onboard those ships that worry me so."

"Can we not parley with them, father?" Stephen asked, fear causing his bladder to empty down his trouser leg. The young men grimaced and stepped back apace from the spreading yellow puddle.

Malcolm's face softened and he placed a firm hand on his son's shoulder. "Nay, there is only leg irons or death in our future! I was not born a captive my son, to grovel at the feet of my enslavers and to truly be free we will have to fight bitterly to uphold it to our dying day. And I fear today will be that day." Understanding shone in Stephen's red-rimmed eyes and he swallowed hard and nodded. The others were struggling to control the whirl of emotions within and it was mirrored on their faces and in their posture. "We shall thwart them for as long as we are able."

* * *

Onboard the Mjöllnir's Might, Gunnar grunted as Olaf blew a short blast on his conch shell. The Vikings were gulping thirstily at their water when they heard the signal. The heads of some of the freemen crew turned in curiously, while others draw knifes from their belts with clammy palms as they sprang to their feet, eager for battle.

"Siegfried, we've almost arrived," he called over his broad, tanned shoulder as another burly Norseman dressed in noble's finery climbed up the vertical steps out of the stern hatch in the decking, clutching a bow and a quiver of arrows. "Open the helmet sacks and see to it that you hand out one to each warrior."

"Yes, Father," Siegfried replied. Like the other Vikings he wore a tunic and baggy trousers, fastened shut with metal clasps, while about his neck hung a protection amulet of bone in the shape of Thor's hammer. Siegfried quickly overturned two of the nearby sacks and a quantity of horned helmets spilled out. He tried one on but despite the helm's sheepskin lining he still found it was too large for his shaven head. Irritated with the misery of the heat and the drying sweat that caused an itchy sensation on their broad tanned faces and along their bare muscular arms, some of the Vikings sailors crowded around Siegfried muttering their misgivings as they swapped their caps of hide for the strange helms.

Wearing exotic lamellar armour and carrying a two handled scimitar in a scabbard, the hilt was delicately decorated with silver inlays, signifying the nobleman's affluence and rank in their close-knit community, the forty-four year old warrior strode forward along the central deck. "Out of my way, coming through," Jarl Magnus Magnússon roared as he elbowed his way past the approaching flow of Norsemen until he came to a halt beside Gunnar.

"So, shipwright; this is the isle you boasted of?" he asked impatiently, slinging the quiver over his shoulder as he stared at their destination through his spectacles-like visor. An iron domed helmet with a spike on the crown and a mail neck-guard concealed most of his aquiline features. "I hope I haven't risked bringing my entire fleet on a fool's errand."

"Aye and I would not play you falsely, Jarl Magnússon," Gunnar replied with appeared confidence, addressing the nobleman by his title and surname. Details gradually became less blurry on the bleak isle until the view grew firmer and Magnússon and Gunnar could make out its most distinguishing features with the naked eye. "The people hereabouts call it Holy Island or Lindisfarne and I have it on good authority that a treasure is stored within the monastery build in the centre of it."

"How vast?" Magnússon asked.

"Enough to even put a smile on your face, Jarl Magnússon," Gunnar replied, knowing the man's greed for gold and the keen relish he had for the good things in life.

"A bold claim, but I and the crew rejoice to hear that," Magnússon replied, flexing the string of the bow as he stared at the drab landscape made up of sharp lines of dwellings in the foreground. "I have given you leeway and a degree of my tolerance, but I'm of a mind to ask isn't it finally time to shed light on shadow and speak of how you came by such tidings, Gunnar?"

Gunnar blew out his bearded cheeks and nodded reluctantly. "You made no secret of your lusty ambitions for raiding religious sites and plunder--"

"Among other things," Magnússon interrupted as dribs and drabs of the crew returned to their oars. "Go on man."

"Well, my kinsman Rolf is a man of humble upbringing and he saw the privileges granted to my family with your patronage and we discussed how he could gain similar favour from you and still the tongues of the villagers in the bargain. So we hatched a plan designed with your interests in mind and he set sail on a voyage on a merchant vessel to gather information."

"I've never had to eat the crust of poverty like your minor house and I do respect a man of purpose, but I know of that ball of grease, he's a skald is he not?" Magnússon asked, reaching back to the quiver and drawing an arrow, his voice positively dripped malice as he conjured up his likeness from memory and he saw Gunnar nod. "You're kinsman is held with little regard, no wonder the villagers think of him thusly."

"It's not an opinion I share, Jarl Magnússon," Gunnar said, bristling at the suggestion before shifting his attention up at the slowly deflating sail and growling to the Viking crew. "Rowers back to your oars. The wind is dying down on us." The sailors quickly cleared the deck, retaking their seats fore and aft. "Ready yourselves on my command." The oar blades extended out into the rough water. "Stroke to the beat!"

"Be not snippy with me, shipwright," Magnússon nocked the arrow and pulled the bow back before fixing the older man with a hard look as the drum beater kept up the tempo and the slowing Mjöllnir's Might got underway again. Sailors in the fleet busied themselves by rolling up the sails and knotting ropes as the rowers pulled on their oars with a series of fluid arm movements. Several archers on the other longships tilted their bows and fired their arrows. "I stand only as much as is bearable even from my obedient ball and chain at home."

"Apologies Jarl Magnússon," Gunnar bowed his head in acknowledgment. "But Rolf has courage and has lived by his wits this season past, scouting this part of England unmolested as a wandering minstrel. He sent messages by homing pigeon and regaled me with his stories of doors belonging to wealthy landowners and nobles normally closed for commoners and yet opened for his lute music--"

Magnússon guffawed mockingly. He took careful aim and fired his arrow. The extensive shoals beneath the water raised the sea bed causing less depth, but the shallow draft of the longships enabled the fleet to continue gliding through the swells without difficulty. Behind Mjöllnir's Might, the first mate aboard the Long Snake shook his head in dissatisfaction and ordered his steersman to swerve to starboard to create more distant space between his vessel and the Bifrost's bow so that both banks of oars wouldn't become foul up, snapping the blades and disrupting the rhythm of the rowers. "The English must be starved for entertainment if they welcome the likes of him to their hearth. My bowels play better music."

Fired by his contempt, Gunnar glared at him, but minded his tongue as he spoke on. "And once he spoke of one evening he even sang for his supper for an audience of monks," he pointed at the looming island, "and gold and silver was plentiful in that walled-monastery, but I think not in the village of Lindisfarne build in the fertile southwest corner of the island. Rolf also heard talk of pilgrims and nuns undertaking a pilgrimage to this holy place to behold some bones belonging to a dead priest for the sake of devotion."

"Dead priest," Magnússon echoed with a shake of his head.

"I would have told you sooner, Jarl Magnússon, but I had to wait for the raid to have favourable sailing weather."

"Hmmm, the isle 'tis like a realm unto itself with monks, nuns and villagers," Magnússon mused thoughtfully and tucked at his forked beard with free hand. "I welcome fortune as a means of obtaining riches for my family and my subjects."

Gunnar nodded in agreement, picking up on the emphasis he placed on the last word. "'Tis known far and wide, you are not selfish in temperament, Jarl Magnússon."

"Nor do I rashly bestow gifts with an open hand, shipwright. If Rolf speaks the truth, it will be a debt not soon forgotten; I shall appoint him my royal skald and food taster." A shadow of a smile sparkled in his blue eyes. "Mayhap if the Gods favour him, he will have the fortune to live longer than his predecessor, but if he is wrong he shall find me unforgiving and I will have him gelded with a rusty blade." Gunnar was unable to totally stifle a shudder. "It has cost me plenty of coin to have you and your sons build most of these ships and supply my poorer bondsmen with food and better weapons than just the knives and the hand-me-down blades they owned."

"Fret not, Jarl Magnússon," Gunnar sighed in exasperation, breaking eye contact to judge the longship's current speed and the continued direction of the wind as he glanced up at the swinging weather vane mounted near the top of the mast. "There will be enough plunder and adventure for all. We'll have several horns of mead at the celebration feast and laugh at the crew's sing the retelling of this tale."

"From your lips to Odin's ears," Magnússon said in a threatening tone, slinging his bow over his other shoulder. A second volley of arrows arched skyward from the decks of the surrounding longships. "Those barbs should be plenty to clear the beach of any defenders."

"Father," Siegfried approached them from behind. Reindeer hide armour protected his muscular torso and now a horned helmet topped his lean, bronze clean-shaven face. He carried one more identical helmet. "The crew has theirs helms and this is for you."

Gunnar nodded his thanks and took the proffered helmet before putting it on and addressing the nobleman to voice his concerns. "These helms are unwise, Jarl Magnússon. The warriors won't be able to properly overlap their shields for the shield wall for fear of gouging themselves with those damnable cattle horns."

"It entered my mind after seeing our priests wearing such protrusions on helmets during their rituals and from what little you did reveal of this raid to me beforehand I judged there would be no need for such tactics when there is nay hope of spirited resistance from the monastery. It will be simple butchery against the pious monks and farmers; they're timid sheep and the only sport we have will be to run them down." Magnússon noisily hawked to clear his throat and spat out the phlegm, splashing it on Gunnar's leather boot. The shipwright gritted his yellowish teeth in disgust. "I like to know my enemies and I've studied these 'Anglisc' Christians. They're as superstitious as the next man, having faith in worded spells of protection and I mean to use it to our advantage. If they can believe in Angels and evil spirits skulking about the night shadows, then the sight of the dragon figureheads, the dyed blood red sails and the horned helmets will inspire fear in their hearts, making the survivors believe we're not just men, but demons that have escaped from some nether-realm, intent on stealing their souls."

"We be leaving behind survivors?" it was the turn of Gunnar to furrow his brow. "Methinks we were capturing slaves and slaughtering the old and weak, Jarl Magnússon?"

"Aye, we are, but I require two or three breathing monks is all, Gunnar," Magnússon replied, folding his sinewy arms above his developing paunch. "I do everything for a reason. My destiny is to be forged in fire and steel and this is where my dreams take flight. I want the name and bloody exploits of the Viking nobleman Magnus Magnússon to ring out throughout the Sagas and annals for eternity, and be also carved upon memorial stones, but for me to build such a reputation I need it to start being spread by word of mouth to the four winds." He paused then, becoming serious and thoughtful in his demeanour. "I must confess though that my mind has been busy with other thoughts of late." The shipwright nodded, well versed in the subject. "I care not of the Saxons or their Frisian allies or mourn for their loses, but this 'White Christ' the flow of exiles speak off and the bloodthirsty tales of war and subjugation befalling their homeland between the Rhine and the Elbe rivers Charlemagne wages against the old religions in order to spread this Christianity of his threatens us all. This raid and the ones that follow shall be my answer to the broken truces and the mass killings his Frankish soldiers have carried out."

* * *

Plump-bodied pigeons jerked their heads and were taking hurried steps towards some scrapes of stale bread lying on the dirty flagstones when the bells in the lofty bell tower unexpectedly rang out to disturbed the peace and tranquilly of the monastery. Startled, the birds flapped their wings and took to the sky. Below in an arcaded cloister a gaggle of voices grew louder as a dozen monks emerged slowly from doorways and corridors - leading to the monastery's central kitchen, the brewery, and smith's workshop - in genuine curiosity.

The shade from the enclosing stone walls made the quadrangle-courtyard cooler and a small number of nuns - who were publicly washing their lathered hair with the sap of the soapwort plant in the water from the horse trough for penance - muttered and grabbed a cotton cloth to wipe their stinging eyes and dry themselves off. Several additional monks of various age and build had been sitting around the central fountain in contemplative meditation, but in turns, they blinked and looked at each other in puzzlement.

"It's much too early for the Vespers bell or to join the choir, Brother Francis," the tall, gaunt Abbot said with a confused frown to an elderly monk whose back was crooked with the rigors of time.

Just then a panting novice in a full length robe and sporting a full head of hair not yet conferred with the tonsured upon, hurried from an adjacent stone corridor, his sandals slapping on the paving. "You're Holiness," the boy said, as he stopped in front of the abbot. No burbling water plunged into the fountain's deep stone bowl because it had evaporated due to the prolonged periods of hot, dry weather. "Strangers come by ships to our shore."

"Is it Pilgrims, Vincent?" Abbot Percival asked as he stood. "Perchance they bring offerings or word from the outside world."

"Nay! Brother Gilbert was polishing the bells in the belfry and from that vantage point he says that they be Norse pagans and the fierce dragon-carved prow on their longship is a harbinger for their hostile purpose and 'tis another dire sign in the wake of the whirlwinds, the famine and the lightning storms to visit this land."

"Nonsense! I think anyone can see monsters in the clouds if they stare hard enough at the sky and I believe that Brother Gilbert has been listening to the Queen's astrologer when he visited the court to teach Bible studies, and he simply misspoke himself," the Abbott sighed deeply. "Those were merely omens sent by the Lord to test the flock and smite the turpitude within."

Feeling a touch of premonition, Brother Francis took a breath and was glad he was already sitting down as his frail reedy voice spoke with emotion. "I've heard a tale of similar tall ships arriving on the Wessex shore four years hence and the local reeve went to greet them but one of the beasts slew him with a single stroke of his sword. I beseech thee, Abbot," he added as if sensing the abbot's feelings and knowing it was in his character to behave and look kindly upon the less fortunate, "keep the monastery gates locked against these foreign heathen. It may be the only chance we have to save our lives."

"Brother Francis speaks the truth, you're Eminence," A bulldogged faced monk with a few remaining teeth agreed; the sharp edges of tension couldn't be concealed from his crackling tone. "Afore I sought deliverance for breaking eight of the Ten Commandments and dedicated myself permanently to spiritual life within the walls of this community, I tasted the terrible sins of the flesh and drank of the grape and these heathens are far worst than when I was a mere cutpurse and bandit."

"I too have heard of that circulated story and of the wicked reputation preceding these ferocious men from the icy North, Brother Barnabas; but I haven't spoken to another living person who actually witnessed the incident and without facts to confirm the truth, I deem it to be idle speculation, which I daresay has been greatly exaggerated with each telling." Abbot Percival shook his large head vehemently as he tried to look for the good in everyone. "I hereby decree that we shall admit them, for it is not the Christian way to turn our back on our fellow man even if they be pagans. How are we to banish our own ignorance and rudeness besmirching your minds and to discover a person's true self if we don't embrace the opportunity to learn all we can about these hardy travellers?"

"But with humble respect--" Brother Barnabas persisted.

"No buts, brother," the bald Abbot interrupted with annoyance, in a tone that brooked no argument. "Your concern is gratefully received, nevertheless by the grace of God Almighty, its best that you cast out such thoughts, for I shall not falter nor will I ever lose my faith in humanity." He glanced around at the rest of the monks and addressed them. "You all took wows of chastity, poverty and obedience to this monastery; henceforth heed me and obey. I shall go out to greet them and be ready my Brothers to enlighten these Norsemen to our religious belief."

Putting their blind faith in the Abbot's words, all but one of the monks bowed their heads in support. Brother Francis' calloused; twitching fingers picked up the chain about his bony neck and kissed the wooden crucifix, praying silently for all their eternal souls to be looked after. The Abbot turned and was about to walk towards his room when Brother Barnabas addressed him with a flat and defeated voice.

"Abbott, our larder is meagre at present what with the extended visit of the Reverend Mother and her nuns," he glanced over at the Mother Superior and winced as her stern gaze glared at him, "and the prolonged drought which has caused extensive damage to the crops grown thus far on the island and replenishing them in the short term will be nigh impossible. But I do have an answer to the solution, we receive a sufficient fish supply from the headman and I would like your permission to butcher two of the pigs and the chickens?"

The Abbott nodded thoughtfully. "The Lord's house can be a warm haven for the weary, but it's not enough to be friendly and welcoming, we have to be generous with our guests too. The fattest of the sows and a few of the piglets can go, but keep the hens, for they be still laying eggs. Catch and kill some of the pigeons hereabouts and they will do for the other meat courses, but use plenty of herbs and spices to give the meat additional flavour; the tastes of these Norsemen are not so refined as say our King, so they won't know the different." He turned again. "I shall change into my ceremonial robes. They are befitting an occasion such as this." He snapped his fingers at Vincent as he set off. "Assist me, boy."

Chapter Two
Brothers and Sisters in Arms

Reaching the shore, the crew onboard the Mjöllnir's Might drew their oars inside and laid them down on the deck just seconds before the remaining momentum sent the distinctive prow bursting from the surf; the hull and keel scraping a wedged furrow into the beach and the few inexperienced Norsemen's that had not held on to something were thrown off their feet. Sand gradually built up before the prow and formed heaps as the timbers groaned and vibration shook the length and breadth of the longship until it came to a shuddering halt.

The Long Snake and the Bifrost's Bow were now also easing towards the shone.

"You all know your tasks," Gunnar barked to the crew as he surveyed the scene. "Forget them not. Good hunting to ya."

The knuckles of Magnus Magnússon's left hand whitened as he tightly gripped his round wooden shield before he hooked a leg over the gunwale and shouted back. "Follow me, you rogues, today we be the tip of the spear and be treading the path to blood and plunder."

Answering with a nod, Lokar laughed and slapped a fist into his other callused palm. His sword was sheathed and having removed his shield from the shield rack, it was now slung across his broad back. Excitement gripped the crew as one and all picked up upon Magnússon's confidence attitude and they banged swords against shields and gave tongue to a cacophony of passionate whoops. Magnússon leaped to the ground, quickly striding up the beach to allow room for his crew to disembark in ones and twos. Sunlight glinted off spearheads, naked blades and the claw-like grappling hooks attached to coils of rope as their hairy owners energetically jumped from the longship and landed heavily, their fierce-eyes darting at their bleak surroundings as they surged forward and out of fear and respect crowded behind Magnússon, who had stopped in his tracks on the slope of a small rise topped with the fishing settlement and surveyed it with calculating eyes.

"Those people ran off like spooked ponies, father," Lokar came up alongside him and was just about to dash forward when Magnússon grabbed hold of him by the scruff of the neck.

"Hold your horses, Lokar; something is not as it should be," Magnússon was listening to his instincts as Lokar struggled against his grip before relaxing. "Take five and ten warriors, and search those fishing hovels for anything of worth. Perchance there will be food filling the cauldrons, clothing and weapons, but burn the thatch not else we signal the English of our presence upon the shore of this miserable outpost earlier than I planned too," Magnússon said bluntly and released him as something suddenly thudded behind the Vikings and several heads turned to see the Long Snake slowing as it ploughed through the hardening sand heaps. The Bifrost's Bow was still a little aways out, but its crew were back-stroking their oars over the dwindling distance, smoothly bringing the dragon prow into shore. Lokar scowled dubiously at the order and felt a strong temptation to speak out. "Your sister has arrived. Once you have completed the task escort her up to the monastery. In the meanwhile I will forge inland with the vanguard of the army to see what lies ahead of us."

"Hmpt, but father, I am a skilled warrior not a mother hen to fuss over Kari so; and as for those dwellings they be dung-heaps,

I question whether there would be two copper coins in there for me to rub together, where is the honour and glory in that. It profits…" Lokar sputtered, his mind reasoning the merit of the tactics that clashed with his own desires of blood lust and greed.

"This is not the time for more of your honeyed words, Lokar," Magnússon interrupted, holding up a hand to forestall him as he felt a flash of annoyance and shook his head, impatience at his son's hesitation. The nobleman sensed the eyes of his Norsemen on him and he knew the men didn't have the tolerance to linger for long when they craved for spilled blood and the tantalizing prospect of treasure lay nearby. Behind them, the Long Snake eventually ground on the beach abreast of the Mjöllnir's Might, about fifteen yards distance separated their hulls. "I feel the weight of eyes upon me from those hovels. They might only seem abandoned and we can ill afford to leave an enemy at our back so ferret them out. You have my word you and your men will receive a cut of the plunder from the monastery," he brutally shoved Lokar away, "Now go."

Lokar laughed, letting the contempt he felt for this unworthy of tasks seep into the sound as he glared up at a hulking, ugly warrior, who made a low growling sound in his throat. He was tucked right behind Magnússon and there was an air of death and violence about him as he clutched a spear in each of his large scared hands. A huge double edged battle axe was strapped to his broad, muscular back. Lokar's face lost all traces of humour and he grew abruptly serious and thoughtful in his demeanour before meeting his father's gaze and nodding. "This squabbling avails us naught, Father," beneath his veneer of politeness lay hostility. "I will do as you command."

"Such enthusiasm and loyalty from you is truly humbling, Lokar," Magnússon said with sarcasm. "Never have I known such a man so fascinated with petty intrigues and mischief. It must be exhausting being you?"

Lokar shot Magnússon a sour look and then glanced at the warriors and pointed at the Norsemen he knew and trusted. "Bárðr Bearcloak, you, Sjolf Ninefingers and Önundr of the Low Hills……" A few of the chosen warriors freed themselves of additional weight in case of a fight by discarding shackles or fetters attached to thick chains before Lokar curled a finger and beckoned them to follow him. Magnússon pointed at the manacles and issued a command for Vikings not carrying irons to pick them up.

Watching Lokar go, the hulking warrior learned his head forward and whispered causally in Magnússon's ear as he hefted up his shield and raised his scimitar above his head. "Just a thought, Jarl Magnússon; you can not command the full respect of the men if Lokar openly challenges your authority. It is ill-advised and only bleeds strife."

"Of that I am well aware, Björn," Magnússon admitted, lowering his sword, signalling his warriors to advance as he set off at a trot, circumventing the settlement in a smooth curve. The loose, soft sand became harder packed and it made their jogging easier. "And yet I can not choose my family as easily as I do my few friends or discard them if I must like an old mantle. Lokar was the runt of the wife's litter and I loathed that weakness in him. I would have left him outside to die had it not been for my wife's refusal. We had already lost one boy to chest disease and another baby boy was stillborn, hence I was stuck with him. I tried to mould Lokar like clay into the son a Jarl deserves, so I could gaze with pride upon him. Alas it was not meant to be. Our quarrels have gone on till I became quite hoarse and the disagreement between us has made me angry. There is more to being a Viking nobleman, 'tis not enough to be born to command, I felt I had to be worthy of the honour. Oh, he vexes me so."

"Lokar can not stop being who he is anymore than you can stop the wind from blowing." Björn ran beside his chieftain along the uneven ground surrounded by the vanguard of warriors as they savoured the tang of brine in the air and the caress of the invigorating wind now blowing in from a southerly direction. "He may be your only son in wedlock, but you have others the wars and disease did not kill who would be willing to take his place if you only admit to their existence."

Magnússon digested the man's words as he considered them. "Aye, I had always intended to beget as many offspring as possible by bedding the servant wenches in my household and elsewhere, while preserving the anonymity of the each bastard's lineage for their own safety after the hemlock mysteriously found its way into Halvar's drinking cup."

"You had the slave killed when I discovered the clippings of the poison plant upon her person. Do you still ponder that Lady Ranveig put her up to it?"

"Aye, my wife is finicky at their mere mention of my other sons and daughters and is liable to suffer from diarrhoea of the mouth," Magnússon replied, the Roman road replacing the sand and dirt beneath their boots. "One night when the ale was flowing freely it loosened many a guarded tongue including hers. I heard of her fears that one of my bastards might one day try to stand in Lokar's way and usurp his right of inheritance and she spoke dispassionately of being justified in doing whatever she could to see that did not happen. I have nay proof, but I know my wife has murderous intentions and is capable of such a task. I am a devoted father, Björn; and seeing each of them grow up has brought me much joy during the past seasons. If I can carve out a large enough kingdom, then all my sons can receive a Jarldorn of their own and my daughters will marry my allies once I finally leave this world for the hall of Valhalla." He was striving to drive away any distractions that delayed his focus. "For now I am content that even Lokar looks nervously upon you and is wise enough to not rock the boat by trying to face my bodyguard Björn Strongarm in open battle. I will keep that thought alive though and then reach a decision."

The peal of the bells continued to echo across the landscape. At the bow of the Long Snake, Vegard, the first mate lowered the gangplank and he hurriedly disembarked from the ship.

A sixty year old Norseman with bandy-legs and clutching a coil of rope followed Vegard onto the sand. "Vegard, where do you want to place the anchors?" A couple of younger sailors came after the old warrior, carrying large, heavy stones; each one was lashed into a wooden frame.

"There and there, Old Sven," Vegard pointed at the left and then the right side of the ship. "And see to it that the lines are tied tightly."

It was the turn of the Bifrost's Bow to thump into the beach next. The remainder of the longships coming in behind it had reduced speed and were promptly shipping their oars as they grew dramatically in size and their helmsmen angled them on a course towards the empty stretches of beach.

* * *

On board the Mjöllnir's Might, Siegfried handed down spears to a couple of older stragglers and was in the process of joining the warriors when he glanced sympathetically at Gunnar standing glumly at the gunwale behind him. There were dark circles of tiredness shading the bags under his eyes.

"Father, I wish you and Lars were coming with me to watch my back," the tall, nineteen year old said with regret, the words caught in his throat as he thought about Gunnar's self-sacrifice and mourned over his loss, "as opposed to him standing in your stead back at the shipyard and you remaining on deck with the other two men to guard the longship."

"Aye, Siegfried;" Gunnar nodded with pent up frustration,

letting it fill his voice. "But Jarl Magnússon decided I was too valuable to lose in battle," he puffed out his chest in pride with as much dignity as his melancholy mood would permit, "that my skill as a shipwright dwarfs any talent I ever had with a blade." His clenched fist thumped the top of the gunwale and he got himself into a terrible temper as his eyes grew shadowy by the miserable memory. "Bah, I curse the day I embarked on that winter hunt to keep an eye out for you and your younger, half brother. The pain of the wound faded with the passing of the seasons and yet the memory I carry will not go away and my suffering endures like my neighbours' noisy children."

"We did not ask you to come on the hunt," Siegfried took umbrage and shouldered the long haft of his battleaxe. Gunnar recoiled as if he had been punched. "For we had attained a man's growth by then and neither of us needed a father's bridle."

"Gods above, Siegfried," Gunnar swore an oath, shock disappearing from his expression to be replaced by a stubborn scowl as he turned his head and regarded his son for a moment. "I was not denying your birthright, but I felt you both were warriors only in waiting. Glad am I you and your half brother finally bonded over your shared fervour for life, but in my eyes my pups were still too young to go and prone in making mistakes that you might not have been able to learn from. Your pride and vanity," referring to his son's beardless face and shaven head, "leaves you with something to prove in battle."

"Growing up, you drummed this speech into our heads, Father. As Vikings we all believe that the dying moment is predestined. If that is the will of Odin then all we can do is face it bravely."

"Aye," Gunnar sighed deeply and his next words were less harsh and kinder as he looked away, his attention drawn to the crews of the Long Snake and the Bifrost's Bow, which were going ashore in twos and threes. "I am not made out of wood. I can not just stop being a caring parent nor can I fail to give guidance and support, be it wanted or not. I promised your mother, Sigrid on her death bed I would do what I could to keep you from harm. 'Twas the reason I shoved you out of the way when I saw the boar emerge from the bushes, his tusk gouging my leg and crippling me instead ere Magnússon's bodyguard slayed it with his spears."

Siegfried's rigid demeanour disappeared and he took a quick breath rich in significance as his eyes strayed behind him at the older Viking stragglers receding up the beach as they tried to catch up to the vanguard force. "Father, I have been wracked by guilt for many moons now," his voice was tight as if he was stifling his feelings, "but by way of a belated apology I shall bring you back gold and silver in abundant."

A ghost of smile spread across Gunnar's lips and he make a dismissive gesture in reply. "I will settle for a plump wench with big milkers," his hands gestured like they were cupping a pair of invisible breasts, "I can chain to the cooking cauldron and keep her bare foot and pregnant. My rutting instincts have not gone away so why should you and Lars have all the fun?" Siegfried grinned, while Gunnar turned serious again. "Remember though when you are with your shipmates their camaraderie is not as strong as our bond of kinship nor are they as deep-rooted as their rivalries. So do not succumb to doubt."

As Siegfried turned to go, Tjernagl approached Gunnar from the stern, "I can not find Fridrik anywhere on board."

"Fridrik and the other boys went with the Jarl," Gunnar said. "Their duties are to run messages relaying his commands to those under him. Battle is fluid and parts of the army can get lost in the chaos, hence its makes sense to use them as a means of communication."

"Huh," Tjernagl expressed his surprise, tearing a chunk

of stale bread in half and handed the piece to Gunnar. "I have posted a new lookout aloft."

"Good," Gunnar took a bite and chewed noisily. "Have him keep a wary eye especially on the mainland; the causeway may be underwater now preventing the people from other local villagers from becoming a nuisance to us, but we haven't the luxury to think it will stop the Northumbria king if our longships are seen. Aethelred will send a fleet of galleys loaded with swordsmen and bowmen after us from Bamburgh Castle."

Tjernagl swallowed his mouthful. "He will signal twice with the conch shell should he see such a fleet hove into view."

Gunnar gave him a satisfied nod and threw down the rest of the bread beginning to discolour with mould. "I am not a person who gives praise freely, Tjernagl, but you will make a fine Sailing Master one of these days."

"I thank you, master steersman," Tjernagl beamed, thinking of the esteem such a command would bestow upon him. "Only Vegard has more lore."

"True, and yet I wager very soon you shall be his equal."

* * *

Brandishing swords and battleaxes Lokar and his Norsemen gathered themselves into an uneven line and moved forward and up among the overturned boats, edging closer and closer to the fishing huts and shacks.

"I tell you my father behaves towards his thralls with more kindness than he offers me. I am Lokar; heir apparent to Jarl Magnus Magnússon, Sjolf," Lokar bemoaned to his sandy-haired friend and confidant, who was a half a head taller than him, "but these senseless tasks are beneath my dignity. I know there is a time for caution to overshadow speed, but after beholding yon place it is in my estimation this is not one of them."

"I grant you 'tis not the liveliest settlement we have ever been in," Sjolf mused aloud with a flat nasal accent. Ahead a hut door swung inward a little on creaking hinges and the sound made pairs of Norsemen eyes stray toward it. "Hmmm, the wind is not at our backs so it seems Jarl Magnússon was right about somebody hiding in the shacks." That made Lokar perk up with casual interest. "We may have some sport after all, Lokar."

"Come on, you English maggots," Lokar taunted loudly with an arrogant drawl at the hovels, his eyes darting left and right as he silently communicated to his warriors with hand gestures to fan out and stay alert. The Vikings put on wary expressions and obeyed. "Show your faces if you have courage and fight us like men."

Malcolm peered out from behind the hut door and he clenched his teeth, breathing through them in a hiss. Stephen poked his head out from the opposite side of the entranceway, holding a bow and some arrows.

"This will be unlike shooting fish in shallow water, Father." Stephen said, feeling sweat trickling down his nose as he notched an arrow to his bow string.

"Aye," Malcolm said, shaking out the fishing net he held, "but fish don't shoot back. Feather those bastards."

"There be two that are to stubborn to run away, Lokar," Sjolf pointed out, his voice bore a trace of amusement. "This will be child's play."

Hunkering down behind one of the huge cauldrons, Doon snarled angrily at the Viking's insult and taking the bait he revealed himself as he quickly stood. Lokar smiled coldly as the Englishmen reacted in precisely the way that he wanted him too.

"And there are more of their ilk," Lokar gestured with his head as Stephen trained his bow at the Vikings and let fly. "Bárðr, take the left flank, Önundr, you the right."

The arrow sprouted from the neck of a well-thewed man with oily golden hair. As he fell, it provided a signal on both sides to act.

Lokar squinted his eyes and knowing more arrows could undermine the confidence of his Norsemen, his voice cracked out like a whip as he became bereft of pity. "Give nay quarter or mercy. Kill them all."

Stephen drew his bow back and released another shaft. It struck a Viking shield, splintering on the pointed metal boss in the centre. Bárðr growled and propelled his battle axe at the doorway framing Malcolm and Stephen. Malcolm heard the weapon whistling through the air and he yanked his son further inside the hut as the axe blade hit the lintel beam and wedged there.

"Now, foul their approach," Doon shouted to three other villagers as he braced his back against his hut wall and grunting with the effort kicked out, toppling the iron pot before him and sending it rolling down the slope at the approaching Vikings. Lokar blinked and leaped to one side as the heavy cauldron spilled the last of its contents and shot past him a handbreadth from his leg before it collided into the hapless warrior with a broad, drooping moustache, braining him and tossing his body aside by its sheer momentum.

The Vikings hesitated in their staggered rush and it took only a moment for them to realise what had happened. Some of the Norsemen shouted in alarm in their mother tongue including Bárðr, who draw his short sax sword, while a couple of others cursed in broken English as they felt the strong urge to look up to see three more fisher folk had emerged from their hiding places. By this time they were using all their strength to heave up an equal number of cauldrons, fish and the preserving salt water plopped and splashed out of the gaping maw onto the ground as the rust-spotted pots was eventually pushed over and trundled at speed down the slope.

Malcolm grabbed the handle of Bárðr's axe and wretched it from the beam before he leaned it against the hut wall alongside a barbed spear before making room again for Stephen to shoot his arrows.

Sjolf Ninefingers lost his sword when he vaulted over a second cauldron with difficulty. The heavy-boned face of Önundr wrinkled as he drew his muscular arm back, aimed at a target and threw his battleaxe with one smooth movement. But before he had the chance to dodge it, the third cauldron crashed into him with bone crushing impact, blood spurted from his mouth onto his braided beard and the Norsemen's mangled body was catapulted backwards, leaving behind a crimson smear. In the intervening time Önundr's axe flashed end over end and the wide metal head buried itself in the chest of one of the young fisher folk. He slammed back against the hut wall and collapsed with a dying gargle.

✶ ✶ ✶

Standing on the beach a man-length in front of the grounded longships, Vegard the first mate of the Long Snake spoke to some of his assembling Norsemen. "Seize everything that benefits us," he spoke and pointed up the nearby heights. Viking eyes glanced in that direction and were rewarded with glimpses of movement. "Jens Three-Torques," he addressed a thickset man wearing two armbands and a metal collar about his broad neck. "Lead two and ten warriors up yon hillside and gather together those goats. Grettir of the Marshland, your task for provisions is similar," he jerked his helmeted head at the fields beyond the hillside, his blond hair plaits did not swish about much because they were weighed down with metal balls. "Capture the sheep and carry back any farming tools you find along the way, bestowing it all hither on the sand."

"Tether them not by my ship, Vegard; I will not have the stench of spilled animal blood and loosened bowels wafting towards where I and my shield maidens sleep," ordered a young woman in a voice that carried over the babble of other vocal utterances. Heads turned partway around to see her descending the gangplank with a bouncing stride, her shapely figure was hidden within her male armour and clothes. A stray gust of wind flicked a strand of her long raven coloured hair flowing down from her horned helmet and fluttered the cloaks of the three women following her down to the sand. The generous curves of their womanliness were equally evened out by their garb and gave them the androgynous looks of both sexes as they gripped spears and shields. A short, scraggly looking boy with an iron shackle wrapped about his neck adhered to the heels of the last shield maiden. "It reminds me of being enclosed in my father's old longhouse in the winter seasons, the reek of smoke from the large central hearth and unwashed bodies and of dung and urine befouling the hay in the stalls housing all his treasured livestock."

"Aye," a petite, pixie-faced young shield-maiden said, forgetting herself as the heat of the sun made her unfastened her cloak. The remaining shield maidens did the same, and handed them to the servant boy. "The Jarl always liked to blow his own horn by flaunting the animal's wealth whenever my father came to visit…." She tailed off to an embarrassing silence as the raven haired woman flashed a dirty look at her. "Apologises Lady Kari."

"What you say is true, Helga, but this not a moment for my sergeant at arms to let loose your hair and speak thus. Close your lips till I say otherwise," Kari watched the shield maiden curtsey with nervous energy and then swivelled her gaze to Vegard. He opened his mouth to say something, then changed his mind and closed it again, knowing Kari was not a person who took orders easily and she was prone to argue if he tried to press the point of who was really in charge of the beachhead. "Well, man what is it to be?" she addressed Vegard demandingly, giving him an arched look, revelling in her fierce independent. "Follow my commands or I hear there is an opening for a second mate on a sheep scow."

"I shall do as you say Kari Magnúsdaughter," Vegard sketched a bow as something low and vague began merging with the background noise. Most of the Vikings shrugged, shifting from foot to foot as they restlessly waited in the staging area for orders, but a few of them were staying alert, listening for the barest sound and their brooding eyes glanced at the shadows and the slanting sunlight around the beach and the heights for any signs of danger.

"Thought so, but I prefer Kari Rune-Master," Kari approached the growing crowd and peered at individual faces, become aware of someone's absent and of a strange rumbling that came within earshot. Flanking her, two of the shield maidens frowned in puzzlement at the deepening sound, while the third fell back apace and fingered the hilt of her sword. "Where is my wretched brother Lokar? He is supposed to be awaiting me here."

Vegard suppressed the urge to laugh at her adopting the name of her new position within the army. "Gunnar said he had been..." his voice trailed off and he held up a warning hand as a loud sound of rending wood filed the air. And then a sudden shout from a warrior broke the tension and caused Vegard to whirl about and the eyes of the crowd peered upward in fascination to see a blood stained cauldron had smashed into one of the overturned boats. More cauldrons were rolling down the slope towards the other boats and behind them there was Norsemen standing and crawling like they were injured, while the rest littered the ground. "The cauldrons be coming from the fishing settlement where Lokar was sent."

"To arms, men and women of the North, to arms I say in my father' name," Kari commanded, taking the initiative as she saw most of the cauldrons have solid impacts with the boats, shunting them and splintering timbers, and producing a series of long gashes in the hulls. The last one though wasn't as direct, only clipping the keel a glancing blow before it trundled on past and off the slope. On the beach, Vikings were in the act of drawing their swords as they got out of the cauldron's path as it finally crashed harmlessly into the sand mounts in front of the Mjöllnir's Might. "Vegard, I am taking half the crew of the Sea Chariot," she added, naming one of the other longships and the first mate let out an exasperated sign, "to accompany my shield maidens up to the settlement, I bid you and your warriors to carry out your assigned tasks." Kari looked at her sergeant at arms and nodded. "Helga."

"I will take the point," Helga held her spear and shield at the ready. "Gyrid," she glanced at the woman's round face and intense green eyes as she was checking the straps of her breast armour, "bring up the rear, Marit," she flicker her gaze to the slimmer woman, who wiped sweat from her high forehead before donning her helm again. "You are on the right flank."

"You heard Kari.... Rune-Master," Vegard corrected himself in time before turning towards where the crew of the Sea Chariot stood. "Every second person step out and join her shield maidens."

Helga barked a command. "Crew of the Sea Chariot line up behind me here and listen to the words of the Rune-Master."

The selected Vikings spread out as they formed up together.

"The English have kicked the wasp's nest," Kari said in a voice sharp with anxiety and drew her sword. "Let's show them the sting of our steel." The sentiment was echoed loud and raucously by dozens of the warriors and it brought a satisfied smile to her face. "Advance my brothers and sisters in arms."

Nervous and tense, Kari set off accompanied by her shield maidens up the slope. The Vikings followed closed behind them.

* * *

A fourth and fifth cauldron rolled harmlessly in-between the spaces separating three Norsemen's, but then another arrow flashed from the hut and sank with a meaty thump into the round bulging stomach of a craggy-faced man on the edge of the line, who saw the sun glint on the arrow head but was slow in reacting to lift his slightly larger shield in time. Lokar and a few others slid on the fish fillets at the top of the rise and stumbled onto their hands and knees. Doon scooped up a barbed fishing spear and threw it at two nearing swordsmen. Sjolf cried out, doubling up as the shaft lodged in his torso and the tip burst out of his back in a welter of blood.

"That was the last arrow, father," Stephen said hinting but not putting into words what they both were afraid of as he discarded the bow and pulled a sharp knife from his rawhide belt. "They be holding their approach and more come behind them. What do we do?"

"Fight on, I shall take the score on the right, you and Doon take the score on the left," Malcolm gripped the fishing net at his side and stress increased the sound of his heartbeat as his gaze strayed briefly at his son and how he was armed. "Take up the enemy axe; it will service you better than that filleting knife you hold," he struggled to control his voice. "Now step back and give me room."

The remaining two villagers near Doon each picked up a bench and converged on the second Norsemen, hoisting them up as makeshift weapons. Bárðr observed the pair lacked coordination as he raised his shield at an angle to deflect a quick awkward blow from the forerunner's bench, the force of it was redistributed over the flat surface, only for Bárðr to still felt the shock vibrate down his arm to his shoulder as he gritted his teeth and counterattacked with a low disabling thrust at the leg of his shorter opponent, severing the muscles to put him out of action so he could concentrate on dealing with the taller villager bearing down on him.

Bárðr grinned. "I have corns bigger than you."

The villager came up and bunching his shoulders, he swung vigorously with all his wiry strength at the Viking's temple, but Bárðr ducked under the swipe and had his riveted helmet ripped off his head, revealing his topknot, as the bench leg caught at the horns in passing. Straightening, Bárðr swivelled his hips and the extended reach of his left arm lashed out with the edge of his shield, the knuckle-duster style punch inflicted great injury to his opponent's face, sending the fisherman reeling. The swordsman advanced and his sax blade sliced down, opening the villager up from throat to navel.

Thirsty for blood and battle, Lokar's face was a brutish mask and as he heard the approach of heavy footfalls from behind, he stared angrily first at the trail of corpses and then at the villagers, who were now slowly retreating into their hut's shadowy interiors. Rattled, he got his feet under him and unslung his shield. "Damn their eyes, I wearily of this. I shall tip the scales in hacked silver to the men who help me take their heads."

"That be a prosperous way to spur the men on, Lokar," said Bárðr as he dispatched the wounded villager with a sword thrust into his neck. "You shall have my support and goodwill when you are Jarl."

* * *

On came the shield maidens and the warriors of the Sea Chariot through the flattened grasses.

Kari's heart beat noisily and her expression flickered with emotion, but she felt some of her anxiety fade as she saw Lokar turned his head to stare behind him at the reinforcements and gestured with his sword to communicate an instruction.

Recognising the sign language, Helga pulled up and raised her arms as she shouted to her warriors in a husky voice. "Stand fast! We go nay closer, you lubbers," the men and women skidded to a halt in two and threes, "this here skirmish be Lokar's until it's over." She glanced at Kari. "We are to stay back…"

"I have eyes, but what is the reason my brother does this?" Kari interrupted her features stony. "I think there is something more in the wind," her raising doubts made her exchanged a confused look with Helga, who shook her head, "and I would know what it is?"

* * *

The Vikings gasped at Lokar's generosity and terrifying war cries filled the air as they eagerly threw themselves over the last half a dozen yards and engaged the villagers. Over excited, Doon lunged out of his hut, over extending himself with another fishing spear, which Lokar turned aside with his rune-decorated shield before stepping in closer and with a wild look in his eyes and working out his frustrations, his low blade cut upward into Doon's groin and continued ripping into his stomach, gore spurted out of the grisly wound to soak Lokar's arm and armour.

Simultaneously off to the left, Malcolm emerged out of his hut and threw the net with a twist, and it entangled itself around Bárðr's arm, weapon and head. Determined to stand beside his father one last time, Stephen ran out of the doorway and his arm muscles ached with the weight of Önundr's axe as he managed to swing it clumsy from on high, splitting Bárðr's skull in twain. Another Norseman with shoulders as broad as the gap separating the horns atop his helmet stomped forward and stabbed his sword deep into Stephen's side, sliding between ribs to pierce his heart.

"Ha-ha let the Goddess Hel know that I Auðun Frostbeard send this mewling corpse to the shore of Náströnd." He ripped out his blade with a flourish and Stephen's body slumped lifelessly to the ground.

"That was my son you butchered," the headman cried out in anguish, his blood boiling. "Upon my oath you will join him in death."

"I be used to family feuds lasting seasons not moments." Auðun laughed and turned to meet him, seeing Malcolm snatch up his spear. "Like my shadow, death for a Viking warrior is a devoted companion."

As grief-fuelled adrenaline coursed through Malcolm's body he sought vengeance by veering around Bárðr's body and launching himself headlong at the Viking. Auðun widened his eyes in an instant of surprise at the fisherman's burst of speed as he saw him preparing to thrust his spear. Gathering himself, Auðun plunged his sword into the ground and held his shield with both hands against the momentum of the strike, but the spear thrust was powerful and the planks making up the shield were already split and weakened from previous battles.

Malcolm's spearhead punched through the outer edge of the wood and armour to drive deep into the Norseman's waist. Pieces of shield dropped at his feet.

"You have slayed me, worm," Auðun grunted in pain and bubbly foamed appeared on his lips as he continued walking up the spear shaft for the purpose of getting to the shocked headman, who hesitated for a second or two, speechlessly and felt goose bumps ripple across his arms and legs at the sight. When Auðun reached him, his arm lunged forward and the pointed tip of the shield boss impaled Malcolm's right eye socket. "As I spit my final breath into your cursed face tell the dragon Nidhogg, we both died well this day, but only your soul shall he have, for mine will be spending eternity, drinking and battling in Valhalla."

Auðun leaned heavily into Malcolm and they fell back into a tangled heap of arms and legs where they were left to bleed out.

Lokar came over to them, withdrew Auðun's blade, before reversing the hilt and placing it into the dying man's hand. "A Viking warrior dies with a sword in his hand."

* * *

Kari studied the killing ground ahead of her, hearing the cries of excitement from the remainder of Lokar's men as she watched them scrambled into the fishing huts and among the corpses like a pack of scavenging wolves. Growling and barking at each other as they ripped off boots and armour from their own fallen shipmates and knelt to run hands rapidly over the clothing of the fisher folk, searching for concealed weapons, trinkets about necks and cutting free pouches holding various amounts of metal coins.

And then the realisation behind Lokar's refusal of help hit her like a slap to the face and she glanced at her sergeant at arms. "Helga, the battle is over; pick out six warriors and sent the rest away. We go on alone, my father or Lokar will see us safely back to the Long Snake."

Helga nodded and she become the focus of angry stares, listening to the disappointed groans and mutterings from the assembled warriors as she pointed at the nearest men and one woman cutting them out like cattle from a herd. "Return to Vegard for further orders."

The crew of the Sea Chariot did not falter in their steps or think twice as they obeyed.

Without saying another word, Helga turned and strode after the other shield maidens.

The six Vikings brought up the rear.

✷ ✷ ✷

Olaf the lookout tried and failed to tug a ring off Auðun's stiffening hand when he caught sight of a familiar Norseman from the periphery of his vision. "Bugger off Ásgrímr," he looked up and snarled angrily at his bearded and Mjöllnir's Might shipmate as he approached him and the bodies of Auðun and Malcolm. "Back I say."

"He speaks," Ásgrímr's bestial laughter rang out at his own mirth, above the sound of scampering feet as they came into earshot. "Are you frightened of me, little man?"

"Only of your stink, herder of sheep, 'tis a pity you were not coming from downwind when you slayed my older brother in the forest."

Ásgrímr's darkening face told Olaf how he felt about that. "I did not cast the first stone, 'twas Oddur who gave unwanted attention to my wife and I was within my right by Jarl Magnússon's law to behead him. But now your insult has wounded me deeply and prolonged the feud betwixt our families unless Bárðr's Bearcloak and whatever baubles you have stripped from the other corpses were offered up by you as payment to heal the rift."

"Covet this plunder you may, but 'tis mine." A new metal armlet decorated Olaf's forearm and a collar of chain of twisted patterns was now wrapped about his neck. The approaching footfalls grew nearer.

"Neither fell beneath your blade and 'tis said by my mother that Auðun was a distance kinsman of mine, my cousin's father's brother," the big man stared back greedily as he continued to ignore Olaf, clutching two spears in one hand and his helmet in the other filled with an assortment of coins, large fibulae-brooches that fasten cloaks, bracelets and silver fragments. "That means I take what I want."

"Hmph, you presume too much braggart, I care not if your mother fell from the ugly tree and hit every branch on her way down. I got to these bodies first." Olaf blew out his breath to regain his composure and drew his throwing knife with every appearance of meaning it as he aimed the weighted weapon at Ásgrímr. "I named my dagger 'Viper' because its bite can slay."

Ásgrímr came on two more steps and then met his gaze and blanched. Pausing in mid-motion, his tongue licked his cracked bottom lip and calmly he eyed the throwing dagger in the younger man's hand. "You have the upper hand for now whoreson, but you will see me again ere long." His mouth twisted and he nodded before turning away.

After watching Ásgrímr go elsewhere for easily pickings, Olaf looked down and he sliced with the dagger's blade through Auðun's finger and freed the ring that way.

"You learning fast boy," Helga addressed Olaf as the small retinue of warriors and shield maidens passed him by. Kari looked around, searching for Lokar and eventually spotted him emerging from one of the hut's entrances. "But be prepared to start sleeping with one eye open, for aggrieved and a bad loser as Ásgrímr is he's liable in the night to gut you like a trout."

"I see Lokar," Kari said, appearing at Helga's shoulder before forging on ahead towards the tannery workshop. Outside, animal hides had been strung on wooden frames to dry in the sun, not so fresh skins were also stretched on frames and were in the process of being scraped clean of hair, before the leather or vellum was softened by pounding in sheep's brains and animal fat. "You have been beset by problems I see, Brother," Kari's mouth quirked into a lopsided smirk as she drew up in front of him, the loud abrupt manner of her tone brought Lokar up short and turn to face her. "I thought you would be expressing relief and tears of gratitude," Helga took her habitual position at Kari's shoulder and listened as the rune-master needled him, "that I brought lots of stalwart warriors to pull your fat from the fire."

"That was my pampered sister trying to humiliate me in front of my men?" Lokar said evasively with a breathless wheeze, putting on a look of exaggerated wonder as fliers buzzed around pails of animal hair and organs. "I mistook you for a beardless youth."

"A beardless youth?" Kari's smile faded at the insult, as warriors behind her began cutting the animal hides from the frames. "Thank you that is the first cold breeze I have felt in days."

"In truth I did not recognise you wearing that helm and armour, sister," Lokar shrugged his shoulders and fixed his gaze on her. Kari silently hurled a look of entreaty at Helga, who nodded discreetly and motioned for the other shield maidens and the warriors to move out of hearing range. "The English though were a challenge to be sure, but they are a thorn in our side nay longer."

"Disperse and secure the vicinity with a perimeter," Helga waved her spear in an all encompassing gesture of the settlement and the warriors grunted or muttered their acknowledgments before angling away. "Make swift work of it."

Kari lowered her brow as she detected the hint of arrogance in Lokar's voice and stared at the tools he held and rested within his inverted helmet. "Father should be pleased you did not disappoint him again, but," she wedged her shield between her legs and then in turn reached into the helm and picked up a couple of iron punches, an awl, a ball of beeswax and an array of needles and gave each the once-over, "to gain such trifling spoils is methinks at too great a price in warrior lives when accompanying me were archers that would have given aid instead you let your stubbornness prevail."

Lokar's manner sobered and he addressed her dissatisfaction. "You and I are Norse nobility and 'tis the bounden duty to the low born to do our bidding and if need be die in our stead. Bows are good for hunting, but in my mind are," he choose his words carefully, putting slow emphasises on them as he talked, personally believing the weapon was only suitable for women or slaves to shoot, "not fit for purpose on a field of battle, there be nay honour in that..."

"Honour? Now you doth jest with me, brother," Kari interjected with a sniff of disdain, "and father calls me the jocular one."

Lokar clenched his jaw and pressed on, "and as for the spoils they are not a mere trifling, sister," he jerked his head at the entrance of the shack behind him. "That hut houses a workshop, inside there be a mound of cattle leather and scraps reveal they have been making boots and straps and repairing belts and pouches. The neighbouring shack is a fish storehouse and I am bound for the source of the smoke plumes we beheld earlier on the beach."

Kari nodded and regarded him suspiciously through level lashes. "I still have trouble believing you, brother, for the reason that follows you are inherently unscrupulous and have expensive tastes for the finer things in life. 'Twas the glory you wanted all for yourself, was that not it?"

There was a simmering second of silence between them and then Lokar spoke in a softer brooding voice. "Few of us are what we seem. How little you truly know me sister. I am many things and I fancy you, Björn and father regularly call me them behind my back."

"In blunt truth, not every day," Kari admitted in embarrassment, her voice cracking a bit as she rubbed the back of her neck. "But I can not speak for father or the bodyguard."

Her sincerity came through and Lokar let his surprise show by baring his prefect teeth in a humourless smile. "I have my own code of honour like not robbing our own dead."

"Pish! But you be willing to overlook your own warriors from plucking such low hanging fruit without criticizing them for it?" Kari shook her head incredibly.

Lokar sighed. "I have not a tax man's heart, sister; my men fought well in the skirmish and I was of the thought that they should not share the spoils with you or anyone else."

Chapter Three
Panic in the Monastery

Using his riding crop, Brother Isaac trotted his donkey through the crowded graveyard dominated by simple weather-beaten wooden crosses and several craved headstones, a memorial to the people buried there. Garlands of daisies or a single flower rested atop of the graves. As the sturdy stones walls enclosing the monastery and the priory loomed in front of him, glimpses of narrow-windowed buildings with sloping slate roofs speckled white with bird droppings poked up beyond the walls, their façade was forbidding in their bareness and lack of any ornament. Silvery snail tracks crisscrossed the flagstones outside the threshold.

The monk yanked on the bridle and his donkey brayed, skidding to a halt before he quickly slid off the animal's lathered back, "Sorry I had to give you the short end of my stick, Julius," he said regrettably, glancing at the angry welts decorating the animal's hind quarters. "It was for the needs of the many." He strode over to the huge double doors and banged the bronze knocker three times.

"Open up, 'tis brother Isaac," the monk shouted, the words tumbling out of his mouth, the steadily growing cries and shouts from behind him did little to ease his nerves. "Open up both portals I say and make haste, for they are coming."

The sound of scuffing footfalls came from the opposite side of the doors and then a wrinkled female face calm, but puzzled appeared behind the cast-bronze grill embedded in the wood.

"What is the meaning for your rudeness, Brother Isaac?" The old woman asked, her nostrils flaring. "I deem your true "self" is held to be encumbered and veiled by imperfections like sin, ignorance and perversion acquired I daresay by spending too much time in the village. There be some women there that are in plain words belike pots without lids. You should dedicate yourself to meditation and spending time in the company of your Brother monks or favour my cause of serenity. I have placed my poetry scrolls in the monastery's library for all to read and they speak of the joy of solitude."

The monk licked his dry lips, aware that any unwillingness to speak would be taken by the Mother Superior as a humiliating discourtesy. "Nay have I the time to explain myself, Reverend Mother," he said, his heart pounding as he cast a furtive glance behind him, half expecting the barbarians to appear among the approaching villagers, wetting their swords and cleaving skulls at any moment. "I beseech thee to trust unto the Lord that he guides my path."

The Mother Superior's confusion deepened visibly between her white brows as she mulled his words over for a few seconds and stood on her tiptoes to see behind the monk. Bronwyn and Arwen were steering a gaggle of village children from a parked cart towards the monastery. Questions swirled in her mind like leaves caught in a gale and her stomach rolled, but the desperate edge to Brother Isaac's voice and the way he averted his eyes told the Reverend Mother not to ask more of him just now. "God's will be done." She looked away to address someone unseen and her scratchy voice intensified up an octave. "Open the doors wide."

Inside the monastery, monks, novices and a couple of nuns in long loose, black habit- gowns hurried to carry out the Mother Superior's order. There was a succession of whumping sounds as metal bolts were unfastened before many hands grabbed the metal rings that served as handles and pulled. The doors creaked and groaned as they slowly swung inward to reveal the quadrangle-courtyard with stone benches arranged around the central fountain and monks and nuns standing in the cloister arches of the inner arcade that ran along the walls and buildings.

"Clear the way," Bother Isaac bellowed at two novices who tarried a second or two longer in the opening as he strode forward. Bronwyn, Arwen and the children followed him inside, and they stared this way and that with wide eyes of amazed admiration at the new surroundings. "There are villagers on my heels and dozens more further back that seek sanctuary."

"Sanctuary is it? From what pray tell will these holy walls echo with the chatter of fishwives and urchins living cheek by jowl?" Mother Superior said to him from the side, her arms folded.

"Indeed, Brother Isaac," Abbot Percival spoke with a wrinkled brow, catching the last part of their conversation as he descended to the bottom of a flight of stone stairs on the left of the Mother Superior, the risers were worn into slight depressions from centuries of foot traffic. "Enlighten us if you please if you don't want to spend the night locked up in your cell, fed only bread and water."

Brother Isaac glanced back at the entrance and beckoned William and the cart driver to him before sadness ebbed out of him as he told the Mother Superior and the Abbot everything that had happened.

* * *

Magnússon's vanguard of warriors followed the cracked, weed-infested roadway, turning in land as it wound its way between the broken countryside crisscrossed by low dry stone walls and sun-baked stands of hazel, birch wood and rowan trees. Set up

Clash of the Vikings

in an approaching field was a scarecrow dressed in old rags. An archer saw it and loosed an arrow at it in passing as a practice dummy, but unbeknown to him the mannequin wasn't entirely stuffed with straw. The shaft pinned the sloughing scarecrow against its tee-shaped back post and a trickle of blood oozed from the concealed man's mortal wound. The bell tower dominated the flat landscape and it gradually grew even higher to match and then surpass the preceding hill behind them. The tolling of the bells suddenly stopped and the Vikings jostled one another as they continued to advance upon the Lindisfarne monastery.

Bronwyn's shawl had fallen off her and was draped over a stile until a young Viking snatched it up and shoved it inside his armour. Shadows flittered across old bleached cattle bones strewn beside a wall and the prickly stems of thistles sprouted from the skull's gaping eye sockets. At a corner a child's doll lay on the edge of the road and William's straw hat rested atop of scrub vegetation choking a drainage ditch. A breeze ruffled some plants with holes in the leaves, wriggling with caterpillars feeding upon them. A sharp yelp came from a golden eagle circling in the sky.

Here and there, four elderly women and a couple of men of middle years had fallen by the wayside, and they were now hiding, huddling behind the walls with taut sinews and extremely frightened faces, daring even to breath, afraid that it would give away their presence to the lurking dangers beyond. The sound of the passing vanguard of warriors faded with distance and the villagers crawled on their hands and knees in the other direction

"I feel like a fox being chase by the hounds, Petroc," one of the men's voice dropped to a conspiratorial whisper as he spoke to the other. "What now? We can nay linger here nor can we go back to whence we came."

"We keep moving and pray to God for deliverance, Saul," Petroc said, clenching his brown teeth and fighting down a sense of futility.

Further on, legs and ribs slowly began to ache at the warriors' tempo and the combined weight of weapons, armour and shackles, sweat dampened their underarms. Bees buzzed among the profusion of wild flowers withering in the heat and the long, browning grasses glistered with the last of the morning's evaporating dew. Crops of wheat and barley were stunted and not developing as they normally would at this time of the growing season, the grain had a yellowish tint and a brittle quality about it, shrivelling up from the lack of rain. A few fields had been left to lie fallow by the farmers after ploughing to destroy weeds and conserve soil moisture.

Within another field a flock of Cheviot sheep were lying wearily beneath splotches of dappled tree shade and they looked up at the clatter and clamour of the Norsemen, but they still had the strength to bleat and stand before moving away in a massed group for safety.

"Björn," Magnússon ordered with a jerk of his helmeted head at the ewes and lambs in the field, barely slowing down. "Detail some men to slaughter those sheep when we return this way from the monastery along with any cattle, pigs, chickens and beasts of burden we find on the island. We will brine the meat in the storage barrels in the ship holds aboard the Sea Chariot and the Horse of the Waves."

"Aye, Jarl Magnússon," the bodyguard puffed and panted, sweat dripping off his bulbous nose and cauliflower ears as bits of fallen apple blossom from Arwen's hair were crushed beneath the lope of his boots in passing. "What about the fields? The hot weather and shortage of water I seen have weakened the crop yield."

"Burn the crops until naught remains but ash as our first offering to Odin," Magnússon gasped for breath. "I want to flaunt our might upon his isle and let our actions speak louder than mere words."

Björn bobbed his head and then spoke his thoughts aloud. "I thought it likely we would chase down some stragglers by now? But the way the villagers have dropped their belongings, 'tis clear they just stampeded along this road in panic as fast as their legs could carry them."

"Forget not where we run; the English seek the refuge behind the monastery walls," Magnússon said, his face reddening from a mixture of anger and exertion. "But we will chop the doors to kindling and rip the monastery apart stone by stone if need be to get at the slaves and plunder within."

Ahead, there was a thick mass of spiny, dry furze that had been allowed to grow without check. It edged the roadway and obscured what lay beyond, but the rear of a parked cart protruded half way out and a babble of voices loud and far-carrying reached the ears of the Vikings vanguard as they rounded the bushes and found themselves entering the graveyard. Magnússon made a calm assessment as he surveyed the enfolding situation before him and then striding onward, scarcely controlling his impatience. Björn moved in beside him as the others followed, bunching the muscles in their shoulders and arms whilst all their attention was focused on the progress of the villagers.

The horses yoked to the cart didn't have their legs loosely hobbled by a rope to prevent them from moving away. The scuff of so many boots and the unfamiliar scents of the approaching strangers caused the draft animals to become restless, pricking up their ears in alarm and whinnying as their hooves started pawing the ground.

Across the way, the Abbot stood in the doorway and waved the flow of people forward. "This way, the Lord's blessings be upon thee, wayfarers," his gaze flickered left and right and saw the ordeal was etched in every passing face, the villagers breaking apart and moving around him. "I, Abbot Percival and Evangelina, the Reverend Mother welcome you all to break bread and have a libation with the monks and sisters after you hath all been settled inside," he added with a comforting tone in his voice and a forced smile.

Hope swelled within the last of the villagers as they quickly threaded through the monastery's doorway, but this ember of happiness of reaching safety and to several parents the imminent reunion with their children Enoch had carted here early was snuffed out when the combination of sounds behind them made heads whipped around to detect movement, seeing the forerunners of the Norsemen scattering from the cart horses as the frightened animals rolled their eyes and reared up before bolting across the graveyard.

The spooked team galloped between a knot of warriors and trampled them all down in a second or two, their hooves dripped with blood and the wheels bounced over the mutilated bodies and the burial mounds.

As the cart and horses moved away, one of the Viking's waved his sword to the fore before they surged remorsefully forward wearing horned helmets, skulls and snakes decorating the shields they carried and the dwindling distance made individual faces discernible, some of the younger warriors had filed straight lines into their teeth and then had tinted the marks with red resin to make them look even fiercer when they grinned.

"We art surrounded by devilish heathens, ready to drag us off to hell." A root farmer shouted in dismay, his face paling at the frightening spectacle.

Women gasped and their eyes moistened, the men's Adam's apples bobbed in their throats and they uttered curses punctuating the tears of frustration and anger as a sudden overwhelming feeling of fear washed over each of them. Abbot Percival had heard much of the pagans but was curious to take a look at them for himself. He stretched his neck in order to get a better view and his gimlet-eyes widened and he exhaled a breath he hadn't realised he had been holding. The Vikings were unlike anything he had ever seen in his limited experience and he knew if he didn't do something these thralls of the devil would run rampant and prey on the innocence.

"Close the doors at once, my brothers and sisters," The Abbot shouted high and unsteadily to the other startled monks and nuns that were standing behind the portals.

Tasting bile that had risen in their throats, the villagers turned and harbouring no illusions to their fate, neighbour frantically shoved neighbours as they tried to get inside the monastery before their pursers caught them. Archers fired arrows at close range, the fletching of one grazed past someone's hand and another shaft hurtled in and struck the wood just below the knocker. The open entranceway was wide enough for four people to stand side by side, but then the doors twitched before starting to move together, the gap narrowing quickly as more monks, nuns and pilgrims rushed from the cloister to join their brethren where they could and lent their strength to their common cause.

Abbot Percival backpedalled out of the way and the quadrangle-courtyard disappeared with every second. At the back of the dribbling people flow two men kept looking over their shoulders periodically at the advancing shadows creeping up their trembling legs until they finally made it through the arm-length opening.

But before the doors could completely close, the Vikings crashed heavily against the portals like a huge ferocious wave, Björn and his shipmates slammed their shoulders against the wood and on the opposite side, labouring nuns and gaunt-faced monks of various ages felt the impact vibrated up their arms as they grunted and their strained aching muscles pushed back for all their worth, some including a villager or two braced their backs against the shifting doors.

Warriors, who had eagerly hurled themselves at the wood, were now standing shoulder to shoulder, trying to force the doors inward; one or two of them pounded their pommels at the cast-bronze grill and a few others thrust sword blades through the shrinking opening with optimism of hitting a target beyond. War cries and battle horns sounded, echoing off the walls.

The struggle was a brief contest of great physical effort. Breaths became ragged and the sandals of the monks and nuns couldn't get any purchase on the slippery flagstones as their resistance started to flounder. Opposite them, the Norsemen pressed harder, their ranks swelling in frenzied, superior numbers as the rest of Magnússon's vanguard caught up and regrouped with the forerunners. The press of bodies' added momentum and brawn and that urged the other invaders onward as they scented victory and the pious defenders finally weakened and fell back under the overwhelming onslaught.

The Mother Superior raised her hands to hide her mouth and a young, plain-featured woman, a novice nun by her garb and the lack of wimple covering for her head and neck, shook from head to toe. Abbot Percival's fragile hope of shutting out the pagans withered in his breast. There was a tangible air of despair and panic in the monastery.

"God preserve us, there be so many of them," Brother Francis cried out in defeat, kneeing beside the fountain as the doors were forced wide open. Brother Barnabas and another of his brethren bent to join him and they began to weep and pray. Monks and nuns turned and ran towards the group of buildings and the cloister, parents and children were out ahead of them, blindly making a dart for doorways and the mouths of corridors leading deeper into the older parts of the monastery.

"Get thee gone, Bronwyn," William hugged his boys in turn before straightening up, "Look after my sons."

"I will," Bronwyn sobbed, tears welled up in her eyes, knowing that her brother and the other village menfolk were the only defence between their loved ones and a certain fate as she grasped the boys by the hands and then with one last lingering look she followed Arwen into shadow.

"Come Enoch," William tightened his grip on an axe he had borrowed off someone. The wagoner nodded and drew an eating dagger. "Let's strike this affliction from our land."

"Aye," Enoch replied.

With howls of triumph and gripped by the imminent fever of battle, the Vikings had a red haze swimming before their eyes as they funnelled through the entrance and fanned out across the courtyard. The Mother Superior and a pair of middle aged monks were paralysed with fear and they were cut down chaotically where they stood. Three warriors caught up with the young, plain-featured novice and grabbed her struggling willowy figure.

"Please don't," the young, plain-featured novice pleaded to the men, "My maidenhead is devoted to my Lord."

"This is a bad business Wulfric," said the man with a pockmarked face, his eyes blazing with frustration, feeling his cock erect as she raised the subject.

The bearded warrior called Wulfric frowned as he helped his companion to restrain the woman. "How so, Einar?"

"I long for the old way of life, when raiding meant a brotherhood of warriors and not the presence of the shield maidens and the other women preventing us from savouring the benefits from the spoils of war like the Carolingians." Einar replied, crouching down to fit chains and fetters to the ankles of the novice nun. "They would be ripping off this woman's gown and deflowering her on the spot, but we are prevented from doing that, because of the terribly dishonour it would mean to the both of us. Huh," he shook his head in disdain, "as if I have a care for honour."

"Be silent, Einar," Wulfric urged caution, his eyes narrowing as he cast about. "The Jarl could have heard you, or worst that Frost Giant guarding him."

Einar looked sheepish from embarrassment and spoke in a lower tone. "I hope there be barrels of mead in here for the taking, for being a farmer I ain't high up on the pecking order and with my gaming debts I can ill afford the price this slave will bring for a bedfellow."

"I can be irresistibly attracted to a-pair of big blue eyes myself." Wulfric nodded and scratched his bulging stomach as he continued to survey their surroundings, letting the third Norseman take the woman away, over to the wall where a bruised and blooded monk and another unharmed nun slightly older sat in chains flanked by Old Sven and another aging warrior. "Such was it in my village of Lillesund and in the neighbouring village Skálholt till Jarl Magnússon annexed the land and had everybody swear an oath of loyalty to bind us to his enforceable rule. To break it carried a death penalty in all of the land he owns and on all the overseas raids he leads. But I see the wisdom of using some women warriors to man the oars and do their share of the fighting, for they free up more men to guard our homes and families from neighbouring nobles belike Jarl Sigvald Foeslayer and Imgrimund of the Axe, who see the fleet gone and believe there art easy pickings to be had if they raid us."

Across the way, nuns and monks shouted to be let in as they hammered their fists raw and bloody against a closed side door locked with a wooden bar on the inside by Brother Isaac. A villager swore and kicked, while others pleaded but it was all to no avail. Norsemen enslaved the English and then began assaulting the door, making short work of it with their axes.

* * *

At the same time, the rest of the Viking vanguard in the throes of bloodlust had first pursued the fleeing monks and nuns to all corners of the compound before drawing near and taking pleasure as they mercilessly dispatched them with an axe or sword stroke from behind. Cries of the wounded and the screams of the dying filled the air as bodies tumbled in a welter of blood. Villagers clutching makeshift weapons whirled about in twos and threes in desperation from the main doors and went to meet the enemy with ground eating strides.

The line fragmented as sparks showered with the clash of steel on steel.

"Put them to the sword," Magnússon shouted to his Norsemen, his shield took the blow of a thrusting pitchfork and he counted by stabbing the Englishman in the face. "And let their God sort them out."

"By thunder, Boromir," A warrior with braided russet hair crusted with sea spray said in awe to his premature bald companion as he dodged Enoch's dagger and opened the man's jugular with a backward swing of his sword. "A few of these sheep have grown a spine."

"Aye, Finn; but 'tis only token resistance at best," Boromir's wart-dotted face grinned, his upraised shield taking the blows from William. "This one chops like a woodman hewing a tree trunk." He laughed, undoubtedly enjoying himself as he timed the slowing swings and the lessening impact as his opponent tired. A few seconds later Boromir counterattacked by bringing his own battleaxe in a curving horizontal arc to break the fisherman's rib cage, burying the blade head deep into his side. William collapsed and the stocky Norseman stamped down with his leg for leverage before ripping the weapon free with a sucking sound.

Off to the right, a tall, slim Viking with an angular face brought his pommel down on the head of the boy Vincent, knocking him unconscious. He sheathed his blade and as he unslung the shackles dangling from his shoulder and knelt to fasten the metal bands to the ankles of the novice, he heard Björn bark at him in warning.

"Rothgar, keep your eye on the battle."

The dark haired and bearded warrior glanced up and saw two villagers bearing down on him with a hammer and an adze. Out of his peripheral vision, Rothgar's one eye caught a glimpse of Björn hoist up the long iron spike spears he held in both hands, drew his powerful arms back simultaneously and then threw the weapons at the men. Both Englishmen screamed in agony and were catapulted off their feet with grisly torso wounds as the spears pierced straight through their bodies, crimson spread where their clothes bulged at the back.

Rothgar nodded his thanks before glancing around for other living opponents. When he was satisfied there were none near him, he went back to locking the shackles in place. Björn unslung his battle axe and went off to find Magnússon as the gathered Norsemen in the courtyard thinned considerable, the rest of the undisciplined warriors dispersed, separating into smaller bands and had paused at the threshold of the arch doorways to allow their eyes adjust to the mellow glow of rush light beyond before they swept deeper into the monastery, each one angling away into rooms and along cold stone corridors.

Behind them in the courtyard, the remaining Vikings were recovering arrows and spears, kicking the corpses over and spitting on wooden crucifixes or snatching up fallen bibles, frowning as they flickered through the pages out of curiosity.

"Lo, Boromir," Finn grinned to his taller comrade, the thirty year old revealing several missing teeth like the openings crenels of a battlement as he tore paper pages from a holy book.. "This will be better than wiping me arse with leaves."

* * *

The abbot hid in the shadows of a building and he muttered a quote he remembered from the pages of Genesis, as he had watched the knots of raiders go off in different directions. "... And there it divided and became four rivers."

The Norsemen in the courtyard were moving closer to him and the abbot turned for a doorway, merely to collide into a red bearded warrior, with waist long braided hair. Rollo Throatslitter's sword immediately disembowelled the abbot and the holy man collapsed to his knees trying to hold in his ropey intestines with his reddened fingers. Showing a glimmer of humanity, the heavyset Viking put Percival out of his suffering by thrusting his blade into his chest, before he looked left and right quickly; seeking out his next victim, only to find there was hardly any monks alive except for three praying aloud beside the fountain. Rollo grinned and stepped over the bloody corpses on his way to them.

"I implore thee to hear the words of thy humble servant," Brother Francis prayed aloud.

"Our Father who art in Heaven, Hallowed be thy name," Brother Barnabas and the other monk said in unison.

"Chanting those dreary dirges won't save you from my sword, monk," the heavyset man said, pulling up to stand over Brother Francis as the old man squeezed his eyes shut so he wouldn't see the blow coming and lowered his voice to a mere whisper. Brother Barnabas and the third monk did the same, as they felt the waves of malevolence exuding from him. "At least you and the other sheep will be able to speak to your God directly." The warrior was about to lunge his gore dripping blade into the monk's midriff when Magnússon appeared from behind a pillar and stopped him.

"Enough, Rollo Throatslitter; sully not your blade with his blood, for I have need of that man to live and his two companions," he snapped, lifting his shield hand. The frustration was apparent on his hard features, but the pugnacious Rollo clenched his yellowish teeth and he stayed his hand as his breathing slowed to normal and there was a sudden lessening of tension in his body language. Brother Francis opened his eyes, but continued to pray with his brethren. "I want your oath on it?"

"You have it, but with respect, Magnus; the old man is in his dotage, slaying him would be an act of kindness, you said it yourselves many times," he said with a shake of his head. "The other monks are much younger and will make better slaves and shall receive higher prices on the Arab's auction block."

"I am glad you were listening to me, but terror is our greatest ally and our enemies' enemy. For the moment his fate is entwined with my own so leave him be, Brother-in-law," Magnússon ordered, Björn grinned at him and hefted up his battleaxe. "Now, go and round up the women and children from where they be hiding. Take Björn and a score of warriors here," he pointed with his sword at the Vikings still in the courtyard, "to accompany you in the search and Rollo, have your pick of one of the nun's to keep for yourself," he added to appease the man's bruised ego.

"You shall get your thralls, I swear it." Rollo grinned and then slipping two fingers into his mouth, he whistled at the men to get their attention and beckoned them to follow as he whirled about and set off through a doorway off to the right. The bodyguard brought up the rear. Magnússon waylaid Einar at the back of the group.

"Stand guard here and protect these monks from harm till I return. You shall receive your weight in silver for missing out on any plunder gathered by your shipmates." The disgruntled man's shoulders sagged on his imposing physique and Einar's square face grimaced sourly at his lost opportunity, as he finally nodded. "When my son and daughter arrive, steer them to the church."

"Aye, Jarl Magnússon," Einar said, as the nobleman began to stride away in a different direction.

"Jarl Magnus Magnússon is it?" Brother Francis suddenly spoke in the Viking's language. "It seems the Devil has many names when he is abroad in the mortal world."

"You dare speak to the Jarl in a disrespectful a manner," Einar was tore with indecision over to react to the old man's insolent and obeying Magnússon's order.

"It's quite all right, Einar," Magnússon gave him the nod before addressing Brother Francis. "You speak my mother tongue, monk," he raised his eyebrows in surprise and turned before walking back to the prisoners. "So you are not senile as Rollo believed."

"I am not. My saintly father was a trader for many seasons and when I was old enough to ride and sail he took me all over God's creation and I picked up a smattering of each language."

Magnússon nodded and drew up, bringing up a fact before the monk could express his gratitude. "Thank me not for sparing the lives of you and your brother monks, for if you think 'twas out of compassion, I say now I possess none. I have taken life as easily as I have given it in the past much like the Gods my people worship, but they would not forsake me as yours did, monk."

"You have erred most gravely, Magnus Magnússon. My Lord is always listening to the faithful and his wisdom is beyond mortal man, but his ways remain mysterious and inscrutable to even this humble vessel that has devoted his life to prayer and contemplation." Brother Francis' hands touched his heart.

"Hmmm, perchance you're God will do naught again, but listen to the crackle of flames at eventide when my warriors put your monastery to the torch."

* * *

"'Tis better to light a candle than to curse the darkness, Wulfric," Rollo Throatslitter said, snatching up a burning torch from its wall sconce backed by a mirror of polished bronze and stride down the dark corridor. Rounded a corner, Wulfric saw the glow of a second torch flickering like distant jewels and he hefted it up when he came to it. Boromir and Finn brushed aside cobwebs and breathed in the smoke pluming up to the barrel-vaulted ceilings as they followed the bobbing flambeaus turn another corner before they poked their heads into a brightly lit side chamber and the stink of death filled their nostrils.

Old Roman oil lamps designed with lions and dolphin handles holding aloft hooks were suspended from ceiling brackets and these shed dwindling light on textiles on trestle tables along with stools, distaffs and spindles. Vikings stepped over the body of a farmer lying in a pool of his own blood; his hair had been parted with an axe.

The dead man's wife had tear streaks down her face and she hugged her young son, only to scream and struggle after dirty nails and rough callused hands bruised and scratched her skin as they parted the pair and slipped shacklers on their limbs. Warriors' grabbed sacks made from goat hair and filled them with extinguished lamps, yarns varying in thickness, and anything else of value in there.

"Don't get distracted from the task at hand," Rollo barked to his men as they marched past a procession of rooms crowded by their shipmates, who helped themselves to resources from workshops focusing on techniques and skills in a particular field.

A small group of monks including Master coopers, shoemakers, and saddlers were not killed nor their apprentices, instead they was chained up and led away. Within the treasury, coffers filled with coins were looted along with imported goods like olive oil and wine in two handled amphora pots, and limited agricultural and sea products in storage chambers.

The corridor ended at a place where three other passageways met: the barrel vaults intersected at right angles to form the groin vault. Rollo took the right hand corridor and it was broad enough for the men to walk two-abreast. Another series of rooms opened onto it and within them was amphora jars of pitch and equipment for various handicrafts. Norsemen had also captured a few trembling children and moisture welled up in Arwen's eyes as she was pulled forcibly from one chamber by a grinning Siegfried.

Knowing in her heart she wouldn't see her baby again, Arwen's fists struck his armoured chest plate, the chains chaining her slender wrists together rattled as she craned her neck back to see her child silenced with a dagger thrust from an older Viking, before he dropped the little corpse beside a dead crone.

Dark arterial gore surrounded the ugly wound, where an axe had cleaved her left breast apart. Bronwyn's open glassy eyes stared unseeingly at the rafters above.

"You did not, even give me the chance to say goodbye, demon," Arwen sputtered in anguish, spraying out drops of saliva into Siegfried's face as she continued to resist.

"You shall have more children, slave," Siegfried said with an undertone of viciousness as he slapped her hard across the face, leaving a reddening handprint on her cheek. He briefly met her eyes: they spoke volumes as she digested the statement. "My father will enjoy many an eve taming your shrewish spirit."

Arwen sniffed and cried quiet enraged tears at the bitter truth of it as Siegfried dragged her away.

Further along specks of dust floated on the air and the walls echoed with their cacophony as the warrior band proceeded, past pools of ruse lights, etched into which were two Norsemen, who busied themselves by rippling down religious tapestries that depicted in vivid detail Saints and a pilgrimage to a holy place. The two men made the corridor even narrower and Rollo went between them in single file, the others followed and their torches began to sputter.

At the end of the corridor the Vikings found themselves within a medium-sized chamber that was a crossing point of three passageways, the doorways of which were edged with frieze like bands. A number of smoking braziers lit the space, charcoal burned and the flickering flames cast dancing shadows upon rows of ornamental pedestals, each one supported a marble sculpture of somebody's head and shoulders. Julius Caesar, Hadrian, Claudius I and other Romans of note, while the second row of portrait busts were of lesser quality and made from clay depicting the male faces of past Abbots.

And there was even a female bust showing the winkled likeness of the Mother Superior herself. It was another gift for the monastery from the mainland convent.

Wulfric glanced at the monks in passing and he almost did a double take when he recognised the face of the woman. "Ho," he said, jabbing his sword point at the bust to draw the attention of the other warriors. "This is the crone I cleaved in twain at the gate." He grinned and with a swipe chopped off the Reverend Mothers beaky nose. Around him, the Norsemen laughed and growled their blind approval, kicking over the pedestals and the clay busts smashed into smithereens. The Roman sculptures were equally defaced but harder to destroy; daggers dug deep to scar the faces, pommels hammered down to crack the marble heads and then the busts were thrown against the walls, damaging the classical features.

Rollo strode across the chamber to the two doorways. "This place be like a rabbit warren," he remarked with a shake of his head as he peered through them in turn, seeing each one leading to a corridor branching off in opposite directions, before he cast a glance over his shoulder to address first his men and then the bodyguard. "Quiet you laggards! Björn Strongarm, I am splitting our numbers in twain to cover more ground to better search and wheedle out more women and children. You and the last ten warriors take the left turn; I shall lead the rest along to the right."

* * *

"Are you certain you locked the outer door, Brother Bernard?" Prior Jabez cast a frightened glance over his shoulder at the storage room doorway. "For without an inner door, we are virtually defenceless."

"I am not pig ignorance, Prior Jabez; for there is a brain under my cowl." Brother Bernard replied tensely, his body fidgety. "I threw both bolts, whist you and the other brothers erected the first barricade in the storage room."

Relieved with the answer and seeing no sign of pursuit; Prior Jabez returned his attention forward and strode across the pottery chamber. Halting, he reached for the decorative three-limbed candle wall holder, fingering the left branch, which tilted at an angle beneath his hand. There was a sudden hiss of escaping air mingled with a harsher grating noise, before disturbed dust seeped out of lengthening cracks in the stonework behind the undulating, frayed edges of a tapestry depicting the pictorial sample of the four seasons.

"What is happening, Prior Jabez," said another of the younger monks, blinking in confusion, clutching a beautiful, handwritten and illuminated bible, as he and the other three holy men crowded around the taller man. Sunshine slanted through the chamber's two low windows and draped across the potter's wheel and the benches standing upon the flagstoned floor. There were distant vibrations rippling a pail of water and round pots in various stages of development quivered upon the trestle tables blocking the doorway leading to the adjacent storage room, but the chamber's other entrance debouched into a neighbouring corridor that was free of obstructions.

"I am opening a secret passage to the catacombs, Brother Biutta," Prior Jabez turned and pointed at the smoke-daubed tapestry, corner candlelight emphasized the stress and age lines wrinkling his raw-boned face and the long nose hairs dangling down like spider's legs from his wide nostrils. "'Tis behind yonder wall hanging and the abbot said 'twas shorter than the other routes and the task you venture forth upon should be interrupted not by the heathens."

Brother Biutta rushed over the tapestry, lifted it up and gasped as he saw a door sized hole had appeared in the unyielding stone. The section of masonry had retreated inward and slid aside to expose a gloomy and silent corridor. "I assumed there would be secret passages given that the monastery was built over the Roman ruins, but the library records are old and not complete, for there is nay a written mention of the tunnels in the scrolls and parchments I read to help Brother Isaac's research in finding the aquifer."

"There would not be; for each former generation of Abbot only puts his trust in a handful of monks and nuns to know of their existence and now Abbot Percival has given you all the same courtesy," Prior Jabez said, signalling the rest of the holy men to quickly follow Brother Biutta.

"Secrets in this order?" Brother Biutta batted his eyelids as he digested the statement and then commented caustically. "And it merely took a host of bloodthirsty pagans invading the monastery for it to happen."

"You have a dry wit and a swift smile that in punishment should have been beaten out of you long ago, Brother Biutta; but neither is suitable for this present situation." Prior Jabez sniffed loudly in disapproval and then returned to their original topic. "Any writings were burned to ashes long ago by the Abbot's forebears when it was decided to store the holiest of relics down there," he explained as he heard the locked outer door shuddered, as battleaxes backed by brute force chopped into the wood, before being wretched free by their owners.

"They are here," Brother Bernard said, "Once through the door the barricades will prove next to useless in slowing them down."

Brother Jabez let out a long hissing breath when axes thudded into the outer door again, gouging a large hole in the wood. "Now, tear your eyes not from purpose and be gone ere the raiders discover the way to the sepulchral and the holy treasures within. Take the first left and then the second passage on the right. That will lead you to the great catacomb stair."

"What of flint and steel to strike a spark, and candles or torches to light our way?" Brother Biutta asked, tightening his grip on the bible.

"You will find shelves in an alcove holding such things after you enter as well as wrappings and twine to bundle up the bible in order to keep out the wet and the grime," Prior Jabez said.

Behind the monks, Viking hands reached into the hewed holes they had made and groped about until thick fingers found the bolts and drew them back to unlock the door. Disdainful, mocking laugher and a loud crash of breakages, bowls and amphora-style vases of black pottery smashed as the warriors swept their weapons through the first barricade to clear their path.

Three of the monks dashed and slipped beneath the tapestry, only Brother Biutta hesitated half way into the secret passage, as the noise of conflict grew nearer; the torchlight and the raiders' long shadows preceding them through the storage room. "What of you, Prior Jabez? Come with us."

"I can not, for I am the sacrificial lamb and need to be seen so I can lure them away," Prior Jabez said, snatching one more look behind him.

"Lure!" Brother Biutta echoed, raising his eyebrows to his receding hairline. "I am younger and fleeter of foot; it should be my cross to bear."

"Nay," Prior Jabez shook his head stubbornly. "Go and cover the opening with the tapestry, but close not the secret passage up to the time I and the army of trespassers have departed, else they will hear the stone panel rumbling as it closes in place."

Brother Biutta nodded. "Godspeed!" He then vanished behind the falling tapestry.

Praying silently that the holy relics could be saved and a little uncaringly that the enemy would show mercy to him alone, Prior Jabez turned and making sure the Norsemen saw him, as they demolish the last weaker barricade - he ran out the corridor doorway.

Covered in blood and gore that wasn't his own, Björn emerged into the pottery chamber, with his men in tow.

"After that monk," he shouted and jogged onward. "This way."

Chapter Four
Secrets and Lies

A smaller band of noisy, energetic, and rowdy Vikings curiously crowded into the monastery's large kitchen, drawn by the smells of porridge, roasting chicken and the sweet aromas of freshly baked bread. Their laughter and voices echoed hollowly in the empty air as the warmth from the roaring open fires washed over them and their appetites swelled. Firewood was stacked in the corners and bunches of dried herbs hung from ceiling hooks.

Boards creaked loudly beneath the warriors shifting weight as they skirted past preparation tables – on top of one was sprinkled flour and knead dough - and crude chairs that occupied most of the floor space, and their distorted reflections reflected back off shiny bronze pots and pans on storage shelving. Boiling cauldrons stood in hearths and rising smoke escaped up the chimneys.

"We shed the monk's blood and we pick their bones clean for plunder, Rigsson," a young, wide faced, barrel-chested warrior commented as he sheathed his blooded sword and plonked his shield onto the trestle table, before snatching up a wooded bowl and eating utensil on his way to the nearest cauldron. "Now, Odin in his wonder hath provided gruel to feed our bellies," he dipped the bowl into the porridge and the thick liquid sloshed over the rim as he lifted the container out and dug his spoon into the dish. Several of his shipmates joined him and not bothering with spoons, simply upended full bowls and wolfed it down.

"Aye, Healfdene," the twenty five year old Norseman chuckled, freeing his hands of his weapons in a similar manner ahead of tearing a round flat loaf in half and taking a bite, crumbs showered his dark beard plaited beneath his square chin. "Not as tasty as what my mother and wife makes," he spoke in between chews, impaling the halves of bread on the horns of his helmet to save for later as he looked around for something else to eat. "But the odour reminds me of life at home and all the weighty labours awaiting my return." He sighed deeply. "The trees have long since been fed to the iron smelts, but stones and stumps remain to be cleared from the land Jarl Magnússon bestowed to my family ere we can grow a harvest for our growing population." A warrior broke open another loaf and then poured a jug of honey onto it to sweeten the cooling bread.

"My friend, if you be lucky you will discover the tree roots have held the soil in place, but elsewhere sheep have overgrazed the pastureland and the rains have eroded the cleared fields turning the ground into useless mud. Every season 'tis harder for a man to eke out a bare existence in the rhythm of short summers and cold winters, for the amount of food falls short of what is needed by our Norse people to say naught of thralls and the flow of exiles migrating into our crowded homeland. The Jarl has annexed territory in the past and now he must do so again, then perchance there shall be land aplenty even for me to come back too."

Rigsson lifted his eyebrows in surprise. "What talk is this? You already live on one of the largest farms."

Feeling the need to reveal the gloomy thoughts eddying in his mind, Healfdene spoke: "'Tis not a place I can call my own, unless my older brother and his bride dies like father did last winter, for being a second son I can not inherit the family farmstead." He spooned another mouthful of porridge and he wiped his mouth and blond moustache with the back of his scarred hand. "My brother is welcome to it though, because I found ploughing land and tending animals is not in my blood. If I is to be bound by servitude and subject to the will of the Jarl, then I do it aboard a longship, sailing and raiding a monastery is more suited to my talents and 'twill be a better life, for the ever restless like me."

Rigsson grabbed a cleaver, tying it to his sword belt, before he and a couple of other men gathered around one of preparation tables topped with trenchers used to serve or cut food upon. "The coin I receive here shall speed up my ambitions of living a life of leisure in the enjoyment of wealth and slaves pandering to my every whim." He took a bite of cheese curd and watery whey was released, trickling down his rugged features. The warriors wiped their sweaty, blood-soaked hands on their leggings before snatching up handfuls of ingredients and shoving them into their mouths.

Healfdene moved over to a corner as he continued to forage, and a few scrawny chickens chucked a ruckus after he hoisted up their wooden cage. "Ease and pleasure are things I would soon tire of, Rigsson," he said, lodging the cage under his arm and turning to the nearest food table. "The freedom to travel over the horizon to new lands and the adventure we find there are more to my likings."

* * *

"Where has that damnable monk fled to in this unholy place?" Rothgar said, staining his good eye against the deep shadows.

"Certain am I that it was the glow of a torch I seen come this way, Rothgar," Björn replied, his own torchlight didn't penetrate far, but when the shape of something eventually resolved in the gloom. Björn caught sight of motion beyond him.

Ordering his procession to halt, the bodyguard plunged down the corridor and was upon the drifting door in five steps. He swung it open and holding the torch before him, Björn advanced to fill the entranceway, extending and then lowering the light at the threshold, playing it across the top riser in a series of steps leading down into the bowels of the monastery. The smell of burning wax wafted up to his nostrils from other lit flambeau set in wall scones at various heights receding into the shadows of clammy darkness and the distant sound of sandaled feet echoed off the stonework.

"Well, does Thor grant us favour, Björn?" Rothgar asked loudly, the waiting seemed to take forever for him.

"One of the Gods hath heard you, Rothgar," Björn shouted back in reply to the rest of his men. "Follow me my sea brothers, our prey seek to lose us by heading deeper into this warren of his. We shall run the monk to ground yet."

Björn disappeared from view and the warriors hared off after him, passing mould decorating the walls, as they descended the narrow stairs through rising smoke until they reached the level ground of a wider corridor, easily twice the size of the previous one above. Cressets in the shape of rusty metal cups mounted on poles stood at various places, the cups were filled with burning pitch giving light to dozens of chambers on both sides, opening onto the corridor.

"I never went so deep underground," Boromir mused, surveying the scene, "even when I accompanied Bárðr Bearcloak into the cave, where he won the trophy he's named himself after."

In a small recess in the nearest wall beside the stairs was a clepsydra consisting of a shiny greyish metal cylinder into which water dripped from a reservoir; a wooded float provided readings against a scale on the cylinder wall. The shorter, broad-shouldered Wulfric saw the gleam in the torchlight and sheathed his sword, before grabbing it, water and the float falling out the open top of the cylinder as he turned it over in a rapid examination.

"Björn, this trinket is silver," Wulfric frowned thoughtfully, speaking around the long, dangling stem of coarse grass he held between his yellowing teeth, as a question burst upon his lips. "But what is its purpose? I have never seen its like."

Björn's gaze briefly strayed from the closed doors to the water clock Wulfric held. "I have in Jarl Magnússon's longhouse, 'tis an ancient instrument for time measurement."

"Björn, can he not just stab a hole in a hanging bag of sand and let the contents trickle out?" Wulfric asked as confusion crossed his features.

"Each bag can be slightly larger or smaller in size, which can contain a different amount of sand that takes an imprecise time to flow. The Jarl found these instruments measured and recorded time more specifically." Björn looked at Wulfric, knowing him like the back of his hand. "And afore you ask Wulfric he came aware of ideas and was taught to understand the workings of such things as a young man when he was a sell-sword paid to fight in foreign armies and in harder times of peace he hired out as a caravan guard protecting silk carried westward, while wool, gold, and silver went east along the Silk Road. Magnússon became one of the few men to ride the entire route, seeking out scholars to educate him to read and observe the knowledge of the world of nature as he accompanied the cargo moved by a chain of traders."

"Well, I wager there be something of worth behind those doors," Finn said, his voice breathy with anticipation. The talk of gold and silver wetting his and others appetites for treasure as he, Rothgar and Wulfric eagerly hefted their weapons and trotted off in their search before Björn could wave his warriors forward.

Just then a few feet ahead of the Vikings, a door opened on the right, and out of it slowly emerged Prior Jabez. Knowing his pursues were near he looked left and then right, breathing in sharply when his close-set eyes sighted the gaggle of warriors heading right for him. Seized by wild, animalistic terror he made a dart for another door at the end of the corridor. Rothgar howled and jostled past Wulfric, and being faster, the one eyed Norseman caught the fleeing monk, bringing him down by cutting through his hamstring, before plunging his sword into Prior Jabez back, twisting the blade to make the wound larger and silencing the pitiful sound of pain coming from the holy man.

The Vikings spread out along the corridor and a majority of them didn't wait for Björn's signal to kick in the doors, which crashed noisily against the inside walls. Torchlight shone into the dingy interiors of very small and simple rooms. Four windowless walls and a low plain ceiling that barely had the height and length of a tall man. Each cell had a straw pallets covered with a coarse woollen blanket lying on the flagstoned floors and a crucifix hanging above it. Often there was a stool standing in a corner with a wooden drinking cup atop of it and a candle stub resting upon a wall niche.

"You can not swing a cat in here," Rothgar said to no one in particular after entering a cell. "And unlike my own dwelling there be nay sign of a rat either."

Occupying some of the cells was only a nun or monk kneeing in prayer. In others were traumatised women and children trembling as they sat, huddled together for warmth and comfort, but their eyes were empty and defeated. Entering the rooms, the Vikings laughed at the frightened screams and pleas of the innocent victims and gauging the worth of the people they found, they either took the English prisoner or struck them down.

Boromir shouted from a cell, "Finn, I have two harlots in here. Give me the manacles."

Finn replied just as loudly from the next room, his sword

brutally slicing through a monk's flesh to nick the bone underneath. "I be busy killing, fetch them yourself."

Within another cell opposite Boromir, Björn wiped clean the head of his blooded axe with a blanket. "There is nay safe sanctuary for the likes of those that lack the manliness and fighting spirit of a warrior born," he said to himself, feeling contempt for the body of Brother Isaac at his feet. The youngish monk had had his skull cloven to his stubbled jawline.

Emerging from the cell, the bodyguard met Finn coming from the opposite direction as he threw down his helmet in a fit of rage.

"Björn, we captured some women and children, but naught else." Finn's vindictive face had darkened a tinge of purple as he bent to pick the helm back up. "How can these kinsmen and the women choose to live like beggars with so few possessions?"

"The monks are brothers in faith, not blood," Björn corrected Finn's mistake, growing quickly bored and restless through lack of interest. "As for their possessions, perchance 'tis an act of religious devotion or a Christian penance, it matters not," he shrugged and turned away. "Slip it from your mind, Finn Baldhead and embrace the small fortune we found here." He strode past the series of doorways and glancing left and right at the slaughter his band had wrought inside the rooms. "Come!" he beckoned his men to follow. Boromir's dagger gestured and the women, miserable and exhausted, shuffled along to join other captures ahead of him. "Let us depart these smothering surroundings; enjoyable as this bloodletting has been, 'tis not a victory my pride will allow me to crow about."

* * *

With his heart beating loudly in his ears, Biutta the monk lifted up the threadbare hem of his cassock to reveal pale hairy legs as his sandal feet waded through the calf-high water submerging the bottom of the cramped, underground tunnel. He paused to cast a glance over his hunched shoulder and still seeing no signs of pursuit, swivelled his dark eyes back around and stared at the angular face of one of his three cowled companions' backlit in the wan light atop of the candle stub he carried in one shaking hand, while he held the wrapped bible in the other.

"It was a masterly move to take the oak coffin holding the relics of St. Cuthbert from their usual home and hide them down in Bishop Eadfrith's dry burial chamber ere concealing the entranceway with rocks we build up from cave in debris, Brother Biutta," Brother Bernard said in a stress pitched voice, his breath pluming visibly in the gloomy, chilled air as his own candle flame flickered in a stray draught of air.

"Before I choice to take the cowl at twenty summers and worked hard to hold my trusted position of hagiographer in the Order," Brother Biutta ruminated. "I was a shepherd tending the village flock and one task was fixing holes within the dry stone walls to keep crops safe and to prevent sheep from escaping the grazing land."

Brother Bernard frowned slightly and asked, "But why in the Lord's name did we not leave the Lindisfarne Gospels there too, instead of journeying deeper into the catacombs?"

"I discovered that 'tis not wise to put all your eggs in one basket, Brother Bernard," Brother Biutta replied, shivering from the cold and fear, the dangling folds of flesh on his arms was goose-pimply. "We have already lost the bible's treasure binding in our haste to get away. If the pagans enter the catacombs by the great stairs and somehow find the relics of St. Cuthbert; mayhap that will satisfy them from searching further afield for the Lindisfarne Gospels and us."

Brother Bernard nodded, accepting the point Biutta made.

"Where do you intend to hide the bible, Brother Biutta?" another slim monk asked with sleepy-eyes and a slightly slurred, muttering delivery. "And is it far ahead?"

"We have a ways to go, Brother Gurkinn," Brother Biutta said. Squeezing past his brethren, he set off and thrust the candle to the fore. "You would think with my penchant to detail as a writer of Saints, describing the lives of martyrs and the accounts of the miracles occurring at their tombs or from their relics by gathering and interpreting the evidence from all manner of records, it would be I that discovered this forgotten knowledge. But it was Brother Isaac, who told me of an antiquated scroll he stumbled upon in his research of the island's history detailing the directions to a burial cavern in use long before the collapse of the Western Roman Empire, 'tis there, where we will hide the bible above the watermark among the remains of the dead."

Brother Bernard then glimpsed his candlelight tint a pale blue before returning back to normal orange as the procession entered and left a pocket of odourless methane gas. "Brother Biutta, my candle flame changed colour again, but on this occasion it lasted merely a moment. How do you interpret this....omen?"

Brother Biutta let out a frustrated sigh. "With the same answer: A deceptive effect of the light and darkness on smoke sensitive eyes, naught else."

"What happens when we reach the burial cavern?" the fourth monk asked, favouring Brother Bernard with a sympathetic smile. "How do we now escape the catacombs when the inbred savages stop us from travelling back whence we came?"

"Aye, Brother Gideon," Brother Gurkinn agreed. "We be trapped like rats in a cage. Should we not pray for guidance?"

"I shall not waste time by asking what Jesus would do, Brother Gurkinn," Brother Biutta smiled despite himself and paused, raising the candle flame to read a small, flat stone plaque fixed to the mouldy brick wall. It had a Latin inscription bearing information that told the monk in which tunnel he was in and a guide to determine his direction. His companions crowded in behind him. "Come brothers! Believe me when I say we are upon the right path." He moved off ahead of them again. "The burial cavern I speak off has an unexpected benefit of having an egress leading to the surface the Roman sappers dug as an escape tunnel in the event of their garrison, ever becoming under siege from warring Celt tribes."

"That is news of good cheer," Brother Gurkinn said, wiping cobwebs from his robe and he inhaled and breathed out to fortify himself for what he was planning to do next, knowing what he revealed would raised questions and caused just as many to bubble under the surface. "I daresay we shall not be able to borrow a boat, given the heathens are as thick as flies on this isle, but if I can escape their clutches I have a coracle hidden between bushes just outside of an bay I use from time to time to visit the mainland in the summer days at high tide. I am willing to brave such a crossing to raise the alarm."

"Indeed," Brother Bernard said suspiciously, arching his eyebrows. "This is a day full of surprises, first news of the secret tunnels and now you do important business for the Abbot or rather the milkmaid on twelve trees farm. I have seen how you look at her Brother Gurkinn, but what of your vows to the Order?"

The overwhelming feelings of guilt gave Brother Gurkinn pause and he let his emotions settle before speaking again. "With too many children to support on a small farm and encouraged by a visiting elder monk, my father sent me, the youngest off to the monastery at the age of seven carrying a bundle holding some food, honeyed mead and the few coins my father owned for the Abbot whose care I was then entrusted.

Growing to manhood I tried to live in accordance with the rules and remain part of the fellowship of my brother monks, endure the whipping and the hours of daily prayer, but associating with the visiting nuns has awaken feelings and instincts within me and I came to understand that a single life lacking the intimate companionship of women was not for me. Simply put I do not belong here...."

"Recklessness and sheer folly," Brother Bernard interjected, his mood darkening when he was unable to remain silent any longer, glancing back to give Brother Gurkinn a disapproving eye as he viewed the whole concept with disgust. "Little did I know you were capable of such secrets and lies? I thought your faith was unwavering like my own and yet it seems darkness can taint even the purest of souls."

"Now, now, Brother Bernard," Brother Biutta scolded the monk, but understanding his discomfort nevertheless, before going on to advise the two monks in particular. "This is not the time or the surroundings to have a discussion of this magnitude or even the argument against such a position."

"But I say it is, Brother Biutta," Brother Gurkinn said hastily, refusing to listen or be mollified. "The cat is out of the bag and I feel a great weight has been lifted from my shoulders. I shall not be returning to the Order once I have delivered the warning."

Brother Biutta sighed deeply at the strong commitment in his voice and with a heavy heart accepted his decision. "I am not keen with your choice, Brother Gurkinn, alas; if your mind is truly made up, then go with God. I shall accompany you a short way on your journey and I will be glad of the fresh air." He deliberately tried to change the subject and wrinkled his generous nose, as he breathed in the strong and unpleasant stench of corruption wafting up from the dirty water and the side recesses carved into the stone walls – shelves holding discoloured, naked skeletons, the clothes they had been buried in had long since rotted away. "For this place smells worst than our cow-sheds and pig sties combined."

"Alarmed was I with the swiftness of these attacking beast men and the trail of death they left in their wake, but I have faith the farm hands and soldiers from the mainland will still come to our aid in this our darkest hour." The forth monk said, following Brother Biutta and the other monks round a bend in the ancient subterranean tunnel, the stink galvanizing them to move faster.

"Possibly, Brother Gideon," Brother Bernard said with a shake of his head as he struggled to come to teams with his friends decision. "But if the filthy Norsemen decide to press on inland I feel 'twould be only after our countrymen have locked up their daughters and buried the odd coins the king's tax collectors didn't seize off them."

* * *

Rollo pushed open the oak door banded with iron and plunged into the sacristy room, his nostrils flaring as they smelt the lingering whiff of incense, before he paused half way in and glanced about him. It was of medium size and windowless with another door set directly ahead of him. There were burning tapers in shelved recesses and in the intervening gaps along the walls were pegs and hanging on these was an assortment of religious dress and vestments. A knot of warriors followed him in and crowded behind him, as something low and vague merged with the echoing background noise behind them.

A broken-nosed Norseman made a disgusted grunt and yanked at his short beard. "Priest's garments, I was hoping this chamber would be accumulated with wealth."

"You are not the only magpie attracted to shine, Erik; but regardless this clothing still has its uses for a resource," Rollo replied, eyeing something he liked the look of and going over to it. Vegard adhered to his heels and the rest came after, splitting apart as they headed towards something which caught their fancy. "Some of my wife's influence has rubbed off onto me over the seasons. Ingrid is thrifty and squanders not even from previous meals, saving the leftovers and making it into a new dish."

"I suppose so," Erik shrugged, showing reluctant agreement as he saw wisdom in Rollo's words. "They be not tainted by monk's blood at least."

Rollo nodded as he walked up to a peg and slipped off a full length robe made of the finest fabric. "See where that other door leads too, Erik?"

"Aye," Erik stamped off gloomily.

"This will make me a fine cloak," Rollo threw the vestment around his broad shoulders and fastened it at the breast by a brooch.

Halting beside Rollo, Vegard took down from a neighbouring peg, a long woollen ecclesiastical garment with sleeves and embroidery work. "And this I shall wear as a tunic," he dropped his shield, removed his horned helm, and then put it on.

Opposite them, the tall figure of a woman knelt before a low table standing in an alcove. On top of the table were a hand bell, a crock washbasin and a wooden box. The latter she quickly opened and withdrew an Abbot's mitre, but discarded the headdress when she saw what lay beneath it. A gold circlet with a decorated band of precious stones. "Heh, Erik will be maddened that he missed seeing this treasure," she picked up the circlet from the box and whirled on her heel, eyes straying her way as she placed it upon her bare head. "I may not be a female Viking of the upper classes belike Kari and her shield maidens," a mixture of jealously and pride entered her voice, "but with this monk's crown I now own, I shall take pleasure when they will say that 'Ellisiv the Millers Daughter' has one of the greatest dowries in the settlement."

Erik was just coming at pace from the second doorway when what sounded like something metallic came into earshot from the corridor beyond the first doorway. It was accompanied by an increasing clatter of boots, reverberating whacks, and braying calls as the sources approached the open entrance of the sacristy room. Heads turns at first and then Rollo and a few others let their curiosity get the better of them, striding over to the door and peer out to see a column of naked monks shuffling along in fetters two-abreast.

"More thralls," Vegard threw his head back and laughed, as he heard a series of shocked gasps and a sharp intake of breath from some of the female Vikings rippling out from all quarters.

"Aye," Rollo nodded. "But these were captured in the workshops and have skills of art and trade to pass on to us."

The backs and shoulders of the enslaved thralls were slouched and their heads bowed, a sign of the extreme state of despair and depression they were in, as the surrounding Norsemen cracked their whips and drove them out towards the front of the monastery. The guards had stripped the male pilgrims, surviving villagers and monks of their habits to humiliated them, and now Viking men and women came out of chambers and corridors to chasten the prisoners, spitting at them and jeering and shouting insults.

"Misbegotten son of a sow."

"With a shrivelled up cock like that 'tis nay wonder he joined the monastery."

"Snivelling weaklings, they are lower than a snake's belly."

"Move yourselves quicker thralls," a guard drew his arm back to punish a monk for being slow with another stoke of his whip. The youngish man cried out in pain as the lash tore a flesh bloody welt in the fresh on his back, causing him to stagger into the two monks in front, the chains on their arms clanked as the links hit each other. Several novice monks flinched when another guard struck the flagstones near them with the business end of his whip and they hurried on into the urinating path of Vegard as he emptied his bladder all over the monks.

Erik elbowed and pushed his way to the front of the crowd, as he let his excitement get the better of him. "Rollo," he sputtered. "The door leads to the church…."

"I daresay 'tis another empty chamber our shipmates have looted already?" Vegard interrupted with a sigh, glaring daggers at Rollo, as he pulled up his trousers and buckled up his leather belt. The guards took the enslaved monks away, around a corner.

"Empty aye for now, but the chamber has not been ransacked yet," Erik shook his head. "There is a sizable haul of riches in there for the taking."

The warriors silently stared at each other, desperation mingling with uncertainty as they were not at all sure how Rollo would react, given he rarely liked anybody and also had a sudden and extreme tendency for mood swings. Ellisiv decided to press him on it.

"Our shipmates will think we be addled if we turn our backs on such wealth again, Rollo?" advised Ellisiv carefully. "Time and tempers are steadily growing shorter."

That statement prompted Rollo to grunt. Gauging the undercurrent of resentment among his followers, he grinned and adopted a magnanimous attitude. "Hah, why not! We found some slaves and they have been sent on ahead along the Sea Road, so I deem I have upheld my vow to the Jarl. All right, let us go and do some honourable thievery."

* * *

The corridors forked and split at intersections time and again taking Kari's shield maidens and the warriors of the Sea Chariot in different directions until everyone was swiftly lost and completely disorientated. The wooden walls were bare and the monotony of the murkiness was barely alleviated by the rush light or from the burning cressets equally giving off smoke. The Vikings rounded another bend and that was when they heard the sound of harsh, sharp voices and their owner's silhouettes flittering in front of the candlelight escaping through the open archway into the corridor ahead of them.

Torches began sputtering in the hands of Ásgrímr and Olaf as they sweep them back and forth before them. The heavy atmosphere of the place was slowly having an effect upon the Norsemen and women and they felt additionally oppressive by the lingering shadows that seemed to have taken on a disturbing quality about them. The torch bearers tightened their grip on the handles and extended their arms as if the flames were some kind of amulet to ward off evil. Other Vikings muttered the names of their Gods as they crossed the shortening distance to their destination.

* * *

In the monastery's quadrangle-courtyard, metal scraped against wood when Vikings heaved the heavy coffers up to the wagon's boxlike body, where onboard their comrades took the proffered chests off their hands, lids opened and banged shut again and on those occasions, silver and gold coins - donated to the monastery from visiting pilgrims - fell to the courtyard as each strong chest were roughly manhandled to the groaning bed.

Seeing that Enoch's wagon was almost loaded to maximum capacity with large casks of ale, hand-woven rugs and tapestries, one of the loaders jumped down, while the second Norseman with a lantern jaw and without a neck took a house-shaped Celtic casket made from red enamel and copper plates off Fridrik, put it down and then helped the boy up.

"Your father is to go to the ships and unload the cargo, boy, ere returning for a third load," the muscle bound warrior said without preamble, before getting off the wagon.

"Aye, Ulf," Fridrik stepped awkwardly to the wagon bench and sat down beside the hunched figure of Grettir of the Marshland, perched on the edge of the seat, grasping the reins tightly. Grettir's heavy-lidded grey eyes shot his son a look and the loud background noise forced the boy to shout Ulf's order.

Grettir nodded and turned his attention forward. He spread his boots apart for better balance and then lashed out with his whip. "Hee-Yahhh!" Fridrik's nimble fingers held on to his seat for dear life, as the horses galloped through the monastery's gateway, axles creaking under the weighty load. Beyond the walls, a knot of Vikings had dug three small, deep holes in the soil of the graveyard and now were pounding posts into them.

Within the walls, the guards herding the column of monks emerged into the courtyard, and at the rear of it a gaggle of young nuns and a few village womenfolk of similar age had also been attached to the chain gang. Links clanged as they lifted up there bare arms to shade their puffy eyes from the bright daylight after spending some considerable time hiding in the dark. The women had been striped to the waist to parade their assets of youth and good health to potential buyers among the ship crews.

Hungry eyes wandered down the length of the women's bodies and back up again with leisurely enjoyment. Sweat trickled down between their bobbing breasts and the wind disturbed their tresses and the black skirts had been cut along the sides to flaunt plenty of leg as they progressed, angling right, following Enoch's wagon toward the Sea Road and the beached longships. Two young warriors nearby stopped what they were doing and ogled the women.

"Gísli, my foster brother, the auction back home will have a lot of bidders, including me."

"And I, Harold," Gísli replied with a nod.

Harold shook his head. "What a waste of woman fresh to keep it all hidden away behind stone walls."

Gísli nodded again. "Alas, showing off the thralls like this is liable to arouse interest and cause competition among the other buyers. Jarl Magnússon is nay a fool; he wants a bidding war to happen between the men so it forces his merchant friend to offer higher and higher bids for the purchase of them."

"Even if the Arab does not know of it yet," Harold grinned.

On the way the monks and nuns passed more of the raiders with their hands full, busy continuing with the preparations of their departure, as they moved in an eddying mass around a pair of two-wheeled carts, heaping up plunder upon the loading areas.

Away to the left, stabled horses and even plough teams from the outlying fields were being brought into the courtyard by handlers to be utilized for the tasks ahead. Elsewhere still, men and women pitched hay from the second cart to their comrades, who in turn used rakes and scoop shovels to gather the dried grasses and move it to strategic spots that would link up the buildings. Shields and spears were stacked nearby.

***

"By the Gods, I pummelled this Christian symbol belike I did the monks heads outside, Floki," boasted the blacksmith's young apprentice, the tall, fair-headed warrior gestured with his spiked mace at one of the columns within the scriptorium. Debris from the shattered cross lay at his feet.

"Be quiet, Tyrker," his older companion snarled with a glance that was part uneasiness and anticipation. "Someone comes."

Heads of fishermen, carpenters and artisans turned sharply at the approaching footsteps and their voices died down, the owners of war hammers broke off from clobbering the room's fixtures and wiped the sweat beading their scowling brows, while the huge hands of other Norsemen paused uncertainty in drawing pictures, knowing it could only be more of their shipmates, but there was a small bit of lingering doubt in their minds that the monastery was a big place to search and maybe not all of the armed villagers had been slain in the courtyard. Warriors dropped the brushes dripping with lampblack ink or simply stopped filling up sacks already bulging with ivory carvings and an ample assortment of gold and silver implements – to finger the hilts of their swords as Ásgrímr and Lokar emerged through the archway and skidded to a halt, before they looked around the large ransacked chamber with curiosity.

There was multiple wooded columns carved with broken religious motifs consumed much of the floor space. Slotted between the supports were a number of hardwood desks that hadn't been kicked over previously like so many others had. They had sloping surfaces and often with compartments and pigeonholes for rolls of parchment, art brushes made from flexible hog bristles, quills made from seagull feathers and inks and coloured dyes cultivated from leaves of plants. A simple stool with no back or arm rests stood before each desk, most of which were topped with open manuscripts that had been in the process of being copied and illustrated.

Lit candles in glass bowls stood on slender pedestals at various places in between the furnishings and along the enclosing windowless timberwork inset with two more entrances. Shreds of cloth was all that remained of the tapestries lining three of those walls, a forth made of stone had a faded Roman fresco showing the sinuous bends of the river Thames meandering through a marshy valley and at a point just north of that was the city of Londinium build between two low hills, with a bridge giving access from land to the south. But the painting had been defaced by the occupying warriors' graffiti.. Drawing of wolves, horses and birds in recognizable forms were mixed in with vulgar images of pairs of women's' breasts along with male genitalia.

"Report what your eyes do see, my brother?" Kari shouted from behind Lokar, who listened to his first instinct and ignored her, addressing someone else instead.

"You have erred yet again, Ásgrímr; for this is not the church either." Lokar hissed in exasperation, giving the bearded man a hard stare, galvanising him into action as the shield maidens and the warriors of the Sea Chariot gathered behind the pair. Olaf eyed Ásgrímr's receding back warily. The scriptorium's occupants visibly relaxed in recognition and returned to what they were doing. "I know you are not the sharpest arrow in the quiver, but brand me a fool if I did not think you had wit enough to have a sense of direction."

"Ooh, branding my brother with a hot, thrall iron," Kari butted into the conversation with her customary bluntness, coming alongside Olaf as they passed through the archway, "if only." Helga smiled inwardly at the wry comment, but kept her expression straight-faced.

"All these passageways look the same to me, Lokar," Ásgrímr growled, deep in his throat and scowled, breathing hard, his brown eyes glistening in the candlelight as he strode towards a lithe, panther-ish figure with long blond hair interwoven into a single, dangling braid behind his head. The men from the

Sea Chariot sniggered at the vandal's cruder artwork and the averting faces of Kari and her shield maidens - already flushed with their exertions - reddened further from a mixture of embarrassment and anger. "One of yonder doorways is sure to lead us to the Jarl." Lokar barked a vocal laugh as he neared the end of his patience. "We shall see."

Floki could see Ásgrímr was clearly irritated from his body language and then he grinned as he heard the bearded man grumble something under his breath.

"Floki, you be a welcome sight," Ásgrímr said, his nostrils flaring in and out as he came to a halt and inserted his torch handle into an empty sconce fixed to a column.

"Well met, Ásgrímr," he said. Turning away to avoid meeting the cold fury and violent burning in the man's eyes, he shoved the Lindisfarne Gospels treasure binding into a bulging sack. "Trouble with Lokar, is it?"

"Aye," Ásgrímr whispered just as loudly in a voice totally bereft of cheer. "If he was anyone other than Magnússon's whelp," veins stood out of his bull neck, as he got himself into a terrible temper, but he still had the good sense to fight the impulse to kill Lokar, finally taking a calming breath and not to let slip the rest of his thoughts. "Can you plot a course that will steer me to the Jarl?"

"Ahead, beyond the left door is the library stair leading up directly into the church," Floki said absently pointing with his shield arm, surprise changing his chiselled features as he became distracted by a manuscript upon a desk top. Licking the dirty fingers of his free hand, he turned the carpet page in the form of a cross with a background overflowing with elaborate designs of birds and beasts in brilliant colours to reveal the next vellum page that had insular majuscule script. "It seems the Jarl and Rollo was neck and neck when they arrived."

Ásgrímr half turned and nodded with confidence, before beckoning Lokar and the others to him. "Can you read that language, Floki?" he asked, focusing his attention forward.

"You jest with me, Ásgrímr," Floki shook his head and flipped over the page to reveal a portrait of an unknown figure standing upright with raised arms in prayer. There was a bright halo around his head. "Like you and most of the warriors here I am illiterate and happy to be so. But thinking have I on the perchance of making coin from these handwritten books."

"How so?" Ásgrímr asked with renewed interest as Lokar and Kari approached accompanied by their warriors.

"By ransoming the manuscripts back to the English."

"Hmmm," Ásgrímr mused. "I count it not as a man wealth unless it can munch on grass or be hacked silver weighed on a trader's scales."

"If you two hens can stop your chucking for the moment," Lokar said with indignation. Pulling up short, he glared at them into silence. "Ásgrímr, show us the way."

Ásgrímr nodded confidently and silently set off towards the doors, Lokar and his sister followed, the rest bunched up and brought up the rear.

"Tyrker," Floki said and he whirled about. "On my authority, detail three men from the granary to haul these church treasures back to the Rune Fire."

"Aye, aye," Tyrker scratch his light coloured goatee in thought. "And what of these desks and stools, Floki? The Jarl wants the monastery razed to the ground before we depart these shores and this," he gestured at the furniture with his mace, "'twould make fine kindling to spread the blaze."

Floki nodded, after mentally evaluating the suggestion. "Aye, along with the supplies of lamp oil and pitch we found in the storage rooms." He pointed at two stalwart Vikings nearby. "Bödvar, you and Hakon, start chopping up the furniture, while I take the rest of the warriors to fetch those amphora jars." Bödvar and Hakon unlimbered their axes and set about the task. "We will then met back here, Tyrker, and set about the task."

Chapter Five
Dug up the Altars

From behind the corner there came snorts of cheerful guffaws and jeers pierced by a sudden loud bang not unlike breaking stone. Einar accompanied by Rigsson stomped along the quiet wooden corridor lit with torches as they encouraged the three monks to keep going onward. The small procession rounded the bend and then went through a wide doorway, only to see the walls recede and the magnificent painted ceiling - showing monumental figures of people and animals rendered with impressive naturalism and grace - lift into shadow as the corridor debouched into the church and the long central nave made up of a pebble mosaics in dark and light patterns stretched out ahead of them.

"The inroads of these heathen men have trampled all the holy places with their polluted steps," Brother Barnabas said, walking between the rows of marble pillars holding up the ceiling, as he cast a glance over his shoulder at Rigsson and Einar, both of whom were letting their eyes stray, taking in the lavish decorations all around them. "Brother Francis, ask the guards what their chieftain wants with us?"

Instead of answering him, Brother Francis loudly gasped, "Sacrilege!" and pointed at a space between the pillars where Kari stood, carving rune graffiti into the wall with her dagger. The early part of the inscription was maledictory in nature, cursing the monks and the Northumbria king, Aethelred, while the bottom part included a verse of epic character and an indirect reference to heroic myth she was putting in a poetic vocabulary. "They slaughter our brothers and sisters and now they wreak lamentable havoc in the church of God."

"'Tis nay more than bird scratching to me," the other monk commented in sorrow, his face livid as he waved away a buzzing bluebottle and retched.

"'Aye, Brother Godfrey," Brother Barnabas agreed, feeling the point of Rigsson's knife press into the small of his back as he walked, bisecting rows of wooden benches, each with a straight back and often a kneeling bench attached to the one in front of it. Runes had been carved into them here and there by the shield maidens, and a number of dead monks lay slumped about. "But the walls still speak to these barbarians as do these pews."

"Rest in peace, brother," Brother Godfrey said and pausing to make the sign of the cross over the body of a monk, before Einar gave him a brutal shove forward.

"I know not what you say monk, but shut your mouth and keep moving to the Jarl," Einar snarled tetchy, as the monks reached the bay, where the transept intersected the main body of the church to form the cruciform. The crossings aisles were narrower than the nave and they had been besmeared by muddy and bloody footprints left by knots of warriors heading towards both ends of the transept where there were erected auxiliary altars that were dedicated to particular saints.

Off to the right, amidst the rubble of the stone slab they had been smashed to get at the hidden compartment underneath one of the auxiliary altars, knelt Lokar, Ásgrímr and Olaf shouting in delight as they thrust their hands deeply into the hole and withdrew reliquaries of various sizes. The caskets were made from ivory and metals such as gold, silver, bronze, and copper, and often embossed with enamelwork and precious stones like: diamonds, rubies, emeralds and sapphires.

The three Vikings opened the caskets and upended the relics: A skull fell out of one to hit the floor, a skeleton foot from another along with fingers, teeth, a lock of hair and even fragments of clothing, before the reliquaries were thrown into bulging sacks.

"Lo, Brother Francis; they have dug up the altars and are seizing all the hallowed treasures." Brother Barnabas said, numb with shock, pointing at Lokar and his warriors as he went on to repeat the exact words from a verse from St. Pauls letter to the Colossians. "The mysteries hidden for ages and generations but now revealed."

"I see the rapine all to well and I fear I shall drown in my own tears ere long at such desolation of the spirit," Brother Francis answered in the grip of strong emotion.

Rigsson growled nonverbally at the monks' constant chatter and his free hand shoved the old, shuffling holy man in the back again. Brother Francis grunted with the involuntary half step and cried out as he lost his balance. The guards chuckled, finding amusement in the old man's clumsiness. But before he could stumble face first into the mosaic floor, the much younger monks beside him reached out with their hands to catch Brother Francis and steadied him.

"My gratitude, brothers, for your kindly assistance," Brother Francis' voice was scarcely audible as he was shaken by nerves and had an irregular pulse. "Could you please help me the rest of the way to the high altar, for age and weakness has made my legs as rickety as a chair?"

The younger monks nodded and with a few encouraging words, Brother Barnabas and Brother Godfrey supported the older man weight as they all set off again. Tears welled in the eyes of Brother Francis and one trickled down his wrinkled, sunken cheek, his gait was unsteady and in silence he focused his mental activity in solely upon putting one foot in front of the other towards the steps leading up to the chancel.

Lighted candles atop of wrought-iron tiered stands stood at various intervals to dispel some of the lingering shadows and soften the sharp-edges of the high stone altar and the Crucifixion above it silhouetted by the light passing through the huge three-sided, stain glass windows depicting The Last Judgement and other scenes from the Old Testament.

* * *

At the front of the church, there was also a flurry of activity that acted to stimulate discussion between the Vikings, who were all pleased with themselves.

"The Gods of the North are smiling upon us, Magnus; and I raise my cup early to honour your leadership, for this has been a rousing adventure thus far," Rollo acknowledged him with a bob of his head as he grabbed a gold chalice from the high altar and sipped the red liquid inside, wincing as he swallowed it. "The wine though is as foul as drinking bilge water," he tipped the rest of it onto the floor in disgust and then began admiring the handiwork of the cup.

"This food the monk's laid out is no better," Magnússon spat out the chewed mouthful of stale consecrated bread as he leaned on the creaking ornate rail of the chancel. "'Tis coarse with grit from the millstones grinding the grain nay doubt. But on the word of my son, we shall eat herring at dusk and on the morrow too till we be sick of it."

"Not I, Magnus," Rollo said, dropping the chalice into a sack. "If fish are so plentiful on this side of the North Sea, mayhap it would be well to consider establishing a permanent settlement upon these shores?"

"Your idea has merit, Rollo; and it will give me something else to gnaw on," Magnússon nodded thoughtfully. "As he put the longships through their paces on their maiden voyages,

Gunnar and his sons sighted and charted over seventy of the Orkney Islands and islets. One all more of them could be well suitable for our particular purposes."

"And from there we shall claim this land of the Angles by right of conquest," Rollo said in good humour. "Noblemen born and bred in their castles and soldiers manning the walls of their towns know naught of sleeping rough, living off the land and marching through mud and rain belike us, Magnus. We could best them with ease, enchaining those that lay down their arms and killing those that do not."

Magnússon nodded again. "If what Gunnar regaled me about the politics of this country are true, the bitter dissension between the kingdoms means that we could divide and conquer by battling several smaller armies one after another instead of facing a single huge army united under one banner."

"Jarl Magnússon, if these monks have accumulated such riches here," Björn said, standing with Healfdene behind them, as they snatched up a plain gold cross, a pair of silver candlesticks, plates, a tray and a small gold bell from atop of the baldachin – a satin canopy covering the high altar - that was greatest in size and importance than the smaller auxiliary altars – before each was thrust deeply into his sack, "then what hoards of treasure await us in the other great monasteries?"

"Aye, Björn; what indeed," Magnússon said, watching Vegard's weather beaten face light up as he tugged the baldachin from the high altar and his grubby fingers at first tested its strength and then he felt the materials smooth glossy finish. "I found a beautiful relic-shrine box shaped like a child's plaything in the other smaller altar. I cleaned out the finger and toe nails and now it shall make a fine jewellery box for my wife Ranveig. I sent the boy Fridrik to take it to the carts outside and keep an eye on it as it heads back to the ships."

"There be handholds at the end of this altar, Jarl Magnússon,"

Boromir said, after walking around the raised, flat-topped structure, the cracked sides were stained with smoke and covered with carving depicting Christ's washing the feet of his disciples. "I think the monks have concealed more treasure underneath it."

Magnússon nodded and Vegard dropped the baldachin at the prospect of better loot beckoning, as he and Boromir bent down to get a firm grip on the handholds. "Björn, Rollo help them lay hold and lift it."

There was a chorus of assenting murmurs as the other two men dumped their sacks on the ground and obeyed; the muscles in their legs, arms and their strong backs felt a slight strain from the heavy weight when the stone box shifted, friction causing the altar and the granite surfaces of the repository to rub together with a grating noise. The great rectangular structure shot upward, until it lifted clear of the container underneath, and then the warriors sidestepped and flung the altar into the apse wall with a loud crash.

Magnússon, Healfdene and Vegard were the first to approach the repository filled with crosses, ivory, gold and silver statues, and sparkling gems set within a myriad of religious objects. Lokar, Rollo and other Vikings crowded around the container.

"I think we ought to fetch more sacks," Olaf said with widening eyes as he beheld the treasure.

"By Thor's hammer, Ásgrímr, I am a man of many jealousies," Wulfric exclaimed loudly and with great excitement over the receding echoes of the smashed altar stone. "I have long coveted my neighbour's fighting cock and dreamed of doing more than fondle the firm breasts of his comely daughter, but this plunder makes all that seem poor quality by comparison."

"Aye," said Ásgrímr, his bearded face spilt with a devilish smile as he grabbed the largest of three emerald goblets. "Let others quaff ale from the skull of their enemies if they want, I will drink the Jarl's health out of this fancy cup."

Sounds of footsteps reverberating off the walls behind them made Magnússon and Rollo look around sharply as Einar, Rigsson and the monks pulled up before them.

Einar bowed quickly. "The prisoners you requested to see, Jarl Magnússon."

Magnússon carefully regarded the monks for a moment, reading their distraught expressions and even their tumultuous thoughts, before addressing Brother Francis in broken English. "When your abbot decided to gives alms to the poor," he laughed jubilantly without a hunt of humanity and waved a hand pompously at the front of the church, "I wager he never once considered how charitable his Order would be with their donations."

The jest caused much merriment among the Vikings rapt faces; some guffawed, while others doubled up as they ridiculed the monks.

Brother Francis clenched his jaw to keep his composure and grief-stricken lowered his head, while the jaunty disregard Magnússon held for the holy men and the sacred objects was too much of an insult for one of the younger monk to bear. Caught up in the moment, Brother Godfrey snapped and releasing his hold on Brother Francis, he flung his hand out angrily.

"Those ornaments are sacrosanct, heathen," he said with a mixture of outrage and anguish. "Only the Angels themselves have the skill to guide the hand of the artisan to create such beauty. We stand in the presence of our Lord," Brother Godfrey pointed up at the cross. The attention of Magnússon and Rollo were briefly drawn to it. "He listens to your blabbering and the sins you have committed this day against peaceful monks and nuns will incur his wrath. In his infinite wisdom he shall chastise you and you're pack of hellhounds for this blasphemes. You won't enjoy your ill-gotten gains for long."

Brother Francis took a sharp intake of breath and looking up, he and Brother Barnabas eyed their fellow monk with obvious helplessness, as Rollo stepped forward and clenching his sword hand, punched Brother Godfrey, sending him sprawling to the ground. A tentacle of crimson burst from the monk's mouth and he coughed, before spitting out more blood and a few of his knocked out teeth.

"I have known many a carpenter, but I wouldn't pray to one of them. We Vikings have a pantheon of Gods to protect us, so I think your 'Lord' will punish us not, and now the treasures are ours, you Christian weakening," Rollo snarled, learning over him. "Norse craftsmen will make pieces of jewellery from the gems and the gold and silver will be melted down into more manageable coins and ingots to recoup the Jarl's fortune."

"Enough, Rollo," Magnússon slapped him on the back. "You know my orders, stand the monk up."

"An oath breaker I am not, Magnus," Rollo nodded with cold indifference and he straightened, hauling Brother Godfrey's short and sturdy figure to his feet, his lip was already beginning to swell. "But still am I of the mind that thirty lashes would bleed the insolent out of them."

"I have a much better idea," Magnússon said, twisting his mouth in a half smile, hearing the tension in Rollo's voice. "You can have more amusement ere long when we break the church windows and pull down the cross."

There were shocked gasps at the Viking's brutality and their casual talk of honour caused horror to transform the faces of the monks. Brother Francis inhaled deeply and glanced at Magnússon, managing to pluck up courage to ask a question that had been gnawing at him. "And pray tell why it is that you and your warriors have so cruelly slain so many of my brethren and to sell others in bondage, and yet you have taken great pains to spare us?"

"You are to do a service for my Jarl, monk." Rollo growled,

averting his gaze to stare at the old man. "Be ever thankful to him, if left to me, I be feeding you your innards."

"If its information you seek from us, Magnus Magnússon," the wrinkled face of Brother Francis twisted in a grimace of disgust, but he spoke on with deliberate calm, "we have little to offer about the upheavals on the land. The monastery contains its own bake house, workshops and a bounty of animals that enable us through our labours to live alone and independently of the villagers so there is hardly a reason to step outside of the walls much less leave this Holy Isle."

"Bah, I have heard snippets of news already about this fertile England. 'Tis fragmented into several separate kingdoms and the monarchs are at each others throats, their armies habitually battle one another over lines on a map - hence any opposition we face when we eventually invade will be not organized and be in vain."

"You forget Magnus Magnússon that each king uses his children's marriages to build alliances and sign treaties that increase the power of every kingdom," Brother Francis said.

Brother Francis' interruption really irritated Magnússon. "You cling to life monk because I want you and your companions to bear witness and record that I Jarl Magnus Magnússon, the Red Plague; and my seafaring crew of Norsemen are responsible for all that has fallen the isle of Lindisfarne this day in retribution of Charlemagne ordering the beheading of hundreds of Woden worshipers in Saxony a season hence."

"Save me, O Lord, from lying lips and deceitful tongues," Brother Barnabas quoted psalms as he believed the account was full of falsehoods.

Brother Francis blinked in surprise and considered for a moment, before answering. "Nay, Brother Barnabas, ignorance is not always bliss when it comes to the outside world, for I know of what Magnus Magnússon speaks, I was privy to the news spoken by a pilgrim in the Abbot's chamber."

"In truth?"

"Verily, Brother Barnabas. The Saxon leaders converted to Christianity, but were discovered to be still practicing the pagan rites of their forefathers in secret. They were found guilty and killed as an example to others, thinking of straying off the true path."

"And you civilized people call us pagan's barbarians," Rollo spat fiercely; there was a dangerous cold light in his eyes.

"I met a Christian missionary once in a foreign land, trying to spread his faith and preaching high principles like 'turn the other cheek' but I say you and your kind feign those beliefs and feelings and behave otherwise. Charlemagne used draconian measures to force the Saxons to accept the worship of the 'White Christ.'" Magnússon saw the eyebrows of Brother Francis lift at the term. "Aye, I know of the Athenian legislator Draco and his wide-ranging code of laws, for you monks are not the only men here to be well-educated. My children are already learning to read and write and soon they will chronicle the birth of Norse history starting with me. Tell your king Aethelred and his courtiers that they are to take heed of my forewarning, for my ambitions reach far beyond these monastery walls. As of now the people of England are living in the 'Age of the Viking' and you won't know the moment when we next come to raid these shores."

Björn retraced his steps and he picked up the baldachin before shoving it into his sack.

* * *

"Most of this monastery is made from timber, Hakon; and it shall make a fine funeral pyre for our dead and the undeserving Christens," Bödvar said, his long tawny hair hanging loosely about his broad shoulders as he threw another jar of pitch upon the scriptoriums wooden walls. It smashed and the black viscous substance smeared a decorative Roman pilaster.

"Aye," Hakon agreed, a frown crossing his heavily boned face, as he and other barrel-chested Norsemen coordinated their actions, hurling pitch on the soot-stained walls above extinguished torches and sloshing lamp oil over the trail of newly-hewed ecclesiastical furniture leading out into the corridor. "But what is to happen to the places of stone that won't easily burn?"

"I know not," Bödvar shook his head; as his brawny arm and large hand reached down to grab the delicately curved handle of another graceful Roman jug. "Bur sure am I at what I beheld from a tower window has something to do with it though, for one of our shipmates took the plough horses from the fields and steered them into one of the columned chambers."

* * *

Elsewhere in the monastery, the clopping of hooves striking hard ground announced to everyone present within the huge chamber that the horses were coming. The space was about eighty paces across from one niveous-coloured wall to the next and marking the tiles here and there were the letters SPQR – meaning the senate and people of Rome. Supporting the ceiling was a central range of columns in the form of statues carved in dynamic poses. Shadowy corners were festooned with dusty cobwebs and shafts of restless sunlight shined down through the clerestory windows onto the ornate, but badly damaged pool. No water filled it, only the dead bodies of monks and nuns. The air stank of their blood and offal.

"You send for my help, Almgren," Floki said, surveying his

surroundings and seeing men and women carrying off lead candleholders and manhandling out a few ornate braziers that had runes chalked on to them, which simply said 'To Take.' A knot of short, sleeveless warriors, reeking of sweat and clutching grappling hooks followed closely on their leader's heels. "Here we be."

"Aye, the monks called this chamber the 'necessarium' and they were tending to the sick and injured till we came and slaughter them all." The short, wiry, angular-faced, Viking laughed loudly, gesturing with a finger as he slid it across his throat. Floki nodded in understanding and dry rushes strewed across the mosaic floor crackled beneath their boots as they moved among the columns. "I had all my axe-wielders chop up the wooden pallets in here for kindling and now they are busy laying out the pieces in a trail along the corridors and pouring lamp oil over it. Once the trail is ignited the flame will go directly towards the calefactory."

"There are other fire trails being laid all over the monastery, Almgren;" Floki said, "and what does not burn will be tore down." Just then, Ellisiv led in two, harnessed horses through an archway easily wide and tall enough to admit the animals with space to spare. She progressed in for several steps, before she pulled up the blind-folded team beside a row of shelf-like flat stones, each one of which had a dusty, dirty fire space underneath, where wood used to be burned to heat up the stones in the garrison's bathhouse and sauna.

"Aye!" Almgren pointed at a great telamon stature, flecks of colour still clung to the bare marble from when the Roman's had painted it. Cracks zigzagged across the slabs of muscle and it was naked except for a loincloth. "Starting with this Christen art."

"Not Christen, Almgren," Floki corrected and he scratched his hairy armpit. "The Jarl mentioned these Atlas statures were carved by Romans, another race of pagan's belike us, giants whose achievements shaped the known world in their image."

"He should know if anyone does," Almgren shrugged his shoulders. "We be knocking that one and its two neighbours off their pedestals."

"You heard him, Alvin, take the one on the right," Floki shouted over his shoulder.

A fat Viking detached from the knot and went over to the first statue, his pudgy hand swinging the grappling hook with smooth rhythmic motions. When his powerful, but flabby arm released it, the rope uncoiled at his flat feet and the iron shaft soared, curving upwards until two of the multiple prongs lodged into the vee-shaped gap between the head and right arm of the telamon figure. The pot bellied thrower and another man with a pony tail gathered up the rope, pulling hard on the line to see if the grapnel slipped, but it didn't, before the pair headed over to the horses.

Floki then beckoned at more of his men and pointed a finger at another grimy telamon figure. "Jens, you cast at that middle one next. And Ulf, you aim your grapnel at its neighbour."

The young man wearing the three-torques nodded and he and Ulf, sporting a wolf head totem on the shield he set down, took several steps forward and swung their grappling irons above their heads as they did. After letting them go, Jens' saw his grapnel arched inward and latch onto the statue's bent leg, one prong attaching itself behind the knee. Ulf's meanwhile hooked onto a stone arm. He pulled the line and the prongs slid from position into the statue's bent elbow joint, but there it held securely after a couple of sharp tugs.

"Rope men, make the lines secure." Floki ordered." Erik, you and Alvin, mount up."

Jens and Ulf scooped up their individual ropes and hastened to the horses, where they interwove the ends through the padded leather collar resting on the animals' shoulders and a few of the harness straps, and tied the knots tight. The fat warrior stood on one of the heating stones and swung his leg up to get astride his Clydesdale.

"Alvin, you mouse about on tiptoes like a pregnant cow and you be trice as weighty, but there is nay a better skilled horseman than you." Erik mounted the other carthorse.

"A backhanded compliment if I ever heard one, Erik," Alvin's belly wobbled in good natured mirth as he made a throaty chortle. "I shall take it, my friend."

"Everyone outside now," Floki ordered, slowly backtracking to the archway. Almgren beckoned to those around him to follow as he did an about-turn and loped from the chamber. A sense of urgency came over the Vikings and they departed, Ellisiv removed the horse's blind folds before catching up with Jens and Ulf heading out into the corridor beyond. The riders wheeled the Clydesdales to face the sole entrance. Watching over everything, Floki bellowed at the horsemen. "Erik, Alvin, give me to the count of ten to get clear and then ride till you succeed or the horses' hearts give out!" He disappeared from sight.

The riders obeyed, both of them shouting "Hyah, hyah." Gripping the horses' manes as makeshift reins, they heeled their boots into their flanks, driving the animals into a charging gallop towards the archway. The fullness in the ropes behind them was quickly taken in and made taut, and when that happened, the team of Clydesdales was suddenly and violently jolted and their momentum floundered, their harnesses dug into their chests and flanks, causing bruising and abrasions.

At the same time the three statues juddered and were becoming less rigid by the second, cracks widened and extended, a groan travelling the length from floor to ceiling in response to the stresses they were undergoing. Erik and Alvin kicked out again and again, intent on keeping the horses struggling onward.

Eyes bulged and high-pitched, frantic neighs from the powerful stallions echoed loudly off the walls as their nostrils expanded to take in more air, tendons stood out on necks and their muscles became painful knots.

Presently, stone crumbled from the swaying statues as the lathering horses began to make quickening headway, and then there was a loud rumbling sound behind them, the fracturing columns disintegrated, collapsing along with the ceiling above it. The heavy thumps vibrating the ground, the crash resonating from the walls and a dark billowing cloud of dust billowed up and enveloped the chamber in seconds.

The riders whooped and hollered as they negotiated the corridor and emerged outside. Viking cursed profanity and scattered from their path in different directions.

Chapter Six
The Sparks and the Flames

Within the spacious Roman burial cavern Brother Biutta had spoke off, the walls were set with dozens of recesses each was large enough to take a single naked skeleton, layers of dislodged soil and dust of the ages covered the bones like makeshift shrouds. Dominating the centre of the chamber was an earthen slope with risers and treads craved into it. Sitting at the top with his knees drawn up to his bosom, Brother Gideon's face was solemn and his dirty hands left stains upon the wrapped bible he gripped.

Brother Gideon shivered in the chill air and worked hard to subdue his irritation of being left alone and abandoned in the dark. Most of all he regretted not speaking out, letting the other monks make the decisions and obeying them, while he silently derived a persistent sense of futility about what they were going to attempt to do. Brother Gideon had sought to keep hope alive and prove to himself that he was wrong to have such dour thoughts about the fate of his fellow brothers, but the longer he waited in anticipation, not knowing for certain, the more he feared his worst forebodings were soon to become realized.

Brother Gideon took another long look over his shoulder when he again heard the undergrowth rustle just beyond the cave's rocky egress. He felt the hairs bristle on the back of his neck and he prayed silently for his brethren to return safely. With his stomach rumbling, the young monk's exhausted mind spun from the changes in his circumstances the last few hours had brought about and he became lost in his reverie.

Once he and his fellow monks had arrived in the burial chamber, Brother Biutta gave the Lindisfarne Gospels to Brother Gideon to hold, before he led Brother Bernard and Brother Gurkinn on a fact-finding mission outside to get their bearings from the lay of the land ere they went off to find the coracle. And yet as the sun continued to move into the west, the sunlight filtering through the trees and briers screening the egress diminished slowly but steadily to a pale wash, deepening the draping shadows and lowering the temperatures in the cavern, his brethren had not reappeared and for Brother Gideon the future was starting to look very black indeed. Brother Gideon had wanted to flee from this place, to take his chances out in the open, but the importance of the Lindisfarne Gospels forced him to push the temptation away.

A twig snapped behind him and Brother Gideon came out of his contemplation. He tensed up and put the bible down, before he turned to face the egress. His eyes flickered at the shadowy undergrowth and his eyebrows twitched nervously as he listened to his own breathing and his heart pumped a little faster in his chest. A second or two later, a low leafy branch swayed out of position and a tonsured-head, emerged with long, bloody scratches from prickly bramble bushes crisscrossing it.

"Are you there, Brother Gideon?" the monk whispered.

"Where else would I be, Brother Bernard?" Brother Gideon said just as loudly, watching the other monk force his way through the undergrowth on his hands and knees. "I was beginning to wonder if you and the others had been enslaved."

"Brother Biutta and Gurkinn have been," Brother Bernard replied tersely, breathing with a hoarse whistling sound.

"What happened to them?" Brother Gideon asked quickly, feeling his patience beginning to slip, as the branch swung back again in place.

"I know not of what happened to the coracle, but Gurkinn was returning to where I and Brother Biutta were crouching in the hazel grove. Gurkinn with accompanied by a cluster of villagers, which he must have come across in his travels and was helping to bring them to our underground refuge for safety," Brother Bernard said, his trembling hands lifted him up to rest on his knees. "Alas, that was when the Vikings search parties appeared, one came from the west and the other the east," he circled the air with his index finger, "to surround them from the front and the sides."

Brother Gideon shook his head in dismay. "And what of the fate of Brother Biutta?"

"I know not. The Vikings must have sensed our presence or glimpsed the faint hint of movement among the tall grasses where nay a gust of wind blew, because they approached us and thrust their spears into the undergrowth to drive us out of hiding like frightened birds. Brother Gideon's eyes rounded as he continued to listen to every word. "As the snare tightened around us Brother Biutta whispered to me to burrow myself deeper into the bushes and he also gave me the duty of helping you protect the Lindisfarne Gospels pending the arrival of the King's soldiers. Then he burst from cover, intent on leading the raiders away and that was the last I saw of him."

"So what now?" Brother Gideon asked. "We can not venture forth and we can not go back whence we came either, for fear of the Vikings finding us in the tunnels."

"The bible will be safe if we just stay here for the nonce," Brother Bernard said. "The lateness of the hour and the lowering tide will force the longships to leave ere long."

***

"Faugh, I like this not, Orm," Hogun the ship's carpenter said in disgust, a scowl wrinkled his smooth brow under the golden curls escaping his horned helmet as he swept the blazing torch to and fro at the darkness ahead of him. The vertical cave conduit the pair found themselves in was a continuous fracture in the earth and the overall width was liable to change, suddenly and unpredictably from three to six feet. The worn stone steps beneath the monastery had been hewed out of the very bedrock and were narrow with only enough room for one person to progress at a time. There was no balustrade and the risers and treads hugged the craggy walls that were sprinkled with veins of light silver-white magnesium. "The zeal I felt at the start of this task is waning belike the moon."

"Aye," Orm remarked, his breath made a faint mist in the chill air as his right hand caressing the pommel of his sheathed sword for his own comfort. Their bodies were working harder to keep warmer in the lower temperature. "When Björn sent us through the door the monk was heading for in search of more slaves and we followed the smudged footprints disturbing the age-old dust in those low-ceiled passageways branching hither and thither, and now on these steps, little did I think it would get so cold in here and this great stair would lead this far down into the quiet with the bottom still lost to us in shadow?"

Hogun nodded. "The slaves could be anywhere or they might have found a hidden exit." Letting the prevailing atmosphere tensed up his muscles, he became swayed by his deep-seated superstitious beliefs from his homeland, and he added. "I be of the opinion we should not be here, Orm. We have invaded an enemy domain and I know they await us just out beyond the light, armed dwarves or kobolds ready to leap at any moment to attack us."

Already feeling insignificantly small and lost in the shadowy surroundings, Orm nodded in understanding. "A sign that shall allow nay a doubt in my mind either that we have left Midgard behind." In the ruddy glow of his burning torch, there was a deeply troubled expression on his long-lined face and a deepening chill stole over his wiry frame as he lumbered sullenly after him, the sound of his boot descended upon another step mingling with the slap of sword sheath on his thigh carried for a moment or two before the reverberation faded and this gave him the impression that the darkness was swallowing up the echoes supernaturally fast. "I feel there is magic about us and at this depth we may not hear the battle horns or raised voices, hearkening us to return to the longships should the tide be on the ebb. We would be stranded here and not know it until much later."

Balking at the prospect of being abandoned, Hogun felt his gorge rise and he looked miserably around, carefully saying. "Orm, were it up to me, we would be turning back, for I have lost interest. We will be able to carry away slaves aplenty another day."

The thought gave Orm pause and he sloughed. "And what is it you would say to Björn?"

"The truth," Hogun replied, giving Orm a means of enabling him to keep his good name without losing face. "We found naught of worth, there is not any shame in that," he hoisted up his torch as an idea came to him. "Look Orm," he released the burning stick and it fell from the edge of the step he stood on, finding it quite difficult as he tried to measure the distance accurately below them. The flames fluttered in the air currents and grew smaller, drawing the attention of the two Vikings, and then the growing speck was gone, consumed by the darkness. "See the bottom is not to be seen or the magic is blinding our perspective, making us see what they want us to see. We have done all we could. Don't let your pride stand in the way."

"You have been listening to Lokar," Orm pursed his lips, his indecision beginning to show as he chewed over the idea. But before he could come to a choice, the cavern shook and a sudden, incandescent light flared and bloomed from the depths to push back the gloom after the sparks and the flames of Hogun's torch ignited a pocket of highly inflammable and explosive methane present in the stale air. The flames were pale, slightly luminous, and very hot by the time it set fire to the magnesium deposits higher up.

There was flash after flash from several loud detonations as the magnesium exploded, blasting holes in the walls and causing cave-in to block off tunnel mouths and bury the catacombs in rubble. The shadows fled ahead of them to be replaced by vibrant colours of reds, oranges and blues. Tension continued to build, settling Orm and Hogun's teeth on edge as they responded to the sound and activity, peering down at the nature of the source and their stunned expressions varied between doubt and a complete lack of comprehension at the ball of fire coming straight at them.

"What is it, Orm?" Hogun frowned thoughtfully. "Some nether-realm beast."

"Not any beast, Hogun; but a fire breathing dragon. 'Tis Nidhogg himself, come to claim us," Orm drew his blade. "Fill your hand with steel and let us die in battle as we lived with a sword in our hand. Even Odin can not refuse our heroic souls a place within Valhalla's great hall after facing a foe such as him."

More veins of magnesium blew up and the climbing flames washed over the Norsemen, cutting their screams short.

✶ ✶ ✶

During the intervening time, Jarl Magnus Magnússon raised the curved hunting horn and sounded a harsh, howling note to signal the fire lighting. Off to his right, Lokar and Boromir nocked the fletching to their bows, before taking it in turn to dip their pitched covered arrowhead into burning coals in the brazier in front of them, pulling their strings back and releasing their shafts at the hayloft above the stable. Each barb was swallowed up by the fodder, but almost immediately a soft steady orange glow was visible from the depths and wisps of smoke was rising from out of it.

Magnússon blew his horn again for those that missed it and from high up in one of the buildings of the monastery, Rollo was already turning from a window overlooking the courtyard towards piles of wood strewed across the floor of the chamber. He flung his flaming torch into the midst of oil-soaked debris and then a flash-fire burst into life, blazing a path over to the doorway and through it to enter the adjacent chamber. Smoke curled thickly and embers were thrown up into the air.

Rollo wheeled around and headed out the remaining doorway, catching the sound of movement approaching from beyond. Emerging into the corridor, he glanced right to see the silhouettes of Finn and Rothgar against a roaring sheet of flame behind them. Motioning for the men to follow, Rollo darted left and hurried along the corridor to its end. At intervals, shadow and flickering firelight danced across the figures of other smoke-stained Vikings appearing from chamber openings on to the passageway or from junctions to join the back of the fleeing band, increasing its overall size until it numbered at least a score.

Coming to the eastern staircase, Rollo and the warriors did not hesitate for a second to look back at the havoc they had wrought, for waves of intense heat washed over them from the spreading fires. They proceeded with haste down the creaking steps; dimly lit candles in wall recesses at different heights just about pierced the splotches of darkness and smoky stretches to show them the way to the lower floors.

From the north of the monastery, there was a loud explosion from the kitchen and the bakery storeroom after Björn and Olaf kicked over a pair of braziers, burning coals spilled from the metal grille work over the threshold and sparks ignited the dry flour dispersed across the floors, the flame front flashing through the dust and whooshed out into the corridors, carpeted by more flour trails or lines of broken furniture soaked in pitch. The air was thick with ash and spewing smoke from all the destructive burning as fires coursed into the workshops.

Within the library - sets of empty shelves fixed to the walls of the western staircase - Almgren ignited the oil-daubed wood and then fled down the stair. At the bottom he torched the heap of scrolls and pages of parchment torn from ancient tomes, and the resulting fires flared up left and right, crackling tentacles angled down from above to turn the scriptorium into an inferno. Charred beams collapsed and the timber walls and ceilings crashed down atop of them.

Some distance away, the perspiring Rollo stood by the monastery's open front door. "Come on, move yourselves faster!" his voice instilling a sense of urgency, waving at the fleeing Vikings as they filed past him. "This is the way out."

Björn and his clutch of followers emerged from around a corner and merged with the shrinking group of coughing warriors ahead of them. "Rollo," Björn said, breathing hard, as he approached him. "Have you seen any sign of Orm and Hogun?"

"I be counting heads not looking at individual faces, Björn Strongarm." Rollo growled, as his nose detected a whiff of smoke in the air, but his darting eyes did not see any encroaching flames from the various directions yet. "There are other exits hereabouts and 'tis possible they left through one of them and have retreated to the rally point outside the gates or even returned to their ships with treasure. Now, off with ya, I will be coming hard on your heels."

Björn nodded and then led his men outside. Rollo followed in their wake.

* * *

As the last handful of Vikings charged outside and went all out back across the courtyard towards the front gates, shouting with glee, Magnússon gestured at Lokar and Boromir before they carried the brazier over the trails of hay and threw it down, the reddening coals fell onto the fodder and a fierce fire sprang up, spreading greedily left and right to ignite the bodies of the dead. Acrid smoke billowed out the cloister arches of the inner arcade and from building after building as the flames took hold; firelight glowed in doorways and windows.

Whirling, the Jarl and his companions raced away, converging upon the rendezvous point just beyond the walls. But when they were just half way across, the three Norsemen heard a far away rumbling noise and felt the world around them suddenly shake from an underground spasm. Buildings began swaying with the enduring rhythm of the tremors as the cave-ins displaced rock and earth higher up. Lokar fell sprawling to the ground, forcing Magnússon to slow long enough to haul his son to his feet. Boromir struggled onward, following the Vikings trickling out into the graveyard.

Clouds of disturbed dust rose in a haze to blur the shape of the complex of buildings. In one corner of the monastery, a spectacular ball of fire erupted out of the earth to instantly engulf the nuns temporary sleeping quarters housed in a timber-walled priory and blossomed skyward, silhouetting the tiny running figures of Magnússon and Lokar as they passed through the gateway. Behind them, the ground slumped in places, collapsing the walls of buildings and toppling the bell tower.

Beyond the monastery's outer wall, Magnússon and Lokar slowed. They were greeted by a gust of merriment and were applauded with the clatter of sword hilts hitting against shields faces as the pair rejoined their warriors, presently gathering around three posts. Manacled to each one of these were the monks: Brother Francis, Brother Barnabas and Brother Godfrey, who was trying to twist his head and get a peek of the devastation behind him, when he saw the Jarl approaching through the crowd.

"What have you done to the House of the Lord, Magus Magnússon?" demanded Brother Francis loudly over the sound of the 'applause' already starting to die down.

"I have razed it to the ground and gave your unworthy dead the ceremony of a Viking funeral, they shall live and spend eternity serving mead and food to the fallen souls of heroes in the great hall of Valhalla," Magnússon laughed in reply as he took in Brother Francis' sad expression, making his feelings clear as ash fell on them like snowflakes. "We are going now, but remember to heed my words monk and take them to your betters."

Magnússon then unslung his hunting horn and blew two long blasts, the same quivering note signalling the withdrawal and then two outriders galloped on ahead of the line of march. Rollo and Björn waved the men and women forward, and the Vikings jogged off down the Sea Road at a steady pace with barely a glance back from any of them.

* * *

Smoke swirled from behind rock walls and embers danced in the windy air as crops and dead animals burnt in the fields along the largely deserted Sea Road. Clouds scuddled across the sky, temporarily passing before the sun and the countryside grew murky. Flocks of carrion crows took flight at the sound of uproar coming towards them. Astride their lathering Clydesdales, Erik and Alvin rode in silence as they galloped past sparse woodland, unmortared barns and crumbling, overgrown shells of one-roomed farm buildings, until they sawed their reins and the whinnying horses skidded to a sliding halt beside gaps in the walls.

Open wooden gates had been swung inward over the threshold of other fields, where Vikings standing in small knots were busy moving through the mud and discolouring spring grass, slaughtering thin milk cows with spears or setting fire to the stunted wheat and barley. Heads turned and a lone warrior near the gate walked unhurriedly up to the riders.

"Where you be running off to, Erik?" asked the warrior with broken veins in his high-bridged nose, suspiciously eyeing both horses for signs of saddle bags full with treasure.

"Back to the beach for departure off this rock, Yngvarr," Erik shouted, conveying a sense of urgency. "Did you not hear the horn blasts?" Norsemen shook their heads and in twos and threes, strode forward with purpose to join their comrade. "We be passing word along from the Jarl himself. He wants everyone on the longships immediately."

That gave Yngvarr a moment's pause and he wiped sweat off his forehead and widow's peak with the back of his hand. "We saw the fingers of smoke rising to stain the sky and the carts heading towards the beach, but we thought we had time to butcher the rest of these dumb beasts and turn the crops into cinders."

"Abandon what you have been doing and muster your men to follow us quickly, for we have at least a league to travel," Alvin put in snappily. "The last task at the monastery is fulfilled and the rearguard is on the march."

"But what about the cattle meat?" the warrior asked anxiously, licking his lips. "We were supposed to wait for a cart to load up and carry it back to the Horse of the Waves?"

"Leave it," Erik replied, loosing the reins. "I heard the Jarl say he was going to make another offering to Odin. A great victory demands a greater sacrifice, we are just making good on his promise."

Erik dug his heels into the horse's flank and it trotted away. Alvin did the same, riding through shadow up to the time the clouds parted and the sun came back out.

* * *

"Now I ask you the same question monk, and I don't want to hear you speaking falsehoods?"

Siegfried Gunnarson snarled, tearing the tattered robe from Brother Biutta's frame, before deliberately striking the captive behind the joints of his legs with the handle of his whip, forcing him to his knees alongside Brother Gurkinn, who was fighting a wave of nausea. The wind blew across the island, carrying the mingling smells of hay and manure in the air. Here and there tree branches swayed, causing lengthening shadows to move aimlessly over the worn, muddy trail bisecting the low stone wall behind the Vikings, leading to the Roman road before them. "Answer me, cur! Where have you and your fellows been hiding yourselves?" he added, feeling a slow burn of anger building within him as he moved around and bent down low, leaning in to peer into Brother Biutta's perspiring face and this close up, the monk noticed that the young raider was wearing eyeliner. "You were in the catacombs beneath the monastery burying more treasure, admit it? This isle is mostly flat and my people have searched every bay and abandoned dwellings, hence where else could you have been that enabled you to flee the slaughter and enslavement for so long?"

Brother Biutta gasped for breath and straightened his cracking back, holding his head high and he tried to put down the fear inside. His wrists like Brother Gurkinn were bound tightly behind his back. There was inflammation of his skin around his thighs and abdomen where he had itched and an oozing red sore below which was a clinging whitish lice. "I can only echo Brother Gurkinn's words. We were cultivating crops and herbs for medicine on fertile soil on the other side of the Lindisfarne when we heard the bells ringing. Discarding our tools and encumbrances, we hastened back to the monastery to investigate, but upon the way we met with a group of shepherds and shepherdesses seeking news from us. When I said we had naught to share, they decided to accompany us to the Sea Road, and a short time later your warriors took us captive."

"Fie, I don't believe their foolish story for a second, for the bell was ringing slightly after noonday," Old Sven said in disapproval. Wider in the shoulder and thicker about the chest than Siegfried, the warrior detached from the guarding group, holding a dripping sword in one hand, while the fingers in his right grasped hair on the dangling, severed heads of Saul and Petroc. "We found a coracle and I chopped it into pieces; was that child's boat the only one? Or have others already paddled away, loaded down with smuggled treasure?" he showed the heads to the holy men in an attempt to erode their will to defy him. "I am called Old Sven by most, because my hair and beard is the colour of winter snow, but I take great pride that my limbs still hold a man's strength enough to man an oar and to betwixt a head from its shoulders, now speak monk or suffer the same fate as these Angles?" That drew grins from the other guards. "Two or four heads adorning the spearheads outside my home, matters little to me."

When Brother Biutta did not answer, Siegfried straightened and kicked the monk in the stomach, flipping the grunting holy man onto his side in pain. "Death is too quick for the likes of these worms. Let's do it slow by chopping off a thumb and then his fingers one at a time till he has naught left but a stump, for you don't have to have both hands to herd sheep."

The face of Brother Biutta became solemn as he looked up at his tormentor, but his suffering eyes held a glint of determination and a hint of mockery entered his voice. "I think you would not shrink away from the task even if we spoke the truth to thee. Henceforth do what you will, fiendish of heathens; you shall not find the answers you seek from us."

At that exact moment, a nearby wailing sound suddenly rent the air followed shortly after by a second blast from a hunting horn. Eyes swivelled in the direction where it came from to assess the situation and then ever so faintly they heard the heavy tread of jogging feet moving nosily along the road. Chalky dust was kicked up and it rose from around the corner.

"That's the withdrawal signal, Old Sven," Siegfried said. "The rearguard will be with us soon."

"Aye," the bearded Viking replied, his hair braids slowly swung with movement as he shifted his weight from foot to foot. "Who does not make this last rendezvous point will be left behind."

The clamour of voices and the sound of motion reverberating off the rocky ground increased, but the pair's line of sight was obscured by tree foliage and overgrown bushes until Magnússon, Rollo and the rest of the warriors surged around the bend in the road and covered the ten yard distance, dust clung to them, and as some of the men and women carried more than one shield or a spear apiece for their neighbour, others had their arms weighed down with sacks filled with dishes, plates, cups and cutlery of Celtic design that had been laid out earlier by the monks for the preparation of a midday meal.

Sacks containing more plunder dangled from their backs of the warriors behind them, and a squealing, saddleback sow was being towed by a rope held by Björn. A bevy of piglets oinked and scurried around and between the legs of the bodyguard as they trotted with their mother. Chickens clucked in cages, and Ásgrímr and Tyrker brought up the rear, each sharing the burden by clasping a handle attached to a large bucket with yew staves banded with brass.

At the front, Magnússon pulled up beside Old Sven and Siegfried, and waved the rest of rearguard onward. "Rollo, lead them to the ships, I shall follow in a trice."

Rollo nodded and jogged onward. Björn handed the sow's lead to Hakon and then stopped in his tracks.

"Did you not see Erik and Alvin ride this way?" asked Magnússon bluntly, his breath short.

"Only the dust their mounts kicked up in their wake," Old Sven replied and Magnússon nodded in understanding.

"We are homeward bound," Björn put in. "The Jarl wants to set sail within the hour, so everybody is to return to the beach to help with the refloating of the long ships."

"Should we take these monks with us or put them to the sword, Jarl Magnússon?" asked Siegfried.

Magnússon stroked his beard thoughtfully. "Slaying them here would not be a remedy that's serves the purpose I have in mind. Bring them along, but they are not to be put in the pen with the other sheep on board the slaver ship. This pair and a few more like them will be fitted with ball and chain and left on the deck of the Mjöllnir's Might. Now, enough of this dallying we need to be off."

Magnússon got going alongside Björn and the guards followed him.

Siegfried crackled his whip and trotted behind Brother Biutta and Brother Gurkinn. "Move it monks or I be decorating your flesh with fresh welts."

Old Sven tried to keep up when the rest of the men picked up the pace, but he was soon falling back to the rear, wheezing and puffing as he went.

***

By the time the Viking rearguard reached the beach, the ramshackle buildings were ablaze along with the empty stalls and the four overturned boats. Bodies of the dead Norsemen had been stacked up in the fishing huts before being set alight for their funeral pyre. A pillar of thick, greasy smoke rose into the air, but it and the flying embers were no hindrance to the flock of bold carrion crows landing among the corpses of the villager defenders still lying where they had fell, and walking about purposely to gather the grisly harvest. Some of the birds quickly made off with a strips of human skin or an ear, while others squabbled with each other in order to be the first to pluck out an eyeball in the served heads of Malcolm and Stephen impaled upon spearheads angling up from the ground.

Magnússon and the guards herded the monks off the road and followed the rest of the rearguard stampeding down the crowded beach, flowing around the abandoned wagons and the two scores of seamen digging out the prow of the Mjöllnir's Might, lifting and tossing sand aside with wooden shovels. Checking his headlong rush as he reached the gangplank, Rollo led his warriors across the wobbling span in single file and boarded, ordering those carrying livestock to take it to the hold.

Ahead, three of the smaller longships: Sea Chariot, Horse of the Wave, and the Rune Fire, were already afloat, their steering oars pivoted through the brine and the banks of oars bit into and took a firm grip of the heaving waters to negotiate the vessels about turn, timbers creaked loudly, as large white-capped waves charged in to crash against the hulls abeam.

As soon as Gunnar saw Magnússon and Björn approaching the Mjöllnir's Might, he wheeled and surveyed the crew. "Stir yourselves, the Jarl is coming. Tjernagl…"

Anticipating Gunnar's commands, Tjernagl barked just

as loudly, "Raise the anchors and prepare to launch the ship on my mark." Men and women jumped up and formed two corresponding lines of four along the port and starboard sides, scooping up the thick ropes lying on the deck before they hoisted up the baskets of stones and took them aboard. Magnússon and Björn boarded the Mjöllnir's Might, via the gangplank and the monks and the guards came after.

"Where are my son and daughter, shipwright?" asked Magnússon, coming up to him. Ásgrímr, Boromir and Siegfried dropped the anchors down a hatchway, before closing it. Healfdene and Wulfric pulled in the gangplank and lay it on the deck. Siegfried shoved the two monks onto their bruised knees, and he gestured at them to stay down by the rail.

"Lokar is on this longship, Jarl Magnússon, Kari and shield maidens are sailing back aboard the Long Snake," Gunnar remarked and he nodded to Tjernagl, who strode over to the prow. "Take your seats we're about to get underway." The warriors did so, making their way amidships and slotting their shields in the rack.

Tjernagl peered over the ship's rail and looked down on the gathered Vikings below, leaning on their shovels, panting. "Launch crews, haul away."

The burly Norsemen immediately dropped the shovels and then with a passion, they threw all their weight and strength against the high prow. The keel shunted forward through the wet sand and scraped over several buried rocks towards the frothing waves.

"Steady now, steady I say," Tjernagl said, gradually feeling the series of sea waves lift the longship off the submerging beach.

Now the Mjöllnir's Might was afloat and edging into deeper water with momentum, the launch crew waded in with a splashing run alongside the hull and scrambled aboard, all except Old Sven, who was showing the stoicism and the flagging animal vitality of his barbaric clan as he finally caught up somehow and then was helped to get up and over the rail by Rigsson pushing from below.

"Crew," Gunnar shouted to be heard over the noise of the pounding waves as he made his way to the stern. "Take your rowing stations."

The men and women quickly put hands to oars, the blades sliding out. Tjernagl took up the drum and struck up a rhythmic rowing tempo.

With his hand on the steering oar, Gunnar bellowed, "Crew stroke."

Chapter Seven
Fjordstad

As the Mjöllnir's Might toiled over the waves, and manoeuvred towards the open sea, the Sea Chariot, Horse of the Wave, and the Rune Fire were rowing away from the isle, their steering improving after the surf had been left behind. On the beach, the Blood Fang, the Long Snake, and the Bifrost's Bow were underway in stages, their launch crews shoving each one into the whitecaps breaking onto the shore, while other men and women aboard the longships, leaned over the gunwales and plied their oars like boat poles, pushing them against the sand to help move the vessels even quicker.

In time, the slower and heavier longships came together with the faster vessels of the fleet and headed back the way they came, putting quite a few nautical miles behind them. Hugging the coastline, oars were shipped and sails hoisted to capture the gusting wind as the speed of the fleet increased from nine to 12 knots in the good weather conditions. Onboard the Mjöllnir's Might, Gunnar was charting their course, determining their speed and the distance run by using the majestic mountain landscape furrowed by numerous wide valleys on the port side as passing geographical features, serving also as a guide to finding the isolated cove where they would beach at the end of the day.

Gunnar beckoned Tjernagl over to replace him on the steering oar, before the shipwright overstepped the withdrawn looms and went over to deliver his progress report to Magnússon, who was sitting on his sea chest within a noisy and rowdy bubble, drinking dandelion wine from a goatskin. "Jarl Magnússon," he interrupted Rollo's story of cunning dwarves hammering on their forges, "we are approaching the small sandy inlet I named 'Whale Cove' with an hour of daylight to spare…"

"I barely understood you, Gunnar," Rollo teased, hoping for an angry reaction from Gunnar to relieve his boredom and past the time. "Perchance your tongue has grown coarse and bloated from licking the Jarl's boots, huh?"

Gunnar didn't rise to the bait, instead spoke on, "'twill be in view once we sail past this wooded, low country," he pointed and heads turned to stare at the relatively flat land fringed with long lines of sand dunes. Magnússon lowered the goatskin and wiped his mouth with the back of his hand before handing it to Rollo. "There's good depth awaiting the fleet inside the inlet. I will order each ship to furl the sails when we come to the entrance and after the oars carry us through, the sail and yard shall be stored on the uprights located fore and aft."

"Those are details I leave in your capable hands, Shipwright," Magnússon said, his mind was focused more on the wine and Rollo's story than listening to Gunnar's prattle, waving his arm to dismiss him. Gunnar bobbed his head slightly in deference and was about to walk away when mischief appeared in Rollo's eyes and a twisted, humourless grin split his features.

"Gunnar; is there sign of pursuit thus far?" Rollo asked, deliberately being brutally direct, the wine dripping from his beard as he handed the goatskin back to Magnússon. "Like you said there may be."

"Nay sign," Gunnar winced internally and grimaced at his discomfort.

"Nor is there likely to be, with the amount of leagues we put at our stern to distance ourselves from them, shipwright," Magnússon remarked impatiently, eager for the topic to end.

"Our surprise and speed overcame the English. and I confess the isle and country behind us will be rife with King Aethelred's soldiers, seeking revenge upon us, but the cove and the land hereabouts is within 'Pict-land' if I am not mistaken and it seems deserted enough to enable us to beach and light cooking fires."

Gunnar furrowed his brow characteristically, making his feelings clear and he hesitated for a moment as he felt compelled to speak out then, "We know not what Pictish tribesmen there be lurking in the hollows or deep glens that sculpt this land, Jarl Magnússon," he pressed on, offering caution. "We have treasure and slaves in the holds that we should not put at risk. I advise we anchor the fleet in the bay and let the crews sleep safely on aboard ship tonight and I shall have my men elect some tents over their heads to give some additional shelter from the wind and cold."

"Blah, I grow tire of this old cripple's talk of forebodings, Magnus," Rollo shook his head, answering before Magnússon could.

Burning with anger, Siegfried leaped to his feet at the insult to his father, stared balefully at Rollo, and he began to draw his blade.

Gunnar blinked and fear crossed his face for the life of his son, but then Björn Strongarm suddenly appeared at Siegfried's elbow. The bodyguard's massive hands shot out; the fingers of his right wrapped around the wrist of Siegfried's sword arm and tightened, while his left hand roughly grabbed the younger man's shoulder.

"Unhand me," Siegfried exclaimed vehemently, his face twisted with rage, and heads of the crew turned at the commotion.

"Don't be so mutton-headed, lad," Björn growled menacingly to Siegfried as his voice then dropped to a whisper. "That's what Rollo wants; he's daring you to do something foolish, because he harbours resentment over the relationship your father has with the Jarl, he thinks Gunnar's advice is influencing far too many of Magnússon's decisions? Listen well to what I have to say, Siegfried; you are nay a match for Rollo, you would be as good as throwing yourself on his blade."

The shipwright did not miss his son's slight hesitation.

"Put away your sword, Siegfried," Gunnar roared in dismay. "I have laboured at my work these past years and made too many sacrifices for you to ruin the fortunes of our House by starting a blood feud we can not hope to win."

Siegfried frowned deeply, letting his father's words sink in, before he took a calming breath and decided to sheath his sword.

Björn relaxed the pressure on the wrist and he forced Siegfried to sit back down.

Rollo grinned and pressed on like nothing had happened. "'Tis bad enough that Gunnar's words holds sway when we art at sea but now within sight of shore the upstart seeks to drive a wedge between us and take my job as your counsellor." Magnússon arched his eyebrows at that comment, but let it pass. "I say we be warriors born and the mountains themselves shall quake when our numbers sally forth onto the beach. I think we can deal with the Picts."

There was muttered agreement from his bare-chested shipmates as they echoed Rollo's thoughts.

Gunnar glanced over at his son to check on his welfare and he saw Björn move around to sit down opposite Siegfried and whisper something, "Learn to shrug off the insults of a reckless tongue like your father is doing, for good or ill Rollo is part of the Jarl's family and Magnússon's allegiance would demand he take his brother-in-law's side in any disagreement. It would matter little how much value the Jarl puts on Gunnar's skill of ship building, there are other shipwrights, and if you had the chance to split Rollo's skull that usefulness would have ended along with all your lives now do you understand?"

Siegfried nodded.

Waiting for the muttering to stop, Magnússon sighed deeply and his expression sobered as his gaze bore into his brother-in-law's face. "I like it not when my decisions are questioned, Rollo," he paused for dramatic effect for those around him, "but it dost not mean that I won't listen to those that have my ear. In my youth I would have been in favour of it myself, were it not for age bringing the weight of maturity to settle upon my aching shoulders. You all know I am a scholarly landsman, having knowledge and experienced in desert and forest warfare on horse and on foot, but the sea is belike another world to me, insight into the nature of currents and winds escape me. To make sensible decisions and judgements I listen to the wisdom of my Master shipwright and that will continue to happen till I am slayed in battle or yield my Jarldom to Lokar."

Rollo sniffed, "But…"

"I know of few Vikings that would eagerly spend the darkened hours on board ship when we be in sight of land," Magnússon spoke on, "and yet Gunnar is right and this is one such time it'll be prudent to do so. We'll feast on cold food and sour milk in the eventide, enduring the hardships to the approaching dawn. Now, hold your peace on the subject, Rollo."

Rollo ground his teeth in annoyance. "Aye, Magnus."

Gunnar grunted in satisfaction and his gaze strayed then to the rigging, running his fingers at first along the forestay and the shroud, checking for signs of rubbing before stepping around the sitting monks to inspect the rail cleats and outer wooden rings those ropes were attached too. "And what of these monks Jarl Magnússon, is there a reason they are cluttering up my deck with their foul presence?"

"Nay, they have but a single usefulness I can see," Magnússon nodded and gestured to his bodyguard, "Björn, stand the monks up." Rising, Björn strode over to the pair, got hold of them by the scruff of their necks and pulled Brother Biutta and Brother Gurkinn to their feet, manacle chains clanked with the movement. "I have read that the 'White Christ' walked on water and to quench my curiosity, I am eager to see if these holy men also possess this Godly gift." The Viking crew chapped and a huge cheer went up in approval. "Björn, toss one of them over the side."

Björn laughed and dragged the weeping Brother Gurkinn over to the starboard rail. "'Tis time for you to be baptised again monk."

"Please I beg of thee to stay your hand. Don't take Brother Gurkinn's life merely for your amusement," Brother Biutta beseeched with emotion, about to follow, but Gunnar stopped him instead by stepping in from the side, thrusting his muscular arm under the monk's corresponding arm from behind and wrenched it up almost to the point of snapping the bone, sending excruciating pain radiating through him and making his eyes water. "Aaagh!"

Gunnar leaned in to Brother Biutta's ear before speaking. "There be naught you can do for your friend, sheep. Observe his suffering and understand that you shall quickly go after him."

Björn hoisted Brother Gurkinn up overhead in a single, continuous, explosive movement, holding him in that position for a couple of seconds, as the heavy ball and chain dangled down and swung a little from his cracking ankle, the shackle biting into flesh and drawing blood, and then the bodyguard propelled the hapless monk through the air. Brother Gurkinn hit the water with a splash and the weight of the iron ball pulled him under the churning surface.

"It seems that monk has decided to swim with the fishes after all," Rollo hooted at his own jest and the crew guffawed and slapped each other on the back.

Feeling a deep sadness over the loss of Brother Gurkinn, a

tear trickled down the side of Brother Biutta's face and he stayed strong and quoted a passage from the book of Genesis. "What have you done? You shall be a fugitive and a wanderer on the earth."

"Ha," Magnússon grinned and cast a glance over his shoulder to beckon Gunnar forward. "Speak to me of something I know not, monk." A dwindling stream of air bubbles popped on the receding surface of the sea, as the shipwright relaxed his arm hold and frogmarched Brother Biutta before him. "I still wonder at the choices of your God and the reason why he has failed to save you." He scratched his chin thoughtfully. "Mayhap, you will suddenly sprout angel's wings belike the ones I saw in your picture books and fly to safety, but I think not, for you shall surely drown and go to a watery grave."

"Only a life lived for others is a life deemed worth while," Brother Biutta said, pausing and almost looking reflective for a moment. "The Lord giveth and he taketh away."

Björn turned and manhandled Brother Biutta's tense figure up to the gunwale and threw him into the sea. A moment later the monk vanished without a trace, his scream was abruptly cut off as water funnelled down his mouth and into his lungs.

"Let's drop another monk overboard," Lokar suggested loudly in between laughing himself silly. "I wager he sinks faster than the others."

A number of young Vikings liked the sound of that and cheered loudly.

Sensing things were getting badly out of hand, Gunnar shouted to be overheard, "Those few left aboard the Mjöllnir's Might have skills in art and trade valuable to us, Jarl Magnússon. Earlier I saw some old monks taken onto the slave ship. We could dump them into the water on the morrow?"

This suggestion was greeted by a deep roar of applauses from those around them.

"Aye, on the morrow it is then," Magnússon nodded. "Now, away with you, shipwright; for I want the celebrations to continue with Rollo's story."

The Mjöllnir's Might forged onward through the waves and the Long Snake followed, sailing into the turbulence of its wake.

* * *

Hours later and far from the land of the 'Picts' upon the shore of a Scandinavian fjord, two cloaked figures walked onwards. With her pretty face and long braided hair hidden in shadow from the lambskin hood she wore, the young woman wrapped the loose outer garment tighter about the sleeveless blue dress encasing her slim frame to hide her pregnancy as she followed her husband backtracking through the bushes, the burlap sack tied to his sword belt make metallic sounds from the gold ingots colliding together inside.

"Have you committed the escape route to memory, Sigrún?" the man asked, clutching a blazing torch and emerging from behind the three metre high wooden statue of Odin the War God standing proud against the earth and turf mount, build high to form the outer-walled ramparts encircling the Norse village of Trøllheim. "My victory is not chiselled in stone. If or when the time comes that I am defeated, you will need to steal away from here at a moment's notice and search for safety in flight."

"Aye, Sigvald," she answered, picking her way awkwardly. The stars twittered often as the clouds scudded across the night sky and the quarter moon cast the nearby clutter of single story, log longhouses and the statue with a silvery sheen. "But we are in the middle of an extremely remote place, there is not much more away than we can get."

"You will be surprised. I shall not have your old admirers say that I neglected you and subordinate my passions and love for scheming and policy for the battle to come."

"I have never heard Ivar Stoneface or Imgrimund of the Axe say that to your face, husband," Sigrún answered, coming up to him as Sigvald halted by the statue, "and as affable and gracious as I know them to be at times, they would not hesitate to do so if they had a mind, for are they not chieftains like you."

"I am more than a mere Viking chieftain, wife," Sigvald's eyes strayed upward for another glance at the War God. Odin's outward appearance showed him to be a tall old man with flowing beard and only one eye, wearing a cloak and wide brimmed hat, and carrying a spear, but the moonlight gave it an eerie quality that he had not noticed before and it unnerved him, sending the same unexpected chill surging up his spine much like a wolf's howl still did to him. "Or have you forgotten you married Jarl Sigvald Foeslayer. Strong in body am I and frightening in reputation."

"I have not forgotten that you said you were extending the old outer ramparts to fit around the new longhouses and barracks to house the Frisians, but it seems you did not mention to me that you also got your men to dig that secret gate through it as well?"

Sigvald ground his bad teeth together in frustration and he tore his gaze from the statue to glance at her. "Nay, the conditions of hardship and the constant fear of being delivered to an enemy by treachery I experienced in my weakened youth has taught me to be not open in my speech or activities, and wary of almost everyone. But not to you, Sigrún; your affection for me is unconditional; I would have told you if I had known beforehand."

"How did you acquire such knowledge then, husband?"

"Magus Volstagg said my paranoid father built it and he used it to smuggle me and my beloved mother out of the village when he was convinced there were uncertainties with his reign," Sigvald turned away and set off again, expecting her to come after him, "and now I am about to do the same by sending off my own wife and unborn child."

"That clodhopper priest disgusts me, husband," Sigrún said, her mouth going dry as she walked behind him. "The man has not all his oars in the water, living with those birds and conducting his dissection experiments on cats and dogs."

"So you keep saying," Sigvald replied tiresomely. "But remember that Magus Volstagg is not just a loyal priest, seer or historian, he is also a healer with the power of the runes at his command…"

"Runes?" asked Sigrún in surprise.

"'Tis an old magic practiced among my tribe and my mother spoke of the priest writing on her palm, showing her the special runes needed to alleviate all manner of pain.."

"Like my aching back and swollen ankles?"

Sigvald gave her a flat look. "..And 'tis that assistant you will want should you go into labour along the way. Also to bring you peace of mind you won't be alone with him, because I am sending a few guards to keep you safe until I send for you."

"Huh, Magus Volstagg has not spoken to me of these magical runes, husband. I shall ask him about that in the morn."

"Why wait, my beloved, we are bound to his dwelling now to make the final preparations for your journey and bestow gold upon him, most of it to use on your behalf. I grew up in a state of poverty and sickness, but I will be damned if my wife and child shall endure a similar fate of abandonment from the house of Foeslayer."

"I see," Sigrún sniffed in surprise. "Am I allowed to take my slaves with me too?"

"One only, Sigrún," Sigvald slowed his pace in order for her to catch up. "The smaller the number the easier it will be to escape through the trees and get to the waiting horses hobbled in the gully."

"And what if I say I won't go with the priest and I would rather take my chances in Trøllheim?" asked Sigrún, finally drawing alongside him.

"Then my love, you will die and our baby will die at the hands of Magnus Magnússon," Sigvald said, making his way towards a simple turf-roofed shack made of logs. "Obey my wishes in this wife, for I only want you to be both out of his reach."

"I still feel if you do not provoke Magnússon further, he will leave us be husband."

"You are becoming impertinent, Sigrún," Sigvald said.

"I tire of being afraid and worried all the time, husband. 'Tis not a crime to feel thus."

Sigvald nodded in understanding. "Magnússon's land expansion plans rival my own, Sigrún, for him it is a growing population, but for me it is for my self-interest and satisfies my desire to profit from the war. Sooner or later we are going to lock horns. Magnússon's fleet sailed out of the fjords to the open sea many days ago and my pet slaver Skarpheðinn has been sighted by General Gudjóns' advance scouts guiding more families of exiles through the Eastern pass of the mountains. On foot it should take those people four days to get here. Now that omens are good this is the time to strike and I am not in the habit of backing down."

Sigvald pulled up at the entrance of the shack and knocked on the door with a clenched fist. Footsteps grew louder from the interior punctuated by guttural croaks that drew the young Jarl out of his thoughts, as their owner approached the threshold and opened the door, stretching out his candle flame to identify his late night visitors and immediately recognising the pair standing there.

"Ah, Sigvald my boy and your good wife Lady Sigrún, come in, I have been expecting you," the much older man smiled and moved to one side so they could enter. Sigrún's throated constricted at the sight of his long beard braided with blades of grass and dead leaves, the white wisps of hair sticking out of his leather skull cap and the wild look in his eyes. "Welcome to the abode of Volstagg the Priest. I was just feeding my ravens rodents and birds eggs."

Sigrún exchanged a nervous glance with her husband, but Sigvald's face was hard to read in the light and shadows. The young Jarl grinned and hooked his free arm around her waist before striding into the shack like he owned the place. She dutifully went beside him and the priest closed the door behind them. The husband and wife took a slow circle of the candle-lit chamber, surveying the sleeping bench along one wall with storage underneath it, the table against a second topped with priest helmets, daggers, and a sheathed sword, while the last two walls had shelving containing scrolls of parchment and of other materials, soapstone vessels and bowls with spidery runes carved on the sides.

"How long have you possessed the birds, Magus Volstagg?" Sigrún asked using the priest's official title as the heavy-billed raven's gurgling drew her blue eyes over to the large wooden aviary cage standing in one corner, their lustrous feathers had an almost purplish iridescence in the glow of the candles.

"I call them after Odin's two spy ravens: Munin and Hugin and I captured the pair as nestlings many seasons past. They are solitary creatures, coming to feed in flocks much like myself when I eat at my neighbour's fire, but you and Sigvald did not come here under the cloak of night to discuss that with me."

"Nay, Magus, the safe passage for my wife can wait a moment longer if you are agreeable," Sigvald paused for the priest to nod before resuming. Sigrún frowned and one of the ravens uttered a sharp metallic 'tok.' "First I must draw attention to the strained relations with my allies…"

"Aye, 'tis an unlikely alliance you forged, Sigvald; old hatreds linger between the clans and trust can not be earned by those warring factors overnight," the priest nodded thoughtfully and sat down on the bench. "Ivar Stoneface is a distant relative to your father and was the next in line by right of succession, but you claimed the Jarldom after beating your last brother in single combat."

"Swords would have clashed then again had you not spoken of my right to rule by my bastard blood." Sigvald said. "The warriors knelt and bowed in homage after that."

The priest nodded. "Stoneface is cruel and arrogant in temper, and your other allies are incompetence, full of pretence, and licentious. I bore you into this world and I felt ashamed when your father Angantyr cast you out when your two half brothers challenged him for the Serpent Throne. I just knew I had to give you the chance to inspire the people and rule wisely."

"And I appreciate you for that, Magus, I truly do, and I thought the differences between me and my allies could be settled amicably, alas there is still dissension that I fear will fester into open conflict once more unless I ask you for another token of loyalty."

"To prevent further bloodshed there is naught you can not ask of me, Jarl Foeslayer. I pledge myself to you."

"You speak for the Gods," Sigvald said with a hint of satisfaction.

"It is my honour and duty to do so, Sigvald," the priest confirmed. "What of it?"

"Then speak when I command it, but the words my allies hear shall be mine alone."

* * *

The next day dawned bright and clear, golden sunlight sparkling on the water and reflected sharply off the pieces of metalwork onboard the seven longships bobbing in the bay. A strip of pebbles made up the beach and caves pockmarked the enclosing cliffs that almost completely surrounded the natural harbour. Seabirds breeding on ledges and in small hollows waddled upon the jagged rocks before taking flight, filling the air with their strident calls.

A kick in the leg or a shout in an ear from the guards on board each vessel awakened their shipmates before the sun rose. The Vikings clambered out of bedrolls and dropped them into their sea chests along with their armour, helmets and sword belts before eyes alert so their neighbours could not pitch the food off them; they gulped their cold breakfast rations of stale-crusty bread baked before the voyage to England and melting buttermilk that had been stored below decks in the cool shade. And then that was washed it all down with water.

As the sun cleared the horizon and began climbing higher in the cloudless sky, deckhands hoisted up the anchors and then one by one, the longships got underway, and carried along by the tide, the fleet moved along the channel in a single file, until the towering cliff walls reared up on either side of them, the banks of oars driving each vessel onward with an economy of movement.

Scarcely had all the longships debouched from the weathered recess when they yawed and arranged themselves into a pair of interlocking diamond shapes as an arrangement. The Mjöllnir's Might led the way, flanked a short distance behind by the Long Snake and the Bifrost's Bow, and then came Horse of the Waves. Looming close on its sides approached the Sea Chariot and the Rune Fire, the Blood Fang followed lastly.

* * *

Over the next several hours the wind came and went, but regardless the fleet pushed northward, keeping in close to the coastline, their dragon prows dipping slightly into the water as the crews rowed for long stretchers at a top speed of only two to three knots in order that the Vikings manning the oars would not collapse from sheer exhaustion. Clouds began to fleck the sky and northern gannets gliding above the masts dived with half-closed wings into the sea to catch fish and squid.

The contours of hills and pine woodlands gave way gradually to spectacular sheer cliffs, rock terraces, and pinnacles as several more prisoners' securely bound in chains took sickening plunges from the different longships to the sound of the Vikings mocking laugher.

"Tyrker, kick that ancient crone overboard next," Vegard jerked his thumb at the rail of the Long Snake. "She has little worth and it would cost more coin to keep feeding her."

"Please have mercy upon an old woman," the Prioress Nun begged, struggling in vein to frantically tear herself away from Tyrker's grip. "My hands may tremble, but they are steady enough to still work needle and thread and I can look after children."

"Never, Christen," Tyrker's handsome face split with a cruel smile and his hand shot out for her wrinkled neck. The prioress screamed as his fingers tightened about her windpipe, half choking her into silence. Vegard rubbed his hands in anticipation. "The weak do not get to choose their path," he lifted her up in his brawny arms, tears welling up in her bulging eyes, before he cast her over the rail.

There was a splash and the nun was swallowed up by swirling eddies. The Horse of the Waves forged through the dwindling ripples and burst air bubbles rising to the surface.

Onboard the Mjöllnir's Might, Gunnar crouched down beside his sun board floating in a large pale of water. Embedded in the centre of the wooden disc was a vertical peg or 'pointer' surrounding by a number of enlarging rings radiating outwards across the navigation instrument. He measured the angle of the shadow cast on the peg from the noon day sun and it barely brushed the first inward circle, bringing a faint smile to his lips as it confirmed his course was true.

At short intervals of rest within the fleet, the crews, their faces bright red from the effort of rowing and exposure to the sun, stripped off their tunics and boots before taking the chance to either drink and eat - whitish cheese with veins of blue mould wild onions, dried fruits and nuts - in the partial shade the mast and sail provided or they simply lay on the decking, sweating, trying to nap in the stifling heat.

"Healfdene, I tell ya that nun's scream was so loud it must have carried for leagues," Wulfric laughed, holding his wooden drinking cup aloft so Fridrik could fill it with water.

"It caused me to think of a pig I once slaughtered on the farm," Healfdene said with a broad grin, his sun burnt skin starting to peel. "She and the animal were hard to tell apart."

Presently, the land of the 'Picts' curved to the west before extending further north again. Instead of following the rugged contours, pivoting blades spun under the water as the fleet yawned off towards the east and the open sea. The shoreline receded into the distance and finally became lost from sight. The next two and a half days passed with the winds continuing to blow intermittent and oars were deployed to propel the fleet of longships further out across the calm, briny vastness.

The third day out from land was creeping toward mid afternoon when weather vanes on the longships turned to point in the direction of the sudden wind blowing in from the west, sending a strong flesh current across the decks and bellowing the sails, pleasantly lowering the temperature and bringing a welcome relief for the tired crews on board each vessel.

Hulls creaked loudly in protest from stem to stern and men and woman braced their bare feet and held onto their oars, rigging ropes and the rail as the longships swept forward at a good 10 knots. From then on the fleet made swift progress for dozens of leagues across the salty waste, drums went silence and oars were taken in and laid down on the decks. Magnússon came striding over to Gunnar standing at the prow of the Mjöllnir's Might.

"We be flying belike one of Thor's lightning bolts, shipwright," Magnússon grinned, liking the reassuring sensation of speed beneath his bare feet as he pulled up and rested his blistered left hand on the rail. "Is the ship still on course?"

"Aye, Jarl Magnússon; Tjernagl is manning the steering oar, while I was using the swells and the flights of the gulls to correct our heading till I saw him yonder," Gunnar pointed, drawing Magnússon's gaze toward a black, fifty foot humpback whale, which was about thirty yards off the longship's port bow. The animal had been blending his cries and moans into a song, but as the fleet closed on its position, the whale hunched its back and rolled steeply forward into a deep dive, and bringing its tail out of the water and slapping it back down through the surface of the sea. "We are entered the whale's feeding grounds. For now that's significant for my navigation."

* * *

On and on the fleet went, sailing due east driven by a strengthening wind which did not let up once until the evening. Likewise crosswinds sprang up, blowing from northerly and southerly directions, making the surface of the sea turn choppy. In time, sails were reefed in and then lowered completely to arrest their speed and while their momentum continued to carry all the longships onward, the deck hands onboard them, pitched the sail fabric into a tent to shelter the crew inside. It was held up by the mast and kept in place by ropes and the rail cleats.

"That's it, now place the second anchor in the bow as well," Tjernagl shouted to members of the crew. "The heavy weight of those rocks should work as ballast to give the craft increased stability in the approaching storm."

The sky thickened with clouds and the sea grew increasingly turbulent with high whitecaps, pounding against the flexibly planking, letting in leaks and crests breaking over the longships shielded-gunwales to dampen the sail and awash the decks. The high wind and waves were making it hard to navigate. A few men broke out a number of wooden pails or used their horned-helmets as containers and started bailing. The rest of the crew members sitting knee-deep in water tightened their sinews before slipping out their oars and plying them again.

Behind the Mjöllnir's Might, the rest of the fleet followed suit, but waves ripped the oar from one Viking's grasp, causing him to drop a stroke in mid pull and that in turn fouled up the rhythm of the Long Snake's port bank.

"Row, you dogs," Gunner shouted to be heard over the thundering drum beat and the crashing of the waves. "Raise the pace. I want Valhalla's great hall to wait awhile longer for our souls."

The rowers did so, stroking away at a good three knots. Sweat and blood strained the oar handles after blisters had burst open and bled. The fleet became scattered by the rough sea and was steadily driven off course. On the Mjöllnir's Might, Gunnar now manning the steering oar turned the weighted-down dragon prow from the trough into the rising swells, because he knew that if he kept the vessel abeam of the approaching waves, they would easily swamp the longship or even worst capsize her, losing lives and everything of worth onboard.

After a while, Helga and the other shield maidens replaced their tiring shipmates on the bucket chain, negotiating the rock and roll of the deck with practiced skill as they emptied the water over the rail. As the dipping sun lay close to the horizon, the wind suddenly died down and with it went the transfer of energy that fuelled the rough seas. Waves collapsed and the surface became calmer. The long sweeps swept through the water and slowly the fleet came together again. The light faded at the end of the day, the crews ate apples from last winters cold storage and raw fish pickled in brine to give it a sharp flavour, and when they finished, draining their drinking cups, night had fallen and gaggles of stars were winking between the scudding clouds.

Through the night, while the crew snored, curled up on deck or leaned over their oars, Tjernagl and Gunner took turns at the steering oars, gauging the height of the bright Polestar as a navigation aid, and correcting the course of the Mjöllnir's Might, and the fleet according.

"The storm blew us far to the south, Tjernagl," Gunnar said, after determining their latitude. "But now we are steering a course back to Norway."

The next morning was hot and humid, burning torches on the longships were extinguished come the dawn. There was a feeble breeze blowing in from the west but it was not strong enough for the sails to catch and as a result the vessels had to rely on the oars to propel them back on course. Bottlenose dolphins leaped from the water around mid morning and accompanied the fleet for a little bit before falling back. But other than that there was nothing else of note for the crew to observe to relieve the unchanging monotony of the sea. Tjernagl gave the drum to Siegfried to beat and then licking his lips nervously he strode to the stern of the Mjöllnir's Might, where Gunnar stood, manning the steering oar again.

"Master steersman," Tjernagl said, halting before him. "May I give you some advice?"

"Do I not encourage you to ask me questions, Tjernagl? You will learn naught if you do not speak up."

Aye, but this is different."

"Like the Jarl I welcome any advice, but it nay means I will follow it," Gunnar smiled. "Now, say your peace."

"There is an hour or so till the sun reaches its highest point in the sky," Tjernagl whispered in order that the oarsmen nearby would not hear their conversation, "if you doubt the position of the fleet we could let loose the crows from their cages."

Gunnar nodded, guessing the meaning behind the recommendation and he spoke very softly. "Unlike you I doubt not our current heading, Tjernagl; but," he emphasised the word, "I shall release them should the need arises later in the day."

Gunner continued to check their heading with the height of the sun and at noon he put the sun board back into the pail of water. The shadow was inching passed the innermost circle and he knew that the fleet was still to far south for his liking and he nudged the steering oar by degrees to starboard to reposition the longship until the new direction changed the angle of the sun, shrinking it to just touch the circle.

A half hour later something appeared ahead of the fleet as the longships sailed towards it. Veins of quartz and purplish-blue cordierite caught the sun's rays and sparkled in the reflection as a mountain speckled with the minerals rose prominently above its surroundings.

"Land, ho," Olaf called down from the top of the Mjöllnir's Might masthead, seeing the mountain was nothing more than a faint hint against the sky.

"Jarl Magnússon; lo, 'tis the bejewelled peak," Gunnar grinned and pointed at the glittering mountain, becoming clearly defined by the second, as a succession of transverse, jagged peaks with steep slopes began thrusting upwards one by one to crowd the sky and form an unbroken rampart that eventually would stretch over a distance of hundreds of miles. "We be home in Fjordstad ere the sun goes down."

Magnússon nodded. "The Gods named the peak well, shipwright."

Tjernagl blinked at the mountain's distinguishing features and ceased banging on the drum. "Master steersman, you told me several of the old stories, but I know not that one."

"Let me then enlighten you with the tale, Tjernagl," Gunnar grinned, knowing the legend he was about to narrate would help the younger man bring to mind the landmark and enable him to retrace their course more easily in the future. "It has long been one of my favourites."

As Gunnar spoke to the rowing crew, the Scandinavian Peninsula grew up out of the horizon and bulged southwards, steadily edging down past the fleet of vessels as ship masters onboard them navigated between the offshore fringe of rocks and islands. The glaciated mountains reached to the coastline of Norway broken by headlands carpeted with heather, and deeply dissected by the mouths of submerged gorges and canyons knifing deep inland.

Gunnar's eyes strayed upward towards the weather vane as it turned to point where a fierce western crosswind was blowing in from the sea at a speed that he judged was around twenty knots. Encountering high winds before, he knew the currents of air would increase in the narrower confines of the fjord, causing the sail to be ripped apart and making the longships incapable of being controlled.

"Strike the sails and unstep the mast," Gunnar ordered and three Vikings standing on the rigging hurried to obey.

"Make certain that my standard is flying elsewhere, shipwright."

"Aye, Jarl Magnússon." Gunnar snapped his fingers at Siegfried. "See to it, pup."

When the 'bejewelled' mountain neared, the mid-afternoon sun cast its lengthening shadow across the seaward end of another fjord. Instead of the longships passing the mouth by like they had with others on three separate occasions, the Mjöllnir's Might rolled and pitched right, leading the fleet over the comparatively shallow threshold into a U-shaped valley. The strong wind was disturbing the surface of the water, roughly breaking it up with many small waves. The walls of the fjord rose vertically for hundreds of feet from the water's edge, and the bottom rich in black mud dropped away from the keels to many hundreds of feet deep.

A glacier cracked in the heat and the sound echoed loudly across the valley, briefly drowning out the roar of numerous waterfalls pouring down from the mountains to foam the water's choppy surface. The longships arranged themselves in single file and sliced along the middle of the inlet, the wind began to strengthen behind the vessels and the shifting waves grew to the height of the oar ports, as the fleet followed the long arm of the sea, the wide channel winding eastward and then dividing into branches leading into several, smaller fjords extending to the south and the north.

The Mjöllnir's Might kept to the main waterway and after rounding a sharp corner,

the wind died away and the waters calmed as the fjord's head and the delta came into view, where a permanent and prospering, farming and fishing town was established.

"Yon is Fjordstad," Olaf shouted down to the rowing crew.

"Aye," Gunnar grinned. "We are home."

Part 2
Payment In Blood

Chapter Eight
The Conquerors Return

Brunhild closed her eyes in pleasure, arching her back and her fingers clenched the lynx pelts beneath her at the sensations she felt from her lover's lips and fingers on her nipples. Lamplight glinted on the sweat beading the muscular flesh of Lars Gunnarson as he raised his leonine head from between her small, perky breasts and becoming gradually overwhelmed with the aching need in his loins, his rough, eager hands reached down to grasp her naked buttocks as he lifted the young woman to the edge of the planking, topping the raised wooden benches that ran the length of the longhouse.

With her eyes burning with wild anticipation and experiencing a desperate urgency of her own from between her thighs, Brunhild's heartbeat thumped faster as she wrapped her legs around his waist and moulded herself tightly against him. A groan of satisfaction reverberated from deep within her throat, mirroring the gasp of Lars' own desire as their bodies joined in ferocious, animalistic passion.

* * *

"Father, why are we wearing Norse clothing," Hārūn al-Ṭabarī objected bitterly in Arabic, his nimble fingers unbuttoning the high keyhole neckline of the over tunic he wore over the long skirt, which was raised up above his white trousers and tucked into the belt to make him pleasantly cooler in the heat of the day. "I care not for these itchy, tight fitting garments."

"It is the native custom and because I wish it so. Did not your brother Aḥmad speak of it on the voyage or was it that you did not listen as of how your mind was elsewhere in quiet contentment, concentrating on your miscellaneous studies of medicine and cooking." Omar al-Ṭabarī shook his head and silently bemoaned his second son's lack of filial duty, foresight and sense of responsibility as he walked between the rows of empty animal stalls occupying the long, broad chamber, each one was large enough for a single cow or horse to live through the winter months and a thick chain-linked barrier was strung across the gap opening. A bed of hay covered the wooden flooring and troughs for food and water were set against the compartment walls. "The dry clothing is a sign of our host's hospitality to the weary traveller and it would be a great insult to my friends clan should we even dare to refuse, Hārūn."

"Father, I say again better had you brought Aḥmad along instead of me," Hārūn complained peevishly. "This may be a bad idea, you know I am…"

"Reserved and diffident," Omar al-Ṭabarī interrupted calmly.

"I would have said uncomfortable in the company of others."

"And yet you are not shy in speaking your mind to me or your brother?"

"That is different my father, I am comfortable in your presence and I have known you both…"

"I blame your mother's maternity instincts for sheltering you all she could from the rigours of life for so long, but you can not hide from your destiny and I will see your Achilles' heel ends this very day." Omar cut in again, his voice dropping to a growl. "I need you to be the man you are and grow up to confront this challenge. Lady Ranveig has already met Aḥmad at noontime and now it is your turn to get to know my bold allies and form a lasting impression with them, so get used to it."

"I shall try," Hārūn said, thinking over the prospect.

"Forget not I am conducting this trade with their aid," Omar said, bending over his sinewy frame to pass through a low and narrow interior doorway opening onto the long passageway bisecting Jarl Magnus Magnússon's longhouse. "I have the contacts and the knowledge of the eastern countries and the people, but the Vikings supply the skill of sailing their longships and the savage experience of their warriors in plundering and warfare. You and Aḥmad are my sons as well as my apprentices and in time my emissaries. Once Magnus returns from his raiding voyage there shall be much haggling as we buy the slaves and the cargos in the Great Hall and it will be good experience for both of you to watch and begin to understand how I deal with the Norsemen."

"As you say Father," Hārūn grumbled and then sighed in resignation.

A tall Viking guard with his long red hair worn in a topknot nodded to the older al-Ṭabarī in passing, but then he gave a broad, predatory grin to the son, flaunting his war hammer as he moved it around. Hārūn became aggravated and glared at him in returned, his nerves were already stretched to their limit and he longed for both his hands to be free so he could feel the reassuring touch of his sword hilt.

Wisps of smoke rose from countless wall lamps, chasing away the clinging shadows from Omar Al-Ṭabarī's handsome face, cast from the wrapped rim of the silken turban and the dome-shaped helmet atop of his head. A woollen cloak fell from his sloping shoulders, jewels sparkled in the pommel of his tulwar on his hip and the silver mesh of his armour shined like liquid streams in the pools of light. The simple leather shoes the fifty-two year old wore echoed dully off the hard dirt floor, blending with the ones made by the grey-haired slave he followed and that of Hārūn bringing up the rear.

"I know you owe Magnus Magnússon a life debt and you have told me his woman said we were honoured guests, but are we safe here from his people?" asked Hārūn, revealing what was bothering him and ahead of him, Omar al-Ṭabarī's face twitched before settling back into impassive lines. "This is an evil and frightening place to behold, my father. Did you not see the strange symbols carved into the tusks outside? They were hard for me to fathom, I fear they are the work of witchcraft."

Omar burst out laughing. "You put to much concern upon those symbols, my son. They are mere drawings; the art of the Northlanders tells of their customs and believes. Insofar as magic is concerned it is a common word uttered to explain a conjuring trick or a desert mirage by people who should know better."

Hārūn nodded at the barb and said, "After I had arrived, Aḥmad told me about more Viking customs, how their warriors accompanied your every movement off the ship and then how your retinue was mobbed when you and Aḥmad both took a walk this morning in their town, some insulting the robes you wore – calling them dresses, and now that warrior back there just looked at me like a hungry wolf would a chicken."

"And yet we left the town unmolested unless you count Aḥmad treading in a cowpat," The older al-Ṭabarī smiled sardonically.

"The way I heard it, it was you that only departed after the warrior escort forced their way through the crowd," Hārūn refuted in reply or is Aḥmad wrong in his assumption?"

Omar al-Ṭabarī organised his thoughts for a moment. "The truth is not always black and white as the written words on the scrolls you carry around with you. This is your first journey from Badhdad, Hārūn, and like Aḥmad and the warriors of my retinue, you have little knowledge of the people in the West. To you civilization is the gleaming walls, the minarets and spires of our home city, but distance and the...rustic character of a capital can differ greatly from nation to nation. With regard to our Northlander shadow, I should have taken you and Aḥmad into my confidence ere we set sail for Fjordstad. But overjoyed as I was to receive the Jarl's invitation to visit and hear that my old friend was alive and not slain yet by a jealous husband that it simply slipped my mind in the preparation for the voyage. The messenger Magnus send said that Lady Ranveig would assign warriors to me as an escort to protect and show us around for the length of our stay. As for the men and women and children in the town, they crowded around us noisily and excitedly because we were simply foreigners to their land much like a snowflake in the desert and in their confusion they touched the darker hue of our skin and curiously felt the material of our robes for the reason of our uniqueness in this cold climate, nothing more than that. I have basked myself in the attention of many villages along the Silk Road over the past seasons, it never lasts long though for the people become used to our presence and our comings and goings."

"And what of the infidel guard back there?" asked Hārūn.

"Bah, Njáll Bloodhammer was one of the warriors in my escort; he is a hot headed dotard, just trying to intimidate you; like most of his mouth-breathing kinsmen, eager to prove his mettle against anyone including you, my second son."

"Well he succeeded," Hārūn said, not ashamed to admit it to his father's ears alone, who acknowledged the remark with a brief glance back. "Was Magnus Magnússon the same when you met him?"

"Yes, a force of nature that one," Omar said. "He fancied himself a great man even then with a clear purpose in life. I exaggerated not when I say he is the most dangerous man I have ever known to wield a blade, but after months in his company on the 'Sea of Sands' I gained a thorough knowledge of him and I found him to be a very amiable and his word is as good as gold. Magnus may be gone from this shore and yet we are still under his protective wing. Have no fear my son, we are in no danger here so heed neither Njáll Bloodhammer nor the other warriors not. Now to built up good will we will only speak in the language of the Northmen so all those who are about to hear our open words can bear witness we have naught to hide or deceive in our business dealings with them."

Hārūn sighed deeply and then spoke in the Viking tongue. "I hear and obey, my Father."

The middle-aged slave finally came to a wooden door decorated with spidery runes; where she paused to knock before pushing it open. "Mistress," she curtsy and spoke Norse with a slight Eastern accent. "Loath as I am to sour your mood, but Omar the Merchant and his son are outside and they request an audience with you?"

"Here and now?" Lady Ranveig said, confusion entering in her husky voice.

"Yes, milady," the slave said, crunching up her oriental face with worry and wringing her hands in case she had done wrong in bringing the foreigners here.

"Very well, let them come and find us as they may. Send them in, Tove."

Tove curtsied and then withdrew to allow the men space to pass unhindered into the chamber beyond.

Hārūn leaned in close to whisper in his father's ear. "We are not expected?"

"No, most of the gifts I wanted to bestow on our hosts in the Great Hall were in the hold of your ship," the older al-Ṭabarī said, walking forward.

* * *

The barrel-chest of Lars Gunnarson heaved with a ragged breath before he untangled his muscular limbs from Brunhild's and rolled off from atop of her.

"Ah, if only I had the wits to wait for you, my lover," Brunhild wheezed, lifting her slender hand to brush away the sweat-plastered auburn hair that had fallen across her florid face. "But now I learn that you woo another in the neighbouring village behind my back, is it true?"

"Ours has never been a normal romance, Brunhild; and I will not lie to you," Lars said absently, raw events still fresh in his mind as he lay on his back and clasped his hands behind his head. "Her name is Freya and I had been seeking her affections during our break up."

Brunhild twisted her petite frame to accentuate the curve of her hip and rested on her elbow to get a better view of him. "I know of Freya and her family; she lives in Skálholt," She said with a hint of jealousy over Freya's unrivalled beauty and melancholy began settling upon Brunhild as her suspicions were reinforced with a sad conclusion at having to share Lars' with this other woman when she only wanted him for herself. "Her mother eats like Ragnarök is on the morrow," she added unkindly, referring to the destruction of the gods, "and carries around with her the heaviness of a beached whale. In truth the woman could smash the skull of the serpent Jörmungand just by sitting upon it. I tell you that the apple doth not fall far from the tree and while Freya may have a desirable figure now, it will turn to blubber belike her mother's in the future."

"Regardless," Lars said in a deep base voice, about to drop the surprise news with an air of pretended casualness. "I have already won Freya's hand and we are to be wed when my father and brother return from the raid in England."

"Marriage!" The startled interjection burst from her sensuous mouth and Brunhild raised herself up onto her knees.

"I'm not one to wallow over regret," Lars spoke on, his heart beat and his breathing was slowly returning to normal. "You did me a service in choosing Björn over me."

Brunhild raised her eyebrows quizzically and spoke calmly, working hard to subdue her irritation. "But why did you keep this news quiet from me after I insisted we resolve our quarrel and rekindle our intimate relationship?"

"'Tis nay different from when you kept me ignorant of your plans last winter or did you forget the pain you uncaringly inflicted upon me, mmm?" Lars said, savouring the taste of revenge as he stared at the mass of dust motes enlightened in the glow of the oil lamps and in the shaft of daylight lancing down from the smoke hole in the roof of the longhouse. A large cooking cauldron was strung up in the air over the fire pit by a thick iron chain attached to hooks that hung from the overhead rafters.

Brunhild stiffed at the accusation, but she managed to bite back on an angry retort. "I admit I was a fool to take the path I trod, Lars; I made nay bones about that. When I wed Björn Strongarm, I did not think about your feelings or of abandoning the happy times we spent together in the corn fields, I only thought of my own selfish ambitions," she pouted her full lips and added in a sulky tone, feeling the need to explain her decision. "It was for the prestige of Björn being the Jarl's bodyguard and the privileges of wealth my husband would provide me from Magnússon's patronage, but I did not expect he would paw me in our love making or when he finally falls asleep he would snore like a hibernating bear or the long days of lonesomeness I'd have to endure while he was off raiding the other villages with sword and fire."

"Tsk," the eighteen year old clicked his tongue against the roof of his mouth in mock sympathy as he enjoyed her misery. "You have his family for companionship."

"A frail old crone and his brutish brother are not the company I now hunger after in my life, Lars; but someone vigorous, who will ignite the fires of passion within me, that will make my heart hammer in my bosom and keep me warm on even the coldest winter night," Brunhild said, her tanned hand reaching over to caress the well-defined muscles of his flat stomach as she asked him an indirection question. "There is talk among the womenfolk that the House of Gunnarson will be even richer when your father finishes building the other three longboats."

"Aye," Lars agreed, with a mirthless grin, having an-inkling where she was going with this as he sat himself up in a cross-legged position. "Born of the Giant will be the grandest ship in the Jarl's fleet."

Brunhild nodded in satisfaction at the answer and then spoke on to reveal her thoughts. "Lars, I have been dwelling upon much of late concerning you and I and I want to put it right." She inhaled and let it out again. "Give Freya the end of your muddy boot and be faithful unto me. I do not want to repeat the past, enduring the furtive glances we exchanged, my love or of keeping our trysts a secret, I grow weary of it all. I will divorce Björn so we can finally be together. I will love you as you deserve, what say you to that most pleasing of prospect?"

Not amazed by Brunhild's boldness or single-mindedness, Lars said, "I won't test Björn's blade for you, Brunhild; you be not worth it. A slattern, who breaks her troth, is not the sort of wife my father would approve off neither." Brunhild's body stiffened at the barb and disbelief appeared on her hardening face as she lifted her hand to slap Lars across the face, but his fingers shot out to catch her wrist instead. "You cared little for me as evidence of your betrayal and I see now that it has ever been lust with you, not the love I crave, but Freya is decent and one day I dare to hope I will receive tender affection and compassion from her."

His words rang maddening true to Brunhild and she found it hard to envisage Lars doing such a thing. "A pox on your manhood, Lars," she snarled angrily, wrenching her arm loose from his relaxing grip and standing up, "You used me, but I know I did not misread the desire you had for me in your eyes," she added with a surge of confusion and resentment entering her voice as she snatched a linen under-dress from a wall peg and slipped it on to cover her nakedness.

"Of course, as you used me, Brunhild," Lars laughed with a hint of mockery, eager to exploit the growing rift between them as he grabbed his clothes and scrambled to his feet. "A man would have to be touched in the head to refuse your freely-given favours one last time."

"I will not forget this insult, Lars Gunnarson," Brunhild spat at him with a feeling of ill-willed malice. She gave her hair a toss and in a fit of temper verging on murderous fury, she picked up a nearby earthenware pot and threw it at Lars head, but keeping his smirk he ducked it easily and the rounded pot smashed against the wainscotting behind him, the water stained the planks and dripped onto the shield underneath it; the shards falling into the furs spread across the bench in the smaller, partitioned sleeping area.

"Was it something I said," humour shining bright in Lars' eyes as he backtracked towards the front door.

"Get out, you mangy cur," she uttered in a loud, furious scream and then looked around for another object to throw. Brunhild hastily grasped the handle of a kettle, but by the time she glanced up and drew her arm back, Lars was long gone.

✷ ✷ ✷

The sight of Fjordstad lent fresh vitality to the rowers steely thews. Onboard the Mjöllnir's Might, near the prow, Magnússon was giving Fridrik instructions.

"Do you understand everything I have said, boy?"

"Aye, Jarl Magnússon."

"Repeated it so I know you have learned it by heart."

"Once the ship docks I am to seek out the first mate of the Blood Fang and tell him you want the captives to be chained up in the barn of Ragnar the woodcutter, and then I am to go to the Sea Chariot and say to deliver four casks of the monk's wine to your longhouse."

"Fridrik, you have pleased me," Magnússon turned and opened his sea chest, rummaging among the objects until he withdrew a sharp dagger sheathed in leather. "Here," he shoved the sheath into the boy's hands. "Let this be your own personal eating knife."

Fridrik's eyes lit up at the generous gift and he sputtered a startled thank you before hurrying away to do more errands.

"Jarl Magnússon," Björn Strongarm called out and pointed at something ahead of the bow of the Mjöllnir's Might. "Your friend's ships have arrived."

"Aye, 'twill be good to see Omar again," Magnússon smiled broadly. "He a sensitive man, but would trade his own mother for coin if he could. After meeting her I can see why."

Björn Strongarm shook his head bemusedly. "Once the merchant sees the numbers of slaves and the other commodities we have in the holds of our ships I have nay doubt he will think his journey to Norway was worth his while."

"'Tis true that Omar is man of business and with us opening up virgin territory, he knows there wont be any competition from other members of the merchant's guild. In part though he comes because of a service I rendered him in the past."

"And what was that, Jarl Magnússon?" asked Björn Strongarm with interest. "You have not me this tale."

"I am being shown the respect I deserve by Omar recompensing me for my heroism in saving his life, Björn."

Magnússon said, about to elaborate upon the mystery. "Bandits had laid in wait at the oasis for the slave caravan we were travelling with; knowing the prevailing north-westerly winds the Arabs call the 'Shamāl' would bring a great sandstorm at our backs and drive us into the flat valley among the surrounding dunes for refuge. I know not where the bandits hid but they sprung the trap when darkness fell."

"What happened then, my Jarl?" Björn Strongarm pressed.

"They slew the guards and the other traders, but fortune was with me that night, for I found it too hot too sleep for long periods of time and my camel must have become excited by the bandit's presence, because it huffed so sharply that spit was expelled over my face. I rouse myself, stabbed the nearest men to me and grabbed Omar ere losing ourselves in the storm. With hardly a drop of water to drink I dragged him two days through the merciless desert until we reached a nomad village."

"So, the merchant is trying to pay you back," Björn Strongarm nodded in understanding. "A life for a life."

"Aye," Magnússon agreed before speaking of his lofty ambitions. "And with the help from my friend, in time I will turn Fjordstad into the flourishing hub of the Western slave trade and the coin he spends to purchase our human cargos and the treasures we pillaged from the foreign raids shall start to fund and create a firm foundation for the empire I want to build."

Behind them at the stern, Siegfried and Fridrik climbed up the steps of the hold, each was carrying a large cage inside which were four or five crows cawing loudly and flapping their wings as the pair approached Gunnar, who turned towards at the disturbance:

"The birds you wanted fetched, father," Siegfried said, pulling up in front of him. Fridrik came to a halt beside Siegfried.

"Now, we have nay further need of the crows," Gunnar answered after a curt nod. "Release them."

Amidships stood Tjernagl and from a sack, he withdrew and handed out tough and pliable fenders - constructed from withy – to a number of the crew, who had been scaling the rigging. "We shall be docking soon, wrap some of these around the outboard trappings like cleats and the oarlocks, and hang the rest over the side of the hull to protect it from rubbing against the pier. Now, move it, while I take over the drumming."

As the fleet of longships glided further into the fjord, the bows and oars churned up the water, turning it white with foam. The rocky walls around the vessels began angling downward and curving inward along the shoreline to form panorama vitas, dark crags changing to forested hills thick with spruce and pine trees and then to the gently rolling delta plain, crops grew on fenced off agriculture land and livestock grazed on patches of grass and plants vying for domination outside a wide ditch and a palisade of sharp stakes enclosing a densely populated town made up from wooden houses and other buildings, roofed in sod.

Thin tendrils of smoke from dozens of cooking fires came from smoke holes in the roofs of the longhouses and plumed upwards into the sky.

At various intervals large mammoth tusks - carved with horizontal lines of runes, the sides of glaring human faces and fantastic birds that twist around theirs own wings - curved over a narrow dirt trail leading from the town's heavy timber gates down to the waters edge. A number of long jetties, close to the length of three average sized longships and about the width of a tall man, were built on stilts jutting out into the fjord. Several fishing boats, clinker-build and elaborately decorated at the prow and stern posts were moored at the shorter docks, and tied by coconut ropes to the uprights of one of the longer piers were two large Arabian dhows sporting long thin hulls, bounced up and down due to the effects of currents.

Alongside the dhows, Arabs on the pier were occupied with manually unloading the ship's cargo and the drabness of the man-size sacks, baskets and pots were in sharp contrast with the bright colours of the men's turbans and fezzes, the long shirts, their pantalooms and boots. Two Viking warriors watched them work with casual interest.

Off to the far right, another palisade was going up about the shipyard where three longships were being constructed on building berths. Among these berths, men cut and shaped timbers and planking, nails were hammered into the wood to fit the various pieces together to form the hull, the masts and the oars. Tar boiled and strands of walrus skin were twisted together to made rope.

A hunting horn suddenly blared from a lookout standing atop of one of the rocky crags and then a second acknowledging signal echoed on the air after the sentry in the town's watchtower saw the fleet of longships - keeping with a brisk and measured oar pace -approach steadily across the fjord towards the jetties.

In the depths of the forest east of the town a fair-skinned noblewoman, her two blue eyed young children and a blonde, twenty year old guard were walking through the trees, carrying baskets of birds eggs and strawberries the foursome had been gathering in the previous hours, as they now returned to Fjordstad, their talking and laughing faded however, halting in frightened hesitation when the low pitch, haunting tones destroyed the silence.

"Drop everything," the mother quickly told her children and the baskets tumbled over as they hit the ground between the visible tree roots. "And be very quiet my little ones."

"This way, Lady Ingrid," the swordsman said, recognising the call to arms as he picked up the seven year old girl. "If we hurry we can get you and the children safely inside the palisade ere the ships dock."

"There is another roué known to few, Bork the Dauntless," Ingrid said, tightening her grip on the hand of her six year old boy before angling away down a nearby slope, "Come!"

The guard and the children followed Ingrid along a wooded hollow until she pulled apart some overgrown vegetation to reveal a narrow opening among two boulders.

"How...?"

"Your questions can wait, Bork," Ingrid said, stepping through the hole. "There is flint and steel to create flame inside to light the wall torches."

* * *

Outside of Jarl Magnússon's longhouse at the same time, the servant named Tove with a soft sheen of perspiration on her wrinkled brow had been kneeing, tending to Lady Ranveig's herb garden, gathering leaves of rosemary, fennel, marjoram, and dill in a deep wicker basket for savouring the food of the evening feast. But once she heard the resonant warning fill the air, Tove stood up and waving a hand to shoo off a bee that had flew over from the nearby hives, she dashed over the paving stones before disappearing through the elaborately-carved front entrance.

On the pier, the line of Arabs put down their objects as the Viking warrior told them to crouch down behind cover and arm themselves.

Elsewhere, within the hill forest above and north of the town, a tree made a loud creaking sound as it toppled and fell to the ground in a shower of leaves and snapping branches, a patch of changing blue sky became visible within the intertwining branches above. Around it, in the semidarkness, men attacking other trunks with their axes paused after they heard the alarm signals sound over the hum of insects and woodpeckers chiselling nest holes in dead wood hidden beyond their periphery in the shadows and vegetation.

"Ragnar, is Fjordstad, under attack from Jarl Foeslayer?" a young man in nondescript clothing asked his older companion in concern, rippling his weapon from the wood and then turning and treading old leaves and pine needles underfoot as he moved out to the dwindling edge of the forest. "It bodes ill for us."

"Nay, if it is he, Leif, then he has spunk, I give him that, but in my mind he has finally made a rash error in judgement. Sigvald Foeslayer will be expecting to face boys, women and old men, not a warrior host at over half strength and the armed men belonging to the Arab," the thirty-eight year old warrior responded, leaping over roots as the pair of Vikings merged into the tail end of a forming group of woodsmen as it hurriedly flowed down the hillside.

"Will Al-Ṭabarī's men side with us against Foeslayer's fleet though?" asked Leif, his thin figure crashing through bushes, here and there rays of late afternoon sunshine began flittering further than ever before into the depths of the woodland between the developing gaps in the tree trunks and their canopies overhead.

"I know him not, but I think the merchant will do all he can to protect the coin he has heavily invested in purchasing his precious cargo and ships, Leif," Ragnar said, dashing between the fallen logs and the thinning tree trunks. "I daresay someone has told him of what Sigvald Foeslayer has done to most of the Saxon exiles flowing into to his lands and he will worry over the fate of his sons should he not support Jarl Magnússon."

The woodsmen' squinted their eyes as they adjusted to the glare of the sinking sun set against an intermingling red and purpling sky, as they emerged among stumps and pulled up on the cliff edge that afforded them a good view of the inlet and the sleek lines of the advancing longships.

"The sails and masts are lowered," Leif said, his palm

shielding his blue eyes, feeling the air steadily cooling as the shades of evening began to gradually draw in. "I can not tell if it is some of Foeslayer's fleet or not."

"The masthead downed is a sign that those vessels were coming from the sea..." Ragnar narrowed gaze peered at the deck of the leading longships and he saw a swatch of red cloth hoisted up on a spear shaft. "Wait, the crew has raised a standard," he called to his neighbours. "I know those vessels anywhere; my wife had a hand in sewing the slogan in the red cloth. They are Jarl Magnússon's fleet, the conquerors have returned."

Below in the town, there was the rasp of swords being drawn from sheathes as the guards on the walls, tensed themselves in preparation for a battle ahead. Some sporting grim expressions clambered onto higher roofs of barns for a better look and survey the activity in the fjord, finally seeing the crows take flight from the deck of the Mjöllnir's Might, and recognising the longships as friendlies.

"Lo, crows fly from the leading longship," a middle-aged guard indicated with an extended finger in order to draw the attention of his companions towards the flock, their black wings glimmering in the sunshine.. "I hazily recall Gunnar saying to me that he used the birds as navigations aids at sea should his vessel lose sight of land. He would follow the direction of their flight."

"You mean that's Jarl Magnússon's fleet, Roald?" asked a bearded man of similar age, watching the longships slow their pace the nearer they came to the shore.

"None other, Knut," Roald grinned a gummy grin. "Past the word around, ye hear."

Knut did so, jumping down to the palisade's walkway and stopping at every third or forth man along to notify them and point at the repositioning longships in the fjord ere setting off again, down the ladder to tell the town people.

The resulting shouts of the guards echoed up and down the wall.

But a second later, the gates of the town were flung open and wave after wave of archers in coordinated order filed down the dirt trail to the cries of "Come back," and "'Tis only Magnússon's ships," from the wall guards trailing after them, swords were moved side to side as a signal to stop. Arrows were nocked and bow strings drawn as their owners bounded off the trail and along the jetties. At the same time, within the shipyard, men with broad sturdy frames downed tools and snatched up weapons of every description before heading towards the waterfront as fast as their legs could take them.

And then, came a third signal from the middle of the fjord, a long howling, reverberating blast from Olaf's conch shell onboard the Mjöllnir's Might and it was answered by the lookouts aboard the Long Snake, the Bifrost's Bow, and the rest of the longships in turn, blowing a musical fanfare of short dramatic series of notes to announce the arrival of their Jarl. The archers relaxed, lowering their bows and arrows as an excited cheer of relief went up from the jetties and the walls of Fjordstad. Mothers with their children together with old couples emerged from their longhouses and began crowding in the open gateway.

The group was in high spirits, talking and laughing.

* * *

"Omar, friend of my husband, I bid you welcome to the chamber I call the stofa," Lady Ranveig said warmly, her high-boned face splitting with a surprised smile. The thirty-nine year old stood up and spread her arm in an encompassing gesture away from the fabric being woven upon the vertical loom; the wide wooden framework leaned against the wall. The warp threads were tensioned with the help of the collection of stones attached to the threads at the bottom. "'Tis a feasting place for my family and friends in the evening and in the day the women of the house gather here to do their daily chores, the loom comes down from the loft where the slaves sleep and we all take turns in telling gossip as said by my lord and husband."

Omar al-Ṭabarī nodded politely and the stride of his long legs cut the separating distance in half before he came to a halt, arching a shaggy eyebrow as he let his liquid brown eyes sweep the assemblage of seated women whose heads whipped around to regard him, noticing that Lady Ranveig had changed out of the formal dress she wore to greet his arrival in the Great Hall earlier on, now she had on was the same as what the free women of middle to lower class wore: an ankle length linen under-dress with the neck closed by a brooch. Over that was a shorter length woollen dress suspended by shoulder straps called a hangerock and it was also fixed firmly by oval brooches. Amber beads were strung between the pins and whetstones, knifes and scissors were hanging by chains from their belts.

Unlike everyone else, Lady Ranveig had a set of house keys dangling from her belt.

The slave standing before the loom was moving the heddle rods forwards and backwards located in the middle of the framework, wore apparel sharing some qualities, but not identical to the other women, cheaper in the way they were made, the fabric was rough to the touch, had not been dyed and bore no decoration or jewellery.

Hārūn had pulled up a couple of steps behind his father and was presently restlessly shifting his weight from foot to foot as he watched more slaves sewing with bone needles and cut various lengths of cloth with iron shears before storing the fabric in the recesses beneath the benches.

"My wife and daughters, my sisters and nieces have a similar place within my home," Omar said diplomatically, a ghost of a smile emphasising the deep crow's feet radiating from the outer corners of his eyes, before curiously he surveyed the large chamber itself. It had a broad space down its centre and unlike the Great Hall he had visited earlier the stofa was less decorated and the tables and benches were shallower and higher off the floor than the ones that were able to be used for several different purposes in the main chamber. In addition, the rows of pillars that rested on floor stones - were nearer to the walls and the weight they supported was not only for the long ceiling beams that extended the length of the dwelling, but also he observed there was another set of upper rafters that gave shape to room space against the slope of the roof.

As if reading al-Ṭabarī's thoughts, Lady Ranveig lowered her cup and with her free hand tucked a stray lock of reddish-blonde hair streaked with grey under her elaborate headdresses atop of her head, which served to draw attention to her high position within the close-knit Viking community and to single out her matrimonial status. "In spite of being the Jarl's wife, I and Magnus do our own fair share of the work load with the other women and men in a spirit of cooperation and solidarity. Planting crops and gathering in the harvest is strenuous labour, but it takes nigh long when we all just muck in together to get the task done."

"Yes, indeed," Omar nodded after a moment of careful thought. "I can see where the long flowing garments you wore at my official welcoming reception would not be prudent while tending the livestock nor would the stiffness and heaviness of the train give you the grace of movement to escape the danger of the material catching aflame if you stepped to close to the burning fire pit in your longhouse."

"So what do I owe the pleasure of your company, Omar?" Lady Ranveig asked, indicating to al-Ṭabarī and his son that they could sit as she herself sank onto a stool. "We have fruit, bread and cheese laid out, and we have some ale to wash it down with."

"Alas my son and I can do neither, gracious lady," Omar shook his head in refusal. "We are both departing to the dhows after this, but I thank you for agreeing to see us at such short notice."

"Departing to the dhows! I hope you have not had a change of mind over Magnus' proposal of the trade route betwixt here and Badhdad?" Lady Ranveig said in concern, part of her exuberance faded as she jumped to conclusions and questioned Omar's word. "The offer I made in my husband's name was in sincerity and in good faith. Magnus would have wanted to speak to you in person."

The merchant's eyes widened as comprehension dawned of what she was applying too. Hurt from her brazen and unkind outburst was like a punch to him and his feelings showed on his face. "Of that I have no doubt, Lady. Let me reassure you that my decision on the issue is unchanged. I shall fulfil my obligation to my friend, you have my vow on it, and I can not wait to have our secret meeting in the lavatory." He said calmly, slightly miffed as he cast a glance over his shoulder at his son and gesturing with his long and grizzled, bearded jaw for him to come forward. "I did not come about that."

Lady Ranveig studied his proud face and her willowy frame tensed up in response, feeling heat in her reddening cheeks from embarrassment. "Apologies, Omar," she inclined her head in an attempt to mollify him, her mind racing as she became anxious to move the conversation on to more practical matters. "Therefore it must be your bed closet. There is a lock on the inside of the door so you can sleep safely, but I am loathed to move you because there be a trapdoor under the rug that lifts to reveal an escape tunnel that leads outside the walls to the livestock barn."

"I can forgive you easily, Lady Ranveig," Omar al-Ṭabarī held up his hand palm out in a forestalling gesture, Hārūn drawing alongside his father and halting again, his arms were laded with bolt of silk and a small receptacle made of interwoven wickerwork. "But you misunderstand me, wife of my friend. I did not have the pleasure of presenting my number two, son, Hārūn, to you in the Great Hall, because the ship he was on was separated from the other vessel, delayed when the high winds in the fjord cracked one of the masts and tore its lateen sails asunder. Dhows generally use sails as their only means of propulsion, but pondering on what Magnus once said in one of our caravan journeys, I refitted both my ships: the Jewel of Arabia and the Thief of Baghdad with oars. It is a shame the captain of the former did not employ them sooner."

Lady Ranveig glanced at Hārūn with a genuine yet practiced smile, her green eyes running quickly over the younger man to weigh him up and saw that he had strong features and closely resembled his father in height and face, especially in the eyes and the mouth surrounded by a short blue-black curly beard, but he seemed to possess a hint of gentleness in his character and he lacked the physical strength of vitality that radiated from his brother Aḥmad and the older al-Ṭabarī. "Welcome to Fjordstad, Hārūn," she said.

Hārūn became withdrawn under the stress of it all but he still managed to give her a noncommittal nod and the slightest of smiles.

She blinked and was about to say something to break the seconds of awkward silence when Omar cleared his throat and resisting the urge he had to threw up his hands in disgust at Hārūn's shyness, he said to cover up his humiliation, "My son is a man of few words, Lady Ranveig, but let me reassure you that we are both cut from the same cloth," he forced a chuckle. "If I may I would like to offer additional gifts to seal our friendship."

"If you insist," Lady Ranveig said, looking slightly bemused.

"The first is a roll of fabric for you and your daughters and the second," Omar al-Ṭabarī glared at his son, as he took the wicker receptacle from Hārūn and opened the lid to reveal a number of the same dark-coloured oval fruit that had sweet flesh and a single hard narrow seed. "Lady, this is called a date, the edible fruit of a palm. It is the core food and chief source of wealth in the deserts of North Africa. A delicacy and it is a favourite of mine and your husband's."

"You spoil us, Omar," Lady Ranveig said, plucking a date from the wicker receptacle and popping it into her mouth. "Sweet," she added after a chew. Hārūn proffered the bolt of silk to a slave and she took it off his hands. Another woman of higher class approached the merchant and she removed the dates from his extended hand before withdrawing. "May the Gods smile their blessing upon you?"

"Allah has granted me a rich life with a large family and I give thanks in prayer each day," Omar al-Ṭabarī bowed his head to her. "Now, with your permission, Lady Ranveig," he said, clapping a hand upon Hārūn's shoulder. "My son and I will take our leave and help Aḥmad with unloading the cargo from the second dhow while daylight remains."

"You have it, friend of my husband." She inclined her head in return. The merchant was ushering Hārūn to the door when Tove rushed into the stofa, carrying a short sword.

"Mistress, ships have been sighted in the fjord," she declared ominously.

"My husband's fleet or doth it belong to Sigvald Foeslayer?"

Tove shook her head and reversed the hilt of the sword in order that it pointed away from her. "I know not, after I heard the alarm signal I detoured slightly to grab your blade ere dashing here." There was a chorus of gasps as the announcement provoked considerable unease among the slaves and the freeborn women, who glanced anxiously at one another, the same terrifying thoughts crossing their minds.

Lady Ranveig strode forward, grabbing the hilt and drew the blade with a flourish. The women stood up instinctively and stared apprehensively at her. "Tove, get my daughter, Sonja out of the long house, you know where she will be safe, oh, one more thing, along the way tell Njáll Bloodhammer I wish to see him here."

"At once, Mistress," Tove said, shoving the empty sheath into the hands of another servant before scurrying away again. A look flashed between Omar and his son.

Lady Ranveig had become vaguely aware of the women clustering about her and the men, her blue eyes roaming their faces as she addressed them. "The rest of you should go too, gather your weapons or find a hiding place where I or my warriors shall come for you in time…"

"What of us if you do not come, milady," interrupted a young freeborn woman; her angular face was framed with long, unwoven blond curls.

"Then, Thora," Lady Ranveig's penetrating gaze coming to rest upon her and Thora flinched involuntary, a sudden chill washing over her. "I dare say that Sigvald Foeslayer and his men will know what to do with you, now go at haste. The walls and the warriors shall stall the enemy till dark, but if Jarl Foeslayer's men hath brought along scaling ladders they could come over the palisade at any number of places and gain a foothold ere the guards can mount a stout defence to repel them."

Lady Ranveig's steely words galvanised the women into action and her own instincts were urging her into motion, but she resisted until Njáll Bloodhammer arrived. Omar al-Ṭabarī and his son watched Thora and the others depart the stofa; waiting for the last one to vanish from sight before speaking his concerns.

"Lady Ranveig, why have I not heard of this Sigvald Foeslayer?" he demanded, his voice containing flint. Hārūn was taking an interest in the developing proceedings in spite of being beside himself with worry.

She made a disturbing sound in her throat and tightened her grip on the sword hilt and her knuckles rapidly whitened as she turned back to face the merchant, lowering the tip of the blade to the ground. "He is a bastard lording of strife and steel from beyond the broken tooth mountains, the unfortunate result of a dalliance between his late father, the Jarl and a concubine." Her anger suddenly got the better of her common sense and she let her feelings slip to a man she hardly knew. "He's presence is like an open insult to me, a scar that is a constant reminder of the crop my husband's own seed has sowed and the cause of me having many sleepless nights in fear of losing everything I hold dear," the merchant frowned at the insight into her innermost thoughts, but he let her continued without interruption, "and I deemed that he was not worth the mentioning in your honoured presence, Omar."

"What else is known of Sigvald Foeslayer?" asked Omar al-Ṭabarī tactfully, as he heard the sound of approaching boots reverberating in the passageway beyond the chamber.

"I confess I have never met him face to face, but his reputation precedes him belike an onrushing spear. It is said from reliable sources that Sigvald Foeslayer sits on the Serpent Throne inside the fort village of Trøllheim after having had his two half brothers slain as well as a few of his distant cousins in the following civil war when they did not openly support his claim to his father's Jarldorn. The other chieftains allied themselves to him out of necessary, bringing ships and many men under his banner, but I presume the hatred they have for him runs deep."

The footfalls stopped outside the stofa and Njáll Bloodhammer poked his head around the doorway. "You send for me, milady."

"Aye, what do you know of the approaching ships?"

"Milady, I was inside the longhouse when the signal went off and the little I have learned is from what your own servant has told me."

"Damnation! If there is a future for Fjordstad, I shall make it my task that not only the guards recognize the different horn notes of our new signalling system my husband has introduced recently," Lady Ranveig shook her head, "but every man woman and child will share in that knowledge too."

"You can not go greatly wrong with a gong, Lady Ranveig," Omar said, "I seen them in China suspended on ropes in a wooden frame and the bell like tones could be used to herald the arrival of a foe. I have one in the hold of my dhow; you can purchase it for the right price."

"I will mediate upon your suggestion, Omar," Lady Ranveig said, her eyes darting to the young warrior. "Njáll Bloodhammer, you are to follow wherever I go understand?" The warrior nodded and she shifted her attention again. "Come Omar and Hārūn," she motioned with her sword towards the doorway. "Walk with me." She turned abruptly and strode out the chamber, brushing past Njáll Bloodhammer. The merchant and his son dashed after her and the young Viking brought up the rear.

Chapter Nine
The Sword I wield

Carrying coils of rope, a dozen boys ran from the shipyard in a wild, disordered charge. Ahead of them, carpenters and labours, plank-cutters and stem-smiths had gathered at the water's edge to watch the fleet of longships. They turned at the sound of their swift and nimble sons and nephews approach and shouted their enthusiasm as they stepped to the side in order to not impede their progress.

Upon the jetties, the archers slung their bows over their shoulders, as the boys group divided into two parts, some taking the nearest pier to them, while the rest heading for the next one along. The youngsters came to the forefront of the archer's formation and started handing out the rope so that the warriors would be set to toss the lines over to the sailors onboard the longships with the purpose of pulling the vessels closer to the dock and tying them securely up to the studier of the pilings.

The array of piers grew gradually closer before the advancing fleet and Tjernagl stopped beating the drum and barked an order to the rowers to unship their oars. The crew obeyed wordlessly, drawing them into the deck before each oar bank was upped into the air. Judging the Mjöllnir's Might speed and the dwindling distance to their destination, Gunnar nudged the steering oar and the keel pivoted by degrees until he had levelled off, easing it into alignment with the wooden structure, the forefront of which slowly ran past the dragon prow in a parallel position.

Now losing momentum, Gunnar brought in the Mjöllnir's Might. Ropes snaked out over the rail of shields and Old Sven, Einar and a few others not holding an oar, caught the lines before tying the ends to the cleats.

"Rope secure," Einar shouted.

"And here, Gunnar," Old Sven said just as loudly.

On the other end of the mooring lines, the archers tightened their grips and grunted as they winded in the rope and pulled the longship gently in alongside the pier. Ropes were then warped about the pilings.

"Drop anchors," Gunnar bellowed after feeling the hull bump against the edge of the pier planking and in the following few seconds he heard the two large, welcoming splashes. "Store the oars and unload the sea chests."

Members of the crew took it in turns to store the oars atop of the rolled up sail stored on the cradles in the uprights located fore and aft. Fridrik stepped on someone's sea chest as a step up before he clambered over the rail and dropped onto the pier beyond.

* * *

At the same time that Gunnar was putting in Magnússon's flagship, the crowds in Fjordstad had to divert their attention as the Long Snake yawed from behind the Mjöllnir's Might, and its flashing oar stokes drove it at an angle towards the next pier across the way. Vegard leaned into the steering oar and brought his longship steadily about before leaving a yard long gap when he eventually heaved to beside the pilings. He dropped the anchors in advance of the mooring lines being attached, and stretched a gangplank to bridge the watery fissure so his crew could disembark the ship. Kari the Rune-Master was the first to walk off the Long Snake, carrying a sack of belongings and plunder. Helga came on her heels, and the other shield maidens all with their hands full of weapons and bulging sacks, brought up the rear.

By now the setting sun had dipped half way behind the mountains tops, colouring the rock and the glacier blood red; the encroaching darkness gradually rippled across the fjord and the odd scudding cloud was in the deepening purple sky. The Sea Chariot put in a lot closer behind the Long Snake, the hull amidships scraping against the sides of the pier's pilings and planking before it came to rest a good distance from Vegard's vessel.

"Hurry up and clear that anchor line!" the first mate of the Sea Chariot shouted to members of his crew.

The Bifrost's Bow and the Horse of the Waves came on in the wake of the Mjöllnir's Might and navigated their way successfully into port.

The Blood Fang had far too much momentum and overshoot the berth between the Sea Chariot and the Long Snake so the longship's first mate extended the oars and back stroked to another pier. The Rune Fire suffered minor damage on final approach due to the tardiness of the rowers in the lateness of unshipping their oars, the blades breaking off when it struck part of the pilings, splitting and twisting the shafts in the oar ports, and the Vikings had to await landing until they cleared away the obstructions.

On board the Mjöllnir's Might, Magnússon spared a glance back at the Rune Fire as he groaned and hauled up his sea chest, heavy with his possessions and some choice pieces of the monastery treasures. "Shipwright, your apprentices need to practice their manoeuvring into port. I expect better from seafarers under my command."

"Aye, as do I, Jarl Magnússon," Gunnar agreed, plucking his shield up from the rack and slipping his arms through the straps till he carried it on his back. "They be young still, but I shall get them aboard a longship and be sailing in and out of the fjord at cockcrow on the first day after the celebrations."

"That if Gunnar has the strength after bedding that comely slave of his all night long," Lokar said, dragging his wooden sea chest across the deck by one of the leather handles.

"I better make it mid morning, Jarl Magnússon," Gunnar said with embarrassment. "I should have my vigour back by then."

"See that you do," Magnússon struggled over to the rail and hoisted the chest into the waiting arms of two archers standing on the pier before addressing them. "Take my chattels to my longhouse...."

"What is the matter, father? Are you suffering pain or stiffness in those old joints of yours," Lokar interrupted with sarcasm. "Is that the reason why you can't carry your own chest?"

"Nay, just enjoying a privilege of my rank, Lokar," Magnússon replied icily. "You don't miss anything, do you?"

"Hmmm, I try not to," Lokar smirked. "If it is good enough for you, then 'tis good enough for me," he manhandled his rectangular box up to balance atop of the gunwale. "Take mine as well."

"You heard him," Magnússon grumbled, jerking his thumb at the chest. "But when you reach the great hall I want you to hide my chest away from the prying eyes of Lady Ranveig; say, in her stofa, for I would like the gift I brought back with me to be a complete surprise when I give it to her."

"It shall be done," the archer inclined his head before turning to go.

"And be careful with my chest," Lokar cautioned the second archer, who grabbed it in his arms and quickly followed his comrade. "There be glory and tribute inside for the Jarl."

"But will it be enough Lokar to earn back the seat you so foolishly lost at your father's table?" said Björn Strongarm, scoffing at his declaration as he walked towards them, carrying spears in one large hand and his other held his sea chest perched upon his shoulder.

"Ha, Lokar shall have to sail far and wide ere that happens, Björn," Magnússon spoke harshly as he vaulted over the rail and landed on the pier. The bodyguard arched his left leg to astraddle the gunwale and then pulled his right leg over to stand beside the Jarl. "And only then it will be at my own sufferance because of his mother's behest."

Magnússon and Björn Strongarm got going along the pier Rollo came up beside Lokar and slapped him heartily on the back with guarded optimism. "You took their remarks in good heart, nephew."

"Aye, I was bruised by the criticism," Lokar whispered so that no one else could hear but Rollo, clenching his hands into fists and glaring daggers into their receding backs as revenge occupied his musings like a black cloud. "But now is not the time to make waves, uncle, it is to hatch future plots."

"'Twill have to be a wise plan if you and I are to cross spears with Magnus and Björn," Rollo spoke in a furtive manner, glancing askance at fellow Vikings carrying armfuls of plunder off the longship.

Lokar smiled at the family support as he and Rollo disembarked. "It will uncle, fret not on that. As good as you and I are with weapons I am at my deadliest when I am thinking."

Lokar and Rollo lengthened their stride to catch up to Magnússon and Björn Strongarm. Behind them, one of the crew carried Rollo's sea chest.

* * *

Considering what he had just heard, the tone of Omar al-Ṭabarī took on a more conciliatory note as he spoke. "I have no doubt that Sigvald Foeslayer is a bitter rival to your clan, yes, but if you permit me to be blunt, lady," he paused while Lady Ranveig inclined her head in assent; "surely the civil war he waged among his own people depleted his warrior strength and now is no match for the force of arms under Magnus' command?"

"If only that was the case, friend of my husband, but Foeslayer has taken his lack of fighting forces into consideration." Lady Ranveig signed heavily, casting a glance over a shoulder as she progressed along the passageway and passed a few side rooms opening up on to it; their doors had small pieces of rock tied to a cord fastened to the doors to keep them pulled shut. "Saxon exiles have swarmed the lands of Sigvald Foeslayer in greater number than here or anywhere else on the fjords and it is also said he has not enslaved them belike other Norse settlements has, instead he has armed and trained these foreign trespassers with the purpose of shoving them in the forefront of an attack." She then directed her words to the young warrior adhering to their heels, thinking the following news would be better coming from an eyewitness than via herself. "Njáll Bloodhammer, speak of what you know."

"Aye, milady" Njáll Bloodhammer said, about to recount the story. "Jarl Foeslayer asserted himself against us in the spring when men under his coiled snake banner captured three of our fishing boats and murdered all but one of the crews. A fisherman named Halldór, escaped by jumping overboard and it was the same man, who was in one of our hunting parties in the woods a month or so later that came upon a score of mystery warriors. By their garments, we saw that they were foreign and from the game trail these spearmen followed, we deemed that they were on a quest of stealth to explore deep into our land."

"Pardon, friend Njáll," Omar al-Ṭabarī said with a frown, daring to look back at him. "I know a banner would be impractical among the trees, but when you say a mystery, does that mean this band of spearmen sported no symbol on their shields, no identifying mark to tell you who they were or who they fought for?"

"Aye, merchant," he replied.

"Then how could you tell they were on a quest? Omar frown deepened. "Did your men capture one of them and you tortured it out of the prisoner?"

"Nay," Njáll Bloodhammer shook his head. "The trail the Saxons trod through the forest was old and had become disused by animal, and Halldór recognized the Norse captain leading the Saxons to be the same man who was in charge of the raiding party that boarded and seized his fishing boat. My warriors ambushed the exiles in the end and Lady Ranveig sent their heads back to Jarl Foeslayer...."

"I have a suspicious nature as all who know me can attest," Lady Ranveig put in; bending her head to slip through another doorway that lead to the animal stalls. The others did the same as they entered the chamber. "And I know that act of slaughter would not discourage Sigvald Foeslayer in the least."

Omar al-Ṭabarī tucked at his beard thoughtfully but he did not baulk in offering aid to the wife of his friend. "How can we be of service, Lady? Hārūn is a healer," Hārūn paled. "He knows about the medicinal properties of herbs and how to tend wounds, and age has not yet dulled the reflexes of my sword arm."

Feeling a measure of gratitude, Lady Ranveig smiled in relief as another doorway loomed ahead of her and she stepped on through it. The three men came after. "You would honour Magnus and me if you would protect our youngest daughter, Sonja and my faithful servant," she said, revealing a rarely seen vulnerable side to her character, her voice carrying further now within the echoing vastness of the Great Hall. "You shall find them in the blacksmith's shop. There is an escape tunnel known only by a handful of people, an old coal mine that leads under the palisade and comes out in the forest east of here. Escort them far from here."

"Granted," the merchant declared smoothly after a moment's deliberation, walking among the benches littering the beaten-earth floor. The main chamber had been designed for the warrior and war rather than aesthetic principles. Shields hung from pillars and weapons decorated the timber walls. On their right were the steps of a raised dais topped with two thrones carved with scenes of the fabled city of Asgard, the rainbow bridge and an assortment of Magnus Magnússon's family sharing a fellowship with Norse deities. Behind the dais was the chamber's dominating feature and in passing the strangeness of the ancient tree once again made Hārūn turn his broad face, drawing his attention in rapt fascination to the elongating trunk that was twisted and full of knots and in his mind it begged the question why was the tree growing inside the longhouse as his eyes wandered upwards to the branches that seemed to him to reach up like gnarled fingers through the large hole in the vaulted, soot-coated roof above. "But what of you, Lady Ranveig, will you not be coming with us?"

"Nay, Omar; 'tis not I to hide myself away in a black hole when others are risking their lives fighting for me," Lady Ranveig shook her head, making her way towards the front entrance of the longhouse. "I am heading for the town gate to gaze upon these ships and judge them with my own eyes," she replied, her eyes burning with determination. "I may be only keeping the throne warm for my husband and son, but I am nay a figurehead to sit meekly upon it. Before I became the wife of Magnus and the mother of his three healthy children, I was and still am a shield maiden of the House of Magnússon."

"If it is the fleet of Sigvald Foeslayer, I am confident that you will prevail, Lady," Omar said, drawing courage from her example.

"That's makes one of us," Hārūn muttered, rolling his eyes dubiously and then the merchant turned his head to glare at him. "There is every sign that age has not dulled your hearing either, Father."

"Let my son, accompany you to where he will be the most good, Lady. I am certain he will warm to the idea eventually," Omar al-Ṭabarī said without a trace of humour, as Hārūn shook his head. Lady Ranveig came to a large wooden door, bound in iron and she shoved it open. "Hārūn shall also let Aḥmad know that he and the warriors of my retinue are under your command."

"I am grateful for both your words and your men, Omar," Lady Ranveig said, blinking in the bright sunshine and she raised her hand to shade her brow, going forward a few steps outside before stopping for a moment. Omar al-Ṭabarī drew up beside her. Hārūn and Njáll Bloodhammer pressed in close behind them. "This is where we part company for the present," she jabbed her sword down the slope in the direction he should take. "See where the horses are kept in the corral?"

"Yes," the merchant nodded and he half-closed his eyes so he could see a little better the horses milling about in the coral and he could just perceived a slight heat haze shimmering on the air from around the dwelling at its rear. Tove preceded a small child with pig tails into the establishment and closed the door quietly behind them.

"The blacksmith's shop lies beyond."

Without another word, Lady Ranveig yanked up the hem of her dress with her free hand, tucking it under her belt to allow herself to walk unhindered and then she set off into the purple shadows with a surefooted stride. Hārūn and Njáll Bloodhammer accompanied her down the slope, a faint, dappled trail parted the grass and lead among the darkening buildings looming ahead of them. Omar al-Ṭabarī watched them go and then his gait angled away.

* * *

Once, Lars Gunnarson had hurriedly departed Brunhild's wraith, he stopped quickly to dress in the anddyri of Björn Strongarm's longhouse. There were farming tools, ropes and harnesses for draught animals filling wooden boxes set against the wall along with a collection of muddy boots below crudely-made pegs on which was dirty working clothes. Buckling up his sword belt, Lars unlocked the bolts and slightly opened the exterior door to peek out the gap in order to see that the coast was clear.

It was.

Lars slipped out the mud room quietly, shut the door behind him and headed along the pathway, casting a stealthy glance around as he went. A second later, he became distracted when he detected footfalls and then caught sight of movement from the corner of his eye emerging suddenly from the side of the longhouse. Fearing he had been noticed by the mother and brother of Björn Strongarm, back early from washing and untangling the fleeces from their herd of sheep, Lars looked sharply to his left and saw Lady Ranveig leading a couple of men.

"You there," she barked at Lars. "Come with me."

Lars nodded and fell in behind Njáll Bloodhammer. Unused to the horn signals they heard, old and disabled people shouted confused questions from doorways to Lady Ranveig in passing and she shook her head in answer, refusing to even speculate as she picked her way through the small fenced plots containing buildings, the eaves of the roofs almost touched their neighbours above a section of narrow paved road, the little company began swelling in size as it collected stray dogs with rough bristly coats and orphan children, a few Arabs sailors, a priest and his acolytes, and women of various ages. Clicking chickens scattered out of the peoples' way and the dogs barked and wagged their tails as they paddled along beside them.

And then, Lady Ranveig and the others began listening to a low hum of voices coming up from the hidden slope, some barns, pig pens and a large grain storehouse were obscuring the view beyond. Aware they were closing upon the main gate and the palisade, Lady Ranveig quickened her pace and the crowd kept up behind her. The voices grew louder the nearer they came and Lars and several of his friends and neighbours swapped uncertain glances with each other as they could now, distinguish the unmistakeable sounds of shouting and clapping apart.

The head of Knut was glimpsed in the diluting daylight climbing the slope through the gaps in the pig pen fencing and subsequently his feet urgently brought him up and along the narrow passageway running between the buildings. Lady Ranveig met him half way in and her heart was in her mouth as she saw the knowing smile that split Knut's features.

"Lady Ranveig, I was coming to knock upon your door next," Knut said breathlessly, the stink of mead assailed her nostrils. "Jarl Magnússon is home."

"Praise Allah," Hārūn muttered in relief. "I thought we would be up to our necks in trouble."

"Njáll Bloodhammer," Lady Ranveig half turned towards him and pushed her sword into his free hand. "Go and tell the merchant and Thora and the rest of the women of my house that all is well. If my brother's wife, Lady Ingrid is back from picking wild strawberries in the woods," she removed the house keys from her belt, "instruct her to prepare the Great Hall for an extravagant welcome home feast to celebrate the safe return of our kinfolk and give her these keys, they open locks to doors and chests she will need to access to do her chores." He took the proffered keys. "Have the feasting tables set up between the benches, dig out the old victory decorations and hang them from the walls, and tell the cooks to empty the baskets in the food stores, I want an assorted of meats, because I know not what our Eastern guests prefer to eat: pork, beef, venison and mutton, served on our finest wooden trenchers, vegetables too and all the barley bread they baked this week."

"Aye," he acknowledged before retracing his steps.

Lady Ranveig fixed her gaze ahead and brushed past Knut, striding down the slope as she pressed onward. Lars and Hārūn lead the rest of the cheerful crowd in pursuit, but the separating gap between them widened until they lost sight of her. Lady Ranveig went around stragglers and glanced at archers coming up from the pier, carrying someone's sea chests, before she soon became caught up with the excitement from more of the town's people heading for the gate, jostling her way passed men lighting torches against the deepening gloom, and jabbering women and children, who tugged at their skirts for them to hurry to the shore in order to greet their family members disembarking the longships and in hope of snatching a peek of the wondrous treasures the Vikings had brought back with them.

✷ ✷ ✷

The tip of the fading sun was just visible behind the mountains now and the steady but weak phenomenon of twilight glow was beginning to emanate from the sky. Upon the longships and the piers the sharp glare of torches flickered into life as the boys returned, handing out the sticks of resinous-wood to guards escorting the prisoners from the holds and then igniting them with their own burning brand they carried to see by.

Outside Fjordstad, the awaiting town folk cheered enthusiastically and the applauds were loud and continuous, as Magnússon and Björn Strongarm strode the last few feet up the illuminated dirt trail and drew to a halt before the crowded gateway. Burning torches were held in wall brackets affixed to the palisade walls and carried by Vikings standing in-between the mammoth tusks.

The Jarl grinned at the acclaim, letting his eyes take in the smiling happy faces of his audience and he raised his hand to make himself heard.

The crowd fell in complete silence.

"People of Fjordstad, I won't bore you all with a long speech..." Magnússon began.

"Nay he will do it with a short one instead," Lokar interrupted loudly, as he and Rollo pulled up behind the pair. Kari and her shield maidens brought up the rear.

There were howls of mirth from the palisade above them and that was punctuated by clapping from elsewhere. Magnússon pressed his lips tightly together in annoyance and raised his arm to summon order and the audience quieted down again.

"I promised you a voyage of adventure and a treasure trove beyond measure," Magnússon resumed, delivering the lines with style. The crowd stared back at him with rapt attention. "I kept my word," his voice rising to a swift crescendo, "victory is ours."

The crowd went wild with animation; women and children applauded and warriors on the piers started chanting the Jarl's surname over and over again, "Magnússon, Magnússon, Magnússon, Magnússon!" Guards either hit their sword pommels against their shields or they ground their spears on the walkway above, thumping them in an honoured salute.

Magnússon grinned and waved as he strode forward towards the crowded gateway, where the town's folk standing in ranks four-deep, backpedalled immediately across the threshold, dividing to form a narrow passage for the Jarl and his followers to proceed through with relaxed easy strides. Björn Strongarm and Lokar each took a flaming torch off the torchbearers, and forged onward.

Behind them, the chanting receded as families looked around for love ones, spotting husbands and sons, daughters' and uncles disembarking the ships in a steady stream before surging forward to reunite with them. A few of the seamen sported bandages on their arms or legs, dropped their weapons and sea chests to lift their children up in their arms. Some wives and mothers waiting on the dirt trail kept staring at the passing warriors in hope of seeing their relatives alive, but slowly oarsmen with an expressions of sorrow and sympathy came up to them and offered their condolences.

Magnússon and the others were heading deeper into town when Lady Ranveig appeared suddenly a short distance ahead after the rest of the people got out of their way. She felt a fluttery little sensation deep in her gut as she saw her husband.

"Come to me, dear heart," Magnússon said, bearing down on her.

"Hail, Magnus my Lord and husband," Lady Ranveig smiled and ran into his outstretched arms, their sudden parting and not knowing if he was alive or dead had caused intense painful feelings to grow within her during his absence and the emotions just spilled out into her words. "The hours of the days seemed to drag without you by my side."

"Well, met, Ranveig my lady wife," Magnússon hugged her tightly and gave her a bruising kiss on the cheek. "I too felt incomplete without you near, but," he added, retaining his indomitable spirit, "embrace the opportunity I shall when next it presents itself to play merry Hel with the English."

Lady Ranveig tasted the salt on his lips as she pulled away and nodded. "'Tis a hardship I have endured without a single complaint when the raiding season comes around again and you go a-Viking. Such is my lot in life," thinking on the wellbeing of her son and daughter, she glanced behind him and saw her oldest children standing there. "How did Lokar and Kari fare in battle, my husband?"

"Their deeds heaped much honour on the house of Magnússon," the Jarl said diplomatically, in order to not spoil the festive mood.

"I don't back down from a fight or a drink," Lokar said, walking with a confident swagger.

"Why are you being so modesty, brother of mine," Kari replied with sarcasm. "You are an expert backstabber as well." Lokar clenched his jaw at the hint of trouble. "You never give yourself a sufficient amount of credit for that."

Lokar sniffed loudly. "I prefer to think of it as a hidden talent, dearest sister. I am certain that one day the man whom father chooses for you to marry will love how your mouth runs away with you."

Kari glared at him. "Hmpt, if and when that happens my husband will hold nay sway over me, brother. I am not a mere chattel to be possessive by any man."

Listening to their mocking repartee, Lady Ranveig arched an eyebrow as she glanced at her husband and whispered. "You have not told her yet about her future marriage to Jarl Henrik Storrvik, Magnus?"

"Nay, I had weightier tasks on my mind, but I shall broach the subject in my own time...."

"Kari deserves to know ere the rising of the harvest moon?"

"She will and you my dear wife will smooth Kari's ruffled feathers and I am certain that you shall see to it that good sense will prevail," replied Magnússon just as softly, his son and daughter's bickering exchanges were growing increasing heated, but before he could say anything, Lady Ranveig beat him to it, casting a glance over her shoulder.

"Ahem," Lady Ranveig expressed her disapproval by looking daggers at her children and making the sound of a quiet cough to attract the attention of everybody back to her. "So, husband," she pressed him, not betraying her own feelings on the matter, as her gaze returned forward, "in your eyes has Lokar done enough to earn the right to retake his seat at your feasting table?"

"Naught would make me happier, wife," Magnússon said through gritted teeth as he snatched a withering glance back at his son, who grinned back at him. "I have nay a doubt that the number of English he slew with increase after each retelling of the story."

"I don't know why men have to exaggerated everything either," Lady Ranveig delivered the line absolutely deadpan as she glanced aimlessly at the gloom and could only just perceive the outlines of the buildings and the shadows of the sky in the torchlight. "Come along, Magnus; the evening is upon us and I hunger for the celebrations of the náttverðr meal. Omar awaits us at the longhouse."

"Aye," Magnússon said cheerfully and held his wife's hand affectingly, projecting the rare blend of physical toughness and emotional sensitivity she had grown to love about him. "I hope my friend can find a Western buyer for the casks of monk wine; because I be trading the swill for whatever I can get my hands on."

* * *

By the time Magnússon and Lady Ranveig entered the Great Hall followed by a number of others, the place was swarming with activity. A skald was limbering up his voice by a graduated series of musical tones ascending or descending in order of pitch as he rehearsed a song stanza, while musicians plucked strings and blew practice notes on their instruments.

Omar al-Ṭabarī sat and watched a slave coaxing the growling coals of this morning's fire to burn beneath an iron cauldron suspended over the centre of the floor. Beside his mother, a young boy was holding a metal poker, ready to use it to stir the fire when told. A smoke hole was directly in the roof above the pair. Somewhere else, two male slaves, one of whom was standing on the benches passed down the wooden slab of a tabletop to the arms of his companion, before he reached up again and grabbed the legs of the trestle from where the items of furniture had been stored overhead on the beams when not in everyday use.

Among all this chaos, Lady Ingrid Sturluson was ordering about servants and free born alike, encouraging and complaining to them in equal measure as she moved from one pillar to another, turning her bony frame to survey the developing scene and pointing here and there to add an ornate feature to a corner and shift another hanging banner, honouring some act of bravery in battle or achievement in victory, further along the wall to conceal the doors of a bed closet.

"Niece," Lady Ingrid said in a brief musical lull, straightening the headdress atop of her sandy-coloured tresses as she showed nepotism to Thora. "Replace the old torches in the brackets with fresh ones and I want candles on all the tables."

Thora clicked her slender fingers. "I believe I saw a supply of tapers in one of the heavy chests behind the dais."

"Be careful in which of the chests you rummage, niece," Ingrid Sturluson warned, her hard obsidian eyes boring steely into Thora, as she handed over the house keys to the girl. "For that's where Lady Ranveig stores most of her personal possessions. If she finds anything missing she is liable to imprison the person responsible or worst."

Thora went pale at the meaning and nodded before hurrying off.

"Lady Ingrid," Njáll Bloodhammer called out as he and another warrior carried a large wooden carving of a dragon, its eyes were decorated with gems which glinted in the torchlight. "Where do you want this ship's figurehead placed?"

Ingrid sighed. "Lay it down in the opposite corner you put the first one in. In truth, I do worry that you have naught, but space under that helmet of yours, cousin."

The skald and the musicians were about to start rehearsing again when Magnússon barked out an order to them.

"Silence you're caterwauling, Fandral." Magnússon felt the eyes of the surrounding people stray towards him as they paused in their work. "Do your practicing outside if you must, skald." He strode forward in the direction of the merchant, who had stood up and was grinning as he went to meet his friend. Lokar and Kari accompanied their father and Omar's two sons brought up the rear. "My head echoes with the clank of the blacksmiths hammer hitting his forge."

"Are you not going to change into your best clothes for the feast, husband?" Lady Ranveig asked.

"Nay," Magnússon shook his head. "Do what you will wife, but I am content as I am."

"All right everyone, back to work" Lady Ingrid said loudly, her voice flat and harsh as she focused her attention on the two male servants setting up the trestle table in the space between two benches to accommodate guests. "Get a move on thralls, this chamber will be packed to the rafters once the town's people assemble here for the festivals."

"Aunt Ingrid," Thora said, holding a collection of candles as she pulled up short and handed her the keys. "I can not find the cloth to cover the Jarl's table."

Before Ingrid Sturluson could say something, Björn Strongarm came up from her left. "I can help with that," he dropped his sea chest with a heavy thump and the vibration knocked over empty drinking vessels laid out upon the tables. Adhering to the heels of the bodyguard, Lady Ranveig jumped in shock mirroring the reaction of her sister-in-law. Björn opened up the lid and withdrew a rumpled satin canopy. "This covered the high altar in the English monastery we raided and I think it would make a finer decoration for the main table."

Lady Ranveig, Thora and Ingrid Sturluson took it off his hands and unfolded the creased cloth between them to reveal an image of a Christen Cross.

Lady Ranveig studied the cloth for a moment. "I agree, Björn. Let's spread it out."

Not far from them, Magnússon finally converged on the merchant, who showed his deep respect by bowing low with the palm of his right hand against the forehead

"Hail, Omar," Magnússon's face softening as the merchant straightened. "You're arrival was sooner than I expected."

"Salaam, Magnus," Omar al-Ṭabarī clasped Magnússon's extended hand with his own in greeting. "We sailed calm seas and the gods sent strong winds to fill our sails. I could not have asked for more."

Magnússon nodded and their hands released. "The years have certainly been good to you, my friend."

"You are too kind, Magnus; I may have a few more laughter lines and flecks of snow in the hair and beard since last we met, but Fatima, my wife says that gives me a confident and dignified appearance," the merchant said, giving the Viking chieftain the once over. "And it seems you are a building a kingdom here as well as a paunch."

Magnússon laughed good-naturally "I am growing fat on the wealth of my enemies, and you will too my friend. On the morrow you shall see the rich bounty of slaves I captured and appraise each one at your leisure."

"Now that is music to my ears, Magnus," Omar said, glancing to the right as another wall decoration was hung giving the chamber an even greater appearance of prosperity. "They will be more than welcome in the slave markets of Baghdad."

"Come Omar; Let us take our seats at yonder table," Magnússon jerked his thumb behind the merchant, who inclined his head and turned around, "and talk more of kith and kin while I am sober enough to do so. How is Fatima, doth she still belly dance for you?"

"My wife is well and she still does on occasion the dance of the seven veils when she usually wants me to buy her something really expensive." Omar al-Ṭabarī smiled, walking alongside Magnússon as they dodged the comings and going of the servants. "I brought my sons along on the voyage."

"Aye, I met Hārūn and Aḥmad en route to the longhouse; they must be a source of pride for you?" Magnússon said. Lokar rolled his eyes in exasperation.

"All my children are, Magnus. I had the pleasure of meeting your youngest daughter Sonja awhile ago, sweet child. She was accompanied by a slave I remember giving you as a present, but she answered to another name, why is that?"

"Her birth name was Mie, but my wife decided that a new life in a new land deserved a new given name, so she called her Tove."

"Ah, I see," Omar said in understanding.

"And the sword I wield is the same one I seized that fateful night out of the dead hand of the bandit leader. The blade is well balanced and it has a keen edge that has never once let me down in battle."

"And may all the Gods, yours and mine, keep it so," Omar al-Ṭabarī said.

Behind them, Lokar whispered to Kari. "I expected someone more impressive after the way father talked him up."

"Don't be fooled by appearances, brother," she whispered back and caught his eye. "I am not."

The pair reached the main table and the Jarl pulled up a chair and sat down, the merchant hesitated for a second or two with indecision over where he ought to sit until Magnússon indicated he should take the bench next to him.

"We normally eat our servings of food while sitting on the benches, but I have the trestle tables set up when we have visits from honoured guests like you, Omar," Magnússon said, as servants hastily came up to the table and laid out a number of wooden cups along with a few copper and silver ones before pouring mead into them, the drink sloshing over the rims from time to time and stained the new tablecloth underneath.

Omar al-Ṭabarī placed his hand atop of his cup and shook his head to the slave. "Alcohol is against my custom; bring me water or milk, the same for my sons and my men."

The servant nodded and quickly departed, as Hārūn and Aḥmad sat down.

Lokar unslung his bow and propped against the table leg while Kari gave her spear to one of her shield maidens before choosing a place to sit opposite their father and the merchant. It was then that Magnússon introduced them to each other.

"Omar, these two rebellious and unruly people are my older surviving children in wedlock, Lokar and Kari. Their favourite pastime is to lock horns with me or each other. Alas 'twas not always this way. For they were closer than two peas in a pod, playing together as they grew, a season separating them is all, but the pressure of family life shoved them in opposite directions as they became groomed for their expected functions within the clan..." Magnússon drew his eating dagger and wiped the blade clean on his sleeve.

"Aye, for me that means the responsibility of being the next Jarl," Lokar put in, smiling at his sister. "Kari is going to be a brood mare."

"Oh, what would I do without you brother apart from be happy," Kari clenched her fists and gave him a dirty look.

Magnússon shook his head, but the merchant saw the funny side and grinned. "Son, daughter, I want you both to greet an old ally of mine: Omar al-Ṭabarī, a friend and brother-in-arms from my time on the Silk Road." The Arab inclined his head at them in turn and they returned the gesture. "He is willing to take most of the slaves off our hands."

"I did not say that," Omar al-Ṭabarī said, his smile fading slightly, "but we were see once I have inspected the merchandise."

Lady Ranveig moved around the table and sat down to her husband's left, wearing the house keys on her belt and some of her finest jewellery for this special occasion. "Björn has gone to fetch his family and Rollo and Ingrid will join us presently, they are starting to let in the first of the town folk."

"Good, "Magnússon nodded and clunked his dagger down on the table top. "We will wait till everyone has taken their seats and then raise our cups and drink to honour Odin and Thor for our safe return."

* * *

At the rear of Jarl Magnússon's longhouse, a large cooking pit had been dug and lined with wood to cater food for all of the town's folk. Meat of every description boiled in the water and to keep the temperature heated to the boiling point, men dropped hot stones into the bubbling surface, while women seasoned the water with herbs and spices. Elsewhere, standing over charcoal fires that cast dim red glows to the bottom of riveted cauldrons suspended by chains, cooks stirred the stew in the pots, and beneath them bread baked on skillets.

"This meat is tender and ready to be eaten," one of the cooks said, over her shoulder as she roasted a piece of beef on a spit resting on fork sticks on either side of the fire.

"And my broth is done as well," a second cook said to the approaching servants, who dipped horn ladles into the broth and served it up into wooden bowls before heading off.

The cook took the meat off the spit and dumped it upon a wooden platter. Tove carried it away through the kitchen of the longhouse. Stone ovens took up one wall and a bread-making quern stood against a second with sacks of wheat, barley and oat flours. Tables lined the last two walls littered with soapstone pots, baskets of bird's eggs; clay jars containing dried red alga, and chopped up vegetables. Smoked mutton and fish hung by hooks from the room's rafters.

Following the number of slaves streaming through the corridors in different directions, Tove sneaked a glance at one of Kari's shield maidens, Marit giggling as she led a smirking Ulf away from the feasting tables and into a side chamber for a little privacy. The music swelled from the Great Hall and wisps of drifting smoke came from simple stone lamps shaped like a box with a more or less concave interior filled with fish liver oil and a reedy stems of cotton grass were loosely twisted as a wick, drawing the fuel to the naked flame.

Tove passed some of the merchant's cargo that had been stacked in front of the armoury doorway before entering the Great Hall and proceeding through the thickening haze of smoke that rose into the air from the central cooking fire and from tallow candles and torches burnt to provide light. The musician's instruments, drums, lyres, lur's and others, and the singing voices from the skalds reciting a poem about heroism and legend, reverberated off the walls, but was steadily becoming drowned out by chatter of conversation and guffaws of hilarity.

Alvin got up and started stamping his feet and waving his arms in crude and spontaneous movements as he attempted to dance to the music and release his pent-up energy. Across the room, a man and woman joyfully grasped each other firmly and turned around and around. In a patch of shadow between the torchlight, Olaf did not see Ásgrímr stick his leg out and the young lookout tripped over.

Off to the right from the main table, Rigsson opened a bulging sack again and placed an orate candlestick on the floor, Lokar raised a heavy double-edged battle axe and brought it down, cutting the tall, slim metal holder in half. A young woman and an older man approached Lokar as he knelt and picked up a piece of hacked silver

"Steingerðr, please accept this gift as a down payment of my appreciation for your husband's lost when he fought alongside me in England," Lokar said, handing the silver to her. "I promised Bárðr and the other warriors more coin and you," he glanced from the woman to the man, "and you, Kormákr the animal doctor shall receive it on the morrow. Pass on my words to the rest of their families and tell them to come to me."

"We shall," Kormákr nodded.

Thank you, milord," Steingerðr said, her eyes red rimmed from shedding tears. "Did Bárðr die well?"

"Aye, he did," Lokar handed the other piece of the candlestick to the older man, "and your son too, Kormákr. Bárðr and Önundr were laid atop of a pyre and had a Viking funeral."

Nearby, Lars Gunnarson smiled and raised his cup to Brunhild sitting on the next table. She glared back at him and then whispered something in the ear of Björn Strongarm. The bodyguard stiffened in reaction and stared intently and angrily at Lars before his gaze flickered to the entertainment in front of him. Gísli and Tyrker were grappling as they wrestled one another, growls and snarls escaped their lips until Tyrker kneed his tattooed adversary in the groin in advance of hauling Gísli up and throwing him awkwardly against a figurehead in the corner, breaking the man's spine.

Everyone burst out laughing including those on the main table.

"Father," Aḥmad said in between chews of his meat sausage, crumbs dotted his curly black beard. In front of him, Slaves lifted the figurehead off the tattooed man and then grabbing him by his legs and under the arms, the men carried the unconscious Gísli out of the chamber. Harold stood up and scratching, he closely followed his foster brother. Tyrker snatched a cup of ale from a passing female slave and gulped it down. "Never have I seen people enjoying themselves so much. Jarl Magnússon must be prosperous indeed, because by my count the feast has been going on for at least two hours now, and they have not stopped eating and drinking."

"Neither have we, Aḥmad; and festivities like this one can last for days," Omar al-Ṭabarī replied after swallowing a mouthful of the thick slices of bread spread with butter and filled with wild boar meat. "Life for the Vikings can be short in the harsh climate of the icy northlands and they do not need much encouraging in celebrating weddings, seed-sowing in the spring and so forth, and I learned from Magnus that Lady Ranveig is thrifty with their food, preserving it in their supply rooms unto the time is right."

Magnússon pulled back his chair and crumbs fell from his lap as he got up, Lady Ranveig gave him a sour look for leaving so earlier in the midst of men and women around other tables singing ribald songs and exchanging joking insults. Dogs under the planking barked and snapped at each other as they fought over the table scraps.

Further along the main table, Rollo drank ale and drummed the fingers of his free hand as he waited for fourths. Tove came up and put down the platters of food, grabbing handfuls of empty flat dishes and shot off again. Rollo cut of the head of the pickled fish with his knife and glanced at Hārūn's platter containing onions, leeks, peas, and cabbages.

Rollo learned over to him and the stink of the Viking's grubby clothes washed over Hārūn. "Have you tried the meat we sacrifice to show our allegiance to the Gods, lad?"

Hārūn wrinkled his nose and he was undecided over what smelt the worst: Rollo or the curdled milk he had refused earlier on in favour of water. "Is it more exotic meat like the potions of stringy moose and gristly polar bear I have already tasted?"

"Nay, my new friend, 'tis horseflesh," Rollo belched, as he removed some fish bones and threw them over his shoulder, "We place much value on the animal in life and the meat is eaten mostly as part of the feasting ceremonies."

Hārūn tried his best not to retch when shouted words drew the eyes of everyone to a quarrel that was within spitting distance of the large boiling cauldron and the fire pit, between two Norsemen standing face to face, an arm length apart "Pay up, Knut," Old Sven crackled his knuckles loudly. "You wagered on Gísli to win the wrestling bout, but he was defeated by Tyrker."

"I knows what I saw, Sven," the intoxicated guard said, the excessive amount of ale he had consumed was making him slur his words and bestow him with false courage. "Knut the Fierce does not need you to keep mimicking the words belike my pet raven. You are mistaken, I said the outcome was for mere diversion and not hacked silver."

"Falsehood, Knut," Old Sven said with a scowl. "I have witnesses."

"Aye," Yngvarr bellowed in agreement, a woman giggled as she sat on his lap and his hand slipped up her skirt. Listening to all this, Alvin and the couple stopped dancing, while a few men and women stood up and wandered over to watch the entertainment.

"I have called you several nicknames, Knut; but Fierce is not one of them and 'tis only after you have left the room," Old Sven said in growing irritation and clenched his fists. "But now I say them to your lying face, you are an unworthy mongrel that is backpedalling out of your obligation."

"A wager I made not to an addle-headed fence repairer like you, Sven," Knut replied insolently, the veins standing out on his neck were turning purple as he straightened his back and puffed out his scrawny chest. "Leave my sight," his voice turned shrill as he shoved Sven and gave him a withering look. "I am a guard of Fjordstad and that entitles me to some respect."

"Knut, the only respect I have for you is in the pig trough where it belongs," Old Sven growled in anger and he punched Knut in his flat face, breaking his nose. Blood flew through the air, splashing on Sven's tunic as the guard's head snapped back and he was send sprawling to the floor. Old Sven bore down on the woozy guard, picked him up and forced him over the cauldron before plunging Knut's head first into the boiling water.

The heat scorched Knut's fresh and he died instantly, the sudden shock to his system caused his heart to fail. Watching from the main table, Hārūn sheltered upbringing meant he was a lot more sensitive to the violence than those around him, and he looked away and vomited as Old Sven pulled the burnt ravaged head out the water and let the body drop onto the floor.

* * *

Magnússon left the Great Hall and strode two-thirds the way down the corridor towards a partially closed door, where incoherent grunts and shrieks were flittering through the gap from the supply chamber beyond. Slaves frowned as they glanced at the doorway in passing, but their current duties prevented them from stopping to investigate.

But Magnússon was not so encumbered. He halted outside

the doorway and to satisfy his curiosity, the Jarl peered into the side room to see a naked man and woman undergoing strenuous activity, their bodies glistening with sweat in the glowing lamplight. Marit's hourglass figure was bent over a large dairy vat partially set into the ground and at the same time Ulf was cupping her heavy breast in one hand and the fingers of the other curled tightly in her hair as he thrust his hips and rammed his manhood into her from behind.

Withdrawing his head, Magnússon grinned and closed the door quietly and then went on his way. A minute later he took a lighted candle from an alcove shelf and strode into the gloomy stofa. Not seeing his youngest daughter cuddling a kitten and the other slightly older children of the longhouse sleeping on the narrow benches around him, he thrust the candle to the fore, the shadows falling back before him until he came upon his sea chest, where the archer had deposited it in the broad space bisecting the chamber.

Wrenching open the lid, Magnússon found his war trophy and was in the process of lifting it out when torchlight shed more light into the chamber and Lady Ranveig's scolding voice rang out behind him.

"Barely back for a few hours in the bosom of your loving family, husband," her eyes flashing angrily as she briefly forgot where she was and who was in there, "and already your wandering eye has lead you here for a secret meeting with your lover."

"You are mistaken, wife," Magnússon sighed deeply, caught on the hop from the tension springing out of nowhere.

"Am I now?" Lady Ranveig put in; her husband's reassurance could not assuage her fears. "Your lips are working and I wager that is not the only thing too."

Magnússon turned slowly towards her, while keeping the beautiful relic-shrine box he held hidden by his body as he shifted it behind his back. "I am not meeting another woman."

"You callous swine, who is she?" Lady Ranveig demanded in agitation, not believing him at all. A few of the children were becoming disturbed and their breathing became less deep as they began to stir restlessly as the noise grew louder in the stofa. The kitten stopped purring and opened one eye. "Some ambitious slave girl I daresay that you smuggled into our longhouse eager to take my place. Why, Magnus, how could you! You said before you set sail to England that you would try to put you're womanising in the past."

"I have so far," Magnússon said. "I do not want you to divorce me, because I would have to give back the dowry payments to your late father's family."

"I desire the truth, but not that truth, husband," Lady Ranveig shook her head in exasperation. "You know I have given you the best years of my life and my womb hath bore you five children. This time you will find me slow to forgive..."

"And jealous and has quite a temper," Magnússon broke in with a smirk in the hope of taking the heat out of the situation and he calmly added. "Those are qualities that still attract my love for you, Ranveig."

It was Lady Ranveig's turn to blink in surprise at his comment and she was unsure how to reach when her daughter Sonja lifted her head and she uttered a sleepy enquiry, still cradling the yawning kitten.

"Is it morning yet, mother?"

"Nay, pumpkin, 'tis only your father annoying me again," Lady Ranveig grimaced in disgust, pressing a finger to her full lips to quiet her husband before gesturing with her hand at him to come, as she wheeled on her heel and headed for the door. "Go back to sleep."

"What are the children of the house in here, wife," Magnússon whispered, following her across the chamber.

"Are you trying to step into my shoes, husband? For you

know the inside of the longhouse is my domain, while the outside is yours. Just say the word if you want to swap roles with me, I shall be more than happy to let you look after the children and do the laundry, and I will drink and gallivant on the longship all day long."

"I was only asking a question, Ranveig," he growled low in his throat.

"Very well, husband; they are in the stofa, because it was quiet for them." She replied just as softly. "Sonja can not slumber in the Great Hall when it is filled with rowdy drunken Vikings, and the other children of servants and bondsmen can not clutter up the space in front of the oven if the kitchen is in use by the cooks and servants can they?"

"I suppose not," Magnússon said, his razor sharp mind was dulled somewhat by the amount of ale and mead he had drunk as he slipped out of chamber and into the corridor.

"Now let me ask you the same question, Magnus," Lady Ranveig rounding on him. "Why are you in my stofa? You hardly ever leave in the middle of the feast and the lavatory is in the opposite direction, which is the reason I became suspicious and followed you here."

"I went to fetch this gift and give it to you in front of everyone, wife," Magnússon brought the heavy wood and metal box into view. "I thought it would make a fine jewellery box and I have even carved a runic inscription on the bottom."

Lady Ranveig felt a tear welling in the eye as Magnússon grunted as he tilted up the trophy to show her what he had written. "It says: 'Ranveig owns this shrine.' but husband I don't see your name on it?"

"Ranveig, you are my woman," Magnússon said, righting the gift, "and you do not need my name to know it is from your lord and husband."

"Oh, Magnus, 'tis lovely, thank you," Lady Ranveig said with great happiness. She closed with him and stood on her tiptoes as her fingers caressed his bearded face and kissed him on the lips. "You will get much more of that later," she added, after pulling back and moving alongside him. "For now we should return to the feast, Omar will be wondering what has happened to us."

Magnússon nodded, and the pair walked back down the corridor toward the music and the light.

Chapter Ten
Shields and Spears

The people of Fjordstad were suffering the worst for wear when they awoke late the next morning after their first night of celebrations. Rising reluctantly from the warm furs covering their hard wooden sleeping benches, family members dressed quickly in the chill, moist air and while the women of the longhouses lit a fire to heat the chamber and dished out a breakfast of leftovers or bread and buttermilk, cheese or oatcakes, the men went to tend the livestock in the enclosures in the adjacent chamber.

Cattle and sheep were driven up to the upper pastures in the summer season to roam free and graze, but the movements of the milk cows, goat does and ewes were restricted from wandering too far off, because they had to be milked every day.

The dawn broke dull with a dark overcast settling over the valley. It began to drizzle steadily shorter thereafter accompanied by a mist that covered the landscape with a thin greyish veil, but eventually the showers stopped and the sun burned off the mist as the skies brightened and cleared by the early afternoon. The bad weather had not dampened the spirits of the excited population nor the vigour of the nervous competitors as they all raced through the marketplace and down to the fjord, where the swimming competitions were taking place.

"We call these sporting games of ours, the leikar, my friend," Magnússon said to Omar al-Ṭabarī and his two sons, pointing at the swimmers in the water, as they pushed their way through the assembled crowds to stand beside Lokar and Gunnar, halfway between the piers and the shipyard. "They are important events for the Norse people and come to pass during feasts or religious festivals, and can last for many days."

Aḥmad's dark eyes darted at the Viking spectators. "I do not see Lady Ranveig or Kari here, Jarl Magnússon?"

"You won't, Aḥmad," he replied, focusing his attention on the activities in the water. "They and some of the other women are visiting a remote spot in the forest where the stream flows from the mountains, bathing and prettying themselves up for the second feast tonight."

"Oooh, I can not wait for that," Hārūn said, feeling the unpleasant sensation of heartburn in his lower chest, caused by stress and the exorbitant consumption of food.

"You enjoy complaining don't you, Hārūn?" Lokar said.

"I find it one of my few pleasures in life," Hārūn replied and glanced askance at his father, the smile fading from the younger al-Ṭabarī face as Omar send him a silence message by shooting him a warning look. Hārūn knew his father was going to give him a stern talking too later on when they were finally alone.

"This water contest you see before you is one of my least favourites, but is a test of a true Viking's strength and endurance." Magnússon said, seemingly obvious to Hārūn's impertinent tone, before he addressed his son. "Who are the opponents' facing one another in this bout, Lokar?"

"That lickspittle of yours: Björn Strongarm and Uncle Rollo."

"Hmmm," Magnússon mused thoughtfully. "Rollo knows he can match Björn for speed any day, but in the water...."

"And what are the rules for this swimming sport, Magnus?" Omar asked as Magnússon's voice trailed off, watching the bare-chested Björn break the surface first and fill his lungs before Rollo finally emerged. Not allowing him time to take a breath, the bodyguard pounced, throwing his great bulk at Rollo and weighing him down beneath the cold water.

"One of the swimmers must hold down his adversary's head underwater longer than the other can." Magnússon said.

"Bah, please do not take this as an insult, Jarl Magnússon, but it should be called the drowning contest," Hārūn said with a shake of his head, "for this is no sport for me."

"None taken, Hārūn," Magnússon reassured him, "loss of life or injury is customary for Viking sport, but competitors know the risks and only have themselves to blame if they suffer harm."

Under the fjord, daylight filtering through the surface dimmed; receding steadily with distance as Björn kept hold of his opponent and kicked his legs to propel them deeper. At the present depth darkness encircled the pair and the cold soaked into their underpants with full-length legs. Black spots began filling Rollo's vision and the last of the air bubbles escaped from his nostrils, his lungs were screaming desperately for oxygen as his numbed hands reached up and tried to ferociously pry himself free, but he could not break away from the bodyguard's clutches.

Realising that the challenge was beyond him, Rollo's head was becoming fuzzy and his face was turning purple. He grimaced in pain and on the verge of losing consciousness; he stopped struggling and frantically tapped Björn on the forearm in submission. Björn smirked at the achieved victory, grabbed hold of Rollo's armpits and then the bodyguard's legs kicked out, simulating the movement of a swimming frog as he made headway against the current. The darkness dropped away beneath them and the sunlight brightened above them as a shadowy line of the shore not far away crept into view.

A few seconds later, the heads of the two Vikings burst through the surface of the water to the cheers and clapping from the spectators standing on the shore. The other swimmers converged on either side of Björn and Rollo, and helped them out of the fjord. Women came forward and offered them cloths to dry their bodies, Björn gasping, took his and rubbed his face and hair, while dripping wet, Rollo fell onto his knees, coughing and sputtering.

"And you believed we wouldn't find any amusement here, Hārūn," Aḥmad whispered to his brother.

"You are taking enjoyment from this, Aḥmad?" enquired Hārūn, arching a questioning eyebrow at him.

"I am not bored, little brother," replied Aḥmad with a grin.

"Come my friends," Magnússon beckoned the al-Ṭabarī family to follow. "Let me show you some more entrainment."

Lokar lingered for a second or two longer as Magnússon and the Arabs left the scene, taking a drying cloth from a woman and handing it to Rollo, who straightened up his torso.

"I failed you nephew," Rollo whispered, drying himself off. "Björn almost drowned me instead of the other way around. If he had known that we had actually planned for his accidental demise he never would have brought me back of the surface."

"Your idea to remove one of the threats to me had merit uncle, but let me do the thinking for both of us in the future, all right?" Lokar said just as loudly, glancing about him to see that none of the slaves were in earshot before he checked for Rollo's agreement and saw his uncle nod his head. "I am going to join Father's party. I like to keep my enemies close and our new eastern friends even closer."

✶ ✶ ✶

Many leagues away, inside the longhouse belonging to Jarl Sigvald Foeslayer, he peered into a sack and counted out silently as he listened to the words of his underling.

"For a replacement, Sigvald; hmmm…" the sharp-featured

man mused until Jarl Foeslayer handled the pouch full of gold ingots to him, "I suggest from what I heard upon the journey hither: a man they call Hansel. He was the villagers' respected lawgiver, they will listen to him."

"You heard the name, General Gudjóns," Sigvald said, casting a look over his board shoulder at the tall armoured soldier behind him. "Remove him from the cellar; I shall have words with the man presently."

"By your command, Jarl Foeslayer," General Gudjóns saluted crisply. "Be it the carrot or the stick, I will force Hansel's cooperation." He snapped his fingers at a young ruggedly handsome guard standing nearby, who was momentarily distracted by a buxom serving girl. "Now, Field Officer Hlod." The general added sharply, before striding off through a door leading off the wide corridor.

Hlod looked sheepish as he darted into another chamber and barked out an order to others within earshot. The underling tied the pouch's drawstring to his belt.

"So where did you gather this herd of outcasts from this time, Skarpheðinn?" Sigvald directed his eyes back at the thin man wearing a clutch of daggers sheathed to his leather belt.

"Sweden, they were migrating along one of the long patterned routes I know out of the Rhineland, heading away from the intolerance of Charlemagne's reign toward kin or tribes in the North still linked by the worship of the old religion. Small families had been taken in by the Swede's, but the rest of the group of exiles had been turned away by spear point, because the locals feared the heavy demands so many extra foreign mouths to feed would create food shortages that could result in bloodshed between the clans. As you can tell the remaining Saxon's did not need any convincing to follow me once I spun my heart warming tale and they gave me most of their livestock in payment. With these people and the numbers of Frisian I brought you, your army must be growing apace, Sigvald?"

"Skarpheðinn, my curious little dogsbody," Sigvald said menacingly, his face darkening as he grabbed the hilt of one of Skarpheðinn's belt daggers, whipping the blade out and upending it until the tip was under the forty-year's old sagging chin, "I am finding your grating voice irritating me far more today than usual. You have been well paid and all you need to know is that everything is going according to plan." Sigvald felt the ground quiver and heard the tumult in the air as he glanced at the activity passing them by. "Is that understood?"

"Aye," Skarpheðinn uttered with sweat beginning to bead his brow.

"Rest up ere you set forth upon your next journey," Sigvald said, thrusting the dagger back into the sheath. "For now I must be away elsewhere."

Sigvald turned and receded down the corridor.

The flying feet of a score of servants carried them into the gloomy audience hall and the flickering yellow radiance of the candles they held illuminated their expressionless faces as they crossed over to the torches in the wall sconces and set them ablaze. Corners were festooned with grey cobwebs and long, narrow threads dangled down like banners. Guards stomping two abreast behind them encroached on the shifting, diluting shadows, their formation breaking apart under the diffused light shining through the smoke holes overhead, all but one of the swordsmen interspersed to take guarding positions between the torches.

The other, a sullen-eyed, young man with his ginger-tousled head bare of a helmet, ascended the three steps of the dais and sat down on an ornate wooden chair, the seat and the arms rests were carved in the design of scales decorating the long, coiling body of a snake. The back support formed the serpent's ribbed neck and the wedged-shaped head complete with glistering fangs was poised in the air and served as the throne's canopy.

Four of the departing slaves paused briefly in the corners to clamber up narrow ladders and seize the edges of animal membranes before pulling the coverings loose to expose small holes where the roof met the wall; the timber frames were moist and discoloured by brown fungal rot. Beams of sunshine slanted in to touch the iron ring embedded into the centre of the stone floor. The strapping, occupant of the throne clapped his hands and barked in a bellicose tone.

"General Gudjóns, bring that scrag end to me, now."

* * *

Across the North Sea in England, in one of the turrets projecting from the corner of Bamburgh Castle, the Northumbria king groaned in strong emotion as he reacted to the letter in his scared hand.

"Oh, woe is me," Aethelred said, the gold embroidery sleeve of his calf-length linen tunic dropped onto the wooden armrest of his carved chair at the head of the Council table before him, and he looked up, his eyes pale and hard. "Will this misery never end?"

Sitting at the King's left the grizzled, ruddy-faced counsellor and scribe laid down the quill beside the inkwell and the scroll he had been writing down a new Northumberland law, and stood up. "What ails you, my Liege? Is it the same malady that forced the queen to be indisposed from Court this morn," he asked in concern, taking in the king's striking features as his long legs carried him around the table towards him. "I noticed you didn't eat your entire roast hedgehog at the mid-day meal. Shall I summon ye a leech?"

"Nay, wise, Wigmund; I am hale and hearty this fine afternoon, I just like my belt notch to stay where it is, that's all,"

Aethelred raised a reassuring hand, palm out to calm the easily excitable man as he came to halt before him. Warm summer sunshine streamed through the long, vertical, archer notches set at various intervals along the circular length of bare stone wall. "Sit, counsellor," he gestured at the empty chair alongside his own. "You know how I loathe looking up at anyone standing over me; it gives me a crick in my neck."

"A thousand pardons Sire," Wigmund said, pulling out the chair and sat down. "Please continue."

"I have received news that weighs heavier than the gold crown upon my wrinkled brow. It seems the attack on the Lindisfarne monastery has even reached the ears of those at Charlemagne's Court in Rome, for this parchment comes from the monk Alcuin."

"'Tis like the ripples I created as a boy when I dropped stones into the lake, they spread across the surface of the water until reaching distant shores," Wigmund nodded thoughtfully. "I have heard of this monk, Alcuin is a poet, educator, and cleric, and studied at York under Archbishop Egbert and since then he has become Charlemagne's chief theological adviser as well as educating the King's children."

Aethelred grimaced to register his disgust, his bubbling anger causing his tone to be sharper than he intended when he spoke. "Well, I care little of the esteem he enjoys at the Court of the Frankish Empire; Alcuin will be swinging from a gallows tree alongside the Viking chieftain Magnus Magnússon if he ever comes back to England, on this I vow upon my father's sceptre."

Wigmund lifted his shaggy eyebrows almost to his receding hairline. "May I be so bold as to ask why, Sire?"

Aethelred leaned forward and proffered him the curling up scroll. Wigmund took it, spread it open and began reading the Latin writing for himself. "He begins by communicating his horror and anguish at the raid," he summarized the contents of the letter in his own words, "and the slaughtering of the monks, including that of his friend Biutta whom he has often exchanged letters with, and yet his fury is actually aimed at you, sire and his own people the Anglo-Saxons nobility instead of at the soulless heathens. Alcuin condemns us for seasons of wicked deeds and says we be worthy of the fate, because it is the Almighty's chastisement."

"You can see why the monk angers me so, Wigmund," Aethelred said, his hollowed cheeks flushing dark with ire. "He sets the wrath of God upon my kingdom now, as if I don't have plenty of erstwhile enemies already."

Wigmund shook his head and glanced up, saying in a gentle voice in an attempt to smooth the friction that had arisen. "You know I am more right than wrong, so heed me when I say they are just the prattling words of a spineless madman that it is said comes from noble English stock," Aethelred raised his eyebrows at that warning, "a saddened old monk that has allowed his grief to impair his judgement. Pay them no mind, Milord."

"Are you saying this monk could be related to one of my Barons? The same nobles who are attempting to restrict my power and build up their own in governing my land."

Wigmund bowed in acknowledgement. "Anything is possible, sire, but if I was you I would refrain from making one of your snap decisions unto you have had ample time to ponder on this, for in the event the monk doth return to England and he somehow dies by your command, you may not be given further assistance from Charlemagne."

Aethelred took a calming breath and nodded his gratitude, as he seemed to accept the sense in the counsellor's words. "Insightful as ever, Wigmund; and now I have had an opportunity to understand I am of similar opinion." He started drumming his fingers restlessly on the armrest. "Let us turn our attentions to the fresh threat of the Viking raiders. It's a boil that has to be lanced otherwise my kingship of Northumbria will last nay longer than my first stint."

Wigmund inclined his head slightly. "Indeed, Sire. Diplomacy is not a choice we have with them. The crux of the Viking problem is where this Magnus Magnússon and his warriors will come ashore is as baffling to us as trying to predict the weather outside. Following your order I have send word for piles of wood to be set up upon hilltops in different places for the greatest possible visibility. Should the pagan's raid at night soldiers on watch duty will ignite the beacon fires and if their longships come in the day smoke signals will alert our ships and your patrolling horsemen of the raiders' general whereabouts."

"The early snows and high winds of the colder seasons ought to prevent the Vikings from venturing seaward to raid after that," Aethelred said, clenching his remaining teeth in frustration. "I like not having some of my soldiers spread far and wide upon duties that take them away from guarding the granaries and the king's road for bandits."

Wigmund cleared his throat. "You will not like what I have to speak of next, sire."

"Proceed my friend," Aethelred said, "long have I known you and our rapport is strong. A lesser aristocrat from a dying house, you may be," Wigmund blinked at that comment and knew the king referred to the two daughters he had, but not a son to carry on the family name. "And yet a toady you are not belike some of the Thanes in my court that uses their position to fawn and flatter me, and agree with everything I say."

"In these private Counsel Sessions where you and I talk freely away from your other ministers and the leaders of your fighting forces, I act as your counsellor and scribe, but it is in my proper role as your Chancellor that I must advise you sire that the beacons will also empty the royal coffers of coin." Aethelred frowned, but did not interrupt Wigmund from continuing. "The men can not be expected to live and sleep in pitched tents, something more permanent has to be constructed up there, shacks for the guards, stables for their horses and sheepfolds and storage areas for although their occupancy is only for the whole of the summer months, you might have to send the soldiers back on the hilltops next year."

"You want me to raise taxes?"

"Indeed. The plans have been drawn up, subject to your final approval, sire."

"I approve, alas it won't make me very popular with either the poor or the barons..."

"Or the church, sire."

"It was the council of lords and the prelates that overthrown my father and had him tonsured, and it seems I may have that to look forward in my future too," Aethelred shook his head and his subdued manner became more despondent and bitter as he spoke. "If I had known the enormity of what I have been through these past few years I would have stayed in exile. When I was a boy I always wanted to sit in my father's throne, but I was unaware of the burdens of kingship and I was not ready to hear certain people whisper that I was a man of straw or that I was "Æthelwald Moll's son". Call it stubbornness or my injured pride if you like, Wigmund," he stared at the chancellor's deceptively passive face, "Since then I have attempted to bury the past along with those who criticised me. Whereas I was once adrift I am now living life with a strength of purpose; my soldiers were gaining confidence in me unto the Vikings came and I can ill afford to look weak or for the barons and my neighbouring monarchs to sense my hesitancy, my grip on the throne is tenuous at best and is only as strong as my sword arm."

Wigmund shrugged his rounded shoulders and his mood grew sombre. "'Tis true that this realm has faced harsh times of late, what with ealdorman Eardwulf surviving the unsuccessful assassination attempt by your soldiers to say naught of your arrogant sons Aeif and Aelfwine plotting deadly intrigues and the challenge of your predecessor Osred to regain the Northumberland throne--" he stated heavily, the images of their faces flashing into his mind.

"Hells teeth, you have a true knack for understatement," Aethelred signed and gestured at the archery slot. "I have more enemies than grains of sand upon yonder beach."

Wigmund resumed after the interruption. "Be that as it may, your sons and Osred did not beget our ruin as the soothsayer predicted; you also did not falter in your judgement when you had all three put to death."

"But not Eardwulf," Aethelred protested.

"In due time you shall and remember sire, you have done your best to reconcile the land claims of our neighbours and the demands of the kingdom."

"Thus far," Aethelred put in.

Wigmund inclined his head in acknowledgement. "You can claim furthermore that you have steadfast allies, the royal house Deiran robustly supports you by reason you are a descendant of Ælle, and your arranged marriage to queen Aelfflaed has forged another alliance with King Offa of Mercia."

"Politics, bah, I did my duty for Northumbria, alas I resign myself to a marriage without love," Aethelred stiffened; the counsellor's comment had done little to dispel his anxieties and nothing at all to lift his spirits. He pursed his narrow lips before speaking forlornly. "To be blunt, Wigmund; Offa's daughter is a hand-me-down harridan that if I had a choice in the matter I would not have touched with a barge pole. She has her mother's stare, has a spiritless personality and passion in the bed chamber is akin to a dead fish. I told her so in no certain terms yesternight and that is the very reason that Aelfflaed is absence from Court.

I am not in the least bothered by her sulky silence though, for she is not much of a conversationalist either."

Wigmund gasped at the king's admission and said the first thing that came into his head. "An uncommon trait in a woman, if only I was so blessed I may have won more arguments."

"Wigmund, you have a wife's companionship and devotion, while I in contrast have neither, in fact the queen spends more time visiting with that simpleton astrologer in his chamber than me. Aelfflaed herself is merely one of a sea of faces surrounding me, but I still find myself alone with my thoughts."

Wigmund was trying to come up with a response to that when there was a knock on the door at the opposite end of the Counsel chamber. It swung open to admit a slender, bandy-legged soldier, brushing road dust from his cloak and his flexible pieces of black armour with his leather riding gloves. The king and the Chancellor fell silent and they glanced at the beardless soldier with interest as he proceeded further into the turret.

"Lo, Captain Cerdic is here, sire," Wigmund said before addressing the soldier.

"Speak, man, how goeth the investigation?"

Cerdic came to a halt before the table and tucked his gloves behind his sword belt before removing a drawstring pouch and open it. "We captured the man called Rolf the skald a few leagues within the land of the Picts and he fits the description the surviving monks gave us. The Viking wore a cross openly upon his person belike many a foreign merchant I have seen and he swore he had converged to Christianity, but searching him for hidden weapons my men found a pagan necklace. Rolf says it gave him added protection."

"Lies," Wigmund said, as Cerdic emptied the contents of the pouch onto the tabletop near the King's family coat of arms carved into the wood. "The skald has loyalty for his old Gods still."

Cerdic nodded in agreement. "We seized a basket of carrier pigeons from the back of the wain the Carter was driving and there were heathen markings on the pieces of paper I could not read," Aethelred leaned over and picked up the Thor's hammer necklace, turning it over to study the workmanship on both sides of it. "But I deem them to be messages about to be sent to his savage brethren."

"Good work Cerdic! On the authority of King Aethelred take this Rolf to the deepest dungeon in the keep," Wigmund said. "We have soon torture the truth out from him."

✶ ✶ ✶

Under the longhouse of Jarl Sigvald Foeslayer, Saxons of all ages and genders shivered as they got up hesitantly and crowded around the cell door, as they heard the distant voices and the sound of approaching footsteps echoing off the stone floor of the torch lit corridor.

General Gudjóns strode along with two guards armed with spears as they past the rows of walled rooms storing casks of ale and meat. The glow from passing torches cast their faces in reddish streaks and often between the brackets were pegs holding chains and a collection of different shackles.

Coming up to the largest cell where the prisoners were being held, General Gudjóns called a halt, and one of the guards passed the motionless Gudjóns to draw back a set of rusty iron bolts and push the cell door ponderously open. The Saxons surged forward in the hope of being freed, stretching their hands out, but General Gudjóns drew his sword and stepped forward, filling the cell doorway. The first guard transferred his weapon to his dominated hand and levelled the shaft, mirroring the manoeuvre of the second guard jabbing his spearhead between the bars, as the prisoners skidded to an abrupt halt.

"Back," the second soldier snarled. "Get back I say."

"Release us," a woman pleaded, cradling her young child in her goose-pimply arms.

"Not yet wench," General Gudjóns growled, feeling the cold cling to his armour and the bare skin of his face and hands.

"Then give us additional coverings to warm us against the chill," a youngish man said, retreating a further step back as the reach of the spears extended.

"You will all share in the vicissitudes of bettering fortune for your children after Hansel the Saxon steps forward," General Gudjóns said, sheathing his blade and moving out of the doorway.

There was startled mutterings and the people's dirty, drawn faces glanced apprehensively around until a stocky man of average height detached from the crowd. The second guard handed his spear to his comrade before turning and taking down the chains and shackles from the nearest wall peg.

"I am Hansel the Saxon."

General Gudjóns nodded. "You are to come with me."

"But what do you mean by unexpected changes in our fortunes," Hansel emerged out of the cell and the guard began fastening the irons onto him. There was the clang of metal sounding behind them as the first guard closed the door and slid the bolts into their sockets, locking the door again.

"You will see," General Gudjóns said, taking Hansel along the corridor. The two guards turned and marched back to whence they came.

"It is Helmut that you want to speak too, not me, soldier," Hansel said anxiously to the grey-whiskered general, who tugged at the length of chain leashed to the rusty shackle encircling the neck of the speaking man. Another set of manacles had been fastened around his wrists and was joined by a thick chain to restrain his hands, but his legs were left unhindered, allowing him to walk normally. "He wears the torc of leadership about his neck," his breathing was becoming shallow, "I am unimportant."

"Soldier," General Gudjóns scrunched up his bulldog face at the insult and showing his disdain for the prisoner glanced back at him. "I am General Gudjóns and you're chieftain died from the wounds he received after my archers and spearman waylaid your people at the border." The tall general shifted his gaze forward and led the prisoner up a short flight of stone steps covered with patches of moss and then through a doorway, a rush of warm light washed over him. "So Jarl Foeslayer is stuck with you, Saxon."

"I am a lawgiver by trade," the prisoner said with a slight whistle through the gap in his teeth as they emerged into the large audience hall.

General Gudjóns made a contemptuous noise. "Your father must be proud."

"Not really, he wanted me to become a common soldier like you," Hansel said, there was a slight trembling in his hands and he felt the beginning of panic taking root, as his dark sunken eyes frantically looked around the chamber, taking in the blazing torches at various intervals casing a reddened glow upon the conical helmets of riveted iron belonging to the soldiers armed with shields and spears lining the walls of logs - laid one upon the another with the spaces in between filled with mud, moss and dried animal dung. A log fire burned in a raised stone hearth in the centre of the chamber and the scent of the wood filled the air. Here and there enormous elk antlers decorated blackened beams and shield-sized wood carvings, rimmed with bark, depicted families of Viking men and women. "Skarpheðinn the hunter and livestock trader whose knowledge my people were dependant upon, guided us here, but I swear by all the Gods above that we would not have wandered so far on this perilous journey had Skarpheðinn not boasted of Virgin timberland up North rich with game and streams that had scarcely been explored by man."

"Ha," General Gudjóns laughed, enjoying the tale. "It seems this Skarpheðinn the weaver of lies fleeced you good, Saxon. The Snake Tribe has lived on this land since Odin breathed into Askr and Embla, the first Norseman and woman and gave them life."

Hansel nodded thoughtfully. "Helmut's first thought was your soldiers were robbers after the last few possessions we still owned and that is the reason why we fought you so fiercely." Pieces of straw dropped off his long dishevelled hair and the dirt stained sleeves and the back of his tunic from the bedding in the dungeon

"Speak of this now to my lord and master, for he is a man who likes a captive audience," General Gudjóns said, finally bringing Hansel to a halt and forcing him to kneel as the middle aged soldier fastened the neck chain to the iron ring embedded into the floor. "The prisoner named Hansel, Jarl Foeslayer."

"Greeting Hansel; welcome to the village of Trøllheim, as General Gudjóns has already mentioned I am Jarl Sigvald Foeslayer," he said and steepled his fingers together as he spoke the Saxon tongue as if it was a second language. "You may have heard of me."

"Nay," Hansel said with a shake of his head, staring at the long ginger beard hiding the lower half of Sigvald's face. "Not until five minute ago."

"Pfft," Sigvald muttered something under his breath. "You breathe now only by my grace. You are in my presence; because I can offer you an answer to your dilemma, but the decision you make will determine the fate of all your people."

"I care not for decision?" Hansel sounded incredulous, as his temper shortened somewhat. "Why have you kept me and my people captive for so long?"

"Because trespasser," there was an unmistakable edge in Sigvald's voice, "your warrior band entered my homeland in great number threatening the families and farmsteads belonging to my Norsemen."

"We are merely exiles not a warrior band, driven from the land of our birth by Frankish soldier who burned our sacred tree groves and destroyed the statues of our gods for not embracing Christianity. We came to your territory in peace in search of a safe place to take shelter and start a new life, but even here in the North we have faced fear and prejudice, while the understanding and the friendship we envisioned from the Swedish clans was not wholly forthcoming as we had hoped. One third of my tribe are made up of women and children," Hansel emphasized their importance as he pressed his point, "and aye, we were armed lightly, but only to defend themselves. You're general did not find buckler or flanged helmet or a soldier's coat of mail among us, did he?"

"You could easily have buried those things before you crossed the border to scout my land and then returned for them later," Sigvald shrugged.

"Nonsense," Hansel shook his head again and could taste something acidic in his throat. "Cunning my people are not."

"Viking men and women are taught as children in the ways of the warrior, and once upon a time I heard that the Saxon race was sword-wielding seafarers like my own Norse people are now. I wager Hansel that your people still cling to those ingrained habits of old and time has not weakened the steel in your veins so much that it prevents you from resolving a dispute between your neighbours, bloodily if need be."

"All of what you say is true, but for the most part the traditions of our forefathers have long been abandoned by my tribe," Hansel said. "We practice a pastoral way of life, content to be farmers, metal smiths, musicians and some of us are versed in the health and husbandry of herd animals."

"Well, those trades will be of use, alas for now I am in obvious and urgent need for warriors," Sigvald said, leaning forward. "There is a threat to my people brewing across the border from a rival Viking nobleman called Magnus Magnússon. I know not what devilry he is concocting in his machinations, but there is a shortage of fertile land in the north and I fear an imminent invasion of my territory. My enemy has already taken control of two villages on the shores of the fjords, Lillesund and Skálholt and my homeland could be next. My army doth not have the numbers to resist him unless your men and women were to join my army and fight for me alongside some Frisian allies."

"What motivation could you offer us that would make us risk our lives, Jarl Foeslayer?" Hansel asked.

"You will be enslaved if my enemy wins, but if my army achieves victory in the battle to come, then you shall have my blessings to settle on the land of Magnus Magnússon."

A wave of shock washed over Hansel as he tried to absorb this news. "Land?"

"Aye, 'tis not all thin soil and stony fields, certain crops can be grown well in the north. My priest told me that Trøllheim began life as a fishing village as many other settlements did; the waters of the fjord and the river hereabouts are rich in fish."

"What about freedom, Jarl Foeslayer?"

"Freedom too can be yours, but 'tis on the understanding your people keep fighting for me in future battles. I will include dwellings in the town of Fjordstad," Sigvald nodded. "What say you, Hansel?"

Hansel pursed his lips thoughtfully. "You're argument has persuaded me. I shall speak of this to my people, but I think it safe to assume I can convince them in doing as you ask. You have your warriors, Jarl Foeslayer."

"Aye," Sigvald grinned broadly. "I believe I do."

* * *

The remainder of the hours of daylight passed swiftly for Magnus Magnússon and his small party as they went about the outskirts of Fjordstad barely noticed by the preoccupied spectators watching the activities arranged at different times throughout the afternoon and into the evening. There was an archery competition in which bowmen and women followed a an uneven course through the forest shooting arrows at wooden and straw targets of assorted size and positioned at varying distances.

Healfdene won by hitting most of the targets and Ellisiv came a close second.

"It is a good idea of yours Jarl Magnússon to use the woods in an attempt to resemble hunting conditions," Aḥmad said with a favourable nod. "Do all your women hunt game?"

"The men of the town do the hunting and fishing, but like my father and his father before him," Magnússon glanced back over his shoulder as he walked alongside spectators going to the next sporting event, "I encourage women to practice the bow and the sword for defence and self-reliance."

It took the spectators awhile to work their way back through the forest to a grassy ridge where they gathered again to provided them with a view of the plain below, but they did not have long to wait for the single bout of horse fighting to begin. Beyond the animals stood a dozen or more Norsemen being picked by team captains, in the midst of weather eroded arches and tapering chunks of rock that looked like the broken ribs of a long dead giant.

"Omar, my friend, we call the fells hereabouts the Hestathing," Magnússon pointed at the treeless hillsides about him and Aḥmad and Hārūn frowned at the unknown Norse words.

"The horse meeting," Omar al-Ṭabarī translated for his sons, as the two stallions circled one another, prodded by their owner's sharpened sticks and stirred up and urged on to complete as rivals by the sight and scent of oestrous mares, their hobbled legs were fastened together with rope to prevent them straying from the odd tree. "And what of the plain itself?"

"Hestavig or horse right," Lokar said, halting beside his father as he finally caught up.

The brown and white stallions clashed, banging their heads together as they neck fought and bit, piercing fresh with gripping teeth, the neighing was high and sharp, punctuating the cheering of the town's people watching the contest. The owners shouted commands, pushing at the horses rumps or hanging on to their tails in an attempt to prevent them from going on the run as the lathering and bloodied beasts torn with the goading and overwhelmed by their own instincts, rushed to meet again, rearing up on their hind legs and kicking out simultaneously.

Hārūn turned away when the hooves of the brown stallion connected with a resounding clack, crunching through bone and the impact send the white horse hurtling to the ground with its head caved in and its right eye hanging out. The audience found it difficult to contain their enjoyment, laughter and applauses broke out. Lokar slapped Hārūn on the back and gave Aḥmad a feral grin. Children jumped up and down in great excitement.

"How do you like our Viking pastimes thus far, Hārūn?" Lokar asked enthusiastically, his eyes crinkling up with mischief.

"Some better than others," Hārūn replied after compositing himself, the ire the spectacle had aroused within him was buried down deep.

"I have seen one such horse fight in the wild," Omar al-Ṭabarī said guardedly, interiorly shaking his head at the waste of horseflesh and noticed some of the Norsemen and a few of his own Arab sailors around him had been wagering on the outcome of the contest, for the grumbling losers were forfeiting coin or pieces of hacked silver to the grinning winners, "the defeated animal did not die though, it just fled."

"Come!" Magnússon beckoned to his small party, setting off down the hillside towards the plain as he followed the younger forerunners of the crowd speeding up to the next event. "We are off to view a game of knattleikr."

"Jarl Magnússon, "Hārūn frowned in confusion as he recalled a conversation he had had. "Rollo roughly spoke yesternight about horses being highly prized in your society and I find it strange and I was curious as to why you permit your animals to be treated in that brutal way if they mean that much to your people?"

Magnússon nodded in understanding. "Horse fighting is a popular entertainment and generously contributes to the fertility rites in this land, the beasts are breed for their strength of spirit and their blood soaks into the ground as an offering to the Gods to make certain there will be good crops for the harvest. It is also a sign of prestige for the victorious owner should his horse best all the rivals and become a champion we call a skeidfol."

The spectators swarmed forward across the plain in a kind of frenzied excitement and after about a hundred yards or so, they pulled up alongside a long row of stones that marked one of the boundaries of the large rectangular playing field. The two contending teams stood tensely facing each other in uneven lines, burley bare-chested men wielding bats tried to intimate their slimmer and wiry opponents who were equally armed, but clothed in poorer brown tunics and trousers.

"You are in for a treat, Omar," Lokar said, as he and Magnússon joisted their way through to the front of the crowd. "The game of knattleikr is usually held in tournaments during the winter months, attracting families from farms and other settlements within the region like metal to a lodestone. But since you won't be here to witness it then father has brought it forward to entertain you and your sons now. 'Tis said a game in the time of my grandfather: Magnus Jokinen lasted the entire day until the mead ran out."

"How do the players win this game, Lokar?" Aḥmad asked, crossing his arms, as Aikku the healer, the wife of Roald the town guard, recognized old friends in the crowd with a smile and a wave.

"By carrying, hitting or kicking the ball and dropping it into the scoring hole," Lokar pointed first in one direction at a long, shallow trench-like cut in the ground and then at the second hole behind the bare-chested team, "There and there."

Magnússon halted beside Gunnar. "Are Lars and Siegfried playing today, shipwright?"

"Aye, they be in the team of brown tunics along with Einar, Bork, Olaf and Ragnar the woodcutter," Gunnar said with a nod, his eyes immediately was drawn to the tunic-less side as their captain started the game by tossing the hard wooden ball to his counterpart on the opposition. "The other side, the skins include Njáll Bloodhammer, Egil and Aunund of the Mill, Finn, Leif the woodcutter, and Ásgrímr."

"I remember being Lokar's age and wearing furs against the freezing wind, playing on the slippery ice of a frozen pond and I miss the rough and tumble of the competition," Magnússon said regretfully, his eyes momentarily going distant as he got nostalgic. "Now my aching bones would not withstand the punishment."

"Aye," Gunnar nodded in agreement. "I often think the wisdom of a greybeard is a poor substitute for youth and vigour."

The rangy Bork the Dauntless rushed forward and swung his bat with a powerful arm, walloping the ball in mid-air and returning it. Instead of hitting it back, Ásgrímr choose to let the heavy ball bounce on the ground in front of him in a bid to slow it down before he caught it and ran with it for a few yards down the field. Seeing Lars and Siegfried converged upon him in a double team, Ásgrímr quickly handed the ball to Finn, who passed it to Egil.

"Gunnar's whelps," Ásgrímr shouted, hoping to catch Lars and Siegfried's attention and take it away from what was happening in the game as he charged at the brothers, who were beginning to veer from Ásgrímr to chase after the new runner.

"Whelps?" Siegfried echoed in outrage, slowing slightly.

"Aye, that's all you two are," Ásgrímr grinned and obstructed Siegfried by body-checking him to the ground before turning to face Lars as he came at him. "Boys with milk in their veins instead of fire; who scrape off a man's beard and hair like a weak willed foreigner."

"Would a weak willed foreigner do this," Lars struck at the laughing Ásgrímr with his bat, but Ásgrímr avoided the blow and then kneed Lars in the groin.

"On the sideline, Magnússon elbowed Gunnar in the ribs. "That was a good distraction tactic from Ásgrímr. It has given his team an advantage."

At the same time the skins team continued to pass the ball from player to player as they headed closer to the brown tunics scoring trench. Einar tackled Egil, but not before he kicked it to Njáll Bloodhammer, who muscled past Olaf and finally threw the ball into the hole to gain the first point for his side.

Over the next two hours, play was thrilling for the spectators and physically energetic for the dwindling members of each team; the only rest they had was after the ball was dropped into the scoring trench or if it went out of bounds. Ásgrímr tripped up Bork and sent Olaf sprawling when he hit the ball at him, causing a blood injury to his arm. Aunund of the Mill received a blow to the head that knocked him unconscious. Lars and Siegfried cut and bruised left the field, having not the animal vitality of the older players.

Disputes leading to disorderly fights began abruptly between Einar and Ragnar the woodcutter against Finn and Njáll Bloodhammer, punches were exchanged over a high tackle or simply being held, but warriors in the crowd judged them to be minor scraps that would not result in serious harm so there was not a need to break them up. Aikku the healer applied balms and wrapped bandages about a player's head, while Hārūn studied her intently.

It was coming up to the deepening shadows of evening and Ásgrímr was carrying the ball, running at full pelt when an armed Olaf burst on the field just in front of him and with a single swipe, drove his axe through Ásgrímr's forehead. Ásgrímr collapsed lifelessly to the ground and Olaf pulled out his weapon stained with traces of blood and brains.

"That's for my brother and for all you did to me, bilge-snipe," Olaf's lower lip quivered as he kicked the body and the ball dropped from Ásgrímr's hand.

"I have killed men for much less, but I always had the foresight to pick a quieter spot to do the deed." Lokar said to Omar al-Ṭabarī from the sideline, as shouts of outrage and curses came from some of Ásgrímr's closest family members and hands went for sword hilts. Olaf glanced about with hesitancy as if pondering whether he should flee or make a stand, his face grew grim and he flourished the battle axe after coming to a decision.

In the crowd, people began making wagers on how many minutes Olaf could survive against five swordsmen and how many of the foes he could cut down before falling himself.

"I say one and one," speculated Yngvarr.

Rollo barged his way up to the betting and said, "Olaf will last one minute and slay two of Ásgrímr's kin."

Before any of the swordsmen could advance on Olaf to

attack him, Ragnar the woodcutter raced back to intercept the ball, scooped it up and then dashed from whence he came along the playing field and recklessly knocked over the exhausted Njáll Bloodhammer. Behind him, Olaf retreated and was quickly joined by his cousins and friends, including enemies of Ásgrímr, causing a standoff.

Ahead of them, Finn chased after the woodcutter deep into the skins half, but could not prevent Ragnar from diving into the trench and scoring another point. The crowd cheered and Finn threw down his bat in temper, and sank onto his knees, that final adrenaline surge had sapped his strength. Ragnar clambered out of the hole and stood up. Magnússon stepped out onto the playing field and held up his hand for silence, and the spectators looked in his direction and gradually quieted down to hear him speak.

"Ragnar the woodcutter is the last man standing; I decree the brown tunics are the victorious team of knattleikr this day."

The crowd roared their approval and rushed forward, grasping Ragnar's legs and hoisting him up on their shoulders in celebration, as they walked and talked, reliving their favourite memories of the day's action and eagerly looked forward to the events on the morrow. Ásgrímr's kin withdrew, dragging the body with them, before latching onto the side of the crowd, planning their revenge as they cast murderous glances back at Olaf surrounded by his supporters as they brought up the rear.

"What now, Magnus?" asked Omar al-Ṭabarī, "Is it back to the Great Hall for the evening feast."

"In due time, my old friend," Magnússon nodded. "First though I thought we would stop off at the barn and show you the prisoners."

* * *

The evening sky was awash with stars by the time Magnússon and his small party sat down at the feasting tables in the Great Hall. Brunhild glared at Gunnar and his sons talking and eating across the way and she shook her head before speaking to her husband.

"Why is Lars Gunnarson still alive, Bjorn? How can you endure the fact that he gave me unwelcome attention while you were gone? Now, tell me when are you deciding to kill him, next week, next year, what is the delay?"

Bjorn Strongarm groaned and lowered his drinking cup. "I was hoping I did not have to do it, that you would perchance change your mind…"

"Never," Brunhild spat, irritation reflecting in her eyes as she brushed absently at a loose curl escaped from her headdress and studied his bearded face.

"Or Lars might die on the knattleikr playing field; alas the gods have not meant it to be." Trouble lines etched deeper into Bjorn's forehead and around his mouth. "I like the shipwright, he is a friend of sorts, many a drinking match we have had together and I even admire Lars' brother, for he showed courage onboard the longship, almost fought Rollo over an insult and I mutely agreed he had the right but not the skill to carry it out. On the morrow I shall have to slay all three of them, because Gunner won't let Lars face me alone in a battle, he and Siegfried will be pitted against me too."

Brunhild and Bjorn regarded one another then, measuring what each saw in the others eyes before pondering what it meant for the both of them.

Opposite them, on another table, Omar al-Ṭabarī was telling a tale of his homeland about a thief, who spirited treasure and the princess out of the bloated sultan's palace on a flying carpet to the exclamations of surprise and amazement from his audience.

"And the thief shouted to the guards you have been robbed by the greatest thief ever."

"What happened next, Omar?" Lokar asked eagerly, engrossed in the tale.

"It is the Arabian custom of finishing the tale off another night, my young friend," Omar grinned, leaving the ending teasingly unresolved. "You will have to wait until then."

Rollo leaned over to speak to Magnússon.

"Magnus, I have met with some of Ásgrímr's kin and they urged me to speak to you on their behalf about his death."

"And what did they say, Rollo? That is if I can not guess."

"They want you to declare Olaf outside the law for what he did."

"So they can seek out my..." Magnússon hesitated, remembering who he was talking too before resuming, "man like prey and kill him, I think not." Rollo frowned thoughtfully. "Olaf will be fined half the plunder he seized at Lindisfarne and bestow it to Ásgrímr's kin in recompense. My word is Law, that is my decision on the matter, let us speak of it nay more."

Not far along the main table, Hārūn, Aḥmad and most of their Arab shipmates throughout the chamber had tried not to frown or gawp at the sudden change in the outward appearance of Lady Ranveig, Brunhild, Ingrid and Kari to name but a few along with some of the warriors. Aḥmad leaned over to speak to it to his father.

"Father, I have noticed that the women's hair braids and the Vikings beards have turned blonde, how can this be?"

"Yes my son, the Vikings use a soap, which I have been told has the properties to bleach all the hair growing on the head and can kill lice too. It is a style that is currently very popular with both men and women."

Tove and two younger male slaves of mixed racial parentage came up to the main table and set down wooden stands holding a number of ceremonial drinking horns decorated in a similar way with silver tips and rims. In their midst were two horns that were made from solid silver. The servants departed to the kitchen, as Magnússon picked up the heavier vessels from the stands and handed one to his friend.

"'Tis only water inside yours, Omar," Magnússon said, raising the vessel and the merchant nodded his thanks and did likewise with his own horn. Norseman and women, and Arabs sailors followed suit. "To drink a special toast I would generally use a wassail bowl, but these horns were gifts and I thought it most fitting to honour you with them." Their horns clinked together. "Be well, and in good health."

Omar al-Ṭabarī gulped down the water and then examined the silver horn. "Gifts you say, it takes a skilled craftsman to produce something of this quality."

Magnússon wiped his mouth the back of his hand and replaced the empty horn on its stand and different servants approached the table and filled the ceremonial vessels for the next toast for the Viking Gods. "Kol the Artisan and two smiths who came from seasonal settlements in the south have set up stall in the market place after they learned that Fjordstad was a permanent town and our trade route starts here and runs to the eastern nations."

"I know of many buyers who would be interested in the wares of this Kol."

"As soon as my people have raised a toast to Odin," Magnússon said, picking up his silver horn again, brimming over with ale. "I shall introduce you to him."

Chapter Eleven
A Woman Scorned

A cold wind blew down the mountain slopes, ruffling the tall grass of the sunlit valley and wailing among the tops of Norway spruce and maple that dotted the surrounding foothills. General Gudjóns spurred his horse away from a row of bowmen, trying to feather shield targets nailed against fallen logs, and trotted along the bank of a brook with a width of a few feet babbling through the pastureland. Cattle and sheep moved aside when he approached.

Ahead of him, burly soldiers in chainmail walked between a motley bunch of bearded men and slender women wearing ragged garments, instructing them in how to hold a shield and thrust with a spear at the same time. Further along the stream, Saxons and Frisians with more experience with handling weapons battled as individuals with wooden swords or fought in small groups against more of the guards, who did not pull any of their punches.

Hansel lunged with his sword, only for his opponent to parry with the one end of his quarterstaff and then smack him in the midriff with the other. The law giver tumbled backwards into the water with an abrupt splash. The laughing guard stepped to the edge of the bank and extended a hand as Hansel took it and was helped out of the brook.

"Dry your eyes, Saxon," Hlod the Field Officer said, "and then you can have another go at me."

A horn suddenly made a long, high-pitched noise. Everyone stopped what they were doing and looked around before catching sight of a glint of sunlight reflecting off armour belonging to the four motionless horsemen upon the ridgeline above them.

"Form up you sea rats," Hlod shouted to the men and women.

General Gudjóns tugged on his reins and steered his mount up the grassy slope, encouraging it to go faster until he finally crested the summit and drew up before the riders.

"My Lords and Lady, you honour me with your visit to the training grounds," General Gudjóns wrapped the reins around the saddle horn and slipped off his helmet.

"So that's them, General," said a fain skinned woman with stately beauty and reserve. "Our gaunt reinforcements?"

"Some of them, aye, Lady Melkorka," General Gudjóns nodded. "The rest are sprinkled among the other valleys hereabouts. They be Saxons and Frisians over six hundred strong, gaunt mayhap, but the persecution and adversity they suffered getting here hath made the men and women hard as flint and put fire in their thews. From what my scouts have seen of the enemy force, our army will greatly outnumber them."

"That's all very well, but how goes the retraining of the foreigners, General?" asked a large, heavy set man before his yellow teeth crunched into an apple.

"Progress is slow for some, but not for others, Lord Imgrimund."

"Now is not the time for you to be your usual laconic and somewhat reticent self, General Gudjóns," Imgrimund of the Axe growled after swallowing his mouthful. "Will they be the equal of the warriors under the command of Magnus Magnússon?"

"Nay, not even close," General Gudjóns replied with a shake of his head. "The Frisian bowmen and spearmen show promise from their hunting and fishing skills, but most of the Saxons need a few weeks of work to get them battle ready. The same can also be said for the lack of cohesion between all your fighting men. There is much bad blood from past raids and your own household troops Jarl Foeslayer: the Huscarls are among those that are harbouring a measure of distrust concerning the reliable of their new sword brothers and their equipment...."

"My people are levies 'tis true and not the eternal Huscarls serving under your banner, my Viking brother," Imgrimund of the Axe told Foeslayer. "But they fear not to stare down death when it comes upon them."

"Nor do mine," The forth rider finally spoke in outrage. "They be not cowardly barnacles, my men will fight for me, of that you have the word of Ivar Longhair, General."

"Perchance the general could use more days to practice and train the warriors in cultivating the solidarity between the ranks?" Lady Melkorka said thoughtfully. "There is nay harm in delaying the action."

"I am an impatient man, Melkorka; so I won't be ordering any delay." Sigvald Foeslayer said, idly cleaning the dirt from under his fingernails with a small narrow blade as he next addressed the general. "General Gudjóns, I can only guarantee that you shall have a day or two at most after our combined forces attack and capture the village of Skálholt, for you know our scouts have seen the enemy fleet return to their anchorage and once he hears of our invasion to his homeland, Magnússon will want to strike back immediately by launching his feeble number of longships against us."

"And our mighty fleet shall be waiting in the fjord to meet them," Lady Melkorka said thoughtfully.

"Just so, Melkorka, but all Magnússon will find is his ruin," Sigvald said with a grin before addressing the general again. "For now just teach the foreigners the fundamental techniques of sword and shield to give them a fighting chance. They are an expendable resource I intent to exploit as I see fit."

"I will quicken and intensify the training for everyone, Jarl Foeslayer," General Gudjóns answered, donning his helmet and unwinding his reins ahead of steering his mount around and trotting back down the slope.

Imgrimund of the Axe shook his head; his voice was as grim as his face. "So you are still hoping that the Saxons and the Frisians will be too many for the warriors of Magnus Magnússon to cope with and easily overwhelm them."

"That is the plan," Sigvald said, "and if we are favoured by good fortune, we shall capture their longships intact as well."

"And whose warriors are you planning to use in this assault of Skálholt, Sigvald?" Ivar Longhair spoke with a deadpan expression, meeting Jarl Foeslayer's gaze without flinching, as the sound of General Gudjóns' horse receded with distance. "For my pride demands my warriors be in the vanguard to show what they can do?"

"There will be time for that later. For now I only want a few of your longships, Ivar Stoneface," Sigvald said deliberately needling him to get under his skin as he sheathed the knife, knowing the long, leaned-faced warrior hated being called that nickname, "and some men belonging to me, Imgrimund and Melkorka."

"Who will lead them, you?" Ivar asked him, quietly fuming inside. "You're ebullient optimism is not a match for my experience on the battleground."

"Nor mine, Sigvald," bellowed Imgrimund of the Axe in a bellicose voice, dropping his apple core. "Do you want to tarnish your honour with an even costlier defeat against Magnússon?"

"Well, I am the Jarl of the Serpent Throne and you three are only my allies," Sigvald said, sawing his reins to turn his horse down the grassy slope, aware that he could ill-afford anymore discord to widen the fractures that are already starting to appear in the peace treaty between them. "But I will leave it to the Gods to decide if it pleases you all."

"The Gods," Lady Melkorka scowled thoughtfully, viewing

his receding back with suspicion as Sigvald spurred his mount and trotted away. She dug her heels into her horse's flanks and followed. Imgrimund of the Axe and Ivar Longhair brought up the rear.

"Aye," Sigvald nodded. "Let us talk to Magus Volstagg; if the visions of the priest say otherwise I shall happily abide by his decision and turn command of my army over to one of you, so sayest Jarl Sigvald Foeslayer."

In the distance sprawled the fort village of Trøllheim.

The riders funnelled their galloping horses down the dirt trail leading between the high boundary walls of sod and stone surrounding the hay fields and meadows dotted with irrigation ditches of limited size.

* * *

Noon sunlight shone down from a cloudless sky upon the fortifications of Bamburgh Castle. Flags fluttered in the breeze blowing in off the sea and from his vantage point on a balcony projecting from the exterior wall of the oldest part of the stone keep, King Aethelred leaned on the enclosing parapet and causally watched the courtyard below, the flow of supply wagons and patrols of horsemen trot over the drawbridge as they came and went.

There was a sudden knock on the door behind him and Aethelred signed in annoyance. "Enter!"

Captain Cerdic opened the door and stepped out onto the wide balcony, drawing to a halt a few steps in, taking in the king's speech that radiated his troubles and resentfulness for being disturbed. "Sorry to interrupt you sire, but I have tidings."

"It had better be bloody well important, Captain," King Aethelred cast a look over his shoulder at him. "Did not counsellor Wigmund inform you that I come here for a spot of tranquilly away from the noisy and bustling activity of the court?"

"He did, my liege," Captain Cerdic replied. "But this could not wait, for the news comes from Leodwald, your chief torturer."

"Come forward, Captain." Aethelred said in a tedious and impassive tone as he straightened up.

Captain Cerdic did so, and met the king's gaze evenly. "Leodwald has extracted a confession from Rolf the skald before he died of his wounds."

Aethelred arched an eyebrow. "So soon; I expected the skald to last longer than a day being as how he was a barbarian."

Captain Cerdic nodded. "The Viking visited countless seaside villages and the monasteries of Wearmouth and Jarrow along with those in Hexham and Whitby."

Aethelred brightened up and a ghost of a smile played across his features. "That is news indeed. Yesternight I was looking for a needle in a haystack, but nay more. Captain Cerdic, you will have to repeat the information in front of Wigmund and the other Thanes, because I am immediately convening a session of the full King's Counsel." The king turned and strode towards the doorway, his mind racing, as Cerdic followed out of the sunshine and into the shadowy interior of the keep. "Your words need to be reviewed by everyone and then we must discuss strategy to determine the next step. I am going to recommend my forces concentrate upon the four monastery towns. 'Tis one of those places that the longships of Magnus Magnússon shall raid later in the year I am certain of it."

* * *

"I swear the priest knew we were coming," Lady Melkorka said, her long braided stark white hair shone in the early afternoon sunlight like freshly fallen snow, as she and her allies stepped from the shadowy shack of Magus Volstagg. Imgrimund and Ivar Longhair became sidetracked by an old woman cook with bones showing beneath the flabby skin of her stick like arms and grey hair hanging in long thin strands from her marriage headdress. She was boiling animal blood, offal in a cleaned sheep's intestines over a roaring fire.

They each snatched a blood sausage from where it cooled on nearby platters, before taking a bite and hurrying to catch up with the others.

"The man consults with the Gods, Melkorka, perchance the mushrooms he ingests gave him a future vision of us coming to his door," Sigvald explained, going around a cluster of young boys of various ages practicing fighting each other with wooden swords and small shields of little weight. The gap separating the foursome was quickly dwindling. "Now that Magus Volstagg has spoken for the All Father himself I hope I hear naught further of you three offering unasked for advice and questioning the decisions I make, understood."

"I think I can speak for Ivar and Imgrimund when I say you have our loyalty and support as ever, my Viking brother," Lady Melkorka said, trying another tactic, passing sitting warriors using grindstones to sharpen their axes and swords. "But I fear you shall not want to listen to my warning and it will go unheeded."

"What warning, Melkorka?" growled Sigvald uneasily, pulling up abruptly and whirling about to face her, Imgrimund and Longhair caught up, as a knot of burly Vikings wheeled a large catapult towards the dock where a double-ended, broad-beamed vessel was tied up to a piling among the many anchored longships, two gangplanks angled down from the bobbing, clinker-build craft to the shore and up these walkways the Vikings shoved the catapult until it touched down on top of the deck.

"Sigvald," Imgrimund of the Axe spoke in a hostile way and poked the half eaten end of the sausage at Foeslayer's chest. "Was it your mouth or did you borrow it from a fool when you offered land to the Saxons and Frisians in return for them fighting for us?"

"Aye," Ivar Longhair said with a much calmer voice, flourishing his sausage about like it was a mace. "Your freeborn warriors are complaining that you made a lapse in judgement, that an easier solution to get what you wanted from them would have been to just threaten the lives of the foreigners' children."

"Oh, that," Sigvald's eyes flashed dangerously as he turned and set off again, striding in the direction of the blacksmith's shop. His allies went after him. "I am clearly quite able to tell an untruth when it suits me, Stoneface."

"But you promised…" Imgrimund of the Axe sputtered in shock.

"And I would have kept it if they were Norsemen, not desperate foreigners," Sigvald said with a thinning mask of contempt and cruelty, over his shoulder. The sound of a clanging hammer was getting louder "My word to them is worth less than a field of cabbages."

"Why?" asked Lady Melkorka.

"Because it amused me," Sigvald said, halting beside a rack of weapons outside the open door of a wooden shack containing the smithy shop. The blacksmith held the flattened, reddened metal with tongs and exchanged his hammer for a chisel to shape the edges of the blade. Soot covered his clothes and he sweated from the heat radiating from the furnace.

Nearby, a boy placed a nail next to a shield and chainmail armour atop of a table and then he started pumping the bellows, as the blacksmith cooled the sizzling metal into a bucket of water. "The cauldrons and pans you donated have been melted down to make these swords."

"And where did you get the rest of the iron, Sigvald?" Ivar Longhair frowned.

"The ore is from the red earth west of here, you can also get iron from digging up the bog east of Fjordstad," Imgrimund of the Axe nodded. "My father saw to it that my younger brother and I had a working knowledge of the craft."

"Now this is where we men leave you for a while, Melkorka," Sigvald said. "I intent to bathe before the battle and I need to finalize the other leadership roles I am tasking Ivar and Imgrimund with." Foeslayer turned and walked to a large longhouse built ahead, and the two Viking noblemen followed. "You my dear Viking sister will sit on the Serpent Throne till I return."

Lady Melkorka saw them go and muttered to herself. "That half mongrel is going to get us all killed."

* * *

"Did you make a wager on this morn's horse race, Hārūn?" Rollo Throatslitter said, gripping his beard and moved one of his pieces on the hnefatafl board game, as he and the young Arab sat opposite each other at a table in the centre of the Great hall. Torchlight blazed from the walls and shadows flickered across them.

"Yes," Hārūn replied, rolling the ivory dice, his eyes straying to his right at the sound of loud purring when a pigtailed Sonja came up to them, cradling the kitten in her arms as he licked its paws clean after just eating a fish meal. "I lost coin on it and the following boat race too." He shifted a pawn and the little girl said.

"Uncle Rollo, do you think my kitten will grow strong enough to pull the chariot of the goddess Freyja?"

Rollo gulped down some ale before lowering his cup and answering her. "My little flower, life is governed by the Norns and only those three maidens living by Yggdrasill," he jerked with his thumb at the ancient, gnarled, evergreen ash tree, "spinning the fate of man or cat knows for certain."

"The tree is called Yggdrasill," Hārūn said, trying to get tongue around the word. "I was going to ask Jarl Magnússon about it."

"Magnus is busy showing your father and brother the shipyard, so I shall tell you instead. 'Tis what he would want me to do," Tove refilled Rollo's cup. "Yggdrasill is the world tree and to my people its branches support the entire universe." He picked the game dice and threw it on the board. "A stag is biting its leaves and its roots stretch to different realms, the world of death, Midgard where we are, Johunheim in which half-witted frost-giants live, and Asgard, home of our Gods." Rollo thrust his playing piece forward and knocked over one of Hārūn's. Sonja blinked and stroked the kitten, engrossed by the story. "Beneath the tree is a well, the fount of wisdom. When Odin drank from the water, he gained knowledge, but in exchange he had to pluck out an eye and abandoned it there."

* * *

"So this is where you construct all your longships, Gunnar?" Omar al-Ṭabarī said, walking beside Magnússon, as they followed Gunnar and his sons into the empty shipyard. They passed two guards of medium height, gnawing on chicken legs and playing knucklebones. Hakon watched Harold toss the sheep's anklebones up into the air and then he tried to catch as many as he could with his outstretched hand, only for two to rest in his palm, the other three fell at his feet.

"Most, merchant, but not all; the Sea Chariot and the Horse of the Waves are general purpose vessels and were captured at anchorage when the warriors of Jarl Magnússon took over the villages of Lillesund and Skálholt." Gunnar said, stepping into a shaft of shimmering sunlight. "Both of these Karvs had rower's benches, but since the oarsmen and women of Fjordstad sit on our sea chest, the Jarl ordered me to hew them apart and dumped the pieces over the side."

"And these vessels also have the shallow draft that enable you to land on a shore and sail up a river?" asked Omar.

"Aye, the Karvs in the fleet are a little slower than the Jarl's warships, but they are still manoeuvrable and driven by both wind and oars." Gunnar said, but it was Magnússon, who saw from the merchant's expression he was immersed in deep thought.

"I have seen that look before," Magnússon said, "what are you mulling over, Omar?"

"One day in the future I was thinking you and I and a boatload of your Vikings might go east again and this time we visit the Slavs."

Bringing up the rear of Magnússon's small group was Aḥmad and Lokar.

"What are the women like where you come from, Aḥmad?" asked Lokar, noticing the guards and angling towards them.

"They are not as bold as your own sister or the others in the town."

"Aah," Lokar said with surprise in his voice. "How dull for you," he halted by the guards for a second or two. "Why don't you go on without me, Aḥmad; I would have words with Harold."

"I will wait, Lokar," Aḥmad replied, drawing up beside Lokar. "I would like to listen in, if it is all right with you?"

Lokar nodded and then addressed Harold. "How fairs Gísli? I am curious after Aḥmad sent his brother to tend to him yesternight?"

"Hārūn like Aikku the healer before him could not meld his broken back," Harold said, his head drooping with disappointment. "Gísli did not want to live life as he was and he begged me to release him so this very morn I slit his throat with my dagger."

"Will you seek vengeance against Tyrker?" asked Lokar, as Aḥmad reached over to pat Harold on the shoulder.

"Oh, how I wanted too, but Gísli made me pledge not too," Harold sighed deeply, unable to purge the guilt he was feeling as he looked up and met Lokar's gaze, "saying it was the will of the Norns that that injury should happen to him during the wrestling bout."

Ahead of them at the first building berth, Gunnar was speaking to the rest of the party; proudly running his hand down the hull of one of the longships. "I named this vessel: Born of a Giant and 'twas made for battle, a Drakkars or dragon ship like my father the great shipwright Arnkel Berg-Helgason called them."

"I can see that compared with the Mjöllnir's Might." Omar al-Ṭabarī said, surveying the longship, as the sound of running feet grow louder before Lokar and Aḥmad slowed down and fell into step behind them. "Born of a Giant is a quarter longer in length; has more oars," he pointed up at the oar holes in the hull's soaring curve, "and if I am not mistaken, it shall carry a larger number of crew."

"Aye," Lars answered for his father. "Born of a Giant has to undergo sea trails in a week's time, but Siegfried and I do not believe her size will be at the sake of speed."

Gunnar nodded in agreement. "But a larger ship will have need of a better anchor to hold it in place in the waters of a bay." Magnússon's brow furrowed, as he and the others followed him over to the half decorated prow, where something large was hidden beneath sailcloth, beside a trestle table littered with objects like a plumb line and a measuring stick called a boat ell along with a shield and part of the shield rack. Gunnar halted at the table, his companions following suit, and he pointed at the five foot, double-hooked device made of wood resting on the ground. "This is Siegfried's creation and he had this shaped while we were gone." He gestured for his sons to lift the anchor so Magnússon and his guests could get a better look at it. The brothers came forward and heaved it up and Lokar and the Arabs blinked at the long handle with curved arms at the bottom. "Explain the working of it, son "

* * *

The gates of Fjordstad opened and a rider emerged, cantering his mount down the narrow dirt trail and onto the long grass, avoiding the streaks of rock between the town and the shipyard. The approaching sound of the horse's hooves made Hakon lower his ale skin and Harold look up in alert.

"The rider is heading this way, but with the beard and wolf muzzle he wears like a helmet atop of his head I don't recognise him from here," Harold lifted his hand to shade his eyes from the early afternoon sun. "I wonder why he is not watching the tug-of-war event like everyone else is."

"You and many others are new to Fjordstad, but you will come to learn few warriors wear the wolf or bear pelt over their naked flesh. Only one man I know sits tall in the saddle like that," Hakon narrowed his eyes to a squint against the glare, as the rider loomed closer, "Bjorn Strongarm. Something is up if he is coming here and has taken his armour off."

Twenty seconds later, Bjorn Strongarm pulled up to a halt outside the second palisade. "I was told Lars Gunnarson is here," the bodyguard dismounted and tossed the reins to Hakon, who caught them and exchanged a confused glance with Harold. "Well," he growled with anger and unslung his battleaxe from his back, "is he within the shipyard or not?"

Hakon swallowed. "Aye, he is with Jarl Magnússon's party."

"Good," Bjorn said, striding forward and bumping into Harold's shoulder in passing. "If you pair value your lives, then don't disturb me, for I have killing to do."

* * *

"…And that is what I had in mind for both of you," Jarl Sigvald Foeslayer said, rising naked from a wooden bench, having perspired enough in the sweltering cloud of steam, and he picked up a twig from among buckets of water and hot stones littering the bath house floor. "Both tasks are equally important, what say you to that, my allies?"

"Aye, I prefer being in the thick of the battle, as does my brother Búi Widowmaker. I am the oldest and he will do what I say, Sigvald," Imgrimund of the Axe said, whipping the reddening flesh of his legs with another twig to work loose the stubborn dirt and remove it. "And I have an idea how I can hide the passage of my warriors for a-ways from the prying eyes of sentries."

Ivar Longhair nodded and stepped into a cold pool of water to wash and cleanse his body off. "I can see that there shall be much honour for those under my command too. But it would have been a lot simper if the defences of Skálholt had been belike that of Trøllheim's long curving wall on the landside with the waters of the inlet for the final barricade. We could have just sailed into the harbour and entered the village that way to catch them unawares."

Sigvald blinked and was about to say something about the chains he had commanded his blacksmiths to make to eventually stretch across the entrance to the harbour when the door of the steam bath opened and General Gudjóns strode inside.

"Pardon the intrusion, my Jarl, the longships are prepared for departure. I came to join you aboard the Swiftwind as I promised your wife."

"Nay, general, you will not be sailing with me, for I trust only you to personally oversee the loading of the Saxons and Frisians aboard the other ships of my fleet and bring them to immediately reinforce us at Skálholt, understand?"

"Aye," General Gudjóns said. "I shall appoint Field Officer Hlod to be your shield bearer then." He bowed and departed.

* * *

Further inside the shipyard of Fjordstad, Siegfried was explaining the anchor.

"As you can see 'tis a different shape from the baskets of stones we presently use, Jarl Magnússon," he said. "The old method used just their weight at the sea bottom, but the hooks can dig into the sand or attach itself to a rock offering us better resistance." He pointed at the top of the anchor. "The chain fastens to the ring there."

"Gunnar, if you are satisfied with this improvement then so is I," Magnússon said. "I think though it ought to be made from iron, not wood."

"Did I speak of this very thing to you, father," Lars said.

"Master shipwright, I would like to see a simple explanatory drawing from which you work," Aḥmad said with undisguised admiration as he studied the workmanship, "something showing the arrangement and relations as of the parts of the longship."

"Aḥmad, the only scrolls I consult for knowledge are from the ancient Greek sea charts Jarl Magnússon brought back from his travels in the east," Gunnar replied,. "Be it a ferry, a fishing boat or a Drakkar, I just have an impression in my head of what the longship might look like before it is constructed and then I start making it from the keel on up from the highest trees I can find."

"Those were the scrolls you bartered for in the Egyptian bazaar," Omar al-Ṭabarī smiled at the memory. "You paid to many gold dinars for them."

Magnússon nodded. "A problem I hope you share at the auction on the morrow."

"We shall see, my friend," Omar said. "I had hoped to haggle out a prize, not bid, but we are in your country not mine, so we shall do things your way, my friend."

Lokar had puzzlement on his face, as he peered at the very large mystery object. "And what is under the sail cloth, shipwright?"

"Jarl Magnússon wanted me to fit a catapult on the deck of the Born of a Giant and the Sun Maiden," Gunnar jerked with his thumb at the longship in the next berth, "Alas, as of yet I have not found a way to do so and store the heaps of stone projectiles without losing too much oar space. I could have it placed upon the broad deck of a knar..."

"We use those ships for trade or exploration," Magnússon shook his head. "'Tis the deck of a dragon ship I want to feel beneath my feet, not a knar."

"Hence, Lars came up with this notion from the scrolls you own, Jarl Magnússon," Gunnar bobbed his head and his sons pulled at the sailcloth, finally revealing a Roman ballistae. It was made of wood, and held together with iron plates around the frames and iron nails in the stand.

"A giant crossbow?" Lokar said, pulling a face as he approached it with Aḥmad behind him. The brothers dropped the sailcloth.

"Aye," Gunnar said, as the others crowded around the weapon, reaching up to touch the slider at the top of the crossbow, where the man-sized bolt was loaded. Its shaft was a man-length and had a blunt metal head. The rope was made from animal sinew twisted around the stiff bow arms, and the two winchers at the rear of the stock were meant to crank back the bowstring to the firing position. "'Tis accurate over distance and will pierce an enemy shield wall, bringing down one warrior or several."

"I like it, Lars," Magnússon nodded, not hearing the approach of footfalls behind him. "How many of things have you built?"

"Two thus far," Lars replied. "I could have one fitted to the bow of the Mjöllnir's Might at the end of the celebrations."

"Three days is too long for me to wait, Lars," Magnússon said with a shake of his head. "I want that crossbow upon the Mjöllnir's Might by tonight and the other one placed on deck of the Long Snake before dawn, do you understand?"

"You will have to pick someone else for the task, Jarl Magnússon," Bjorn Strongarm answered just then for Lars. The sound of his gruff voice brought all of Magnússon's party about, and they blinked, taking in the almost naked bodyguard wrapped in a wolf pelt, his murderous expression and the axe he was carrying, before Omar, Aḥmad and Lokar, who freed his blade from the scabbard, stepped back. Bjorn sneered at Lokar. "Worry not Lokar, I have not come for you, but Lars Gunnarson. I going to cut out his giblets and feed them to the wolves in the forest."

"And why is that, Bjorn?" Magnússon asked, folding his arms, as there was a barely perceptible tightening of his facial muscles. He remained where he was along with Gunnar and his sons, fingering the hilts of their swords as the bodyguard tightened his grip on his weapon and strode forward. "Has he done some wrong to you that I don't know about?"

"Not to me, but my wife," Bjorn Strongarm snarled, pulling up, as Magnússon stepped in front of him and held up his hands in a placating gesture in an attempt to intervene before blows were struck. "Brunhild says she was sitting outside my longhouse while I was away, combing to untangle the fibres of a fleece when Lars sat down beside her, pawed her and gave her three undesired kisses."

"Is this true, Lars?" asked Gunnar, as he and Siegfried sneaked glances at him. Lokar shifted his weight from one foot to the other.

"Father," Lars said, drawing his sword and his relatives on instinct did the same, "I am guiltily of exchanging more than kisses with Brunhild, she came to me willingly and I have been proughing her field for months."

"Falsehood," Bjorn bared his teeth and pushed against Magnússon's hand. "Let me go now, my Jarl, ere I lose complete control of the berserker rage brewing inside of me."

"My son doth not lie, Bjorn Strongarm," Gunnar slapped his palm against his forehead and muttered a curse, and despite the tension, a ghost of a smile plunked at the corners of Siegfried's mouth. "Lars, you are as wilful as your mother."

"Wait, Lars Gunnarson is a valued engineer to me, Bjorn," Magnússon placed his hand on the bodyguard's shoulder, in conflict as he scrutinised his flushed face and heavy breathing. "Is there any recompense I could offer to stay your hand and solve this dispute?"

Bjorn Strongarm shrugged of his hand. "Brunhild wants blood and I intend to see that she get's it one way or another. 'Tis a good day to die."

"I tried shipwright, I am afraid that Bjorn's has made up his mind," Magnússon sighed and moved aside, as the bodyguard set off again. "Hel hath nay fury like a woman scorned."

"Well, I can not stand around idly and watch one of my pups be butchered," Gunnar said, going to the table to pick up the shield.

"Nor I," Siegfried agreed with a nod.

"Thanks for the vote of confidence, father; but this is my fight not yours or Siegfried's," Lars steeled himself in anticipation.

"Listen to the dead man well, Gunnar greybeard, you too Siegfried the beardless boy," the bodyguard taunted them, bunching his muscles and gauging the dwindling distance, but he was not so preoccupied to take notice of Gunnar and Siegfried, as he quickened his pace and bore down on his prey. "This is his day of reckoning; don't insist I make it yours as well."

"Our decision stands, she gnat," Gunnar turned to face the bodyguard and frantically swung his blade at his head. "Family is everything to me."

"Bah, I will make certain those words are carved upon the memorial stone commemorating my victory," Bjorn answered, checking his advance and ducked out the way of the sword stroke, but had the projecting wolf nose sliced off atop of his head.

In response Bjorn thrust with the horn of his axe, hopping to stab Gunnar in the throat or hook the top of the shield with the curved interior edge. When the shipwright had managed to avoid both of these tactics, the bodyguard raised his weapon above his head and chopped down with wild unrestrained aggression, splitting the shield in two halves, the blow was enough to cause Gunnar to stagger backwards and stumble into scaffolding in the form of two barrels topped with a plank.

But before the bodyguard could follow it up with a killing stroke, he heard the scuff of a boot coming from his left flank and pivoted on his heel as the brothers dashed forward to meet the axe-wielder in combat. Bjorn furiously parried Siegfried's thrust on the haft of his weapon, only to feel the blurring edge of Lars' sword bite into the meat of his upper arm, drawing crimson from a medium-sized cut. Bjorn did not swear, he just kept his opened-mouthed grin. Behind them, Gunnar stood, flinging the shield down to the ground, before taking his sword in both hands and limping in towards Bjorn's exposed back.

From the sidelines, Omar al-Ṭabarī solemnly watched the fight and spoke to Magnússon in confusion. "Magnus, can you not stop this senseless battle from continuing? After all you make up the rules."

"Aye, I did, and yet even I can only lightly interfere in a quarrel once it has begun. If this duel was between ordinary men to the first spilling of blood, then I could," Magnússon told him, "alas my friend, Bjorn is a berserker, his rage can come over him suddenly and 'tis not safe for any of us to be in front of him while his eyes are veiled by the red mist of battle. He wanted the Holmgang to be to the death so I shall honour his wish."

A sheen of sweat coated Bjorn's furrowed brow and his eyes tracked the circling movements of the brothers, as one went left and the other crossed right, using his feet and fast hands to swat his axe in glittering arcs at his opponents, sparks flew and crashing metal resounded loudly on the air from over a half a dozen vicious thrusts and parries; blocking or deflecting the most damaging effects of each man's blows. For the bodyguard, he ignored the pain of his wounds, but he knew if he lost too much blood, it would weaken him.

"You boys have proven surprising resilient, but I grow bored of toying with you all," Bjorn said, feeling a little bit more of his confidence erode the longer the duel went on for, and now doubt was beginning to slowly enter his mind because he was not as certain as he once was over the outcome. "I am a nut you will never crack."

"You talk too much, you arrogant oaf," Siegfried panted.

Lars then deceived the bodyguard with a feint, luring him one way, which gave Siegfried the opportunity to lunge in to attack from the opposite side, but even off balance as he was, Bjorn still succeeded in twisting around and his axe swung out, smashing into the blade and breaking it into shards. The bodyguard laughed and drew his axe back for an underhand swing aimed at Siegfried's groin.

With his son holding just a jagged hilt to defend himself, Gunnar choose that moment to shout a war cry and charged in, Bjorn hesitated and was in the act of turning his head when the shipwright buried his sword deep into the bodyguard's thigh, the edge nicking bone.

Bjorn cried out in agony, the last of the anger and adrenaline that had been fuelling his muscles left his body. He let go of the axe and closing his fist, backhanded Gunner across the jaw, the impact sending him flying through the air. A fountain of blood gusted forth from the grisly wound, and as the bodyguard's legs began to buckle, his flickering gaze beginning to blur as he saw Lars approaching quickly at an angle and his blade thrust with all his strength to pierce Bjorn's heart. The bodyguard fell to his knees and toppled onto his side.

Magnússon held himself very still; the only movement was the fast beat at the base of his neck, while Lokar shouted in triumph, and finally sheathed his sword, as they and the Arabs set off, converging on the others.

Lars placed a foot on Bjorn's body to anchor it, before pulling his sword free and wiping the blood on the dead man's clothes, as he watched Siegfried dash over to their father. Gunnar tried to get to his trembling feet, but he dropped back down to a sitting position and spat out a tooth before rubbing his aching chin.

"Are you hurt, Father?" Siegfried panted in concern, extending a hand.

"Only when I breathe," Gunnar replied, letting Siegfried help him stand before he shoved aside his supported arm and that of Aḥmad's with as much dignity as he could muster. "I can make my way back to home from here."

Omar al-Ṭabarī shook his head. "Gunnar, the only place you and your sons are going is to the Great Hall. You all have received nasty cuts and they need to be cleaned and bandaged by Hārūn."

"I won't forget that duel in a hurry," Lokar said to his father, enjoying the satisfaction off irritating him.

"Neither shall I, Lokar."

"You know I can hardly contain my grief," Lokar grinned, and then wheeled on his heels and strode off.

Omar al-Ṭabarī cast a glance over his shoulder and caught the sombre expression cross the face of Magnússon, reflecting his troubled state of mind, as he picked up Bjorn's battleaxe and took one last look at his confider and loyal housecarl before he strode after the rest of his party leaving the shipyard behind.

Chapter Twelve
Widows In The Village

Since late afternoon four Viking longships and a couple of smaller watercraft belonging to allies of Jarl Sigvald Foeslayer, nosed their way along the middle of the latest in a complex system of fjord channels. Untroubled by floating logs, the vessels formed up two abreast when the waterway widened, meandering east and west through magnificent, but desolate scenery. Fierce gusts of wind blew across the high cliffs hemming in the submerged valley, but a hundred and forty foot down at the becalmed waters edge, the air was still.

Unlike the longships owned by Magnus Magnússon, these vessels had a higher half-deck at the stern and the rowers sat on benches in the centre of the craft. The banks of oars flung up spray as they regularly dipped in and out of the fjord's surface in perfect rhythm, and seabirds wheeled and swooped above the mastheads with furled sails. Little by little the landscape changed to become less inhospitable. Mountains with jagged peaks and barren ridges yielded to crag and tail formations, where tufts of grasses sprouted from cracks in the rock, which in turn gave way to a range of scrub rounded hills strewn with boulders and a succession of small rapids-streams occupying a broad peat bog valley, tracts of tangled forest and pastoral land.

By then, the dusk was approaching, the blazing sun had began to dip behind the western mountains, painting the sky and outlining the shape of the low clouds with swathes of red, gold and purple, and reflecting the fjord with shimmering colour. A shading effect crept over the longships, smothering the glittering sunlight on spearheads and helmets owned by the silent crews. On board the foremost vessel, the Sleipnir, Imgrimund of the Axe stood at the high prow, atop of loose planks used as steps. His fingers stroked the strikingly-carved, painted figurehead and he grinned as he made a fresh appraisal of where the small fleet was from the landmarks he remembered from his past journeys in this direction.

He was extremely familiarity with this stretch of waterway and where its course curved sinuously into a bent ahead of him, he knew that their current position to be at a point below the village of Skálholt, he glanced back at a burly warrior with bulging muscle and nodded wordlessly, pointing the horn of his axe at the port shore. The tall Norseman turned and strode down the deck, gesturing at the oarsmen that the time was now to carry out the first of the instructions their captain Imgrimund of the Axe had given the crew back at Trøllheim.

The prow of the Sleipnir veered left, out of midstream and bore in towards the looming trees. A second longship called the Valkyrie's choice trailed it on the same course, gliding into its wake.

The Sleipnir's port oars were immediately shipped as the hull swung close into the pooling shadows under the lefty canopies and then a few sailors at various positions along its length, whirled grappling hooks fastened to rope lines and threw them among the densely grouped trunks, the prongs embedding into bark and wood before the lines were pulled tight by the crew and the longship slid abeam until the planking touched the rocky bank.

Imgrimund of the Axe slipped over the gunwale and as quietly as a big cat, he disappeared into the undergrowth beyond. The tall Norseman leaped down from the longship onto the shore. He was joined by scores of archers, spearmen and a standard-bearer holding a limp flag at the end of the pole, depicting the horse-head emblem of Imgrimund of the Axe. The tall Norseman loosened his sword in its scabbard and gestured for them to follow before he ran forward. The warriors steadily loped off in pursuit, leaving two men to watch over the Sleipnir, the Valkyrie's choice pulled in behind it, the end of their taut grapnel lines were equally secured to the rail cleats, and the gangplank was lowered for its crew to disembark in a hurry.

"We are losing the light, Búi," Imgrimund of the Axe whispered to the tall Norseman, as he caught up and ran alongside him.

"Aye, brother," Búi said, glancing about him. "We don't want to stumble through these woods in the complete dark."

"We won't have too. From what I remember before we be on the upper slopes of the valley," Imgrimund of the Axe said. "We shall espy the walls of Skálholt ere long."

"Good to hear, brother," Búi said with a vicious grin, clasping his sword lightly. "I look forward to stealing closer and making more widows in the village."

Imgrimund of the Axe grinned. "Perchance this will be the day I live to see you move your mouth less than your sword arm."

The forest was gloomy and the ground sloped downward, as Imgrimund of the Axe and his men penetrated their way through its depths, abandoning caution for speed. Birdcalls ceased abruptly as conifer needles were carelessly trampled underfoot and small animals scurried away from them in the surrounding undergrowth. A few of the Viking raiders carried unlit torches and touchwood tinder from an oak tree, soaked in days old urine and the sodium nitrate let the fungus hold a smoldering spark that could permit the men to ignite the torches on the move instead of stopping to use the fire-making equipment insides the pouches hanging from their belts.

Eventually the raiders neared the edge of the timber line. Streaks of crimson set against the silvery-white of the western sky had begun seeping through the spaces in the vanishing canopies, slowly brightening the gloom ahead, as the trees thinned about them to reveal what lay beyond. Imgrimund of the Axe raised his shield arm to halt his war band where they were, while he and his brother Búi zigzagged from the cover of each trunk in furtive spurts of pace, crouching down when they reached the last ones and let their gaze sweep across the entire valley.

It was edged in with mountains on three sides and the fjord channel on the other. The lower grassy slopes were occupied by three wooden crofts with fences enclosing small plots of land. Here and there a little brook ran down the slanted ground, mostly turned into fields for cultivation that stretched down onto the long, board flatland squeezed between well-manured meadows and the walled palisade protecting inside the farmsteads that had clustered together to create the village. An empty pier jutted into the water beyond.

"As expected, nay sign of movement at this late hour," said Imgrimund of the Axe. "Farmers tend to be in their dwellings by now, preparing to sit and eat their evening meal."

Búi's eyes strayed to the nearby field and examined the plant's slender stalks and the stems. "Imgrimund, lo you there," he pointed at them, "the farmers are growing flax."

"An important crop indeed, brother," Imgrimund of the Axe nodded. "Drop back to the men and tell them to await my signal to attack; naught is to be burnt, not the fields or the buildings by order of Jarl Foeslayer. We slay only those of the enemy that raise a sword against us, the remainder of the villagers shall be offered clemency if they give their words to submit to his rule."

* * *

As the rowers of the Sleipnir and the Valkyrie's choice manoeuvred their oars in preparation for landing, the Swiftwind and her sister ship the Shield of Ullr eased their way past them, each longship had their oars in motion, a taut towrope tied to each of their stern post's, pulling along behind it, a single barge loaded down with men surrounding a large, firmly-secured catapult and a number of stone projectiles.

It did not take long for the towboats to sail around the bend and almost a quarter of a mile further on, the village of Skálholt came into view lit in the dissipating light.

The sun was sinking fast and a breeze sprang up, blowing in across the fjord, making small waves in its surface and sending them to lap against the near bank. On board the Swiftwind, Sigvald Foeslayer jumped to his feet and strode to the rail of the high, half-deck deep in thought, quickly surveying the indistinct lines of the timber palisade in the near distance as a range-measuring aid. Determining it and the current speed of his longships, he watched the changing angle of their line of sight, and took into account the farthest limit his catapults could operate effectively.

He turned and snapped off a series of commands to his crew.

* * *

Upon the walls of Skálholt, a young guard beckoned an older, portly comrade to join him as the officer's shaking legs climbed the ladder up to the walkway, bathed in pools of fluctuating light cast by the blazing torches atop of long poles erected above the parapet.

"Look, Captain Tjörvi; 'tis ships, did I not tell you," he pointed at the Viking longships on the shadowy fjord. "But who…"

Coming to stop alongside him, Tjörvi, red faced, peered over the palisade and in the fading light his roaming gaze managed to glimpse the catapults being towed on the two barges. "I care not if they be mysterious, Atli. Those craft are attacking us, sound the alarm. I want all the guard turned out and manning their stations."

* * *

Hlod dipped the head of an unlit torch into the glowing coals of a nearby brazier and the combustible material set on fire, before he walked across the high, half-deck to the stem post of the Swiftwind and waved the burning stick to-and-fro to signal the men on the barges ten feet away. Ivar Longhair saw the sign, as wailing horns suddenly rent the air from the village's walls, putting the populace of Skálholt into frenzy.

"Light the torches and prime the catapults," Ivar Longhair ordered, watching his warriors lay down their oars and clustered around the ballistic device and the projectiles, working with an competence born out of a great deal of practice. The same process was happening on the second barge.

* * *

About thirty seconds after hearing the alarm echo from the peaks, the doors of the three wooden crofts outside of Skálholt were flung open and stocky men emerged quickly to be silhouetted in the faint rectangles of orange lamplight spilling out through the doorways. A flight of arrows flew from the edge of the forest targeting the men and one farmer let go of his axe and torch, as two shafts embedded themselves in his chest and forehead. Screams were uttered from his frightened wife and children, but the thirty-one year old woman did not dither next, for she briefly shoved her grief aside and put out the lamplight, before drawing a knife and gathering her four children together in a tight huddle inside.

The glow of torches bobbed up and down in the enclosing murk, and muffled shouts and pounding footfalls increased in volume as their owners approached. Presently, Búi and six swordsmen came into view, heading for the croft, the lines of their armoured frames sharpening in the guttering flames of the farmer's burning stick.

Outside the humble building, two swordsmen detached themselves from the small column and entered the interior with drawn blades.

"Declare yourself defeated and Jarl Sigvald Foeslayer shall be merciful," one of the warrior's said. "Resist and your children will die before your eyes, wench. What is it to be?"

The woman mute and apprehensive looked at the upset faces of her children and dropped the knife.

Outside, Búi and his men rushed onwards and the darkness wrapped around them again. At the neighbouring farm, a man also lay twitching on the ground in a pool of his own blood; his mother knelt and wept as she cradled his head in the hollow formed by her bony arm. Two more warriors dropped off the pace as the rest went on.

When Búi and his men reached the third croft there was not a body in front of the doorway, only drops of blood on the bare ground and the broken arrow shaft ending at the fletchings. Thinking the farmer had gone to ground; the warrior three fanned out and searched the illuminated interior and the surrounding animal enclosures.

"I found naught within, Búi," a clean shaven warrior shook his head, a little later as the trio met back up.

"What about you?" Búi asked the bearded swordsman

"I followed a trail of blood to an empty pen, and I heard horse's hooves galloping towards the woods yonder."

"The farmer has ridden off to warn Magnus Magnússon of the attack," Búi nodded to himself, feeling the urge to hasten back to his brother, as he paid heed to the sounds of battle coming from the village. "The fool does not know it, but he carries out the next task for us. Come! I shall leave the others to guard the prisoners, while we join the fray."

* * *

The prows of the Shield of Ullr and the Swiftwind suddenly yawed towards the pier drawing the barges with them. Aboard both longships deck torches had been lit and the flames flickered in the increasing wind as the sun set and a pall of darkness began descending over the landscape.

It was in the time of twilight when the first barrage of heavy rocks was hurled from the creaking catapults. One cleared the water and fell several yards inshore just short of the village with an earthshaking thump, but the other projectile was aimed directly on target, it crashed into the palisade, knocking down a sizeable section of wall. Blood sprayed on the air as a guard and one of the newly-arrived defenders were flung lifelessly off the parapet.

"Breach!" Captain Tjörvi shouted to all those within earshot. "The parapet has been breached."

"Captain Tjörvi, even with the additional warriors Jarl Magnússon stationed here, we can not hold the town, not against those catapults and the army coming from the longships."

Captain Tjörvi swore. "Detail some men to get the injured and the children inside the longhouses, Atli. Everyone else is to fill their hands with steel and fight in the breaches. We can not stop the raiders, but we can give them a bloody nose."

Instead of cringing in fear or moving backwards defensively to the sounds of shouts and screams from below, the villagers on the parapet, swore oaths and stood their ground, and those carrying bows and quivers, nocked arrows and drawing on the sight of the torchlight on the decks of the approaching longships, released their bowstrings. Shafts arched over the dwindling distance between Skálholt and the vessels, raining down hard and fast. Some thudded randomly into the shields wedged into the shield racks or the hull or the masts, but the remainder of the barbed missiles got through, striking flesh and armour alike, several rowers fell dead across their looms, silencing the cheer that went up after the catapults had scored a hit upon the wall.

The Swiftwind came in close to the pier and two of the deckhands tossed their anchors overboard, while the captain of the Shield of Ullr ground the prow against the rocky shore. Hlod blew a long, mournful, high-pitched blast on his horn and Viking standards were hoisted on the decks of both ships. The arms of the catapults lifted up again, launching another volley of stones. Both throws were equally accurate as they came down, the impacts destroying the gate and punching another ragged hole in the palisade, crushing defenders behind it, and propelling splinters of wood to wound others nearby.

In response fewer arrows streaked skyward from the town, but those that did left a flaming trail through the deepening dusk, as they dropped among the raiders getting off the longships, Vikings grunted, falling backwards from the gangplanks into the water and onto the pier, clothes blackening where the flames ignited the textile. Raiders with bows fired shafts back at the walls; an exposed woman with mahogany hair and two men were struck with mortal wounds and toppled from the parapets.

Steadying his breathing, Sigvald Foeslayer drew his two swords and followed his archers and axe-wielders across the gangplank and accompanied them, Hlod protecting the young Jarl with his upraised shield, as they made their way in a fearless swell along the pier and through the breached gates, savagely cutting down male and female defenders left, right and centre. The two standards of the raiders unfurled in the wind, revealing the distinctive designs. A brown Stag on a green background was the emblem of Ivar Longhair, the second of a coiled snake against a field of white belonged to Jarl Sigvald Foeslayer. The standard-bearers carried them further into the town.

In a bid to slow down the attackers, women opened the gates to livestock pens and with shouts and waving their blazing torches about, frightened the cattle and horses, driving them out in an uncontrolled headlong rush, carving an abrupt, unnavigable path across the advancing line of raiders, evincing alarm within their numbers. Archers and spearmen tried to get out the way of the mooing, neighing stampede, but a dozen of the forerunners including the standard-bearer of Ivar Longhair were caught between the animals. Vikings screamed as they were gored by the bull horns and flung away or the horses bodychecked men over and they fell under their trampling hooves.

Village bowmen and women perched on rooftops shot their shafts down at the congestion, picking off the raiders with head and neck wounds. Arrows thudded into Hlod's shield. Enemy archers seeking similar heights, climbed up ladders to the parapets they held and returned fire. Bodies from both sides thumped to the ground. More defenders that had been cut off from their neighbours in the ensuring chaos, chose that instant to thrust out with their spears from doorways and behind fences, impaling an invading warrior, only for his vengeful comrades to repay the injury suffered by dragging down the men and skewering them several times over.

The passage of the animals passed quickly and they fled through another breach in the wall. Raiders dashed forward, jumping over their dead comrades and the villagers went to meet them. Elsewhere, the beleaguered defenders found themselves being pressed from a different side, as the crews of the Sleipnir and the Valkyrie's choice streamed in through the third large hole in the wall, pouncing upon them like a storm. The defenders could not slow the enemy down and they survived only by fighting a rearguard action. The raiders clambered over rubble and flowed between structures, hot on the heels of the retreating villagers, who were squeezed persistently and without mercy into a gradually diminishing circle as the invading sides merged, cutting off any means of escape.

Captain Tjörvi turned and lunged his sword at the nearest enemy. Imgrimund of the Axe caught the blow on his haft, and then he swung his weapon sideways and buried one of the double-edge blades into Tjörvi's breastplate. Seeing his captain fall and thinking of the welfare of his mother and sister, Atli's resistance crumbled and he threw down his sword in surrender. Those villagers alongside him did the same and inside of a dozen seconds it had caused a rippling effect that spread away from the midst of the conflict until all the defenders had disarmed. Sigvald Foeslayer wiped the blood and brains from his blades before sheathing them.

"Now, that you have laid down your arms," Sigvald Foeslayer said, his voice calm, but held a warning note as he walked past the assemblage of captives, his men were scooping up the fallen weapons, "you will not be harmed further, as long as you bow to me, Sigvald Foeslayer, your new Jarl."

Chapter Thirteen
Struggle and Strife

An owl hooted and then he swivelled his large, forward-facing eyes downward, drawn by the sound of hooves. A pair of greyish badgers with large black-and-white facial stripes had been foraging for food through the undergrowth the colour of moonlight, but when they heard the approaching commotion, the medium-sized animals scurried down their nearest burrow hole. A bare-backed rider emerged between dense clumps of bog mosses forming around a pool and feeling restless, he weakly heeled his horse forward again, splashing through the shallow water to the opposite side.

Blood dipped steadily from the arrow wound in his shoulder and the young man, breathing hard, had developed an ashen cast to his angular face. Sweat trickled down from his blond top-knot to his short, pointed goatee-beard. His eyes were wide with pain as he stubbornly fought the worsening dizzy sensation in his head, holding onto the horse's mane with the last of his strength in fear he should suffer another fainting spell and finally fall from his mount.

As the moon climbed into the sky, a wolf howled behind him and that was followed by a second. The rider urged the horse to go faster and galloped over the high barren moor before descending to the Hestathing fells on a heading that would take him to Fjordstad.

* * *

The doors of the Great Hall were flung open and they smashed nosily against the walls. The musicians stopped playing, inebriated shouts and coarse laugher quieted down, couples stopped canoodling in dark corners, as a sudden change of mood came over the prevailing atmosphere. Vikings and slaves paused and swivelled their heads to look at Jens Three-Torques stamping into the torch-lit chamber. He led Einar and Boromir over the threshold; they were half-dragging and half-hauling an arm apiece belonging to a young wounded man between them. His body was undergoing a violent shiver.

Members of the curious crowd stood up and whispers broke out among them, but they kept a respectable distance.

"Where is Jarl Magnússon?" Jens Three-Torques asked urgently, his eyes darting to the empty chairs drawn in against the main table.

"My father and mother have retired for the night," Lokar said with a frown, a mug of ale forgotten in his hand.

"'Tis vital I speak with him at once, milord," Jens Three-Torques pressed. "Before this messenger passed out from his wounds he told me ill tidings that the Jarl must hear."

Lokar frowned, standing up and snapped his fingers at Tove. "Rouse him woman."

Tove turned and rushed off behind the tree to where the Jarl's bed closet was located.

"You there," Jens Three-Torques pointed at the occupants of a nearby table. "Clear space for a wounded man. He needs help."

The town's people abandoned their table, carrying their food and drink over to the fire pit, as Einar and Boromir approached and lowered the messenger onto one of the benches. The round-faced Aikku and her husband Roald the guard got up from the back of the chamber and threaded their way between the tables to the wounded man.

"Get him water," Rollo said, pulling his chair back and then glancing at Hārūn's lean, hawk face, as he was already getting to his feet.

"I shall take it to him," Hārūn replied to Rollo's unspoken question, lifting up his own water cup. "Aḥmad, please fetch me my bag of instruments from my bed closet."

Aḥmad nodded and sped away in another direction.

A banner shifted on the far side of the chamber as the door of a bed closet opened and Omar al-Ṭabarī emerged in wisps of smoke, his long hair stretched down the back of the bright red, Oriental wide-sleeved kimono he wore. It was girdled at the waist, falling in voluminous folds around his bare feet and the silken fabric reeked of sandalwood incense. He sheathed his sword when he saw a sweaty Magnus Magnússon appear, wearing only trousers held up by the belt he was buckling, followed by Tove and a flush-faced Lady Ranveig with unbraided, dishevelled hair and garbed in a loose fitting, wrinkled nightdress she was struggling to pull the hem lower with one hand, while gripping a naked sword in the other.

"Is this the messenger, Jens?" Magnússon asked, looking questioningly at him, as he halted beside the table. Roald and Aikku reached the wounded man and she drew her knife from the belt she wore, skin pouches dangled from it holding all her charms and seeds and leafs of medical plants, while her husband anticipating his wife's needs, beckoned a neighbour to fetch him the poker from the fire. The sharp end of the rod was red-hot from where the boy had been stirring the fire to make it burn better. Roald grabbed the poker by the handle and quickened over to Aikku's side.

"Aye," said Jens Three-Torques, as Magnússon gazed down at the wounded man and appraised him. His body shiver had abated, but he breathed with laborious effort. "He said he was farmer Laufey from Skálholt…."

"Skálholt!" Rollo echoed, as he, Hārūn and Lokar strode up to them, quickly joined by Aḥmad and Omar al-Ṭabarī from different corners of the chamber. Waiting until her husband had joined her, Aikku turned towards the inflamed wound, cutting at the man's flesh to make the opening slightly wider. Blood spurted up over her hands, as she dug around the arrow head and then finally pulled the broken shaft free. Roald inserted the red-hot end of the poker into the bleeding wound and cauterized it.

"Nnggg," Laufey groaned loudly and curled up onto his side.

Jens Three-Torques nodded to Rollo and went on to condense the story into his own words. "He and his neighbours were attacked, but he managed to flee his croft on horseback to the woods. It is there where he tarried briefly and watched the raiders invade the village through breaches made by catapults."

Magnússon and Rollo were the first to exchange glances, curses and oaths burst forth from surprised lips, as the news was taken up by the people around them, the troubled mutters spreading like wildfire through the others in the chamber. Hārūn took the bag from his brother and he began carefully examining first farmer Laufey's glassy eyes and then his skin, discovering he had an unusually high body temperature and an increased pulse rate.

"Father," Siegfried Gunnarson said, glancing around at him with anguish in his eyes. "Lars' betrothed, Freya and her family live in Skálholt."

Brunhild's lips curved slightly upwards.

Gunner's mouth contorted into a grimace. "I shall go and tell him the news after I have heard the rest of the story."

"Did Laufey say who commanded the raiders?" Magnússon said with a sombre expression, the news had rattled him and cast a dark cloud over his emotions.

"Nay, Jarl Magnússon," Jens Three-Torques said, scratching his broad nose with a mole on it. "But he caught glimpses of the designs on the standards in the torchlight as they fluttered in the wind. A brown Stag was one...."

"That's the emblem of Ivar Stoneface," Rollo said, rubbing his chin thoughtfully. "I wager his allies Imgrimund of the Axe and his brother Búi Widowmaker have joined him."

Magnússon nodded. "Birds of a feather."

"And the other emblem, Jens?" asked Lokar. Lady Ranveig and Kari pressing close behind him.

"A coiled snake!"

"Sigvald Foeslayer, he darest risk my ire and might," Magnússon said loudly, a shadow traversed over his features just for a moment and then it was gone, an outward hint of his worry and resolve, as he peered down to focus on his clenching fists. "Blood begets blood; death will be the kindest fate that awaits him and his allies once I have finished with them."

"Ill tidings indeed," Lady Ranveig said and then addressed Magnússon, forcing him to speak. "Husband, what is our response to be to this dilemma?"

Magnússon looked up and his gaze wandered across the sea of expectant, grim faces, assessing their spirits as he observed the doubt and concern in many of their eyes. "Fellow warriors.... we find ourselves yet again coming up against the challenge of Jarl Sigvald Foeslayer and I grow weary of it. He and his allies have this time taken hold of Skálholt and his army of foreigners has slain our kith and kin alike in his ill-judged conquest." He spoke with clarity of expression, using exactly the right words in precisely the right way as he was about to drive his first point home. "This was meant to intimidate us from facing his men in battle when his ships sail on to Lillesund and Fjordstad," his voice rising in a crescendo as he reached the end of the sentence, "except for the fact we will not yield meekly belike the monks."

"Aye," a drunken warrior uttered, and Magnússon saw other men nod at that.

"They have wounded us 'tis true, but we are far from being crippled," Magnússon resumed, trying to raise their spirits as well as stirring up their pride and anger. "Struggle and strife is what we are born into and used too in life, while this enemy is naught more than an insect to be swatted away." There were additional nods from the town folk, and defiance began showing on individual features as they hung on to his every word. "As your Jarl I have long since demonstrated my prowess in going to war with frequent victories and you all know I am slow to make a promise and yet I am quick to keep it. Fight for me! Fight for the honour of your House and fight for your home. I swear on Odin's one good eye that we were avenge ourselves on this Sigvald Foeslayer," his voice rising in volume again, "take back Skálholt and the plunder of Trøllheim will be ours. Are you with me?"

The people cheered in assent and chanted his name; cups of ale were raised to Magnússon in honour before being drunk by men and women in hasty gulps.

Lokar clapped his hands to get every ones attention. "All right people, go to your homes, the celebrations are over for the time being. Warriors sharpen your weapons and then get some sleep."

"Tjernagl and Vegard," Magnússon shouted out their names. "Tarry a moment at the fire pit, for I would have words with you."

"Gladly lord," Vegard said.

Men and women stood up and let themselves be shepherded away from the tables and slowly out the Great Hall by Lokar, Rollo, Kari and her shield maidens.

Jens Three-Torques was merging with the exodus when a thought struck Rollo and he stepped forward to pluck an arrow from the guardsman's quiver. "I borrow a shaft from you, Jens. The Jarl will be needed it to gather his warriors."

Behind them, Lady Ranveig sided up to Magnússon and planted a kiss on his cheek.

"A rousing speech, my husband," Lady Ranveig said. "You had them eating out of the palm of your hand."

"Just reminding them of a few home truths, wife," Magnússon glanced around for certain faces. "Go and tell Rollo to assemble the war council in the lavatory. We have to craft a plan of counterattack in private ere we engage Sigvald Foeslayer and his allies."

I shall tell him," Lady Ranveig said, her eyes darting about, before catching a glimpse of Lady Ingrid among the shifting mass of people and heading off towards her.

"Will Laufey recover, Hārūn?" Omar al-Ṭabarī asked.

"He has no broken bones, but he has symptoms of a fever, father."

"Perhaps you can make one of your elixirs', Hārūn?" asked Aḥmad.

Hārūn nodded. "I shall have to consult the ancient scrolls in my ship's cabin."

"Bah! I will make a poultice to ease Laufey's pain, but I have seen this malady in the past and I have nay knowledge of an earthy remedy," said Aikku. "Some warriors from different clans dip their arrowheads in animal dung before they go into battle and if the wound doth not kill the enemy outright the inflection will eventually cause a slow and anguishing death. His fate now is up to the Gods, but I think one of the twelve Valkyrie is already riding to escort the soul of this slain hero to Valhalla."

Magnússon went over to the fire pit where the first mates waited. "Tjernagl and Vegard," both men straightened up their slouching postures. "Ready all of my ships for departure. The Sea Chariot and the Blood Fang need to be prepared first. We set sail for Skálholt at cockcrow."

"Aye," the men uttered together before departing

"It seems like we will have to postpone the auction until you get back, Magnus," Omar said, coming up from behind him and placing a hand on his shoulder.

"Aye, my friend, I am afraid so," Magnússon said. "But with their blood and sweat my Vikings crews ought to earn more gold and silver by then to try and outbid you on the slaves."

"They can have the ones worth a goat, I am after those my sons' value at a camel or two," the merchant's smile faded. "What of these catapults I heard Jens Three-Torques mention? Are you not worried Sigvald Foeslayer will use them against your fleet?"

"Nay, my friend," Magnússon said. "Viking leaders put much value on their longships and like me; Sigvald Foeslayer will want to capture my fleet intact."

"It would be my honour if I and my men could offer protection to Lady Ranveig and little Sonja again."

"Aye, it would be one less distraction for me, for should we lose, Foeslayer will come to Fjordstad and slay them," Magnússon said. "Take them aboard one of your dhows by sword point if you have to and give them safe passage to the land of my wife's brother."

"It shall be done. But if I may ask what is it that troubles you, Magnus?" Omar al-Ṭabarī spoke in a whisper so no one close by could over hear; a look of compassion in his eyes. "Is it going into battle without your bodyguard?"

""The death of Bjorn Strongarm was a great shock to me, Omar," he replied in a soft voice. "He had become a friend and a faithful supporter, he was at my side for a long time and my strong right arm. But I now recognise the truth of just how widely I had depended upon his talents to do my killing and entrust him enough to secretly confide and discuss my personal problems with."

"You speak of Lokar," the merchant nodded in understanding. "It would take a blind man not to notice the friction between you."

"Aye, for the most part! My son is growing more brazen by the day and now that Bjorn is gone I suspect our next clash of opinions shall not stop short of violence."

"What will you do?" asked Omar. "During the time I have spent here I have observed him and I take no pleasure in telling you this, my friend but you will only see Lokar coming if you have another of eyes in the back of your head."

Magnússon nodded and said. "I shall end his life without his mother knowing about it, perchance an accidental fall off his horse and hit his head on a rock." The merchant winced at the coldness that crept into his friend's voice. "But that will have to wait, because I can only deal with one battle at a time and I am focusing my grief and rage upon Sigvald Foeslayer. He has to be vanquished, because he has endangered the lives of two of my favourite illegitimate children I send to the village of Skálholt for safety away from the murderous intentions of my wife."

"What?" Omar al-Ṭabarī blinked. "Now it is I that is in shock, Magnus."

"'Tis a long story, Omar; one I will freely share with you when I return to Fjordstad,"

Magnússon saw Lady Ranveig approach, now wearing leather shoes and wrapped up in a long cloak. She beckoned him to come. "I have to go and take my seat at the war council."

* * *

Behind the tree was a short corridor with the bed closets belonging to the Jarl's family and a side door leading to a large lavatory. Inside the Viking war council of Fjordstad were discussing the strategy Magnússon was going to employ, as each member sat perched on the edge of benches with bum holes chiselled out of the wood, positioned above slanted stones gutters that carried away excrement and urine outside.

"I am uneasy about this battle, husband," Lady Ranveig said, warming her hands over the blazing coals heaped atop of a corner brazier. Old Roman oil lamps stolen from Lindisfarne lit the chamber, dangling down from the hooks attached to the ceiling beams. "It smells like a trap."

Magnússon shrugged. "I can do naught but take the bait, wife. Given the lay of the terrain around Skálholt 'tis more likely we shall face Sigvald Foeslayer upon the water."

Kari still wearing her feasting dress decorated with her best amber jewellery, nodded. "Mother is right. What if this plan does not work, father? Our scouts say that we are outnumbered two-to-one in ships and warriors?"

"If you have not got a hammer for the nail, you have to improvise, as your father will too," Rollo said, looking grumpier than usual as he came to Magnússon's defence.

"Well, if I may have my say, Jarl Magnússon," Gunnar said in misery, looking up after consulting with a charcoal diagrammatic drawing of a route through the network of fjord channels between Fjordstad and Skálholt. "I saw you talking with Halldór the fisherman earlier, and he is a capable sailor, but in my opinion he is not a navigator and doth not fit as a replacement on a steering oar aboard any of your Drakkars especially not on your flagship."

"Halldór is not your replacement, shipwright," Magnússon laughed. "I ordered him to sail his fishing boat towards Skálholt to probe what lies ahead of us there."

"Clever," Lokar mused, his features etched into a wary respect.

"I did not survive this long by marching blindly into a beast's maw, Lokar," scolded Magnússon.

"If what you say is true where shall I be if not on the deck of the Mjöllnir's Might, watching over one of my pups at least," said Gunnar in frustration.

"Shipwright, for this one occasion, you shall be steering aboard the Horse of the Waves," Magnússon confirmed. "Unlike Tjernagl, Vegard and the others, you are tasked to manoeuvre individually of my fleet and your skill in navigation will be handy as you seek strategic positions between mine and the enemy ships whereupon you can disembark your warriors to do the most good either to strengthen my weakened forces or attack a vulnerable vessel on Foeslayer's flank."

"You say this is for just one time, Jarl Magnússon?" queried Gunnar.

"Aye, you shall be back on the deck of the Mjöllnir's Might when we sail to England, but for now I need only the strongest able-bodied and seasoned warriors behind me, as I lead them aboard the enemy ships where we will encounter the thickest of the fighting."

"And that is where I shall be right by your side, father," Lokar said. "With Bjorn Strongarm slain, you need someone trustworthy to guard your back, and who is better suited to the role than your own son."

"I wish you would reconsider, Lokar," Magnússon replied with ill-concealed irritation. "You are an age to lead warriors and the Long Snake needs a captain."

"Lokar is a fool," Kari said with a shake of her head, before Lokar could reply. "I have ambition, father; appoint me captain. My shield maidens are on board the Bifrost's Bow, but we can move over...."

"I have heard enough daughter, don't be bothering your father, he has too much on his platter as it is," Lady Ranveig snapped sternly, sweeping away the remainder of what she had to say with a swift, chopping gesture of her hand, glaring at her, as she then addressed her husband. "Magnus, you mentioned to me another task for Rollo."

Still clearly conflicted, Magnússon nodded and directed his gaze towards him. "Rollo, I want you to set sail a few hours ahead of the fleet onboard the Sea Chariot, you will be accompanied by the Blood Fang," he said, snapping an arrow shaft in half and proffering the arrowhead-end to him, "to deliver the war-arrow first to the villagers of Lillesund and gather all the warriors you can there, load them on board the longships ere you go and visit the seasonal settlements in the south and do the same there."

Rollo scratched his hair thoughtfully. "I need an experienced steersman who has knowledge of the route through the inner passage."

"You shall have Almgren, he knows those waters well."

"What am I allowed to offer any man or woman that is willing to fight for us?"

"Coin and a permanent home within Skálholt or Trøllheim," said Magnússon.

"Where will the fleet rendezvous, Magnus?"

"Show him shipwright," Magnússon ordered.

Gunner jerked his head at Rollo to approach and he pulled a face as he did so, crossing to the opposite bench and plonking himself down beside the shipwright. "Here Throatslitter is the place of meeting," he pointed at a spot on the map. "Jarl Magnússon and the rest of the fleet will emerged from this fjord channel I call 'The Narrows' onto the 'Inland Sea' and your longships comes out of that other branching waterway that connects with it. This is the rendezvous point."

Rollo rubbed his chin. "Tell Almgren of the location as well."

"We shall be there about noon," Magnússon said, "We will spread the archers and spearmen evenly between the longships. 'Tis barely half a dozen leagues from there to Skálholt and somewhere in between I daresay Sigvald Foeslayer and his allies will be at anchor awaiting us."

"Good, I would not have liked to miss out on the bloodshedding in this battle," Rollo said, almost drooling at the prospect as he stood and strode towards the closed door. "The skalds will be singing of this first big clash of the Vikings and the heroes for years to come."

Rollo opened the door and guarding outside, Njáll Bloodhammer hastened out of his way. Gunnar, Lokar and Kari got up and filed into the corridor beyond. Lady Ranveig paused to let them all go and then turned to waylay her husband.

"Try to come back to me, Magnus," she said, her hands clasping his tightly and leaning forward to give him a peck on his mouth. "I want you, Lokar and Rollo back to hear those stories for yourselves."

"I will do my best, Ranveig." Magnússon bowed his head and pressed his nose and beard against her cheek. "But a hollow promise I will not make to you, my love."

* * *

The moon had been down for about two hours and the gaggle of stars twinkled like diamonds in the darkness. Vikings dressed in furs against the bitter cold untied the mooring lines from the pilings and jumped aboard the vessels into clouds of visible breath, as the rowers of the Sea Chariot and the Blood Fang eased away from the piers. The meagre torchlight on the palisade faded behind them as the two masts-less longships glided across the waterway in single file, before rounding the bend and nosing into the first side tributary they came too.

By daybreak, the rest of Magnússon's fleet set sail under a bright and cloudless sky speckled with auks and gulls as they briefly followed in the direction that Rollo's longships had taken. The appearance of the calm, blue fjord sparkling in the sunlight reminded many of the crew of a lake they had seen in their previous voyages, as porpoises and seals swam for fish in the saltwater. Side channels began intertwining with the main, long arm of the sea and the vessels were edging past the mouth of the shallow, fjord-type estuary, when a burst of headwind blew across the decks to disturb the rowers' braids, but the masts did not vibrate, because they had also been unstepped.

Tjernagl turned the steering oar to starboard and the Mjöllnir's Might headed into the next side channel along. This was a lot wider and wound north and west amid cliffs towering above the fleet on both sides, shaped by the faulting and shearing of the rock strata. Here and there patches of greenery climbed up the rock. The row of longships arranged one behind the other, kept apace with each another, the crews' oar strokes in rhythm with the echoing beats of their drums, and as the hours crawled to mid morning, the sun warmed the grim landscape and a long-winged, osprey flew over the water of a connecting bay to hunt.

All of a sudden the Vikings uneasily became aware of the forbidden cliffs in front of the Mjöllnir's Might advance inward, shutting out the sun and casting dark, fingers of shadows over everything, with only the pitiful glow of a brazier able to push away the gloom, as the width of the winding fjord channel decreased considerable to the extent of one and a half oar-lengths.

"We have entered 'The Narrows', Lokar," Magnússon said loudly, blinking in the diffused half-light as he leaned on the giant crossbow set in the bow. "Once we emerge onto open water, keep a weathered eye out for the Sea Chariot and the Blood Fang."

Lokar nodded and uncorked his half-filled goatskin, extending it over the gunwale to refill it under a passing, small waterfall; pieces of blue sky were visible above the misty spray. "You lit the brazier, father. Are you rethinking the capturing of Foeslayer's ships?"

"Not if I can help it," Magnússon said. "But my enemy has the advantage in the encroaching battle and if we are not able to turn the tide in our favour I shall see all the ships burn."

The signification was not lost on Lokar as he took a drink of water and then stoppered the goatskin and voiced his reservations about the decision. "I still believe the Mjöllnir's Might and the Long Snake should be in the forefront when the two fleets come together. The crews expect their Jarl to show the most courage in leading our warriors in the fighting."

"You are putting too much faith in old customs, Lokar; but when you are leader, you can follow your own advice, I however will not," Magnússon grinned without an iota of humour. "Let Rollo or his berserkers have the glory of doing the initial boarding. We shall be causing chaos elsewhere."

Shadows immediately fled and sunlight once more bathed the fleet as the cliffs fell away on either side of the oars and the channel debouched into an 'Inland Sea' – an expanse of still saltwater stretching from west to east, enclosed by distant hills, asymmetrical ridges and snow-capped mountains. Cloud hung low on the horizon.

Alert and focused, Magnússon ducked under the giant crossbow and climbed up the plank-steps in the prow to get a better look at the horizon. He shaded his eyes with his hand and was in the process of taking a quick survey for signs of movement when the harsh, mournful sound of a horn pierced the air, making him cast a glance over his shoulder.

"Father," Lokar pointed astern and to the far right at a bowshot away, the Sea Chariot and the Blood Fang under full sail emerged from a second fjord tributary that divided the forbidden cliffs apart. Spears bristled from the decks of both longships and three small fishing boats followed them out in the watery expanse, their blue and yellow striped sails slackened as the wind died down behind them, a few round wooden shields depicting drawing of runes, weapons or sea monsters were hung from the gunwales. "'Tis Rollo."

"Tjernagl, spread the word to the fleet, all stop and drop the anchors," Magnússon said, seeing the oar banks of Rollo's vessels extend from their hulls into the briny surface.

"Aye, aye," the blunt-featured first mate raised his battered horn and blew a long, discordant blast.

Magnússon jumped to the deck and an idea came to him. "Lokar, place the mast in its step and fix up the riggings, but keep the sail furled till we are in motion."

"Has the sun addled your brains, father? There be nay a wind," Lokar threw his head back and laughed, his free hand having to reach up and readjust his conical helmet, placing it more firmly on his head as he remained where he was in defiant. Watching Vikings were enjoying the ridicule and contempt between Magnússon and his son.

Magnússon grinded his teeth and scowled angrily behind the spectacles-like visor of his iron-domed helmet, and then without hesitation he clenched his fists and punched his son twice solidly in the face, knocking him down. Rowers took in a harsh sibilance of breath as mutters erupted and glances were exchanged between them, each one knowing better than to doubt their Jarl. "You dare to undermine my power for the last time, Lokar." He rested his hand on the pommel of his Arabian sword. "I won't take that from any man especially kin."

"You should not have hit me, father," Lokar said menacingly, getting up slowly and wiping away the rivulet of blood to reveal his spit lip, and running his tongue over his chipped teeth he found one of them had loosened. "I swear you will not lay a hand on me again."

"A vow easily kept if you but obey me without question, do you understand, you insolent runt?" Magnússon said his voice and word terse.

"Aye," Lokar snarled with hatred in his eyes, a storm raging deep inside him as resentment drove him to the point of rage.

He wheeled on his heels to carry out the order. "Ulf, Floki, Bödvar, set to."

The men fitted the looms into hooks and then leaped to their feet, their skin glistening with sweat after toiling at the oars.

The fleet heaved to in a ragged arc and dropped anchor. Soon the Sea Chariot and the Blood Fang angled in to join them, their sails were rolled up and secured, but hearing the horn blast and watching the coordinated action on the decks of the other vessels, Rollo decided not to order the lowing of the masts as his port oars were drawn inward; the steersman brought the overcrowded longship on the parallel course alongside the Mjöllnir's Might with hardy any space left to separate the two hulls.

"I bring you good tidings, Magnus," Rollo said, as the Blood Fang lost momentum and draw up between the Long Snake and the Bifrost's Bow. Between gaps within the necklaces of shields, gangplanks were immediately slid from gunwale to gunwale to bridge the watery divides. Captains shouted over requests to their counterparts, who in turn instructed numbers of the warriors to move out to the other ships. The fishing boats ploughed on, their oars weaving a slower path between the vessels until they came to rest. "Eight score of warriors from Lillesund and the settlements answered the call of the war-arrow."

"And the fishing boats, Rollo?" asked Magnússon with an arching eyebrow.

"I thought that cowards who jump overboard rather than face our swords could be speared or feathered by arrow by the men and women onboard them," Rollo's eyes strayed to his nephew and the rest of the grunting Vikings manhandling the heel of the mast over to its step and fix it place.

"Not one of your worst ideas, Rollo. Beside that, have them also launch attacks against Foeslayer and his allies, aim for where their standards fly upon the raised decks," Magnússon said. "If they can whittle the chieftains down on their flagships it could mean the battle will end quicker in our favour."

"Alvin, relay that command to the fishing boats" Rollo said to the black-haired man, before turning back to Magnússon. "How many warriors do you want aboard the Mjöllnir's Might?"

"Seven and ten," Magnússon said and pointed upwards as the longship began to be fitted out with rigging. "Archers mostly: anybody, who is skilled to go aloft and shoot at the enemy from the roped-shrouds. The rest of the crew I have hand-picked myself."

"That's why you are erecting the masts, they be perches for our snipers," Rollo pondered aloud, behind Magnússon he glimpsed sailors preparing the boltropes sewn in to the luff and foot of the sail "but the unfurling of the sail escapes me, Magnus?"

"You will see when the time comes, Rollo," Magnússon said with a mysterious grin.

Frowning, Rollo turned to address the Vikings standing and sitting on the deck of the Sea Chariot. "Bowmen raise your hands." Plenty of his crew and the other warriors did so, and Rollo picked those he did not know at random. "You and you and you...."

"Tjernagl," Magnússon said, turning to him as archers vaulted over to the Mjöllnir's Might. "Any sign of Halldór's red striped sail?"

"Nay, Jarl Magnússon. Halldór is never late. In my opinion something has happened to his boat."

Magnússon nodded. "Once all the tasks are completed, you have my permission to weight anchor and get the fleet underway again. I shall array our battle formation en route."

Chapter Fourteen
Floating Islands

S igvald Foeslayer looked left and right to survey his surroundings and said, "It seems you have or are in the act of carrying out all my orders, General Gudjóns?"

"Aye, my Jarl," the general replied, walking beside him. Slightly behind the pair, Hlod brought up the rear. "Your notion of anchoring our fleet of longships in two, deep bow-to-bow ranks to create floating islands to fight upon and also blockage the fjord was not difficult to do."

"With the hills and ridges hereabout, there is not a flat piece of ground for leagues," Sigvald said, "Regardless of my aversion to battling on the water; this was the only way I and my allies could think of to meet the ships of Magnus Magnússon head on and end the rivalry between us."

General Gudjóns nodded. "We have tied-together the fleet here and there with strong chains so each vessel can not be freed easily and set adrift in battle if our opponents..."

"And my standard?" Sigvald interrupted, not wanting to hear the rest of the general's pessimism, as he went ahead of the others first, crossing the gangplank over the narrow gap between the Swiftwind and the Valkyrie's choice, and stepped down onto the busy deck.

General Gudjóns blinked in annoyance of what he felt was a trifling task for Foeslayer to be so fixated upon. "It shall be unfurled within the hour on the half deck of the Sleipnir,

Jarl Foeslayer."

"Good. I want my best archers on the upper decks and my swordsmen and spearmen occupying the lower ones without stumbling blocks to hinder their footwork."

"As you can see," General Gudjóns drew up next to Foeslayer and made an encompassing gesture to take in the work the number of warriors were doing on the deck of the longships, using an assortment of tools to ply loose the twin-seated, rowing benches without breaking them. "Several of the masts have already been unstepped from the foremost rank and belike their oars will be carried off then and placed on the near shore. The rowers' seats are being removed intact and put in the hold along with the rigging so we can use them again later."

Sigvald nodded and observed the brown stag emblem decorating the flag fluttering from the longship's sternpost. "I notice that Ivar Stoneface has chosen this vessel as his flagship, while Imgrimund of the Axe has taken over the Shield of Ullr in the second rank, but has not even started to undertake the activities I have bidden him."

"Your ally refuses to do so, my Jarl," General Gudjóns sighed deeply. "He said to me that the Shield of Ullr is the faster vessel in your fleet and once you have gained victory over Magnus Magnússon, he has volunteered to sail immediately to Trøllheim to let the rest of your people know of the courageous deed."

"'Tis nice of him, but tell me General should I believe him?"

"I think Imgrimund of the Axe is hedging his bets as this in his reckoning may be your last gambit, moves towards fruition. Magnus Magnússon has a smaller fleet of Drakkars and Karvs, 'tis true enough and we captured a goodly number of his warriors in Skálholt, but it takes not a seer belike Magus Volstagg to see that Magnússon will send the war-arrow to Lillesund and muster all the men and women who can wield a blade from there."

"Begging your pardon, Jarl Foeslayer," Hlod butted in to their private conversation, "But can I ask the general a question?" Sigvald nodded. "How many warriors that will be?"

"Hard to say off hand, Hlod," the general shrugged his shoulders. "Beside the rowers, Magnússon's longships could hold anything from sixty to one hundred and fifty Vikings."

"Hmmm, it matters not," Sigvald said, mentally calculating each other's chances. "My host will wreak havoc among his."

* * *

Four nautical leagues dropped behind the fleet of Magnus Magnússon as it continued to sweep across the sun-glittering fjord at three knots in a pre-planned attack pattern. At the forefront and arranged line abreast of one another were the Sea Chariot, the Bifrost's Bow and the Blood Fang, while positioned at the rear and to one side of the longships in front were the Horse of the Waves and the Rune Fire, Mjöllnir's Might and the Long Snake, forming a wide stepped effect that allowed each vessel a clear view of the way ahead of them.

The fishing boats lagged in the wake of the longships, all hands aboard them were labouring to keep up with the pace. Flora and fauna was sparse along the bracketed shoreline of bare peaks and pinnacles, ridges, spires, hummocks and the odd dwarf tree. Ahead in the channel, a trail of brown, floating specks silhouetted against the blue expanse was disturbed when they came into contact with the turbulent current of an exiting stream - carrying enormous quantities of silt from higher ground, which muddied and clouded the clearer waters, causing the enlarging flotsam to flip and scatter apart in the eddies.

The first of the debris approached the port side of the Horse of the Waves.

Harald stopped singing a jaunty tune on his lyre and scanned the odds and ends atop of the water, asking Gunnar a question. "Is it driftwood?"

The shipwright leaned over the rail and cast his experienced eye over the pieces of drifting plank, rope and a carved painted prow just out of range from being struck by the long sweeps of the oar bank biting into the surface of the fjord. "Nay, 'tis wreckage from a small boat," he answered, pulling back. "And I wager 'twas Halldór's."

"'Tis as if Thor's hammer descended from Asgard and smote it with one blow?" said Harald.

"Or Foeslayer fired a stone from one of his catapults," Gunnar said, "A fishing boat is not a sort of thing he would want to capture intact."

On board the Sea Chariot, Rothgar registered a sighting directly ahead and he shouted down to his shipmates, from where he stood on the rigging overhead. "Ahoy, in the distance."

Drawing the attention of Rollo and knots of warriors not manning the oars; they stood up and poked their heads over the rail or sought height, stepping up the prow steps and climbed the rigging rungs to get a better view of what awaited them in the great blue yonder. The featureless and desolated horizon was now broken by a long, dark, flickering line that broadened across the surface of the fjord. A war horn blared from the Mjöllnir's Might that indicted Magnússon had seen the blistering barricade slowly split and materialise, resolving itself into the lean, rakish hulls of enemy longships beside one another in a column of eight, faint figures were etched in the sunlight, ascending the stairs to the upper decks.

"Prepare for battle, the fleet of Sigvald Foeslayer is ahead of us," Rollo said over his shoulder to the first mate but he kept his gaze on the fore. The drum beat started to quicken and the rowers onboard all the advancing longships picked up the pace significantly, propelling the fleet at about an average speed of about 8 knots. Warriors of Fjordstad and Lillesund occupying the central walkways between the rowers as well spilling out into the prow and stern, donned their helmets and knelt, arms hoisted up shields and hands palmed spears and battleaxes.

Another column of abreast, enemy longships appeared behind the first and after checking their progress or the lack thereof for several seconds, Rollo nodded to himself. "They are at anchor and wait upon our arrival. Let us not disappoint the dogs. Almgren, keep on this course."

"Aye, Lord," Almgren replied, his hand resting lightly on the steering oar.

The distance went from far to middling, and deckhands standing upon the rigging saw dead bodies from Halldór's crew and pieces of fishing boat wreckage that had already washed up on the port and starboard shores like jetsam. Out on the fjord, a breeze rose behind Magnússon's nearing fleet, stirring the sails, and rippling the waters surface, as the three fishing boats shrank to rapidly receding dots.

A sleet of arrows whistled out from the decks of Foeslayer's anchored fleet and undaunted, Magnússon's longships drove onward towards the lethal cloud in perfect rhythmic union. Finn and Rothgar, Bödvar and Hakon to name but a few on those vessels, organised bands of warriors to raise their shields above their heads, some overlapping others to form a crude dome. Shafts splashed in the water, struck the prows and the men and women felt their shields buffet as they absorbed the thumping impacts. Here and there oars missed a stroke, as the rower crumpled, until the body was manhandled over the gunwale and into the water before another Viking took their place at the loom.

Snipers and lookouts aloft; also sought protection by descending the rigging and getting the mast and sail in-between themselves and the barrage of stinging death, the barbs after travelling so far did not have enough power left to pierce the tough, flickering sail, instead they bounced off them to clatter on the decks below. The reeling archers on Magnússon's longships returned fire in spits as their vessels' came onward; the flights were over-hasty and erratic because of the wavelets and the swaying decks ruined their marksmanship. Ahead, the perimeter of the battle was looming large now, bringing out the outline of the anchored Drakkars in sharp contrast against the sky.

"Lord Rollo," Olaf said, pushing his way forward through the knots of warriors, "the wounded are many, where do we put them?"

"Down in the hold, move the warriors off the hatch," Rollo shouted. "The dead go over the side."

Another incessant wave of arrows arched into the sky to darken the sun and fell among the approaching fleet, sails were holed at this closer range, but the barbs did not get all the way through. The shafts that hit the decks had better luck of finding creaks in the armour, causing flesh wounds from stem to stern, and downing rowers by the dozen, but it did not slow the impetus of the longships charging headlong across the diminishing open water as they bore down on the centre left of Foeslayer's line and finally passed inside the reach of the enemy archers.

Just then, aboard the Mjöllnir's Might, men and women dropped their battle axes and shields, and took up vacated oars, as Magnússon issued an order.

"Now, Tjernagl, bear hard to port."

"Aye, aye," Tjernagl worked his steering oar, and the Mjöllnir's Might and the Long Snake peeled away from the rest of the formation, angling along and to the right in single file upon a long curving course that brought the two longships closer in to shore as they carried out a flanking manoeuvre, heading for the end two vessels on the eastern extremity of Foeslayer's two lines of Drakkars.

***

Upon the half-deck of the Sleipnir, Jarl Sigvald Foeslayer and General Gudjóns were making use of the height to scrutinize the disposition of the enemy's fleet as it raced towards their own lines.

"I thought his longships would behave like bee swarming, but," Sigvald said. "Magnus Magnússon has arrayed his ships into a formidable echelon formation."

"Lo, my Jarl," the general pointed, "Magnússon's fleet is breaking up as I knew it would. He is aboard the foremost longship with the red banner atop of the masthead and he's intentions are to outflank the Thunderbolt and the Odin's Spear, and attack us on two fronts. I still think you should have allowed me to set free-moving flanking vessels so they could have blocked his path and prevented Magnússon from boarding that way."

"I am of the opinion that to win victory you have to be bold and take risks," Sigvald sighed deeply. "I want him to think I am still wet behind the ears and have made a costly mistake, general. Won't he be surprised when he locks horns with Búi Widowmaker and half of my foreign host?" he grinned. "I will see Magnússon's face when I humble him."

***

"Even from here I can smell it," Búi Widowmaker sniffed the air, standing on a gangplank behind his Viking bodyguard and the other warriors swarming the decks of the Thunderbolt and the Odin's Spear like an infestation. "'Tis the reek of their fear," he added, hearing the sceptical, nervous laugher from the foreigners, as he gauged the narrowing, diagonal distance between them and the approaching Mjöllnir's Might and the

Long Snake, giving a signal to some of his men to begin the onslaught "Impale them my spearmen."

* * *

"Rowers, bend to it heartily," Magnússon exhorted loudly on the Mjöllnir's Might, as a flurry of spears were thrown at his vessel and the Long Snake. "Take cover," he shouted, descending the bow steps, but most of the spears plopped into the water foaming about the prows and a few others smacked into the hull. The muscles of the rowers knotted with exertion. Archers fired arrows at lower trajectories from the rigging and picked off enemy warriors on the high, half-decks. "Lars Gunnarson," he added, "when you have a shot, take it."

"Aye, Jarl Magnússon," Lars replied, he was striving to bring his large crossbow to bear, and the small detachment of sweating warriors under his command were intent on loading it. Siegfried was doing the same with the second ballista on board the Long Snake.

In the space of minutes, Ellisiv fell onto the planking near Magnússon and she was hurled into the water shorter afterwards. Oars were shipped along the length of both longships. Men and women breathing heavily, snatched up weapons and crouched down behind the gunwale in readiness to attack, as the Mjöllnir's Might glided smoothly with the remaining momentum on a sideways approach up to and begun to overtake the Thunderbolt on a parallel course.

Búi Widowmaker and Imgrimund of the Axe had formed their warriors into two uneven lines two deep and fifty across the seventy-five feet length and the twenty-foot width of each longship.

"Release the next volley," Búi Widowmaker shouted to his warriors.

From the deck of the Thunderbolt throwing axes were propelled, humming through the air at the slowing Mjöllnir's Might. The weapons embedded abeam into the rail and the portside shields of Magnússon's flagship. Lars fired the crossbow and the thick rope banged, sending the iron-headed bolt careering among the rank of Frisians facing him, wrecking great losses as it mowed them down like grass.

Sling-hurlers on the passing Mjöllnir's Might came out of their crouches then, twirling stones in loops of leather to build up velocity before they let go off one of the thong ends and released their missiles. Saxons already alarmed about what had just happened to their sword-brothers on the Thunderbolt did not have the time to react to the next barrage and dozens slumped to the deck with head injuries.

Flinching inwardly and half suppressing the worry in his voice, Búi Widowmaker shouted at the back of the men. "Close up ranks." He felt the furtive looks from Hansel and several of the Saxons, as they hesitated and the sudden tension permeating the Thunderbolt. The shields of his Viking bodyguards surrounded him. "And be ready to repel boarders."

Muttering, the Saxon and the Frisians drew their swords and edged closer together.

Following closely behind the Mjöllnir's Might, the Long Snake glided into the vacated space before it. Two of its crew were skewered with throwing daggers, while Siegfried fired his ballista at point-blank range at the thinning lines of warriors, the bolt streaked away, smashing through a rail shield and cut in half the men behind it. Blood and entrails poured onto the planking and the pieces of body including Hansel's fell spasmodically next to their comrades-in-arms.

"Hold the rank," Búi Widowmaker commanded, but the shocked Saxons and Frisians did not respond. Instead they glanced momentarily about them, listening to the screams of the dying and the wounded writhing in pain, before a few jumped ship, throwing themselves into the water and endeavouring to swim to the nearest shore, while most of the others turned and fled, crossing the gangplanks or leaping over the gaps onto the next longship and to even the one after that in the foremost row, treading upon rail or shield debris and the mutilated remains of Norsemen lying on the decks, underneath the crimson shafts of the ballista bolts.

Forced into a decision he did not want to made, Búi Widowmaker ordered his bodyguard to retreat. Onboard the Long Snake, Vegard grinned as he saw the rout and he cried out an encouraging battle cry and the crew replied by uttering a loud incoherent cheer, brandishing their weapons in the air. Gangplanks were dropped like drawbridges to the opposite gunwale and the Vikings of Fjordstad and Lillesund dashed across to the corpse-choked deck, first stabbing the enemy wounded and then catching up with the stragglers, and hacking at them.

"Come back here so I can slay you," Njáll Bloodhammer shouted in glee, as he led the charge, caving in the skulls of two of the Norse bodyguard with his warhammer, shattering their spines in the bargain; gore spraying him from head to foot, before he parried away a sword thrust from Búi Widowmaker and crushed the nobleman's barrel chest, rig bones snapping to perforate his organs. "I thought naught would make me smile this day."

* * *

In the meantime, the rest of Magnússon's longships crossed the remaining distance that separated the two fleets. Rowers backstroked to reduce speed and then they withdrew their sets of oars to let their momentum carry them into the length of shadow cast by the tall enemy prows; steersmen adjusted the steering oar for drift, and the grapnel hurlers were now swinging their hooks in readiness as spearmen, axe-wielders, swords-women shouted battle cries and eagerly crowded around them.

Crews braced themselves as the Sea Chariot, the Bifrost's Bow and the Blood Fang drew together at last with the Sleipnir, the Valkyrie's choice, and the Swiftwind, the former breasting their way into the gaps between the latter; the overlapping planks groaned and flexed, the wood splintering a little around the nails as the high prows of the Drakkars scraped against one another in a grinding halt, thick chains were stretched taut and the masts quivered. Rollo ordered the anchors to be dropped and the grapnels to be released; the soaring grapples hooked the curving gunwales above them.

Vikings bounded over to the lines, yanked them taut before climbing up in steady streams in an attempt to board the enemy vessels, their hands took most of the weight strain as their boots found hardly any purchase on the slippery-wet wood, gripping sword blades with their teeth. A Saxon appeared in the bow of the Swiftwind and with a thrust drove the head of his spear into the eye socket of a sailor. He fell back onto his grumbling comrades below, as Healfdene twanged his bowstring from the masthead and send a shaft into the spearman's brain. One of Foeslayer's Norsemen came into view and chopped off the grapple line, the rope and the warriors ascending it plunged into the fjord.

The Rune Fire and the Horse of the Waves veered sharply to the left and eventually there was a dull, reverberating impact as they came to a shuddering rest, near and alongside the Sea Chariot, the Bifrost's Bow and the Blood Fang. More grapples shot out from the port and starboard sides of those two anchoring vessels, the prongs latching on the rails of the chained longships in front of them. Archers in the rigging tried but failed to keep the defenders at bay as their comrades clambered up the lines and leaped over the rail onto the decks of the enemy longships, where Norsemen and Frisians were quickly upon them.

The hand-to-hand fighting was particularly fierce at the bows; boarders came and went with puncture wounds, but some like Rollo and Grettir managed to stand their ground by trading blows with the defenders, parrying with shield and thrusting out to cut instead at exposed kneecaps, buying the time needed for reinforcements to scramble up the ropes and help to secure the position. From there, Magnússon's growing group of men and women continued to fan out and shoulder-to-shoulder, they engaged the enemy, and make further advances along the blood-soaked decks.

A small number of naked, howling berserkers armed with only a sword, also established a foothold on the two longships at the left of the Sleipnir. They showed their teeth in a grin and weaved erratically among the defenders.

"Berserkers," a pensive Frisian shouted the Norse name with a mixture of superstitious fear and awe before he and more of his countrymen and women surrendered their position by jumping overboard rather than confront the maniacs. The braver souls in their company came on and had their shields kicked into their faces, bare feet straddling the prone warrior after he had fell backwards and the berserker dealt him a death blow or seizing defenders helmets with one hand and then the frenzied boarders slammed their opponent's heads into the rail. But for every Saxon they struck down, two of Foeslayer's flesher Norsemen took their place.

Ignoring the pain of their wounds from shoulder to waist, the berserkers continued to charge at the Norse defenders, who in the ensuring chaos had their battle formation break apart, wits dulled and discipline was soon forgotten as the warriors of Ivar Longhair blended with those of Lady Melkorka: old clan hatreds resurfaced along with the absence of trust in their new sword-brothers, each one happily preferring to act like a lone wolf and attack instead of cooperating with their neighbour, a tactic that the berserkers exploited, feinting and using the enemy numbers against them, striking to debilitate the defenders: a slashing stoke dismembering an arm or a leg, leaving the injured warrior to bleed out as they moved onward, only for the boarder vanguard to get slowly butchered by men lead by General Gudjóns as they succumbed to exhaustion and their own blood lost.

Behind those berserkers, ordinary Viking warriors such as Erik and Wulfric raised themselves up the ropes from the Rune Fire and the Horse of the Waves, and boarded the enemy ships; one or two had additional ropes fastened about their waists. These they untied and pulled on, heaving aloft bulging sacks containing spears, shields and battleaxes.

After claiming their extra weapons, Magnússon's Vikings moved forward with urgency, thrusting with spearheads and even the broken spear shafts themselves against the defenders shields with the intention of disrupting their enemy's formation and create openings before they cleaved their way through the lingering Saxons until Ivar Longhair replaced General Gudjóns in command and his Norsemen rallied around the standard-bearer waving the brown stag flag to became more of a cohesive force, gradually slowing the boarders progress but not halting their advance altogether.

* * *

Ahead of the Long Snake, the Mjöllnir's Might had cruised forward a little further, skirting perilously close to the Odin's Spear, and then Tjernagl dropped the anchors. By this time, Lars had been winching and ratcheted the crossbow rope back into the arming position and three strong men manhandled the bolt into the top slider. Throwing axes were immediately exchanged between the sides and casualties collapsed on the decks on both longships.

Magnússon's sling-hurlers stood and propelled more stones at the Frisians and Saxons lines on the Odin's Spear, but expecting that battle tactic after seeing its use, the projectiles bounced off raised shields, only claiming the odd helmetless victim after three men had broke ranks and rushed forward, trying to cut Magnússon down with their swords. Lars fired his crossbow again and Norse warriors were hurled back one after another, as the bolt pierced flesh and bone.

* * *

"A curse upon Magnússon and his detestable ballista bolts," Sigvald Foeslayer said in anger, watching his warriors fall in swathes. "My men are in disarray and to attempt to slow down the advance of the enemy rabble I will have to sound the signal and summon up my loyal…."

An arrow quivered as it struck the rail of the longship.

"Arrows! Get down my Jarl." Hlod shouted, quickly stepping in front of the nobleman as he squatted down on the half deck. Another warrior of Foeslayer's bodyguard joined him. Three shafts embedded themselves into their shields. "They have our range."

"Where are they coming from, Hlod?" Sigvald asked as his standard-bearer suddenly gurgled and collapsed with a shaft jutting out of his neck. A stout Viking picked up the flag pole and bravely stood beside it. "After we abandoned the Sleipnir, for this Drakkar in the rearward line I thought we would be safe from arrows for the moment at least."

"Magnússon has warriors on fishing boats out in the fjord swinging around the western flank of the barricade," Hlod replied, trying to stare with one eye past the edge of the shield at the scene beyond. "From what I can see not only are they clubbing our deserters in the water, but they have archers aboard taking shots to us too."

General Gudjóns ran in a low crouch across the oar deck among the ranks of Foeslayer's Huscarls and scrambled up the stairs to the occupied heights. "Jarl Foeslayer, we have lost another longship to the enemy and the Frisian and Saxons are surrendering in droves."

"This is not how I foresaw the battle going against Magnus Magnússon, General," frustration making his mood and voice grim, as Sigvald shook his head. "I did not listen to you and now my leadership had made a serious error of military judgment that has doomed us all."

"Then hear me now, my Jarl," General Gudjóns pleaded. "Release the Huscarls reserves to me and I will check the enemy advance and hold them, while you proceed to the Shield of Ullr, you should still make it before Magnússon's forces manage to cut off the route from the west."

Foeslayer became indignant. "Let Imgrimund of the Axe and his brother suffer that humiliation, not I. I can yet shift the tide of events back into my favour if I but slay Magnus Magnússon. Sound the horn, General Gudjóns; we march to battle this very minute."

* * *

"Make the enemy pay handsomely for your lives," Magnússon shouted to his crew, whose eyes lit up with fierce enthusiasm and they applauded, banging their sword pommels against the edges of their shields.

Magnússon drew his sword, grabbed a rigging rope in his free hand and gallantly swung across to the Odin's Spear on the rearward row, splitting the collarbone of the first young

Frisian he met and then slitting the throat of a howling, Saxons woman rushing towards him. Lokar launched himself by rope and he came across right behind his father, treading onto the dead and slashed accuracy in every direction a foe appeared, burying his sword into a Norseman's abdomen. The rest of the crew followed, vaulting over the rail, a young defender thoughtlessly threw his shield at them and Tyrker leaped over it, swinging his sword as he did, eviscerating the defender in passing.

Along the line of boarders, battleaxes flashed about, disembowelling and decapitating defenders on both decks, as they pushed Foeslayer's host back from the Odin's Spear and onto the longship behind it. Being farmers with a limited weapons skill and inexperienced in battling upon the decks of the longships, the Saxons and Frisians borne the blunt of the attack. They were slower and clumsier, stumbling over the dead underfoot and their movements were restricted further by their comrades in arms getting in their way in opposition to the nimble and confidence of Magnússon's warriors stepping atop of the bodies with a predator's quickness.

"Their numbers are becoming fewer and we outmatch them in close combat, Hakon," Bödvar shouted in amusement, his axe crunching into an enemy's side, as a horn blared loudly ahead of them.

"True enough, Bödvar," Hakon replied, his grin fading somewhat after bringing his sword up to lash into the vitals of his opponent. "But what is Foeslayer signalling for?"

"The withdrawal of his forces nay doubt," Bödvar ripped his weapon out with a powerful yank and then buried the axe-head into the man's neck, and the body slumped.

"They be losing the will to fight."

Like the Odin's Spear, the second longship in the rearmost rank was cleared by sword athwartships and then Magnússon ordered his men to cut away the anchors and the bow and stern chains tying the two Drakkars to the rest of Foeslayer's fleet. Lokar glanced at Magnússon and a look of understanding passed between them.

"Father," Lokar whispered close to his ear, "casting those craft adrift cuts off all possibility of retreat for us should the need arise?"

"It also motivates our warriors and us to fight harder for victory is life, Lokar," Magnússon gave him a tense and humourless smile. "I have found that there is naught more dangerous than a cornered animal."

Magnússon waved his warriors onward and they scrambled over to the third longship in the rearward line. The boarders encountered limited resistance from the defenders until the allies' cooperation collapsed altogether. But then as the Vikings of Fjordstad and Lillesund were hacking indiscriminately in the back's of the Saxon and enemy Norsemen alike, following the retreat of Imgrimund of the Axe and his bodyguard, Magnússon pulled up his warriors and ordered them to raise shields, for he recognised the approaching number of young men clambering over the gunwale of the longship in front of him to belong to Foeslayer's Snake Tribe.

The novice warriors started to spread out on the deck of the forth Drakkar in the rearward line in readiness for combat. Older veterans were trying to arrange themselves in a supporting line behind them. The standard of Sigvald Foeslayer was fluttering above them. At the same time, the tense boarders clustered around Magnússon and Lokar, hiding them from view by a curved phalanx of shields.

"They be goat-shaggers," Hakon insulted the enemy Norsemen loudly to the laughter of his comrades in arms before dripping with sweat, he and several others threw spears at the defenders and a great chorus of angry oaths and agonising shrieks echoed in places on the left and the right of their lines as the missiles pierced reindeer-armoured breastplates and ploughed into shields and the arms behind them.

The veterans and the novice soldiers peered warily from behind their double line of overlapping shields, now standing side by side for the most part, except where the defenders were gathered in knots at the flanks of a small breach, swinging their arms and releasing throwing axes at the boarders. Their own people were let through as well as the last of the foreigners, before the knots of Foeslayer's warriors opened out, shifting sideways, slowly closing the breach in their wall of shields.

"Father," Lokar felt the impact of a throwing axe thud into the shield he held close to his head as he pointed with his sword at Foeslayer's standard. More axes lodged solidly in neighbouring shields. "Our prey is dead ahead."

"Aye and his Huscarls are between us and it, but if we are able to break them ere they can mount a stout defence, we will win the day yet," Magnússon grasped, peeking through the small gaps in his own shield wall, before glancing about at his warriors, who were all exhibiting a restless quality, selecting one before addressing him. "Bödvar, you are the head of the 'Boar's Snout,'" he then spoke to the rest of his audience. "Form up on him, now, and prepare to charge."

* * *

Upon a longship in the first anchored rank, the defenders overlapped their shields and their spears stabbed upwards with unerring precision, staving in ribs and running through hearts, as the boarders continued to press forward by climbing onto the dead and attacking, keeping up the pressure up to the point the warriors of Ivar Longhair buckled under it. Judging the available options to hasten the victory for his side, Rollo ordered knots of his men to gather up the grapnels and quickly return to the front lines.

This they did, before casting them at the foremost enemy rank, the prongs hooking on to the shields or digging into the fresh and bone of the owners holding them. Boarders hauled sharply on the ropes and six screaming defenders were pulled from their rank, only to perish beneath the fall of numerous axes. Archers belonging to Magnússon's forces prowled along from one upper deck to another and used their arrows to whittle away at enemy Norsemen trying to escape by clambering up the ladders to the stern platforms of the next longship over or swinging by ropes to the prow of the vessel behind it.

In twos or threes, the defenders withdrew regularly across the gangplanks to the next longship along and once it was time of Ivar Longhair to cross, he cleared space around him with a sweep of his sword and backtracked, but he stepped onto some spilled guts and blood, slipping and falling hard onto his back. Rollo charged over to the nobleman and was just going to shorten his frame by a head when he blurted out an appeal for clemency.

"Quarter! I say quarter for Ivar Longhair. I have information in exchange for my life."

"Bah," Rollo growled with weary resignation as he contemplated his decision, not liking to show mercy to a defeated enemy, but he stayed his hand nevertheless, knowing full well of what Magnússon's law said on the matter. "You have my word on it."

A few of Ivar Longhair's warriors laid down their weapons like he had done seconds previously. Other defenders under his command were not so inclined to surrender for the fight had not yet deserted them and they briefly shot the nobleman a withering look before pandemonium suddenly sounded behind them.

It started with loud, panicky voices accompanied by the echoing stamp of running footfalls and the defenders - timorously hunched behind their shields in fear of Rollo's men launching an attack against them - stole a glance over their shoulders and spotted their Saxon allies heading towards the longship they stood upon, fleeing by leaps and bounds across the series of decks in front of another pursuing band of rampaging Vikings led by Njáll Bloodhammer.

The defending Norsemen threw down their swords at the horrifying sight of these new boarders and knelt, adopting a supplicant attitude and their voices called out for mercy.

***

Heeding Magnússon's words, thirty of his strongest fighters upon a longship in the second anchored rank, repositioned themselves from the Viking phalanx, the edges of the shield wall suddenly appearing torn to enemy onlookers as the pieces of arm-armour dropped out. The warriors breathless with anticipation and growing more restless by the second formed the angled walls of the wedged-shaped formation behind Bödvar. Aware of the potential for chaos in battle, the festering hate for his father boiled over and Lokar made a firm decision to have the vengeance he sought and there was no better place and time to finally kill him and blame it on the enemy. The thought along gave Lokar a great deal of satisfaction and he knew it would diminish any further complications he had.

"If Foeslayer slays you father, I shall see to it that he will not live long enough to brag about it."

"That is reassuring Lokar; may be I was wrong to think you had the thin blood of a foreigner," Magnússon gestured to the remainder of his men and a second later, the ragged shield wall parted at the sides to reveal the 'Boar's Snout', as he, Lokar and the other boarders swept around it and joined it up at the rear.

The Viking formation advanced to the rail, trod in pools of blood crossing the gangplanks and charged at the opposing lines, aiming for a spot where Foeslayer's standard-bearer stood roughly behind. Magnússon knew there was not enough distance to acquire a good running start for his warriors to forced their way through the defenders lines like they would if this battle was on the land, but he was quietly confidence that the accumulation of his men's momentum and their sheer weight of numbers rushing in from behind the 'Boar's Snout would crack the shield wall asunder.

There was a deafening sound of metal colliding with wood as the two sides came together in battle. The Huscarls' absorbed the charge effortlessly, but then the opposing battleaxes and swords aggressively rained down blow after blow without any let up upon the roof and side of the defensive barrier, penetrating shield planking and cleaving through the helmets and the skulls underneath. In response, defenders in the second rank stepped forward to replace their wounded comrades, treading on them as they counter-attacked with the rest, their spears thrusting with fast, jerky motions and stabbing home in the boarders faces and necks.

Sensing victory was almost within their grasp, more whooping boarders caught up in the excitement slammed into the rear of the advancing throng, forcing the defenders line to bend inward, the shield wall came to be less rigid, narrow spaces widening and multiplying, neutering Foeslayer's boldness and sending overpowering fear to spread among his warriors who stepped backwards, their legs suddenly hitting against the rail and tumbled over it, into the stumbling laps of the Huscarls' behind them. Men fell through the gap separating the one longship from the next and became submerged in the water.

Once the shield wall collapsed, the frantic battle disintegrated now into much smaller melees and one-on-one contests as the boarders ran riot and made inroads within the defenders shambling ranks. Foeslayer had one sword shatter in half and his other torn from his hand in the thick mauling, jostling press of Vikings before he grabbed a warhammer off the man he slew, as he and his shrinking number of Huscarls' gave up ground to the relentless pursuit from Magnússon's warriors, retreating across the oar-decks of the fifth and sixth Drakkars in the rearward row.

But when Foeslayer arrived to step on to the Shield of Ullr, the horrendous situation he was experiencing plumbed to new depths of despair for him, because the longship was no longer there, all he could see was piles of chains and cast off ropes lines on the gunwale and an empty water berth beyond, separating the vessel he was standing on and the last longship in line on the western extremity of his Drakkar barricade. He glanced at the expanse of fjord to his right and saw the oars of the Shield of Ullr propelling it further and further away, closing the distance on the low, shadowy outline of Skálholt that could just be made out on the horizon.

"I be trice-damned, you were right again, General," Foeslayer said in infuriation at the receding longship. "Imgrimund of the Axe has taken every fighting man we could have used aboard his ship and sailed off, leaving us marooned upon this deck."

"Now, we make our last stand here," General Gudjóns pivoted around and lowered the standard pole atop of the hold hatch amidships, watching as Foeslayer and Hlod silently turned and threaded their way forward through the struggling, cacophonous scrum of warriors.

Losses continued to mount on both sides as swordsmen whirled as they fought; because death was coming at them from different angles. The odd defender and boarder dropped their shields over wounded kin or even a friend to protect them. Soon enough, Rollo and Njáll Bloodhammer appeared at the prows of the longships on the rearward rank, followed by dozens of their warriors shouting their battle cries to scare the enemy. General Gudjóns noticed them and he blew his horn in an attempt to rally his tiring veterans around him, but Lokar snatched up a fallen spear and hurled it, impaling the grizzled soldier in the heart. As he fell to the deck; Lokar glanced at his father's back, transferring his sword back to his dominant hand before creeping closer to deliver a killing thrust.

It was then that Lokar's saw a flicker of motion in his peripheral vision. He raised his shield and quickly turned his head away as Foeslayer's borrowed warhammer powerfully clipped the edge of the shield and hit a glancing, ringing blow against Lokar's helm. The leather and wool padding inside it reduced the force of the impact, but the young nobleman still fell with a lost of consciousness, blood trickled down the side of his face. Magnússon dispatched Hlod on the gangplank after their swords had met twice and then he spared a look for his son and saw Foeslayer standing over him, preparing to end Lokar's life.

With a roar, Magnússon spun on his heel and leaped onto the deck. Around the pair, warriors on both sides resisted the temptation to continue fighting; slowly relaxing their guards and their attentions wavering, becoming distracted as they focused on the two chieftains about to do battle, knowing this was the determining factor that would decide the outcome of the struggle.

Foeslayer grinned and hefted up the increasing heavy weapon as he raced to meet him. "You have come far to die by my hand, Magnus Magnússon."

"Nay Serpent," Magnússon ducked under the bone crushing swing from the warhammer and then his slashing sword's upper cut missed Foeslayer's groin by the breadth of a finger as he sprang backwards. "'Tis your life candle that is guttering this day."

Foeslayer swung his warhammer again and his puffing opponent sidestepped to get out of the way, content to use his flagging speed and agility in this individual fight rather than parry the stroke with his sword, because Magnússon knew the metal of his two handled scimitar would not withstand direct contact with such a weapon. Magnússon closed in and brought his scimitar across from the left, adding the momentum of his twisting hip and torso to the swing and shearing it deeply into his enemy's side.

Foeslayer grimaced from the pain and his skin paled as he lifted the warhammer above his head, intending to bring it hurling down to crush his opponent's head, but the older warrior ripped out his sword and kicked out with his boot, knocking Foeslayer off balance and sending him sprawling over to the rail. Magnússon lunged at him, crossing the intervening space between them in moments, following up with a mighty slash, as his shallow-breathing enemy turned to face him and attempted to raise his weapon to parry the stroke.

But his wound was weakening him, slowing him down and the warhammer was becoming increasing harder to lift as Magnússon opened up a second gaping mouth in the younger man's neck where his Adam's apple used to be. Foeslayer's eyes rolled up and his dead body slumped to the deck.

Magnússon's looked around at the sea of faces, some grinning, uplifted in the jubilation of triumph, while others were quietly miserable, their shoulders sagging. "Here me Huscarls, with this victory I have united our two lands and made our people one clan. Fight nay more against your new sword brothers. Yield to me and have a home life under the Red Plague banner of Jarl Magnus Magnússon or die and be food for the fishes. What say you to that?"

"I will not live with the shame of defeat," a young man yelled in defiance, spittle ejecting from his mouth, as he raised his sword at Bödvar in front of him. "Foeslayer was my Jarl..."

Only to be interrupted when he had his legs suddenly chopped away by Hakon standing behind him.

"Anyone else?" asked Bödvar, his alert gaze darting left and right.

The rest of the Huscarls saw that and made snap decisions, reversing the hilts of their weapons and handing them over to the nearest boarders as they eagerly gave up.

Epilogue
In The Aftermath

Lokar shook his head in surprise and surveyed the ongoing scene from where he stood alongside his father and uncle on the upper deck of the Odin's Spear, watching Magnússon's warriors in the aftermath of the battle, loot the dead, picking up weapons and Wulfric bit into a coin to test its firmness and grunted with the pain before grinning when he realised it was gold.

Lars clubbed a moaning enemy Viking about the head until he breathed his last and then helped his brother grab hold of the man's arms and legs before they joined their comrades, hauling the bodies of the Saxons into the water to clear the decks of the captured longships. Another line of Vikings from Fjordstad and Lillesund were also carrying their own slain to the holds of the Rune Fire and the Horse of the Waves, while Magnússon's wounded sat on the decks of the Sea Chariot, the Bifrost's Bow and the Blood Fang, and drank water from their goatskins.

Elsewhere masts and oars were being ferried from the shore by the fishing boats to refit the captured longships.

"I lost my senses for ten minutes and when I awaken covered by a shield I find out Sigvald Foeslayer is dead and the battle is over."

"Aye, Lokar;" Magnússon said, interrupting his ruminations, as he turned away to view the low, distant outline of Skálholt and the fjord sparkling in the late afternoon sunlight. "It has given me time to reflect on what to do next."

"Reflect on what, father? Naught should be simpler," Lokar asked, furrowing his aching brow and casting a glance at him over his shoulder. "We hold course and strike while the iron is hot by retaking Skálholt by tonight and then sailing on to Trøllheim on the morrow. Foeslayer's bitch shall be the first to feel the edge of my sword."

"That won't be easy, nephew," Rollo butted in, "although Magnus has doubled his landholding with Foeslayer's and Stoneface's Jarldoms as well as increased his shipping fleet, our surviving warriors require rest and time for the bereaved to grieve over our own dead. The bodies we haven't fished out of the fjord are ripening in the heat and stinking up the holds. There are also our warrior losses and the Norse prisoners for your father to consider...."

Lokar abrupt laughed halted Rollo's utterance. "How so, uncle?"

"To replace the dead we need to take the prisoners back to Fjordstad in order for them to swear an oath of loyalty to your father in the Great Hall in front of witnesses before we can trust them within our warrior ranks," Rollo resumed, easy to see Lokar's frustration in the way his fingers fidgeted on the hilt of his sword, "and Ivar Stoneface has told me that Skálholt is being held by fighting men faithful to Imgrimund of the Axe and the she devil, Lady Melkorka, the same holds true for Trøllheim."

"To make matters worst there is the strong possibility that the surviving Frisian and Saxons that escaped the battle are now roaming the countryside like bandits, looking for food and shelter," Magnússon said, "with our forces spread so thin, Fjordstad, Lillesund and the other settlements are dangerous under manned and vulnerable to attack until we can get the crews and the prize of Foeslayer's Drakkar fleet safely back home."

"I think most of the foreigners will go to Skálholt, where their allies still hold sway," Lokar counted truculently, knowing the prestige his father would receive from his own people after bringing Foeslayer's fleet into port. "With so many more hands for the tasks, they will make light work of repairing the catapult holes in the palisade wall. They shall also use the time to bring in fresh provisions and that means our army will have to lay siege to the town."

Magnússon sighed and nodded, conceding the point. "Let the sky darken with the smoke from the burning pyres of our dead and in a few days when I have come up with a plan of attack I shall send out our men and women to win back Skálholt, but I dislike killing fellow Vikings especially the young and those that can not defend themselves." A stubborn look appeared in his eye and a rigid grimace of disgust contorted his expression. "I won't end a House by slaying Foeslayer's wife and it is my wish that you do not either Lokar, understand?"

"Aye," Lokar turned and strode to the top of the stairs. "I thought you were older and wiser than me, father," he descended to the lower deck, "seemingly I was only half right."

...And so endeth the first Viking chronicle...

To be continued...